THE RAGE OF SAINTS

S.A. KLOPFENSTEIN

For my good friend, Peter B.

———

CONTENTS

Watcher Magic
Corporeal Orders

Regenero: the regenerators
Medici: the healers
Cerebro: the mentalists
Enduro: the ultra-swift
Metamorphi: the shapeshifters

Watcher Magic
Material Orders

Fieri: manipulators of fire
Conjuri: manipulators of matter
Lumeni: manipulators of light
Sonora: manipulators of sound

FOREWORD

Writing a sprawling fantasy saga, it turns out, is no easy feat.

The first book is difficult in its own right. But there is also a freedom that comes with writing the first book in a series. No one has read it. No one has opinions, or characters they wish had lived. Or died. No one has been crushed by a certain character's decisions.

Expectations are lower, I suppose.

Writing the second book is different. Particularly for an epic fantasy in which the plot explodes at the end of the first book.

The Rage of Saints features more POV characters; we see much more of the New World and its history and cultures; and the action is taken to a more epic level. It's also significantly longer than the first book, and that proved another challenge all its own.

But, I'm told, challenging yourself as a writer often leads to the best outcomes. So, I tried to lean into the challenges with this book, and I believe it paid off. It is often cited as a reader favorite. For many readers, it was the point at which they got fully hooked on the series. It is my wife's favorite book in the series as well.

As for me… well, you can't have a favorite child, right?

Rage of Saints certainly remains one of the toughest books I've written, but I also had an absolute blast writing this story. It was a labor of love, filled with thrilling battles, plot twists, and some of my favorite character moments in the series.

But once you put a work out in the world, it is no longer yours. It belongs to the readers and their own interpretations. One of the challenges that comes with creating works and putting them out there is learning what feedback to listen to, and what to tune out.

I've learned not to listen to individual feedback too much, but I do pay attention to the broad sweep of feedback over time. With a new edition comes the opportunity to revisit the past. And even, improve upon it.

As I worked through this book one last time, I made a few minor adjustments and additions, based on some feedback that resonated with my ultimate vision for the series. I dropped a little more foreshadowing for some things to come, tweaked some spellings of names and other minor things.

The story remains the same. These changes are only meant to improve immersion into the New World, and improve the experience of the series as a whole.

Now, it goes back into the world one more time—the definitive edition of *The Rage of Saints*.

Dive deep. And enjoy all the gorgeous artwork!

S.A. Klopfenstein
Rapid City, SD
Jan. 2025

THE RAGE OF SAINTS

S.A. KLOPFENSTEIN

THE SHADOW WATCH SAGA
— BOOK TWO —

DELUXE ILLUSTRATED EDITION

FROZEN SEA
GREAT WH
Iqala
Crooked Teeth
Mouth of the Gods
Spine
Grey Wa
OSHA
Stormfall
Everwinter Forest
MARO'EL
YAN A
GLACIER SOUND
The Fringes
Forest of Ghen
Hatia
Barra'El
GREATER OSHA
Pendra
BOUNDLESS SEA
Klavash Mountains
Fangsport
Ravencrest
N
MORGATH
W
E
GORAN'EL
S
RUINED EMPIRE of FAERE
V
RUN KHAEN
BAY of TRIUM
The Necropoli
ELYA
SOUTHERN ISLES

Map of the
New World
FROST ISLE
NORTHERN PASSAGE
Crimson Mountains
EPPE
JURKA
KERCIN
LOST SEA
NDERING
DUNES
BAY of JALLAA
ISLE of JALLAA
Canyons
Dimh
KINGDOM of MALAI
SILVER PALACE
Southern Rim
Saltlands
Kerren
PARJHA
UM'VEL
Bhalai River
Jhenai
Vel Tereth
BHALAI
MELANESIA
SILVER SEA

1. The White Citadel
2. Maro Square
3. Citadel Road
4. Sky Guard Headquarters
5. Noble District
6. West Wall District
7. Merching District
8. Lower Citadel Road
9. The Meridian Bridge
Maro'El
Crooked Teeth
Forest of Ghen
The Fringes

PROLOGUE

Cyrus Maro—the sixteenth Chancellor of Osha—should have been pleased. Exuberant, even. The leaders of the Shadow Watch lay in the dungeons beneath the White Citadel, their magic-rich blood filling him with power each day. Many of the Watchers had chosen to serve him rather than suffer this horrid fate, which made Cyrus Maro even more powerful. Monsters ravaged the New World for the first time in centuries, and the people of Osha looked to their chancellor as though he were their god.

And he *was* their god. When the chancellor revealed his magic to the people of Osha, the day he paraded the Watchers through the streets of Maro'El, their mouths had gaped with awe; they'd knelt in reverence as he'd ridden past. Magic had returned to the world at his hand.

Nothing had gone according to plan, but everything had turned out better than he ever could have dreamed.

The monsters that had come through the portal between the worlds had been unanticipated, but they had turned into a precious opportunity. Rulaqs and Nosferati had returned from the realm of nightmares and myths to ravage the world. The people of Osha were afraid, and fear made them loyal. Their chancellor wielded power unknown in all the New

World, and his new magical army, the Sky Guard, would keep the empire safe from hellish beasts.

While other nations plunged into chaos, Osha would remain strong, and the people of the North would be grateful, worshipful.

Cyrus Maro was more powerful than his father, and his father before him. He was far more powerful than Loras, his precious, perfect brother, had ever been.

But it was not enough.

It was as though Loras had returned from the dead to taunt him with this fact, as he had taunted Cyrus with his magical prowess when they were children. Of course, like their parents, Loras had not practiced his magic… much. It was this self-denial that held the empire together, their father had liked to say. Cyrus had showed no prowess to deny himself of, but he had always thought it a ludicrous notion. Self-denial had made his father—and all his forefathers, and especially Loras—weak, far weaker than Cyrus had ever been.

Cyrus had fashioned his *own* power. No longer would an Oshan chancellor be mocked by foreign dignitaries as a vestige of another time. No longer would the nobles rule the empire like puppeteers.

Now, more than ever, the chancellor was revered and feared. But for one thing:

The Gallows Girl.

Cyrus Maro had hoped that in the turmoil of Old World monsters ravaging the New World, the Gallows Girl might be forgotten. It had been weeks since she'd been lost in the catacombs beneath the Crooked Teeth. And many months since any common person had seen her. Yet here he was, on the balcony where he first drank the Gallows Girl's blood, and it was time to inflict pain on her account once more.

There came a knock on the balcony doors. A Morph announced the arrival of his visitor, and Cyrus motioned for them to enter.

"The noble traitor, Ren, of House Andovier," the attendant announced.

"That's Captain Andovier," murmured Ren weakly but defiantly as he entered.

The Watcher was escorted to the balcony by a traitor to his own cause. Dajha Bhati had been one of the first Watchers to join the chancellor's Sky Guard, and the dark-skinned Parjhan seemed all too eager to demonstrate his new loyalties. He led Ren with a shove that sent him to his knees.

"Careful," said the chancellor. "Your captain might break."

Despite his quick tongue, the captain of the Watchers looked like he'd been inflicted with a plague—his skin hung loose and was tinted a greyish hue, as though he were beginning to rot. Even his eyes had lost their lustre. Brilliant blue now appeared dull and faded.

"Yeh're my captain now, milord," said Dajha, bowing his head. His long dreadlocks whipped through the air with the movement. "Reckon the best thing for Ren might be breaking."

The chancellor chuckled, pleased with the young Parjhan's unabashed loyalty. Nevertheless, he motioned for Dajha to help Ren up. Ren moaned.

"Had enough of my dungeons?" said the chancellor. "Dajha's doing quite well."

Dajha stood behind his former captain with arms crossed, his expression hard. The chancellor loved the anger that flared up at the mention of Ren's own soldier's betrayal. Suddenly, the Watcher captain didn't look so pitiful. *There's fire in him, yet. Good.*

"Am I ready to betray my own kind?" said Ren bitterly. "Like my… brother?" He spat the words, and the chancellor grinned. "Like you?"

Cyrus Maro's lips curled. "Betray? Your Gallows Girl sets monsters upon the entire world, and you accuse *me* of betrayal? You sought to return the glory of the Watchers to the New World, and I have done that. I am sorry to have stolen your glory, but it is time you accepted the world as it is and moved forward. The Sky Guard awaits you, my friend. It will welcome you with open arms, as it did Dajha."

At this, Dajha nodded coolly.

A table had been set out on the balcony, and the chancellor gestured to Ren. "Sit. Eat. You must be tired of the stale rations of the dungeons. Replenish yourself. I insist."

Ren sat and replenished, tearing into a leg of roasted venison. The juices splattered from his lips, staining the white tunic he'd been given for this meeting.

As he ate, the color returned to Ren's cheeks, only a little, but nothing was missed by Cyrus Maro. "See, I'm not all blood and horror," the chancellor said.

Ren did not answer, but he did not stop eating.

"You know, you might have been a part of all this," said the chancellor. "The return of our kind."

Ren coughed up his wine. "You're no Watcher. You're a parasite."

The chancellor tensed, though he tried not to let it show. Instead, he smiled, reached out with his sense, and summoned a second goblet. It floated through the air to his hand, and he drank a glorious red liquid. It was not wine.

As its coppery taste left his tongue, he could already feel his power increasing like a stoked fire.

"Yes," said Cyrus Maro. "Our kind. Or are you naïve enough to think that magic is restricted to your Old World orders? It was that sort of thinking that led to the fall of the Watchers, my friend. I thought you were more sophisticated."

"I know what happened in the Old World. My ancestors were there," said Ren.

"Yes, they were. As *you* were there when I discovered what can be done with Watcher blood. So was Scelero. And yet both of you have the audacity to paint yourselves righteous."

Ren's expression grew hard, and the chancellor was pleased. He knew Ren regretted serving him those many years ago—those events had led to the death of the royal family, all but Cyrus. Much as Ren might hate to believe it, he had helped make the chancellor what he was.

"We are more alike than you think, Ren. We both created a problem."

"Astoria may be the one who let those beasts through your portal, but you made it possible. Don't *you* paint yourself righteous."

The chancellor laughed. "Still bantering, even after weeks of bloodletting. Your strength is returning. Good."

"Why are you treating me well?" said Ren bitterly.

"I'm reminding you of the finer things. The things you have longed for ever since you fled the city. You may have spent the last few years out in that gods-forsaken tower in the woods, but you are still a true noble of Osha. I'm trying to seduce you, of course."

For a moment, Ren looked taken aback. The chancellor enjoyed surprising people with the naked truth. Ren recovered and took a loaf of bread. It steamed as he broke it open. "And why else are you treating me well?" Ren said.

The chancellor was pleased. Nothing got past Ren Andovier. "There's something I need you to do for me. And for that, you will need to be strong."

The chancellor procured a parchment from his robes. It was such a little thing, found in the pockets of a mere servant boy. But if Tori had taught him anything, it was that servants could pose a considerable threat, even to him. Especially to him.

Ren unrolled the parchment. Inscribed on the crumpled paper were no letters or words. Servants were rarely literate. No, there was only one symbol. Small, in the bottom corner of the page, so small it might have easily gone unnoticed—mistaken for a scribble by one of the scribes.

The symbol was that of a gallows, the overhanging beam cleft in two.

Though it was not his writing, Ren's face betrayed horror at the sight of it. "What do you want me to do?"

"Commander Redvar! You may enter."

The servant boy, who had been brought up from the dungeons, did not tremble when the commander of the chancellor's Sky Guard forced him into the chancellor's presence. The boy was expressionless, and this infuriated the chancellor, though again, he tried not to let it show.

"Here is your insurrectionist, milord," Darien said, shoving the servant boy to his knees.

Sparing the Gallows Boy had turned out to be one of Cyrus Maro's greatest decisions. When the chancellor appointed Darien Redvar as commander of his magical army, the people of Osha had been in awe. The chancellor had proven cunning even in his own apparent grace. The Gallows Boy—who once had defied him before all of Osha, who had triggered the Gallows Girl's very demonstration of forbidden magic last year —had turned into his most feared servant.

Darien's expression was cold as he stood over the defiant little rebel.

This will be interesting. The chancellor smiled at the boy, offering his hand, and the boy looked dumbly at it. "I am helping you stand," Cyrus Maro said.

Like Ren, the boy was dressed in a fine-spun tunic, better than anything the boy had likely worn before. He took the chancellor's hand and stood.

"What's your name?" the chancellor said.

"Me name's Liam," the boy said, his lowborn accent thick.

"A Morgathian," said the chancellor, noting the boy's sun-specked pale skin. "But it would seem, one not so blessed by your god." Red hair was seen as a blessing from Nafta. Hollsted had been thus blessed, and yet Nafta had not spared the Rebel King at the hands of the Gallows Boy.

Cyrus Maro mussed the boy's plain, tawny hair. He gestured to Ren. "Show Liam what we've found."

Ren's expression was visibly pained as he regarded the boy, but still, he obeyed and handed over the treacherous parchment. Liam clenched his fist around it, crumpling the poorly drawn gallows into a ball.

"You do not deny it is yours?" said the chancellor, amused.

Liam's knees weakened a little, but he stood tall for one no older than thirteen summers. He shook his head without hesitation. "I don't deny it. Don't regret it, neither."

The chancellor chuckled darkly. "You realize that the Gallows Girl is a traitor, a dark sorceress who brought back the terrors of the Old World?"

"She's a saint," Liam said obstinately. "And she's coming to save us."

"Save you? A horde of Rulaqs march toward the city as we speak. At her behest." The chancellor grew cold, gripping the boy by the collar of his tunic. Despite his bravery, little Liam was shaking, and this pleased the chancellor. "*I* saved you. My armies keep the beasts at bay."

"No," said Liam. "You en't no savior. You're a tyrant."

His grip tightened on the boy. A part of him admired his brashness. It was such a spark that had prompted him to spare the Gallows Boy not so long ago. But this boy would receive no such grace.

"Yes, well, we become what we must, my boy. And you are about to become exactly what you must. That symbol is a sign of treason. Do you know what happens to traitors, boy?"

The boy swallowed, but nodded. "Y-you're going to kill me."

The chancellor released his grip on the boy. "Actually, Ren, here, is going to kill you. He's a traitor too. And it's time you both understood what that entails."

Ren backed away from the boy. "I won't," he said.

"Ah, now that is just charming," said the chancellor. "After all that's happened, Ren, you still believe you have a choice."

The sorceress Medea appeared behind Ren, stepping from a sudden rise of mist—the path of the godstones. Before Ren could react, her pale, tendril-like fingers extended from billowy silks and latched onto his skull.

"You don't want to serve me again?" said the chancellor. "Ren, I am afraid, you have no choice." The chancellor took hold of Liam by both arms and held him still. "This is the fate of those who hope in the Gallows Girl."

At Medea's command, Ren began channeling his Conjuri power in a way he had never done before.

First, the boy's tunic was wrenched from his chest, exposing his torso. And then, the incision began, starting at the center of his scrawny chest. The cut ran slow and deep, compelled not by a blade, but by pure, unadulterated magic. It was the cleanest cut the chancellor had ever seen. The skin split open so smoothly, it was as though the image were being painted on a canvas rather than carved from flesh. It was beautiful.

Throughout the process, the servant boy screamed in agony, crimson life gushing from the growing wound.

By the time Ren had finished, the boy was dead, his life poured onto the balcony floor.

The chancellor turned the boy over so he could examine the finished product. The image carved from the little rebel's chest had come out perfect. An exact likeness. A piece of art. Etched into the dead boy's chest was a broken gallows.

The symbol of the Gallows Saint.

PART ONE
MOUTH OF THE GODS

Little was known about the Great White North, nor the people that inhabited it. What was told of the Alyut was mostly legend. Wild men. Ancient savages. Harsh people befitting such a harsh place. No one knew, because no one ventured into the North. It was a place even the gods had forsaken.

—from *Dawn of the Third World*

CHAPTER ONE

The North stretched out like a great frozen sea, powerful and infinite, beyond the Mouth of the Gods. Between two mountain ranges, the northeastern reaches of the Crooked Teeth and the westernmost peaks of the Spine of the North, stretched a gaping glacial valley of ice and crevasses, known to have swallowed many who dared venture through its treacherous passage. This was the Mouth, and it was the only way to the Great White North.

It had been three weeks since Astoria Burodai had joined Alyk dul Baruk and his company of Alyut and Crooked refugees. They had covered many miles, but it was slow going across the frozen scree of the Grey Waste with such a large company.

Tori had begun to wonder if they would ever reach the North. For days she'd longed to finally spot the infamous Mouth of the Gods that Alyk described, but as they neared, Tori began to wonder again if she'd made the wrong decision to journey to the Icelands in pursuit of revolution—or Restoration, as Alyk liked to refer to it.

"I see why they call it the Mouth," murmured Tori's closest companion, Mischa Sufai.

With the looming peaks of the Teeth and the Spine towering on both sides and the jagged pillars of ice rising to meet them, Tori thought the Mouth ought to have been more aptly named. "More like the Fangs of the Gods."

Alyk dul Baruk chuckled, sidling beside her. "I told you it was magnificent."

"Not sure that's the word I'd choose," said Tori.

"Terrifying?" offered Mischa.

"Bloodcurdling?"

Alyk took their jests in stride. "It's a vicious beauty, my grandmother says. The North is cruel, but there's wonder too, if you've eyes to see it."

"We'll work on our squinting, then," said Tori, smiling. It was strange to smile at such a time. Great storms would soon be approaching, but it felt good to joke and laugh, and Alyk had a way of bringing this out of her.

Alyk shook his head. "My people resented being forced to flee to such a harsh land—some still do—but I see magnificence. I see a place that's made us resilient."

"Then why go to war against the chancellor? For some old bit of land?" Mischa asked.

Alyk smiled. Tori had quickly been growing to appreciate his incessant grin. Despite the weathered countenance of a hard existence, his smile shone with childish genuineness. A smile of wisdom and persistent hope.

"For some, it is revenge, justice. But for me it's spiritual. The heart and soul of my people lies in Osha. I love the North, but I feel like a part of me is missing as long as I live anywhere else."

"Have you ever been there?" asked Tori.

"Few living Alyut have. I've heard the tales of the traders in the Ice City. But no, I've seen Osha only in my dreams. Yet I still feel its absence. It is my home."

"Guess I've never felt that way about a place," Tori muttered. "I'm a bastard. No place has ever felt like home."

"What about you, Mischa?" asked Alyk.

Mischa had grown quiet. Her short black hair whipped up in a gust of wind. She gazed off at the massive forms of rock and ice known as the Spine of the North—the natural barrier between the known world and the mysterious Great White North.

"I miss the islands," Mischa said eventually. "The sand and swimming in the Silver Sea. I miss the scent of flowers, the taste of citrus and salt kisses. But not the castes and the codes of my people, or my parents and their damned honor... It's the people that make a place. I never want to go back to Melanesia."

Alyk's expression softened. "Well, you will both just have to trust me.

Nothing is more sacred to the Alyut than our homeland. Someday, maybe it can become home for us all."

They continued in silence, and with each step the Mouth of the Gods seemed to gape wider and wider, as though they were willingly walking down the throat of some gargantuan Old World beast. Tori had already seen enough of those to last a lifetime. With Rulaqs and Nosferati ravaging the world, and the chancellor sure to be hunting for her, the Great White North might be the only safe place in the New World. But looking at the yawning chasms before them, Tori wondered if there was such a thing as a safe place.

When they reached the edge of the valley, Alyk dul Baruk blew a whalehorn, and the company set up camp. The nights were growing colder as the brief season before winter set in. Mammut furs and insulated sealskin yurts helped, but Tori imagined it would only get colder beyond the Mouth of the Gods. As the sun fell behind the Crooked Teeth, the jagged shards of glacial ice that formed the Mouth glowed with a bloody hue.

"A vicious beauty," said Tori. She sat down beside Mischa as the Alyut set fires and prepared supper.

Mischa nodded absently, staring after a young Crooked girl attempting to ignite a pile of kindling for the evening fires. "Yeah, er, beautiful…"

"Tell you what," Tori went on, "I'll sleep a lot easier once we get past that ice maze."

Mischa was troubled, Tori could tell. There were worse things going on, and Tori knew her friend would never bring up her own anxieties, but Mischa had been solemn ever since Alyk had begun speaking of home-lands. Mischa never spoke much of her life before the Watchtower. She came from a highborn Melanesian family, judging by her light olive skin and her ability to read and write. Tori assumed Ren and Kale Andovier had stolen Mischa away without event. So Mischa let it seem, but Tori realized there was more. She felt it, as though a dark storm hovered over her friend's past life.

Tori kept talking, trying to distract her from her troubles, but Mischa didn't respond, her attention fixated on the Crooked girl and her failing fire. The wind rushed and doused the third attempt.

"What do you think Iqala will be like?" said Tori, more to herself than anyone. "I don't imagine the Ice City can truly be made entirely of ice, do you think?"

Suddenly, Mischa shot to her feet without so much as a grunt in answer. She hurried to the fire and knelt beside the Crooked girl. "Let me help." Mischa held out her hand as though to block the wind. "Strike your flint again."

The girl did, and this time the flame roared to life with a flare of Mischa's Fieri power. The kindling hissed, and then the rest of the wood caught. Mischa patted the girl on the shoulder.

"Nice work," she said, and returned to Tori.

The Crooked girl followed. "It's all right, you know," the girl said. "I know you did it. You're magic too."

"Am I?"

"Sure. You came with the Gallows Girl, so you must be. Anyway, I seen you tending the fires the other night, when we were running out of timber before we reached the Ever Winter Forest. Those fires should've burned up by midnight, but in the morning, they were still burning, and you were still tending them. Magic."

Mischa could not hide a smile. "Maybe that was the Gallows Girl."

The girl rolled her eyes, but dared a questioning glance at Tori.

Tori shook her head. "Afraid not. I don't know the first thing about fire. What's your name, little lady?"

The Crooked girl could not have been more than ten or eleven summers old. But she was already growing into long, gangly limbs. "Tesleh, and I'm no lady," she said, unfazed at being addressed by the Gallows Girl. "My brother thinks you're one of the old gods, but I don't really think so. You seem too normal."

"Normal?" said Mischa, chuckling.

"Er… I mean… not normal. Human, I guess." Tesleh glanced away, showing the first signs of timidity.

"Well, that's because I *am* human," said Tori. "You're very bright. Tell me, how do you know so much about fire?"

The girl beamed. "I like to burn things. Mum always says I'll burn down the house one day." At this, her expression turned. "But I guess she don't have to worry about our house no more."

Tori was filled, once again, with fierce shame for the destruction she had caused in the Crooked Teeth only a few short weeks ago. "Your home…"

"The Rulaqs," said Tesleh. "Crushed it to pieces. Killed my papa too."

"I'm so sorry," Mischa said, clasping the girl's hand.

Tori could tell Tesleh was holding back tears, and she could not help but admire the girl's strength.

"Me and my brother do all right. But my mum… she's torn up something awful. She tries to hide it and tells us to keep strong, but I seen her at night crying all alone. It en't *your* fault, though. It's the chancellor that done it."

But is that true? Tori could not convince herself it was. She had been weak. She had let the monsters through the chancellor's gateway between the worlds. She had stirred them up in her failed resistance. And who knew what destruction lay ahead.

A nagging question returned to eat at her gut: *Where did the Nosferati come from?*

Had they come from the Old World as well? And if so, had Tori been the one to let them through? Some by-product when the portal had been opened?

"Don't worry," said Mischa to the Crooked girl. "We'll deal with the chancellor soon enough."

A smile returned to Tesleh's lips. "That's why you're here, en't it?" she said to Tori.

Before Tori could answer, they were interrupted. "Ey! Tes!" A woman with a weathered face came hurrying over and took Tesleh by the wrist. "You en't got time to be bothering our Gallows Saint, and you know it!"

"Oh, no, she's fine," said Tori.

The woman scowled. "She en't fine! She's s'posed to be helping her brother fix the stew! The fire's going just fine, Tes. There's meat to mince and taters to skin. Get on!"

"Gods, Mum, I'm sorry!" cried Tes. "I must've forgot."

"Hmmm, yes, well, I forgive your forgetfulness, but your brother may not. Now, get!"

"Yes, Mum!" Tesleh turned to Mischa. "Thanks again for the fire." Then, she turned to Tori, the firelight flashing in her hazel eyes. "And thank you too."

"For what?" said Tori.

"For coming with us to the North." Tes scampered off to find her brother.

"Hope you'll pardon my daughter. Afraid she takes after her papa."

"Her papa must've been a fine man," said Mischa, still watching the little girl run off. "She was no bother at all."

The woman smiled, though there was sadness in her deep brown eyes. "Well, in that case, you both best be hurrying off yourselves."

"Ma'am?" said Tori.

"Didn't you hear? There's food that needs cooking." Tes's mother shook with a laugh.

Mischa and Tori laughed along with her. For days they had tried to help the company with preparations, but everyone refused to let them assist with trivial duties.

"Of course," said Mischa, the normal lightness returning to her voice. "We'd love to help!"

There was a darkness looming over Astoria and Mischa, more threatening than the Mouth of the Gods—death, guilt, betrayal, fear. But for a few moments, they both felt light again.

———

THE WOMAN'S NAME WAS GWYNETH FALZEN, AND TOGETHER WITH Tes and her brother Jordie, Mischa and Tori prepared a fine stew of hare, potatoes, and a strange spice bark, which fed nearly half the company. It felt good to contribute, for once. So many saw Tori the way Tes's brother Jordie saw her—like a god. It was a relief to be treated as a human again.

Gwyneth reminded Tori of Ol' Merri, which filled her with a strange combined sense of sadness and joy. The woman was sharp and snappy, yet Tori could easily see the love she bore for her children.

When dinner had been served and cleaned up, the fires were stoked, and an old Alyut man began telling ancient stories of frost giants and magic stags and dragons of the sea. Tes led Mischa by the arm to the fireside, and together they listened, enraptured.

Tori stayed back and observed. She was glad Tes had managed to distract Mischa from her haunted memories, though every time Tori saw her, she thought of the godstones and the Rulaqs, and pangs of guilt surged anew. She was responsible for what happened to Tes's village, and who knew what else?

Though, out here in the wild, even those recent horrors felt like something from a dream. Tori loved the simplicity of their company: march, eat, and sleep. Out here, it seemed there was no Osha, no chancellor, no need for magic or wars. She was not sure she believed Alyk, that a land could be worth the bloodshed that would inevitably come with a revolution.

Suddenly, a hand grasped her shoulder from behind, and she leapt, barely stifling a shriek.

Alyk chuckled.

But Tori did not. The unexpected touch took her back to the catacombs beneath the Crooked Teeth, to dark chambers where the soldier, Jujen, had shoved her against a damp cave wall and very nearly had his way with her. In all the chaos and mourning that had followed, Tori had thought little of the terror and helplessness she'd endured in those moments, but at Alyk's touch, it returned in full force. Jujen's twisted gaze roared to life in her memory, and she could feel his wiry hands again, clawing at her clothes, searching for skin and tender places.

Tori jerked away, instantly feeling foolish.

"Tori, it's okay," Alyk said, confused. "It's just me."

She tried not to reveal how shaken she really was. He touched her shoulder again, reassuringly, and she forced herself not to pull away in spite of herself.

Alyk seemed to sense her uneasiness and quickly withdrew his hand. "I'm sorry I startled you."

Tori sighed. "Gods, no, I'm sorry. It's just... I keep going back... to the catacombs."

She had told no one of what Jujen had nearly done, not even Mischa. In the wake of the nightmare they had survived, it had seemed unimportant in comparison to the betrayals of Vashti and Kale and the others, the deaths of Merri and who knew how many of their friends from the Watchtower. Alyk knew about the Nosferati, and she let him believe that was what she meant.

"It's like reliving a nightmare, isn't it?" he said. "Once you've seen death."

Yes, death is much worse. But that was not what haunted her just now. Tori merely nodded.

"When I was young, my youngest sister and me went fishing at the place where the ice meets the Frozen Sea in summer. There was a hole where seals would come to the surface. We'd fished places like it a hundred times before. I dropped our bait on our way there, and asked Lysa to get it while I set up the lines. I heard the crack when she fell through. By the time I got there, she was already gone beneath the ice... It was three years before I fished again."

"Alyk..." Tori did not know what to say. *What can you say about nightmares?* And she felt guilty for being haunted by a terror that almost happened. Why didn't she see flashes of Rulaqs or Nosferati at a startling touch? But no, it was that pig, Jujen. "I'm so sorry."

"Thank you," he said softly. "Though that's not why I told you. I guess we all have nightmares, but… none of us should have to carry the burden of them alone."

Tori smiled. "Maybe one day I'll take that offer."

"It's always there," he said. Tori noticed him reach to touch her again, but he caught himself and pulled back. "The reason I startled you was because I wanted to show you something." He pointed toward the edge of camp, out into the darkness of the Grey Waste.

"What could you possibly need to show me out there?" she said skeptically.

"Well, technically, you'd probably see it inside camp, but the fires tend to pollute it."

"Pollute what?"

"The Lights of Anora—goddess of the northern sky. We're far enough north, we should see them, even this early in the season."

Tori followed him out past the circle of yurts, beyond the ring of light emanating from the evening fires. Twice in her life, she had seen traces of the Lights, but only in the deepest winter upon the Northern Steppe. In Osha, there were too many lamps and they were too far south, but even traces were extraordinary to behold.

Alyk led the way across the frozen scree, never faltering, and soon, the camp was but a flicker in the distance. He found a large boulder that suited him, and he sat with his back to it, the rock blocking out the light of their camp. Tori sat beside him. She enjoyed the young Alyut man's company, and she trusted him, even though, at times, it felt foolish. But it was those times she reminded herself that Alyk had almost killed her— with his blade and his strange shaman's power that negated her own—but when he realized who she was, he had saved her life.

She could sense his kind heart and see it in the way he treated the people in his company, the way he did not pry but was willing to share about his own tragedy and hardships. And so, her flashback to the catacombs fading from her memory, Tori scooted closer to him so she could feel his warmth through the furs of both their parkas. They sat in silence for some time, waiting to see if the Lights would come out.

Finally, Tori broke the silence. "Do you really believe revolution is the answer?"

"Don't you?" he said softly.

"Can more darkness bring light?"

"Night comes before day, doesn't it?"

Tori sighed, staring off into the darkness. Somewhere the Spine and the Teeth were looming. "I know the injustices of the chancellor's rule. I've lived them. And yet I wonder: How much bloodshed will it cost to fight it? I don't know how many of my friends died in the catacombs. All of them, it is possible. All in the name of revolution. Sometimes, I wish the Gallows had never happened. Sometimes, I wish I was still just a servant girl in Maro'El."

Alyk went quiet. He gazed off at the inky night, watching wisps of cloud drift into the valley from the peaks of the Spine.

"You won't be forced to join us, you know," Alyk said. "If you want to leave when we reach the Ice City, you can. You can sail off to the Southern Isles with the traders in the spring, or the Trium'vel—anywhere in the world, if that's what you want. But it won't stop this revolution. This isn't about you, or the Gallows. It has been brewing for decades, centuries, since the days of the Old World. My grandmother envisioned it before I was born, and long before she saw you. Whatever blood has been or will be spilled, it is not your doing. No one can carry the dead."

Tori said little else for a while. Truth be told, she wanted to believe him. She wanted to hope, but she was not sure she knew how. There was too much darkness in her mind to dream of a better world.

Suddenly, Alyk nudged her, and she looked up. It was subtle at first, like traces of dye dropped into a bucket of water, but then, the colors spread. The sky lit up with magnificent waves of purple and green threading across the northern sky—the Lights of Anora. The colors were far more pronounced than any Lights that had ever shone upon the Steppe.

"It's the most beautiful thing I've ever seen," Tori muttered, her eyes following the dancing ripples of light, formed as though a child's finger were tracing in the sky.

"Even in places like this, at the end of the world, there is beauty and hope." At this, Alyk's gaze moved from the Lights and settled upon Tori. His brown eyes twinkled with the colors of the sky, and his olive skin flushed slightly. Tori suddenly realized how close the shaman was to her, and realized that she did not mind his nearness.

But quickly, they broke apart.

From beyond the great shards of ice towering over them, a sharp groaning sound filled the night, reverberating off the peaks of the Teeth and the Spine, building. It sounded like a dozen great beasts roaring to life.

And then, the sound faded.

"W-what was that?" said Tori.

In the distance, she could hear worried murmurs rising from their camp.

"Th-the Mouth is a glacier," said Alyk finally. "The ice is always shifting. I…" He sounded as if he were trying to convince himself. "I'm sure that's all it was."

Nevertheless, they both hurried back to camp. The Lights of Anora rushed now, with violent shifts of color across the sky, as though a storm were raging.

A vicious beauty.

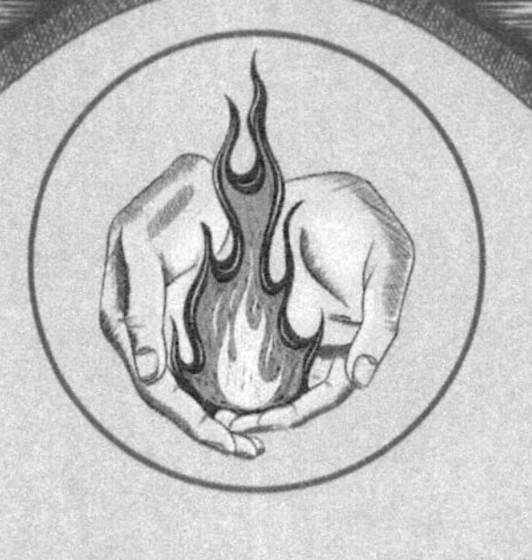

CHAPTER TWO

The Mouth of the Gods gaped wide in the soft dawn light and swallowed them up as they passed from the Grey Waste into the jagged valley of glacial ice that spanned between the mountain ranges of the Crooked Teeth and the Spine of the North. The Mouth stretched north for miles before tapering off into the Icelands beyond.

The groans of shifting ice had lasted less than a minute before quickly waning in the too-still northern night, but still Mischa Sufai had slept lightly. In truth, she had not slept well since the fall of the Watchtower. Since Zaya's death and Vashti's betrayal. Stings that buried themselves into her mind, and even her dreams. Every day, she became more accustomed to the foggy existence of sleep deprivation and night terrors. But Alyk dul Baruk and the Northmen—along with the girl, Tesleh—had rekindled vanished hope in her.

Tes bounded through the snow like a hare with endless energy, pausing often to marvel at the towering pillars of ice looming around them. The girl distracted Mischa from the memories of nightmares, living and imaginary. Still, Mischa longed for a cup of the bold coffees of Melanesia to rouse her in the bitter morning. Her family's kitchen master had once brewed some of the finest in all the islands. But she did not want to think of home either. Those memories haunted her as well.

Tes came running up, grinning. She'd disappeared for a short while, exploring the maze of ice, and now, she gripped Mischa's gloved hand and pulled her along. "You've got to come see this!" Tes shouted for a few of the other children to follow, and they wended through a narrow cleft in the pillars of ice, which towered over them like giant fangs.

"Tes, you shouldn't be wandering in here," said Mischa, regarding the sharp drop of a crevasse on her left. It plummeted for thirty feet at least. "The ice moves. Didn't you hear it last night?"

Tes laughed. "It's not far!" She ran ahead with one of the other Crooked girls.

What does it hurt? Mischa thought, hurrying after them. Tori and Alyk were up ahead, anyway, leading the company through the Mouth. The way was narrow, and so the line of Alyut and Crooked folk stretched long and moved slowly. The children were not likely to stray far enough to get lost from the group, but they needed looking after, and their joy lightened the burdens Mischa carried.

It seemed impossible that, at seventeen, it had only been six years since Mischa had been a similar young girl with endless wonder and energy. So much had changed so quickly with the coming of her first bleeding and all the rites that womanhood brought in the islands of the Silver Sea. Mischa's first blood had occurred during her thirteenth summer, and by fourteen she had fled for the trade cities of the Trium'vel.

A scream jolted Mischa alert. Tes and a pair of Crooked children had just disappeared around a boulder of ice. Mischa raced to them, praying she would not be too late, but before she turned the corner, she heard Tes chortling.

The screaming stopped, and there was more laughter. Around the corner, the children gathered around a gap in the ice. Protruding from the glacier was a frozen human arm, jutting out from an invisible body, buried beneath the ice. Emerged nearly to the elbow, its fingers stretched out like icy daggers, grasping for something just out of reach. Tes grinned at the disgusted expressions of the other children.

"Eww!" cried a young boy, no older than seven.

"Is it real?" asked a girl, who proceeded to poke at the fingers.

"Alyk says the Mouth can swallow people whole!" Tes informed them enthusiastically. "I bet this one died a hundred years ago!"

"But it's still got skin," protested her brother, Jordie. "Can't be *that* old!"

"Don't matter if it's in ice," said Tes. "The skin will stay forever. It could be a thousand years old!"

"Afraid she's right," said Mischa, mussing Jordie's shaggy locks of dark hair. "This far north, I doubt it ever gets warm enough to thaw out, let alone decay."

Tes shoved her brother playfully. "Told you!"

"What are you kids doing all the way out here?" It was Alyk dul Baruk, and the kids all shot to attention at his stern voice. "The group's moving on. So should you."

"We found a hand!" said Tes boldly.

Alyk knelt to examine the frozen limb. "An ancient Northman—Northwoman actually, judging by the hand… might be a thousand years old." Mischa noticed his sly smile as Tes's eyes lit up.

"See?" cried Tes again, pointing at her brother.

"Ah, you just had a lucky guess," said Jordie.

"A thousand years!" said Tes.

"And you might join the frozen people down there for another thousand if you keep wandering off. We're nearing the end of the valley of ice. I want you all marching with your families until we're clear of the Mouth, you hear?" Alyk's face grew stern, and he looked right at Tes.

The Crooked girl wilted under his gaze. "Y-yes, sir. Sorry, sir."

"Now get moving, all of you, or you'll have us all wandering out here into the middle of the night!" The children ran back the way they'd come, and once they'd gone, Alyk laughed.

"It was my fault," said Mischa. "I let them come. Don't be too hard on them."

Alyk smiled. "They could use a bit more fear in a place like this. Though, honestly, I miss the days I could walk through such a place so fearlessly."

"Me too."

"Thank you for watching after them, Mischa." The shaman fell in step beside her as they returned to the group. "They look to you as well, you know."

"What do you mean?"

"The children. Tori may be the Gallows Girl, but you give them hope also. Particularly Tes."

"You notice much," said Mischa.

"I try to know my people, old and new. I am their shaman—a shepherd of souls. I must know them the way our divine parents know them."

"The old gods," said Mischa knowingly. "Few people worship them still, you know."

"We have not forgotten our past. We still pray to them by their old names, what we called them long ago, before the Oshans stole them and distorted them. Shalam is god of the day, and he provides us with food, strength, and peace, when it can be found. Anora is goddess of the night. She followed us to the North and gave her Lights to guide our way, to give us courage and hope, even in bitter darkness. And I must do the same for my people."

"You really believe in them, don't you?"

"Don't they have gods in the islands of the Silver Sea?"

"My people believe the gods left this world long ago. The souls of our ancestors remain to protect us, give us wisdom, and intercede with the gods on our behalf."

"Sounds like the tales of the Watchers of the Old World," said Alyk.

"Melanesians believe the souls of our ancestors spring forth in the trees in our gardens where we sprinkle the ashes of our dead. But I have not prayed in a Garden of Souls in many years."

"Your people pray in gardens. In Jurka, they sacrifice doves in temples. The Watchers burned incense and prayed on rugs."

"I bet we all get it wrong," said Mischa.

"Perhaps…" said Alyk. He thought for a moment. "Or perhaps we all get it a little right. Like shades of the same sunset. My people believe the gods are all around us, and so we pray wherever we are. Perhaps it does not matter where you pray."

"That doesn't sound like a holy man."

"I suppose I am not like most holy men in the New World. I point others to the great mysteries beyond our world. I don't care if you call them by the same name. You do not seem to care for the Gardens of Souls, I sense. So… what then?"

Mischa thought a moment. She had given little thought to gods of late. And since the destruction of the Watchtower, she had often wondered how any gods could stand by and watch powers of evil continue to rule over the world.

"In the Trium'vel," Mischa said at last, "people pray to gods from many lands, and there are temples and shrines throughout the cities where traders may worship any god they desire from any nation in the New World. But there is a temple at the outskirts of the Holy Center dedicated to the Unknown One—the forgotten god. It is said she watches out for strangers and orphans—the people we've forgotten, just like we forgot about her. Somehow, she always made the most sense to me."

Alyk smiled at this. "Then I shall thank the Unknown One for remembering you, and leading you and Tori to us."

Mischa and Alyk reached the rear of the stream of people winding through the maze of ice.

"Where is Tori?" said Mischa.

"Leading the way," said Alyk. "I thought it would be good for her to be the one to lead us into the Great White North."

"You told her where to lead them, didn't you?"

"Of course. Tori has never traveled through the Mouth, after all, but her followers don't need to know that."

Mischa laughed. "Some gods we Watchers make, huh?"

"I imagine even your Unknown One was young once."

Mischa never had the chance to respond.

The ice trembled violently and sent Mischa to her knees. A jarring pain shot up her thighs. From the depths of the Mouth came a horrendous groan and a boom like thunder, and suddenly the ground disappeared from beneath her feet.

A crevasse split wide like a massive wound in the earth, rent by some giant invisible sword. Instinctively, Mischa caught herself, reaching out with her sense, and flew to the edge of the expanse. Her heart thundered in her chest. The rumblings increased, the crevasse stretching wider, and Alyk went plummeting.

Mischa's entire body tingled as her senses honed in. She caught his wrist just in time and pulled him to safety.

They collapsed in the snow. But there was no saving the Alyut and Crooked folk ahead. The Mouth of the Gods swallowed up four that Mischa saw, and who knew how many in the maze beyond. Screams echoed from all directions.

The rumblings faded, the ice groaning like a dying beast, but the crevasse did not grow any wider. It fell away at least a hundred feet, narrowing into the dark innards of the earth. There was no hope for those who'd fallen.

Mischa rose to her feet and held out her hand to help Alyk up. The shaman stared at her dumbly. His hands quavered as she took hold of them. "We have to help the others," she said. "Come on!"

But there was no time to help anyone, for no sooner had the thunder faded than it was replaced by a new sound. From the depths of the gash in the earth, there ushered a mighty roar, followed by a horrid scraping sound like nails upon glass.

A great grey hand, which looked to be composed of ice and scree, emerged from the abyss.

Another hand followed, and then a great icy head with massive tusks protruding from the sides of its vicious face. The thing heaved itself up from the pit, standing taller than four men. It lifted its mighty head, revealing jagged teeth of ice.

"A frost giant!" cried Alyk, suddenly jarring to life.

The Mouth of the Gods fell into madness as the Alyut and the Crooked folk tried to flee. Several more fell to their deaths as the chasm yawned wider.

Alyk and Mischa raced along the edge of the drop, but the monster paid them no mind. It had already found its target.

Fifty yards ahead, a girl was pinned beneath a shard of fallen ice. Her mother and brother tugged frantically at her arms as the beast neared, but the girl was held fast.

Mischa realized with horror that the girl was Tesleh.

CHAPTER THREE

The maze of ice shuddered with the echoes of dying screams. The earth had split wide, the ground falling away beneath the company of Alyut and Crooked folk. The world unraveled around Tori, and in the madness it struck her, strangely, how few names she knew of her followers, and how many she would never know. She fought back welling sickness in her gut. These people were helpless. *I have to save them!*

A Crooked woman vanished before Tori's eyes, and she was unable to reach her. The woman had green eyes like Tori's own, and they locked for a moment before the end, a calm sense passing between them. Tori seized hold of the woman's young son, but she could not save them both. The mother did not scream when she vanished. Survivors screamed. The woman merely slipped away and was gone.

Tori choked back tears. Her son wailed with horror as Tori pulled him away from the growing abyss.

"Mama! Mama!"

Tori did not even know the boy's name. Yet she was all he had left.

An aged Crooked man was pressed against the side of the ice maze nearby. Tori did not know his name either.

Where in the Abyss is Alyk? she thought helplessly.

The man's eyes met hers, but he seemed to be staring through her.

"What's your name?" Tori demanded, the poor orphaned boy sobbing in her arms.

"My name?" the man asked obtusely. He was in shock. A dozen of their company had fallen to their deaths before his eyes. *He's got to snap out of it. All of us do, or we're all dead.*

"Yes!" Tori said, taking his hand. "I'm Astoria. What is your name?"

"Benja," the old man managed.

"Benja, can you walk?"

"Walk?" he said, coming out of his daze. "Yes, yes, of course."

Tori squeezed his hand. "I need you to get this boy out of here safely. Can you do that?"

The old Crooked man seemed to realize who she was, because he straightened up and his eyes went wide. "I will, my saint."

Tori handed the boy over to Benja, brushing the hair out of the orphan's wet eyes. "You are going to make it out of here."

The boy nodded. "O-okay."

And without another word, Tori left them. She had to find Mischa and Alyk. There was another loud boom, and the world shook. Tori staggered forward.

An Alyut man came running from the passage behind. Tori had been at the front of the company, nearly out of the Mouth, when the rending of the world had begun. Everyone else in her company was behind her. Seven others followed the Alyut man, stumbling forward with the trembling of the ice. The leader shouted for them to hurry. He had a spear strapped to the back of his pack, and suddenly, Tori remembered his name. "Meryk!"

He was a hunter. He'd killed two stags in the Ever Winter Forest. She grasped his shoulder and looked him in the eyes. They were wide with fright.

"You must lead the others out!" The hunter was shaking. "Do you hear me?" Tori touched his shoulder. The rumblings faded, and the chasm ceased its expansion for the moment.

The hunter nodded to her, a peace coming over him at her touch. "Y-yes, my saint. I will not fail you."

"Take Benja and the others, the end is half a mile farther." Tori pointed north. "You have to get them out!"

Meryk nodded again. "What about you?"

"The rest are behind us! I can't leave them!"

It was then Tori heard a roar, and she knew it was not the sound of shifting ice, just as she'd known the night before, deep down, when she and Alyk had heard the rumblings. It was the sound of a living beast.

"Go! Get them out!" Tori cried, then took flight. She hadn't flown since the fall of the Watchtower, but her body took to it again as though she'd still been practicing with Ren every day on Orran's Mountain. *That feels like another lifetime,* Tori thought as she flew. And it was. It was before the end of the world had come upon them.

Below her, people scrambled frantically through the passage along the narrow cleft beside the yawning crevasse.

Tori crested a towering pillar of ice, and she saw the creature. A mighty roar echoed through the Mouth of the Gods, sending shivers darting across her skin. She knew it only from the old sage's tales around last night's fires, and a faded memory of one of her mum's old stories. But she knew without doubt what it was.

A frost giant!

The beast held a woman in its massive hands, and Tori realized with horror that it was Gwyneth, Tes's mother. Below, Mischa launched a gust of flame at the beast, but it was of little use. There was nothing to ignite —the giant's skin was frozen solid—and the flame was doused in a great rush of steam. Alyk stood beside Mischa, jabbing desperately with a useless spear.

Gwyneth looked like a doll in the giant's grasp. With its free hand, it launched a chunk of ice at Mischa and Alyk, who leapt aside just in time.

"My daughter, please!" cried Gwyneth.

Tes was trapped beneath a fallen shard of ice at the giant's feet. Jordie tugged helplessly at her arm, but she was pinned down.

Mischa let fly another ball of flame, distracting the beast. It spun away from Tes to face her, and Tori seized the moment and landed.

The ice flew free of Tes's body with a flare of Tori's Conjuri power, and Tori helped Tes to her feet. The girl's leg gave out, crushed beneath the weight of fallen ice, and she screamed. Jordie gave the support of his shoulder.

"Get her away!" Tori shouted.

"No, m-my mum!" cried Tes.

A shard of ice came flying at them, missing Jordie and Tes by a foot and exploding against the side of a pillar.

"Now!" Tori commanded.

The two hobbled feebly along the narrow ledge. Tori turned back just in time. A great icy arm the size of a tree trunk swung at her, and Tori leapt aside. The monster roared.

"Leave me!" cried Gwyneth, still in the giant's clutches. "Get my children out!"

But there was no way Tori could leave her. She had already lost Merri, and the Watchers, and probably half their company here in the Mouth of the Gods.

Tori reached out with her sense, and everything seemed to slow. She could feel the makeup of the world—the tiny frozen droplets that composed every grain of ice. Her heart filled with rage at all the death, all the suffering. A massive shard of ice broke away, with a twinge of Tori's sense, and launched into the giant's legs. It dropped to its knees. But it was not enough.

The shard of ice she'd thrown came flying back at her from the giant's hands. She dodged to the side, tumbling in the snow, and in that same instant, the giant tossed Gwyneth aside, and she disappeared, swallowed up by the crevasse.

Just like that, Tes and Jordie's mother was gone.

The beast lumbered toward her, ice flying at her like cannon fire. Mischa launched another ball of flame to no avail. Tori blocked a few shards with a flare of Conjuri power, but it was too much. The giant launched chunk after chunk of ice the size of boulders. The earth trembled again, and Tori stumbled to her knees.

When the ice hit her, Tori could feel the crunching of her ribs, the collapsing of her left lung, and the rush of blood within her chest. She lay in the snow and tried to move, but her limbs had been rendered immobile. Her head felt light, and she felt herself fading.

The giant reached for her with icy paws. Vaguely, Tori could feel the pieces of her body fitting back together, her Regenero power keeping her alive, but it was slow, and she had no time. The beast's fingers wrapped around her torso, and Tori was too weak to fight it.

Someone behind her screamed. *"NOOOOOOOOOOO!"*

High-pitched, like the shriek of a falcon, the sound seemed to build and build, filling every space in the glacial maze. It reverberated off the ice, building louder and louder. Louder than any scream Tori had ever heard. Her ears rang, and her head pounded. As the horrific shriek built even louder, the Mouth of the Gods shuddered, the crevasse groaning as it gaped even wider. Ice cracked beneath the giant's feet, and it fell backward, taking Tori with it. With every bit of remaining strength, Tori reached out with her Conjuri sense, and the great icy fingers released her. She leapt to safety, collapsing in the snow, and the frost giant disappeared into the abyss.

The scream echoed for some time before dying away. When Tori turned, she found Tesleh standing at the end of the passage, her fist clinging to her brother's cloak. The Crooked girl's chest heaved frantically. The scream had been hers.

Slowly, Tori's body healed, and Mischa and Alyk helped her to her feet. When they reached Tes, the girl collapsed from exhaustion.

"M-my mum," Tes murmured, tears welling in her eyes.

Mischa knelt by the girl's side, brushing the hair out of her face. "Shh... You're all right."

"NO! I'M NOT! SHE'S DEAD!"

The ground trembled again at Tes's scream. Tes broke into sobs, and Mischa held her tight and rocked gently.

"W-what did I do?" Tes whimpered.

Tori took the girl's hand, realization dawning on her. That scream was magic awakening, just as it once had in Tori, so long ago, on the day of the Gallows.

"You saved us, Tes," Tori said. "You saved us all."

PART TWO
THE UNRAVELING OF THE WORLD

There was a saying that arose after everything was over: The world must be undone before it can be remade.

But no one believed that in those days. There was no hope. No world to come. No world to remake. To those who lived through the unraveling, it was the end of the world.

—from Dawn of the Third World

CHAPTER FOUR

Kirra Fehn was in a constant state of anguish, and therefore, so was Kale Andovier—for he felt responsible for what the chancellor had done to her, and there was nothing he could do.

For weeks, they had been secluded in the Den of the Ilya, buried deep beneath the Yan Avii capital, Vlyanii. But this time, not as prisoners. Kale had not seen Salla Burodai—the newly crowned Great Soltayne—since he had been chosen in the twisted game of power that was masked as the Choosing of Arayeva. But it seemed his *old friend* bore some guilt for Kirra's physical state, for Kirra was attended daily by the Burodai family's very own *thrasii,* an elderly tribesman named Azrahi, who administered an array of herbs and healing spells. Still, Kirra's eyes were irreparably disabled, and she lived in that strange limbo between pain and sleep, death and life.

The severe burns she'd sustained under the chancellor's distortion of her own Lumeni power had rendered her eyesight useless and scarred the right side of her face beyond recognition. The tender, swollen skin was dressed with linens and oozed with pus. The room reeked with the smell of death, but Kale hardly noticed, nor cared. Kirra was alive, if barely. And that was all that mattered.

A few days ago, she had shot up in bed, shouting and cursing, seemingly unsure what was dream and what was reality. It had taken the *thrasii* and Kale both to keep her from harming herself. Afterward, she slept a full day before waking to violent delusions.

Kale feared she might never recover. Each time Azrahi tended her wounds, he said, "She is marred by a fierce magic, stronger than my own."

Some days Kirra looked to be improving, and other days, she thrashed about, plagued by dark fever dreams. Truth be told, Kale feared what would happen if she did recover. What would they do? Where would they go now that he'd betrayed all their fellow Watchers? Betrayed her?

Ashi, Salla's most trusted servant, had delivered the news that the Watchtower had indeed been defeated.

"My brother?" Kale had asked.

Ashi shook her head, a strange look on her face. "Ren is alive. In the chancellor's dungeons."

Kale had been overwhelmed by a confliction of guilt and relief. He had betrayed the location of his brother's rebel army, but at least it had not cost Ren his life. But what of the other Watchers? The symbol of the revolution? "And the Gallows Girl?"

"No one knows," Ashi said. "It seems the Legions were attacked by Nosferati while escorting her to Osha. The Gallows Girl was lost in the mayhem."

Now Rulaqs *and* the race of cannibalistic demons had returned to the world of men, and Kale had enabled it to happen.

But if he had not, Kirra would be dead. The chancellor already had the godstones, so it would only have been a matter of time before Cyrus Maro discovered the Watchtower. At least, that was what Kale tried to tell himself.

———

IT HAD BEEN NEARLY A MONTH SINCE HER ENCOUNTER WITH THE chancellor when Kirra began to stir. She was soaked in sweat and clammy to the touch. Kale fetched a bowl of water, took her hand, and helped her drink, uttering a prayer that she would not slip into another violent hallucination. She coughed as she tried to swallow, but the next sip went down easier. She leaned back and sighed. It was more life than she'd shown yet, and Kale dared to cling to hope that the worst might be over.

"Thank the gods," he whispered, squeezing her hand.

Kirra moaned and muttered something unintelligible.

"What do you need?" he said.

"W-where is he?" Her voice was a mere rasp.

"I'm here," said Kale.

Kirra coughed and pulled her hand away from him. "Not you, the *thrasii*."

Azrahi appeared in the archway and knelt at the bedside, his tunic of small beads rattling as he moved. He held his hand to Kirra's forehead and smiled.

"I believe your fever has finally broken, my dear," he said. "Arayeva be praised."

Kirra coughed again, and the *thrasii* helped her sip some more water. "Praised... I'm still blind, aren't I? That wasn't part of the dream?" It pained Kale to hear her speak the words, confirming his fears. It would not pass.

"No," said Azrahi carefully. He passed his hand in front of her eyes, but the sudden movement stirred no life in them. "I...I'm afraid that was no dream. But you must remember, you could be dead, my dear."

"Like my friends?"

The *thrasii* did not seem to know what to say. He helped her with another drink. "I believe the worst has passed." Azrahi patted her hands. "You will be in pain for some time, I expect, as your face continues to heal. But the infection has waned. Can you sit up?"

Kirra was still terribly weak, but she managed to shift herself upright in bed. The *thrasii* began unbinding the wraps about her face. The oozing had eased up, and now the ruined skin shone red and swollen.

He treated her wounds with a healing salve, then wrapped her eyes with a fresh layer of linen, thinner than the last. Tender flesh was left visible at the sides of the bandage, but it was good to see more of her face. It made her seem more like a person and less like a corpse being prepared in burial cloths.

"Thank you, *thrasii*," Kirra said sincerely. "I owe you my life."

"I'm afraid I did precious little. The dark magic binding itself to you has lightened, though not by my doing. Arayeva is not finished with you yet. But you are welcome, all the same." He patted her hands, once more, and then left them alone.

Suddenly, the gravity of everything they had endured together washed over Kale. He loved her, and she was awake, and he knew they should speak. But he feared what she might say, now that she was coherent.

"How do you feel?" Kale said weakly.

"Hungry. I've had nothing but broth in… how long has it been?"

"Nearly a month."

"Gods," said Kirra. "Is there any lamb in this pit?"

Kale smiled, grateful she'd not lost her sense of humor along with her sight. "Maybe you ought to start with *ylkii*."

He fetched her some of the Yan Avii flatbread, and she ate voraciously. As she chewed, she winced, but it did not stop her eating. When she finished, she lay back against her pillow. Kale hated the sight of her like this. But he was desperately grateful she was alive.

Is she *grateful?* he wondered.

"You hardly left this room," she muttered. "All the time I've been out. I could sense you, even when I was lost in some terror." He could not tell if she was pleased by this fact. Her tone was flat, somber.

"You were on the verge of death… I couldn't leave you."

"I wanted to die," Kirra said.

"You're tired. You should rest."

"Don't tell me what I need." She was growing angry, though he could sense she was holding back a rage far greater than her voice showed. "I knew what I was risking, going back for the godstones."

Kale did not know what to say.

"I was willing to die to protect the Shadow Watch. This time, I was going to protect the others. Why did you come back?" Her voice quavered. "Why?"

"I… I couldn't let you die."

"It wasn't your choice to make!" she said bitterly. "After what happened before, how could you take that away from me?"

Kale knew she was referring to their greatest regret, their failure to protect the young Watchers on the Isle of Jallaa all those years ago. Watchers not unlike Ren's Shadow Watch. Young sorcerer refugees led by a charismatic man from another age of the world. Even their leader had died.

"How many are dead at the Watchtower, Kale?"

"The chancellor didn't kill them. Just as he promised."

"I heard," said Kirra, her anger subsiding into sadness. "I may have been half delirious, but I heard when Ashi came to tell you. About the Nosferati. The Gallows Girl. All of it… However many died this time, however many are being bled dry in the White Citadel, that blood is on you, Kale. All of it is on you." Kirra trembled with sobs, her ruined eyes unable to produce tears any longer. "You stole my sacrifice."

"Kirra, please! I... I..." He reached for her hand. All he wanted was to hold her, but she pulled away. A chasm greater than Jallaa, greater than the span of the Great Canyons of Dimh, opened up between them, and Kale felt she was back in the other world, where Medea had taken her with the godstones. Kirra had never seemed so far away.

"Leave me," she said hollowly. "And let me grieve in peace."

Kale knew it was futile to argue. So he left her. When he returned an hour later, she had drifted back to sleep, though this time it was not in fits. And for this, Kale thanked the gods.

———

Kirra improved more each day. A week later, she was able to get up and move about the room with Azrahi's assistance—she would accept no help from Kale. He remained close, but often found himself in the main room of the Ilya Den when she was awake. At times, he would reach out for her mind, wishing for some connection, but she had walled herself from him more than ever.

Azrahi was tending her wounds when Ashi came to see Kale, while he sat outside Kirra's chambers. A few Ilya milled about the central hall of the Den, discussing how to deal with the son of Xander Mynah—the *soltayne* Kale had helped Salla kill during the events of the Choosing. It seemed that Salla saw Kale as an ally, for the Ilya did not try to mask their plot from him. Or perhaps Salla recognized Kale for the spineless, unthreatening coward he was.

Ashi brushed his shoulder from behind, startling him. "For someone who gave up everything for love," she said, "you look like *shenzah*, Sky Blood."

She took the seat beside him at a round table bedecked with platters of roasted lamb and rice. Ashi was dressed in black Ilya garb, her hood drawn back to reveal a bronze face and curly dark hair pulled tight behind her head in a braid.

Kale should have been appalled to see the Yan Avii slave. Ashi and her master had betrayed him, after all, and yet, he was relieved to be spoken to without revulsion. He and Ashi had formed a curious bond during the events of the Choosing. Despite her betrayal, she was about the closest thing he had left to a friend. A miserable truth. "Kirra despises me. And I don't blame her. I betrayed my own kind. Betrayed her."

"The chancellor gets what he wants," said Ashi. "I imagine he'd have gotten the information from Kirra eventually, even if you'd abandoned her like she asked."

"She'd have died before she betrayed them."

"Perhaps," said Ashi. "Even if she had, he'd have found your Watchtower in time."

"Spoken like someone defending their own betrayal."

Ashi glared at him. "You don't pick up on apologies, do you? Your list of allies is small, it seems to me. So don't act like you have any place to judge me. I did what I did for the good of my people. So did Salla."

Kale sighed. "Why are you here, Ashi?"

She rolled her eyes, her lips drawn tight. "To make a peace offering, Sky Blood. I don't regret what I did, but I wish it might have turned out differently for you… and for Kirra." Ashi glanced at the archway to Kirra's chamber at the end of the room, her normally settled expression turning with something like remorse.

"A lot of good it does us now."

"It may yet," said Ashi. "I am leaving in the morning."

"Leaving the Red City?"

"My chief has asked me to attend his sister in the White Citadel as she prepares to become the chancellor's queen. I'll be joined by a company of servants and Ilya charged with looking after Vashti Burodai."

"What?" said Kale. "Doesn't Salla trust his closest ally?"

"Salla would be a fool to *trust* the chancellor."

"Why are telling me this?"

"Because you and Kirra should come with me."

"You can't be serious."

"I saw what Vashti could do before her father tried to burn her at the stake. I know how she healed. Your healers could help Kirra."

Kale longed so very much to be able to help her.

"It is not too late to ally yourselves with the chancellor," said Ashi. "You already gave him the Shadow Watch. If you join him, he will heal her, Sky Blood. I am sure of it. Besides, Salla says several of your Watchers have already joined him. Your brother's revolution is over. But Kirra's sight need not be."

"My brother is there. All the Watchers I betrayed," said Kale. "I couldn't face them." His dreams were already tormented by Ren, his mother, and the dead Watchers from Jallaa. It was like the ghosts of Ghen, ever dwelling in his nightmares to remind him of the countless times the Exiled Lord had failed those for whom he cared the most.

"Not even for her?" Ashi whispered.

"She would never go. Not even to regain her sight."

Ashi held up a vial. "You know this draught." Kale did. Ashi had used it to render him unconscious on more than one occasion in the past couple months. "Sometimes we must choose what is best for the ones we love, in spite of their stubborn ideals. Neither of you can do anyone any good down here."

Kale took the vial and stowed it in his cloak. "I'll… consider it."

Ashi smirked. "Consider quickly, Sky Blood. We leave at dawn, with or without you." And with that, she was gone.

When Kale returned to Kirra's chambers, he found her sleeping again. Her wraps had been removed entirely, and her wounds were beginning to scar. The *thrasii* applied a salve twice daily to aid the process. Her right eye was nearly closed over with scar tissue. Her left eye was in tact, but clouded over. It still moved, but saw none of the world. The thought that all this could be undone was nearly more than Kale could bear.

Perhaps Ashi was right. What good were they down here? What good was Kirra in such a pitiful state?

Kale eyed the vial. He held it up in the soft lamplight and considered the crimson liquid. Kirra would never go to Maro'El willingly; he knew her too well for that. Her blindness was the curse of a failed sacrifice, and she had accepted it. Perhaps she thought it was her punishment for her failures, just as Kale saw it as punishment for his own.

Should he accept her desires, then? Was that best? For her? For the rest of the Shadow Watch? For himself?

There, he knew, was the truth of it.

To take her to the White Citadel would be to temper his own guilt. It might restore her sight, but it would not bridge the chasm between them. To drug her would be to betray her all over again…

———

THAT NIGHT KALE DID NOT SLEEP. INTO THE WAKING HOURS, HE watched over Kirra. It was the one time she seemed at peace with him there, and if he tried, he could catch glimpses of her dreams. Her subconscious was not lined with the walls she constructed when she was awake.

But he quickly withdrew. With his Cerebro magic, he sensed she was dreaming of being able to see again, and this pained him beyond his capacity. It was all he could do not to slip the Ilya draught into the bowl of water beside the bed.

It was what she longed for deep down. To see, to be able to help the others.

But no, he could not do it.

Scarred and blind though she was, he still found Kirra beautiful. So strong, so fierce. He stroked her hand tenderly as she slept. How he loved the feel of her smooth olive skin.

The touch brought back torturous memories of the night he'd beheld her in all her beauty—before the world had filled with horrors and guilt —when his entire world had been nothing but her lips, her skin. Her love.

The night on the Isle of Jallaa.

So many times, he had wished to return to that night and never leave, never go beyond it, but never more than now. The space between them was filled with blood and nightmares and betrayal, but once, they had been as close as two people could be. Back before the night of the slaughter. The night they were both trying to redeem, both trying to forget.

And now, because of Kale, they had one more night to regret. Their chasm was expanding wider and wider. It was said the Great Canyons of Dimh, which spanned miles in some places, had once been mere gullies carved by rain, but over time, they grew. Each snowmelt, each rainfall, each spring flood, cut deeper and wider, deeper and wider, until the other side of the maze of canyons was like another world.

Kale stowed Ashi's vial in his cloak again, and vowed to dispose of it as soon as possible. He was about to find Ashi and tell her they would not be going to the White Citadel, when Kirra began to seize violently in bed.

He took hold of her hand as she trembled. Her skin was cold. And then, she shot up straight and screamed.

"Sh-sh," said Kale. "It's all right. It was only a nightmare."

Kirra's head shifted back and forth, as though trying to see, caught between a dream and her sightless reality. Her grip was tight on his hand.

"Kale, you need to get the others!" she shouted.

"What others? It was only a dream. Everything is fine."

"No!" she shrieked. "Can't you hear them?"

Chills pricked his skin like hornets at the sound of her voice. He had never heard such terror. "Kirra, hear what?"

She shoved him away. "Get Ashi! Warn the Ilya! We have to get out of the city now! They're coming!"

Now, it was Kale's turn to tremble. "Who's coming?"

Kirra's voice was firm and steady, fully awake now, and there was no mistaking the dread in her words. "The terror of the Wandering Dunes," she said. "Xa'Rila!"

CHAPTER FIVE

Xa'Rila, thought Kale. *It's not possible.*

Though Kale heard nothing, he did as Kirra ordered, hurrying to find Ashi before she left the Red City for Osha. The urgency in Kirra's voice left him without doubt. He did not understand how Kirra could hear Xa'Rila, but her tremulous voice had filled him with terrible chills.

The monsters were the most notorious beasts in all Yan Avii folklore, said to have plagued the people during their years wandering the desert, at the dawn of the New World. Kale had always thought them nothing but a superstitious explanation for the sandstorms and sinkholes common in the Wandering Dunes. The thought that the beasts might be real made Kale's stomach lurch. *First, Rulaqs and Nosferati, and now this?*

He found Ashi in the Den of the Ilya, loading supplies with a pair of young Ilya boys. The moment Kale told her what Kirra had heard, Ashi begged him to fly to the Red Palace to warn Salla before it was too late for the entire city.

But Kale hesitated. "I... I can't leave Kirra."

"You must!" Kirra came stumbling blind into the room after him.

Ashi took hold of her hand and led her to a table for support.

"Kale, hurry, please," Kirra murmured, clutching at her temples. "It's getting louder. They are almost upon the city."

"I'll get her out," said Ashi. "Or I'll die by her side. But only you can get to Salla in time."

"I don't know the way from the Den," Kale said.

Ashi took his hand fiercely. Her skin was searing. For the second time, the Yan Avii slave let down the mental walls Salla had taught her to build against Kale's Cerebro gift, and she opened her mind to him. Through her eyes, he saw vividly the network of tunnels beneath the Red City—the Ilya's secret path. "Now fly, Sky Blood!"

And Kale did.

He flew down dark, winding chambers, following Ashi's intricate mind map. When Kale emerged from a drainage grate outside the Red Palace, it was dawn, the Sol glowing blood red as it crested the Wandering Dunes. The sudden light stung his eyes. He had not seen the sun in weeks. It was a red dawn—a sign of Arayeva's anger and despair.

And Xa'Rila are approaching Vlyanii? Kale thought. *Perhaps there is something to their goddess after all.*

Kale flew from the earth and rose above the radial formation of streets and sandstone buildings. The Red Palace rose above everything, the heart of the Yan Avii capital, with the Golden Temple of Arayeva at its zenith. The temple glowed in the early light. Kale knew the Great Soltayne's chambers were situated beneath the temple. He had saved Salla from assassination there only weeks ago.

Kale could sense Salla's mind dimly. It was still guarded by subconscious walls, but Kale sensed enough to know he was in his chambers. Kale flew to a ledge on the western side of the palace and entered through a high window. The Red Palace was well guarded. Through normal entrance, Kale would have had to pass through seven gates and several companies of guards, but Salla's window surmounted a sheer wall of sandstone, which towered two hundred feet over the awakening city. Even if someone could fight through all the security below, it would be nearly impossible to scale the smooth stone tower. Kale flew the distance with ease and landed softly in Salla's chambers.

Set before the western window was a statue of Arayeva—a beautiful sandstone woman with a flaming Sol held at her waist. Outside the eastern window, the Sol crested the dunes, and Salla knelt in prayer before a second, identical statue. Odd, considering the man's lack of fervor toward his people's faith. He wore only a plain white tunic. His dark hair was unkempt, and his face unshaven. A stark contrast to his normally well-maintained appearance. His lips moved with inaudible words, and he was apparently oblivious to Kale's arrival.

But then Salla spoke aloud. "Have you come to kill me, Sky Blood?" Salla sounded at peace, despite the potential threat. Or perhaps he was simply not afraid of Kale.

"No," he said.

Salla chuckled strangely. "I would not blame you, if you were. A red sun rises, just as it did the day I killed my father." Was that regret in his voice?

"I'm not here to kill you. I'm here to warn you. Xa'Rila are descending upon Vlyanii."

Salla breathed heavily, rendered silent by the vile name. "That… can't be possible…" His voice rang hollow.

"You don't have time to find out. If you hesitate, it may be too late."

Salla was still kneeling. He seemed almost in a trance. "How could you possibly know Xa'Rila are coming, old friend?"

"Kirra heard them from the Den," said Kale.

"She… heard them?" He stared out the window, perhaps listening for them himself, but the morning was as still as the uninhabited valleys of the Crimson Mountains of the Far East.

Kale was baffled as well. *How could Kirra possibly hear them?* Kale had heard nothing in the Den. At first, he'd thought she was hallucinating, caught in the remnants of a nightmare. But Ashi believed her. And so must he.

"I don't know how, but Kirra heard them approaching. We have to go!" He took Salla by the arm, firmly, and jerked him to his feet. At this, Salla came back to life.

Salla cursed, took one last glance at the rising Sol, and murmured another prayer. "Jeshu! Daven!" he cried out, and two Ilya appeared immediately through the immense socha doors to Salla's chambers. When they saw Kale, they drew their sabers.

"Filthy Sky Blood!"

"At ease," Salla said, raising his hands.

Daven stammered. "But, my chief, how could he—"

"We have not left your chamber doors all night, I swear it!" pleaded Jeshu.

"He flew," said Salla simply. "And now, so must you. Sound the Horns. We must evacuate the city. The bane of our people has returned."

At the mention of Xa'Rila, both guards nodded fearfully.

"My chief," said Jeshu. "What about you?"

"I am with the Sky Blood. Now hurry!"

The Ilya regarded Kale skeptically, but withdrew at a sprint to sound the ancient Horns of Xa'Rila. Vestiges of the Old World, the Horns were the only thing that could warn the people in time.

"Ashi and the others…" said Salla.

"They're fleeing the Den," said Kale.

"I realize it is much to ask, Sky Blood, but my fate lies in your hands once more."

"Ashi is getting Kirra out alive. I promised to do the same for you. And fortunately for you, I am through with betrayal." Kale took Salla by the wrist. "Let's fly!"

Kale and Salla leapt from the window of the royal chambers. Flight was agonizing with another in tow, but he hoped he could reach the edge of the city. They soared over the gates of the palace. That was when he felt Kirra's cry in his mind. *Oh gods! They're still in the tunnels!*

Without explanation, he descended.

"What are you doing?" Salla protested.

"I... I can't bear you any farther!" Kale lied.

Cradling Salla in his arms like a child, Kale slowed their descent at the last moment. He landed in a crouch outside the palace walls and set Salla down. The Horns of Xa'Rila began booming across the city. Giant tusks of an ancient behemoth, the Horns were set along the walls of the Golden Temple, situated beside much smaller horns that rang out each morning and evening to call the Yan Avii to prayer.

"The Horns have not blown in over three hundred years," said Salla darkly as they hurried through the streets. Kale felt sick. They had to reach the tunnels quick.

The deep bellow of the Horns of Xa'Rila resounded across the city, distinct from any other sound Kale had ever heard. The guttural booming made the streets themselves vibrate. At least, Kale hoped that was the reason. Though the people of Vlyanii had never heard the Horns in their lives, they responded immediately—with terror and panic.

The streets of Vlyanii became teeming chaos, like a colony of war ants after their hive was destroyed. People screamed, flung belongings into the streets, and made frantically for the northern gates of the city, which led to the vast plains of the Steppe. The Horns bellowed beneath it all like a marching beat no one was following. The city seethed in one throbbing mass of mayhem, and Kale and Salla were stuck in the middle, weaving through walls of pressing bodies. No one even realized that their Great Soltayne was in their midst. Salla was shoved aside like anyone else as the Yan Avii fled.

Kale seized Salla's wrist and jerked him down a side street, both of them shoving their way through the crowd. "We've got to go underground," Kale cried. He gestured to a cleft in a wall, similar to the one Kale had emerged from only minutes ago.

"What have you sensed?" Salla demanded, stopping in the narrow vacant alley of red stone.

"Kirra and Ashi are still in the Den!"

Salla nodded, his eyes growing fierce. Kale didn't know for certain that Ashi was still with Kirra, or even alive, but his words had the desired effect. Salla cared for his devoted servant. "Let me lead the way."

They slipped through the cleft in the sandstone wall, slinked through a narrow corridor, then Salla opened a grate, which led to the network of hidden tunnels beneath the Red City. Salla gripped his wrist and led the way in the dark.

They reached the Den to find it empty. Tables were overturned, provisions and crates and clothes were strewn about the room, and in the far wall there was a dark chasm that hadn't been there before.

Xa'Rila was here! Kale pushed back bile and reached out with his senses.

No sign of Kirra.

Salla grabbed his wrist, and they hurried on down the twisted labyrinth of tunnels beneath the Red City. The noise of the fleeing masses faded, and Kale finally heard what Kirra had somehow sensed from afar: a horrid grinding sound like soldiers marching upon a field of skulls. The ground trembled beneath their feet.

It was the approach of Xa'Rila.

"Arayeva, have mercy," Salla murmured. He gripped Kale's wrist harder, and they pressed on as quickly as possible through the dark. Salla's prayer filled Kale with a greater terror than the sound.

The grinding grew in intensity the deeper they ventured. Soon it was a mighty roar, and the ground roiled beneath their feet as they staggered forward.

Without warning, Salla shoved Kale to the ground. The roar reached a fever pitch; there was a great rush of air, and a horrid stench permeated the chambers. And then, all at once, the roar ceased.

The monster was directly ahead.

Kale could sense its mind. Or rather, the mind of the many Rila. He could not tell whether they shared one mind, or were simply tethered together by some mysterious telepathy. But in one glimpse, he unraveled a mystery that centuries of myths had only guessed at. Xa'Rila were many individual beasts, interconnected, functioning as one, sharing their knowledge as they ascended from the depths of the Wandering Dunes. The onslaught of their dark sentience overwhelmed him.

Kale swore he could see silver eyes in the darkness ahead. A slithering sound echoed off the cavern walls as the beast tasted the air. It was searching for one thing—the scent of humans.

Deep breaths echoed through the caverns, a throaty wheeze that left a rancid, sulfuric odor in the air. Kale and Salla held perfectly still, but Kale felt the foul breaths, hot and humid, upon his face, as though a wall of stench were pressing in on him.

The beast sensed them.

The slithering sound grew until Kale could taste the Rila's stench. His stomach churned. But then, he sensed an awakening in the shared mind of Xa'Rila. Some of the horde had reached the surface, where a delectable human feast awaited, all gathered in one place for the slaughter. And in a moment, the grinding sound returned, the stench faded, and Kale's sense of Xa'Rila drifted until it was but a vague anticipation of blood and violence.

He let out a long-held breath of relief.

Salla was trembling. "I thought we were dead, Sky Blood."

"Let's pray the others are not," was all Kale said. He felt nothing in his senses. They were too overwhelmed with the countless dying minds in the world above, mixed with the bloodlust of Xa'Rila.

He and Salla pressed forward once more. The beast left a yawning chasm in the tunnel, just as it had in the Den. It had burrowed straight through the earth, cutting a brand new channel. Kale wondered if Xa'Rila had cut the passage they were in now, centuries and centuries ago.

Kale flew them across the gaping space, and they surged on into the dark.

It took what felt like hours of weaving through the winding maze of tunnels, but eventually Kale and Salla reached the end of the depths. He knew they were close and let out a deep sigh of relief when he felt Kirra's mind open to him.

They came to the end of the tunnel. A large stone shifted forward at

Salla's behest, and they emerged in a red sandstone tower a league outside the city walls.

Ashi and Kirra and the other Ilya were waiting for them. Kale rushed to Kirra and took her in his arms, beyond grateful that she was alive. And for once, she returned his affection. Kirra gripped him tight.

"You took so long," she said. "I worried you didn't make it out of the city in time. Why did you go in the tunnels?"

"I heard you cry out."

"One of the beasts attacked the Den. We barely made it out alive."

Kale held her tight. Ashi and Salla greeted one another in the way of the Yan Avii, clasping forearms. It was the formal greeting of equals, not of a king and his servant. "Thank you, Sky Blood," said Ashi, glancing over at him, "for saving my chief."

Kale nodded his own thanks, grateful to have Kirra safely in his arms.

CHAPTER SIX

The Red City roiled like a den of serpents, whirlwinds of sand and debris rising from the streets and shrouding the infamous Xa'Rila as they consumed the city. From a distance, atop the sandstone tower at the edge of the Steppe, Kale and the others watched helplessly as buildings crumbled and the sky filled with screams. After many hours, it seemed like the Red Palace would survive the onslaught, but then it, too, was shrouded in whirlwinds of sand, and when they had settled, half the palace had fallen away. And then, just as suddenly as it had begun, the crumbling of stone and the wails of the dying ceased.

The attack was over.

A stream of survivors poured onto the plains. That night Ashi lit a beacon at the peak of the tower to guide their way to refuge. Thanks to Kirra's warning, many had escaped the city before Xa'Rila arrived, and soon there were thousands of Yan Avii gathered at the banks of the Spillway, before the outpost tower where their Great Soltayne resided safe and sound.

Over the next few days, Salla sent out teams to search for more survivors, and miraculously, there were some found in the debris. Kale's gift proved vital in locating them. With his Cerebro sense, he found many under piles of rubble and lost in gaping crevasses left behind in the sandstone. The city was riddled with a thousand such holes, making it look like one great corpse after a firing squad had done its dark deed. The search was slow work, and it was many days before Salla called a council of the surviving *soltaynes* to declare an end to the search, to anoint successors for the dead chieftains, and to decide their next move as a people.

Five of the *soltaynes* had been safe on the Steppe with their tribes at the time of the attack. Of those in the city, three were lost, and it fell to their eldest sons to rise up in their late fathers' steads. When the anointing ceremony had been completed, the Great Soltayne gathered the chiefs of the twelve tribes in the commander's quarters in the sandstone guard tower.

Kale and Kirra were not invited.

They waited by a cook fire outside, amidst the large refugee camp that had formed on the banks of the river. The Great Spillway was the life source for the Yan Avii. The mighty river, formed from the runoffs of the Crooked Teeth and the Spine of the North, weaved and built for hundreds of miles across the Grey Waste to the Steppe. The Spillway ran all the way to the Bay of Trium at the southwestern edge of the continent. It was the largest river in the New World, and without it, the Steppe would be an arid wasteland, and the herdsmen would be able to maintain no livelihood upon the Steppe.

Littles were playing at the shore of the river, boys and girls running naked and splashing one another as their mothers washed clothes on the bank. They were squealing with laughter. It seemed absurd after so many dark days.

"It's amazing, isn't it?" said Kirra. "How littles can find such joy, even at a time like this."

"Childish ignorance," said Kale. "Their world is in shambles. Their chieftains meet to decide how the tribes will survive this travesty. And they laugh and play, oblivious."

"It's a gift. What would the world be without laughter?"

Kale could not remember the last time he had laughed out of such pure joy. But he remembered a world before this darkness. He held onto the memory, though he did not dare entertain the notion that its world would return to him. He was grateful Kirra was speaking to him again. It was joy enough for now. Kale squeezed Kirra's hand briefly. She flinched ever so slightly at his touch, whether from surprise at the contact or subdued disdain, he did not know.

"It would be a world without littles," he said at last.

"A world with no future. One not worth fighting for. Gods…" Kirra's face turned toward the children's squeals. "I wish I could see their faces.

I've always thought it was one of the most beautiful things. The bright eyes of a child."

Kale did not know what to say to this. Kirra's blindness was still such a strange concept to grasp. He could not imagine how hard it must be for her. She had not spoken of it since she'd awoken, at least not to him.

Your sight could be returned if we went to the White Citadel.

But he did not say it. Ashi paced nearby, muttering irritated curses, but she soon grew tired of it and joined them around the cook fire.

"Well, you were right, after all, Sky Blood, weren't you?" Ashi said, taking a seat.

"About what?"

"That Salla's alliance with the chancellor is in shambles. It just did not show until after the Choosing, until after he'd gotten what he wanted from my prince."

"How so?"

"How else do you suppose Xa'Rila rose out of the desert to attack our city for the first time in over three hundred years? The chancellor brought back Rulaqs to the North. And now this."

Ashi gestured at the skeletal remains of Vlyanii in the distance. The sight reminded him of the ruined cities of the Ancient World, the Necropoli of the Ruined Empire of Faere. Once magnificent centers of a sprawling empire, now crumbling wastes overgrown with foliage and time.

"I thought there were attacks reported in the New World," said Kirra. "When your people were exiled in the desert."

"Tales," said Ashi. "There have been such claims since. Any dead body found in the desert is blamed on Xa'Rila. But no one has ever seen the attacks, because no one ever survives, they say. You saw how they killed. They swallowed people whole. Real beasts would have left no bodies behind out in the desert for us to find. This is the chancellor's doing. Just like the Rulaqs and the Nosferati."

Kale wanted to agree with her. *But why would the chancellor order a slaughter like this, right after forming an alliance with the Yan Avii?*

"Salla sent ravens to Osha," he said. "They are fighting their own war with the Rulaqs."

Ashi spat into the fire, which aroused a glare from an old maid tending the kettles. "*Shenzah!*" Ashi swore in Yan Avii. "You sound like Salla. An army of Rulaqs. Yes, I heard. If it's true, I hope they raze the city. I hope they turn his White Citadel to crimson."

Kirra reached out and found Ashi's hand. It amazed Kale how she was adapting to life guided by sound rather than light. "Don't wish vengeance upon all at the chancellor's expense. There are innocents in Osha, just as here."

"Pah!" But that was all Ashi could muster for some time. She stared off at her ruined city, glowering silently. "Well, something must be done. There are ten thousand dead at last count. Thousands more will be added in the end. Arayeva, I wish I could sit in on the *soltaynes'* meeting." A sudden thought came to her, and Kale sensed her question before she asked. "Sky Blood, you have your sorcery. What can you make of their council?"

Kale had been catching portions of it for some time, though he did not particularly care what they decided. His thoughts were on Kirra and where they should go next. Kirra was near fully recovered, except for her blindness. It was time they talked of their own next move. They need not be ensnared in the affairs of the Yan Avii any longer.

He shook his head. "You won't like it, Ashi."

"Tell me."

"The chieftains don't know of the chancellor's godstones, nor the door they open between worlds. And Salla does not plan to reveal that knowledge." *They helped Salla steal his way to the Great Saddle,* he thought. *If they knew, Salla would be a dead man.* "All they know is that Salla sealed an alliance with Osha. They have no reason to suspect the chancellor."

Kirra's jaw tightened at the conversation. She quickly caught herself, but it was not lost on Kale. Was it because of the godstones? How Salla had twisted her search for ancient magic toward his own game of power? Or something else?

"But they protested the alliance," said Ashi. "We have always despised Osha, ever since the First Chancellor exiled us to the desert."

Kale almost laughed at the irony. "It would seem that most of the chieftains are rethinking their hatred. Most of the food stores in the city have been laid to waste, and winter is fast approaching. Aid from Osha looks suddenly quite appealing."

"The councils are never that united!" Ashi protested. "There must be *some* dissent."

It was true. The tribes of the Yan Avii were not known for their unity. They often warred against one another, usually territorial squabbles. And Kale knew all too well, when it came to the Choosing of the Great Soltayne, they were not beneath murdering one another.

"Disaster has a way of subsiding old rivalries," said Kale. "From what I can gather, Xerdan Mynah is the only opponent, and since his father's manipulation of fate was exposed at the Choosing, he is not exactly a convincing voice on the council."

Ashi spat in the fire again, and the old maid shooed her away. With a heavy sigh, Ashi stood. "We'll fall groveling at the chancellor's feet for aid? All this reeks of the chancellor." She stormed off and left them alone once more.

Kale watched the children playing again for a while. One sprinted from the pack and raced to her father's arms. He'd just returned from guard duty, judging from his attire. The father twirled the little girl around. She squealed with joy, and together, they made their way to their tent.

Kale despised the *soltaynes* and the corrupt workings of the Red Palace. Their system was riddled with cruel injustices, generally originating from the chieftains. But the Yan Avii people were much like all others. Littles, caring mothers, and doting fathers. Still, he was ready to be done with the Yan Avii.

"The council's nearly over," said Kirra.

"How can you tell?" said Kale, surprised.

"I can hear them rousing in the tower."

Kale had been wanting to ask from the moment she'd told him about Xa'Rila. In his heart, he already knew the answer. Her hearing had never been so acute before. "Kirra, how can you hear them? How did you hear Xa'Rila?"

Kirra did not answer at once. Her eyes blinked without sight, and she shifted her posture. "My Lumeni gift is worthless now." She touched her scarring face and winced. "I... I think a new power is growing... as though to replace it." Her voice betrayed her anger at accepting the finality of her lost sight. She crossed her arms and leaned against a bundle of supplies and said nothing for some time.

A new gift?

Kale did not understand how that could be possible. According to the traditions of the ancient Watcher order, the realms of magic were static. Kale was a Cerebro. He ruled the realm of minds, and that was all. Kirra was a Lumeni, and she ruled the realm of light. There was no transcending that gift. Kirra had never shown an affinity toward any other realm of magic before.

There were some who did. The Mages—those with more than one

affinity. His mother had told him tales of such sorcerers. They were reviled by most leaders of the old Watcher order. They were seen as unnatural, too ambitious, but they had always fascinated Kale as a boy. *Perhaps it is true, what Mother said, that magic has no limit.*

How else could it be explained? Kirra had never shown it before, but with her Lumeni gift rendered useless, she was showing sure signs of the Sonora—who ruled the realm of sound.

And Kirra was right about the council being finished. Moments after she'd heard them, the *soltaynes* emerged from the tower and returned to the camps of their respective tribes.

"How is that possible?" he responded finally. "How could you possess another gift?"

Kirra sighed. "I don't know, Kale. Before I lost my sight, I never heard a thing out of the ordinary. But as I lay in that bed in the Ilya Den, I found myself focusing more on sound to gain any knowledge of my surroundings. I could tell when you entered by your gait, by the timbre of your breaths. Azrahi was distinct by the soft rustle of his beads. Ashi steps lightly, on the balls of her feet, and her breaths are slow and restricted, as though constantly trying to pass unnoticed. The more I focus, the more acute my hearing grows. Subtle shifts of clothing, footsteps, heartbeats, all betray movement. I can't see it, but... the world is alive with sound."

"That's incredible," he said.

Kirra was not smiling. "I know I should be grateful. But I find myself resisting it. Trying not to hear things. As though, if I do, I will accept the fact I will never see again."

"You saved us."

Kirra was silent for some time. She bit her lip, and he could tell she was fighting tears. "Lumeni power has always been part of me, just as much as my eyes themselves. This hearing feels like a pegged leg. A sorry excuse for a replacement. I'd give anything to be a Lumeni again."

When the council was finished, Salla adjourned to confer with the Burodai elders, but not before Ashi accosted him with inquiries about the meeting. She came away disappointed, and stamped off to the edge of camp.

Kale and Kirra ate with the Burodai tribesmen, and it was during dinner that Salla approached them. Despite residing within the safety of the tower, Salla Burodai still ate with his tribe. A trait Kale respected about the man. He was smiling as he took his seat. Kale offered some rice and roasted kela, but the Great Soltayne waved it away.

"No, eat well, old friend. You both have offered more than enough already."

"Have we?"

"My people owe you a great debt, for warning us, for helping us locate survivors in our ruined city. The tribes have always been suspicious of the Sky Bloods who wield magic without spells, fly without wings. But you have shown them that all the horrid tales of the Old World are not true."

It was known that the Yan Avii bore no love for the Watchers. They blamed them for the War Between the Worlds and the ensuing fall of the Old World—the events that led to their exile.

"There is honor among Sky Bloods. And I hope we *all* may put aside past… differences."

"Like an alliance with the chancellor?" said Kale.

Salla smiled resignedly. "I'm afraid we need the aid of Osha more than ever, old friend. The chiefs are unanimous on this matter. We will cross the Steppe and seek refuge at the city of Pendra. As soon as affairs are settled and provisions are secured for my people, I will journey to Maro'El, and my sister will be wed to the chancellor as promised."

"The sister your people believe dead," said Kale. The Yan Avii were superstitious when it came to the dead. Vashti had been publicly burned by her father, because of her Watcher magic. For her to, apparently, rise from the dead now would be seen as grossly unnatural.

"The Zora tribe lives on the southern Steppe, near the Great Canyons of Dimh. Only one hundred leagues from the Trium'vel. Fer Zora's daughter, Sheva, is pledged to a great merchant in Vel'Kerren, and has spent the last five years in the city being trained in the customs and languages of the Trium. Now, she is a woman grown, and her people have not known her looks since she was but a young girl. Fer Zora is an ancient ally of my family, and he has agreed. In the eyes of my people, a marriage between Sheva and the chancellor will seal our alliance."

"And what will become of the *real* Sheva?" asked Kirra suspiciously.

"She will marry the merchant as before. She was to be lost from the tribe anyway. Fer Zora may even go to see his beloved daughter when they journey to trade in the Trium'vel."

Salla always had a plan; Kale couldn't deny that.

"Then all is well, isn't it?" said Kale pointedly.

"My city is in ruins, Sky Blood. Do not make light of what we have lost."

"Why are you telling us all this, Salla?"

"Because while all may *seem* well with this alliance, I fear it stands at the edge of a cliff. And right now, my sister is all alone in the White Citadel."

"You're still sending Ashi to attend her, I trust."

Salla nodded. "She told you."

"And you want us to join her," Kale finished for him.

"Yes, Sky Blood. Ashi is strong, and there will be other Ilya in her company, but we know little of Watcher magic. I need you to see that Vashti is treated well until the wedding."

Kale could not believe the man's audacity. "We may have aided your people in the middle of a cataclysm, but we are far from allies."

"You will make me beg? So be it," said Salla. He clasped Kale's hand between both his palms. "I wish it might have happened another way, Sky Blood. My sister, one of *your* kind, needs you."

"Forgive me if I'm not sympathetic, but your sister betrayed her kind."

"And you did not? We all do what we must with what we are given."

"Then, why must we help you, Salla? What are we being given?" Kale's eyes bore into the Great Soltayne's. He was through with the man's manipulation.

"I think you know, Sky Blood. Did you think Ashi's proposal came only from her?"

"What proposal?" said Kirra.

"That was your plan all along, wasn't it?" said Kale, disregarding her. "To get us to go."

"Now, more than ever," said Salla.

"What proposal?" Kirra demanded, grabbing his wrist.

"Ashi asked us to come with her to the White Citadel. So your eyes might be healed in exchange for our pledged loyalty to the chancellor."

Kirra was silenced. Her mouth hung open.

"The offer still stands," said Salla. "I will send word of my confidence in your loyalty, along with a request that Kirra be restored. There were healers in the Shadow Watch, were there not?"

Kale nodded.

"Then, go. Pledge your loyalty. And restore your sight, Kirra."

"We will not betray our friends again," said Kale.

Salla was clenching his fists. "You are no good to any of them here,

Sky Blood. What is your plan? To wander the Crooked Teeth with a blind woman in search of the Gallows Girl? To run away from it all?"

Kirra reached for him and missed, her hand patting at the ground until she found his arm. "He's right, Kale." Her voice trembled as though she were convincing herself.

"What do you mean?" He felt sick.

Kirra squeezed Kale's arm. "We would not be the first Watchers to join his Sky Guard. Most of the others have done the same."

"Kirra, the chancellor can't be trusted."

Kirra released his arm with a slight shove. She pointed to her scars. "Do you think I don't know that? No one can be trusted!"

Not even me...

It stung, but he knew she was right. He couldn't believe she was saying it, but he could not argue with her. He had lost that right.

"The chancellor will truly restore my sight, Salla?" Kirra asked.

"In exchange for your pledge of loyalty," said Salla. "I will make sure of it."

"Then, we will go with Ashi," said Kirra. "We will go to the White Citadel and pledge our loyalty."

"Excellent," said Salla. "You leave at first light."

PART THREE
THE ICE CITY

The Alyut people once inhabited the lands now known as Osha. Long ago, in the ancient days of the Old World, they were driven from their lands by fair-skinned Elyans with strange and powerful gifts from the gods. Alyut hatred for the Southern peoples ran deep in their blood, passed down generation to generation, for centuries.

—from *Dawn of the Third World*

CHAPTER SEVEN

Nineteen of the company died in the Mouth of the Gods, leaving forty alive, but they had no time to mourn. Only the gods knew how many more giants lurked in the depths of the crevasses. Tori and her followers fled the treacherous maze of ice and headed north, toward the Alyut settlement of Uluq, and no sooner had they set out across the sprawling Icelands than a fierce roar rose up from the Mouth, followed by a series of others, building and building off of one another into a haunting cacophony. Tori shuddered.

"The giants are calling to one another," Mischa muttered.

"I think it's a cry of mourning," said Tori, unsure why she thought it, or how she could know it, but she felt strangely sure. Tes had killed one of their brethren. *And we must get far away quickly.*

Mischa shrugged and pressed on, dragging a sledge filled with supplies behind her. All of them were shaken to the core. No one said more than a few sparse words. Tes was pulled along on a sledge due to the injuries to her leg. Mischa kept close to her, but the Crooked girl remained speechless, withdrawing into her own mind, eyes staring off at a formless world. Her young brother, Jordie, was shell-shocked, but occasionally Tori noticed him regarding his sister with a querulous look, his eyes narrowing at her.

Alyk would not let them rest until they were well clear of the Mouth of the Gods and the frost giants that were rising there. The company trekked into the dark. The nights were growing much longer, Tori had noticed. Alyk said that in the depths of winter, there were times the darkness never ended, one black night bleeding into the next. Tori hoped she would not remain in the North long enough to see such unending darkness.

Finally, they made camp, their work illuminated by the Lights of Anora, brilliant streams of haunting green hues. When the yurts were set, Tori took a look at Tes's injured leg. It had been nearly crushed by a shard of ice.

At the Watchtower, Tori had brought Ren back from the brink of death, but she wasn't truly a Medici healer. The bones in Tes's leg had been shattered, and Tori couldn't hasten the body's growth of tissue and fusion of bone. She could only fit things into place. And when she did, Tes felt every bit of it. But the young girl never screamed. She bit down hard on a strip of leather and held still until it was over.

"You're very brave," Tori said, squeezing her hand when it was finished. "And strong as an ox."

Tes nodded, but said nothing. Tori could tell she was trying hard not to cry, and she felt helpless to comfort her. What was there to say? Tori had no answers for what had happened. And Tori hated the trite things people often said when they were desperate to comfort others.

The gods have a plan.

We all have a time to sail on to the next world.

What a load of shenzah, Tori thought. If the gods were real, they had lost all control over their plans for the world. *Or perhaps we were wrong about the benevolence of the gods. Perhaps death and destruction was their plan all along.*

After all Tori had seen in the past few weeks, it was difficult to see the world any other way. Yet Merri's last words stuck in her mind: *Keep believing there's good left. In Darien. And in all this world.*

But Tori could not bear the thought that the gods would allow a lovely girl like Tes to lose both her parents in a matter of weeks.

Using pine from a damaged sledge, Tori fashioned a splint for Tes's leg and a crutch to help her walk. "This'll have to do for now. Until that leg heals properly."

"Thank you, my saint," said Tes feebly.

"You can call me Tori," she said, touching the girl's cheek. "We're no different, you and me. You're a Watcher."

"Okay." Tes stood, supporting herself on the crutch.

"I'm sorry I can't do more, Tes. You'll need to ride in the sledge until we reach Iqala. But the crutch will get you around camp. Don't try to use that leg, you hear?"

Tes nodded. Tori wanted to talk to her. Surely she was full of questions about the meaning of her gifts. Tori had certainly been when her own powers emerged. But she sensed that it was all too overwhelming for the young girl. *She needs to mourn. There will be time for questions later.*

They both went to join the others, but Tes left the supper fires without touching her food and hobbled to the outskirts of camp, alone. Tori knew she was continuing the late-night mourning ritual her mother had begun for their father. Now, Tes had both parents to grieve, and the confusion of an unknown gift arising moments too late.

Mischa watched her go and quickly rose to follow.

"Misch, perhaps it'd be—"

"I'm just going to be sure she doesn't wander off too far. You heard the Alyut. Giants aren't the only things we have to fear this far north."

Rogue Alyut clans wandered these plains. They had raided more than one trading company on this route, according to Alyk. Even in this bleak world of nothing, there was war and betrayal. A fact that had Alyk more on edge than Tori had ever seen him.

Jordie watched his sister leave, as well, his face tightening with visible anger, then softening to the point of tears. "Sh-she might have saved her," Jordie whimpered. "Our mum…"

Tori squeezed his hand, overwhelmed with sorrow for the boy. He was little older than she had been the day her own mother abandoned her. "I'm afraid it doesn't work that way. There's nothing Tes could have done."

But could I have saved her? The thought had been nagging at Tori's heart the entire trek from the Mouth. If only Tori had reacted quicker. If only she hadn't been overtaken by the beast's onslaught of ice. She was strong. She could have beaten that monster. But she hadn't been prepared, and it all happened so quickly…

"Why not?" said Jordie, an edge to his voice. "She's magic, like you."

Tori forced a kind smile, in spite of the guilt rising within her. She thought of the ghosts of Ghen. How many would haunt her now in that place? *The boy should be blaming me.*

"You've heard how I first revealed my power, haven't you?" said Tori.

Jordie nodded, wiping freezing tears from his cheeks. "You destroyed the chancellor's gallows in front of the whole world."

"Did you know that was the first time I ever used magic?" It was a subtle lie. Tori could not truly remember a time before then that she'd used magic. She simply knew there had been a time. But those memories had been taken from her.

The boy's eyes went wide. "Really?"

"My magic was revealed to me much as it was your sister. I was trying to save someone too."

"Who?"

"The boy they were hanging on the gallows. He was my friend, but… I wasn't able to save him, any more than Tes could save your mum."

Tori didn't tell Jordie that the boy had lived, that Tori *had* saved Darien, only to have him turned into a monster.

"We both were just a little too late." Tori squeezed Jordie's hand tight. "Don't blame your sister. You need to be strong for her. You need each other more than ever."

The boy nodded to his saint. "Should I go find her?"

Tori smiled. "Right now, I think Tes needs to grieve alone, but be ready when she returns."

"I will," said Jordie. "I'll be strong."

"Your mum died to *save* you, Jordie. Never forget that."

"Now, you should rest," said Benja, the old man from the Mouth, coming up from behind the boy. "Leave our Gallows Saint to her own thoughts a while."

Jordie thanked her and then went to the tents with the old Crooked man.

The Lights of Anora had calmed to mere traces of color, thin ribbons that wrapped around the twin moons of the New World. The Sisters glowed with a violet hue.

The others soon retreated to their own tents, and Tori was left alone at the fire for several minutes before Alyk dul Baruk took a seat beside her. He, too, seemed to be in shock, staring off into the sifting flames. His lips moved with silent prayers.

"I led those people to their deaths," he muttered eventually. It was the first time since they'd met that Alyk had lost all traces of optimism.

Tori shook her head. "You cannot carry the weight of the dead, Alyk."

"I insisted those rumblings were just the ice moving. I've traveled that passage a dozen times. We came through only weeks ago on our journey south. I've lived my entire life on the ice. I should have known. I could have stopped this, but I… I didn't want to believe it. The guardians of the Great White North were only myths."

"You couldn't have known."

"No one's seen a frost giant in hundreds of years."

"Not since the Old World?" said Tori.

Alyk merely nodded.

Tori's stomach knotted up inside her, a dark fear creeping up.

"The world is coming apart," Alyk said. "It's like someone drove a spear into a crack in the ice, and now the entire sheet is breaking at the seams."

Tori grasped his hand. "There is still hope, Alyk." The words seemed to come from outside her, just as they had the day she'd first embraced her role as the Gallows Saint, back in the caverns in the Crooked Teeth. They were the words Tori wanted to believe, though she knew she did not deep down. But a saint had to inspire others, so she spoke the words, as much to Alyk as to herself. "Look at Tes. She's a Watcher. Our order believes the gods are bringing magic back to the world for a reason, bestowing gifts once more on ordinary boys and girls to raise up a new generation of Watchers. There will be more. The world may be breaking, but it's not lost."

Alyk chuckled. "Now, you're sounding more like me than myself."

More like Ren, actually. She pushed the thought from her mind.

"She sounds like a saint," said Mischa, returning from the edge of camp. She took a seat beside Tori.

"How's Tes?" Tori said.

"She's tough. But on top of her mother's death, I think she's pretty shaken by what she did in the Mouth."

"Can't blame her for that," said Alyk.

"It's always a shock when you discover magic," said Mischa, perhaps remembering the day she, too, had unearthed her Watcher gifts. It struck Tori that she had never heard how Mischa had come into her abilities. It was strange. They had been through so much. In some ways, Mischa felt closer than a sister, and yet there was so much Tori did not know about her friend.

"I wish it didn't take tragedy to make it reveal itself," Tori murmured.

"Magic shows when it must," said Mischa. "That's what Ren would say."

Gods, is he even alive? she wondered. She hoped desperately that he was. That all of the Watchers were, even the ones who had betrayed them.

Alyk poked a stick into the fire, stirring the coals. "Well, that's good news, considering the state of the world. There should be a lot of magic rising up."

The three of them grew silent. The Lights of Anora surged in the northern sky, as though the ribbons were trying to choke out the light of the Sisters.

Mischa finally broke the stillness. "Tori, where do you think these beasts are coming from? First, the Rulaqs…"

Then the Nosferati, now frost giants. All the legends from the Old World suddenly roaring to life…

Tori could tell Mischa already knew, the way she touched her arm as she waited for an answer. But even so, it was difficult to muster words to the fear that had been gnawing its way out of her since they'd escaped the Nosferati.

"I don't know how," said Tori. "But I think it happened when I fought the chancellor in the Old World… I think I let them in."

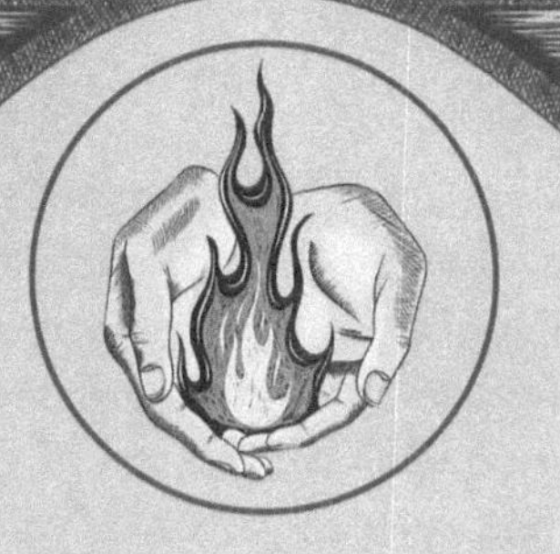

CHAPTER EIGHT

In the village of Uluq, the company of Alyut and Crooked refugees rested for three days to recover from their passage through the Mouth of the Gods. The isolated Alyut village was situated at the edge of the Last Forest—a small outcropping of tall, narrow snowpines in the northernmost foothills of the Crooked Teeth. The Tu'va clan—*treefolk* in the Common Tongue—was glad to house the weary travelers in cabins made of logs and sod. The village was situated within a fort, with a tall and fierce-looking wall made of logs carved with points like massive spears.

"To protect against the rogue clans," said Alyk, when Mischa asked during their first supper.

"What happened? Why would they attack their own people?"

"The Alyut are one family, but like most families, it is a dysfunctional one. When we were exiled to the White North, we banded together better than ever. But over time, there were quarrels. Many believe the Ice City is not our way. They say we are becoming like the invaders. The rogue clans left the unified people long ago. They wander the North, small bands of hunters and warriors. They fight with one another. They fight with us. Sometimes their numbers are small, but they have been growing recently. Rumors have been spreading of a fierce warrior who has been uniting them. The elders have been growing worried. If the rogues ever banded together, they could threaten Iqala and forever change my people."

Even within the walls of Uluq, they were not safe.

In contrast to the sealskin tent Mischa and Tori had been sharing, the cabins, with their roaring hearths, felt as warm as Melanesia. There, the stilt huts were little more than a thin lining of reeds enclosing a bamboo frame. During the hot summers, Mischa would sleep out on the beaches of her village. It was one such night when Mischa had first seen Ala Sumai. And it was on that same beach—at the end of that glorious, horrific summer—that her father had discovered their moonlight trysts.

After that, nothing could be the same…

Here in the North, all hints of summer had drifted away like a morning fog. Despite a year in the Crooked Teeth, Mischa had never grown accustomed to the northern chill, and in the Great White North it was even worse. She had never been so cold in all her life as on this journey, and she mourned the day they left the warmth of Uluq's cabins to continue north once more.

"There are few logs in Iqala," said Alyk, as though reading her mind. "It lies beyond the northern tree line. But the walls are layered with furs and the hearths stoked with firestones. You'll be warm again, soon enough. Don't worry."

Mischa smiled. "What you and I consider warm are quite different things, I think."

Alyk clapped her shoulder. "Stay strong, island girl." He laughed as he trudged ahead to join their saint.

Tori had said nothing more about the beasts from the Old World, and Mischa had not pried. But Tori was retreating into her own thoughts more and more after what had happened. She had begun embracing her role as saint, and Mischa knew she hated that she hadn't been able to save the Alyut and the Crooked folk in the Mouth of the Gods.

Mischa shared her guilt. But the people in their company did not. They saw the Watchers as their saviors. They had killed the frost giant. The people seemed more devoted to Tori than ever, and Mischa had a feeling this had contributed to her mood.

Uluq villagers outfitted the company with a pair of mammuts to haul their supplies. Immense sledges were loaded high and rigged so the beasts could pull them. The white wooly beasts stood fifteen feet at the shoulders and left tracks that Jordie could have climbed inside. Alyk claimed that wild mammuts could split you in half with a swing of their mighty tusks, but those raised by the Alyut were more loyal than any horse. These two were docile and liked to have their trunks scratched while their sledges were loaded down with tent poles and provisions.

The trek across the Icelands took two bitterly cold weeks, and Mischa kept close to Tes, who was begrudgingly riding the entire way on a sledge. At night she hobbled around on the crutch Tori had made for her, and each evening she left the supper fires and escaped to the edge of camp to mourn her parents' deaths as the sun set over the mountainous sheets of ice.

When Mischa asked her how she was doing, Tes always quickly changed the subject. The girl loved Mischa's tales of the islands, however, where there was no snow, and the world was green and warm year round. The girl was stubborn and strong, and Mischa found herself caring for her as she once had her own little sister, Leina.

Tes and Jordie shared their tent each night, along with the old Crooked man, Benja, who had taken a grandfatherly liking to Jordie, as well as the boy he had saved in the Mouth. Tori said that when she'd encountered him in the Mouth—when the ice split wide during the frost giant attack—the man had seemed like a shell-shocked child.

But Mischa never would have guessed it to look at him now. The orphan boys clung to his side as if he were their father. There were others left without parents after the attack, and soon, all the orphans looked to Benja. The old man grinned at the children, told them fantastic tales, and helped them press on in the increasingly harsh conditions of the North. Benja had grown stronger from the horrors of the Mouth.

They all had. They had survived a frozen hell, and they would keep surviving.

If only Tori could realize that...

———

As they neared the Ice City, they made camp in an outcropping of porous black rocks that felt like they were from another world. Violent gusts of wind made it difficult to raise the yurts. Snow whipped at their faces, hard as specks of rock. But even still, Tori wandered to the edge of camp. It had become her nightly ritual, and normally Mischa left her to her thoughts, but not tonight. Alyk said a storm was stirring.

Tori crested a hill and looked out at the great white plains of the Icelands. Plains was an inaccurate word. It made the place sound like a peaceful snow-dusted prairie. The Icelands were harsh. Jagged shards of ice and rock jutted out at harsh angles, making it difficult to maneuver the sledges across the gnarled terrain. They were forced to weave between the obstacles, and Mischa guessed that their twisted path had added days to the journey.

Mischa reached the top of the hill and stood silently at Tori's side. "Not sure I see the beauty that Alyk does out here," Mischa murmured.

Tori nodded. She said nothing for a long time.

"It's not your fault, you know," Mischa said. "The chancellor took you to the Old World. He did this."

Tori nodded wordlessly.

Mischa was about to leave her alone when Tori finally broke the silence.

"I've been thinking about Ren and the others. Anyone who didn't join the chancellor, any that survived the catacombs. They're rotting in his dungeons, their blood getting sucked out of them every morning."

"Just like the chancellor did to you."

Tori turned to her and held her gaze. "We have to help them, Misch. This world is only getting worse and worse. We have to end it."

"We will." Mischa pointed to the camp behind them. Snow was beginning to fall, darting violently on the wind. "Look at them. They will follow you to war."

"But will the others? Alyk says that not all are as eager to—"

Mischa's heart nearly stopped. She grabbed Tori's hand and pulled her to the ground.

"What's wrong?" Tori hissed.

Mischa pointed out across the plain. Far off in the distance, near the horizon, there were dark shades. Figures. A great host of them. Riding on strange white beasts.

"Rogues," Tori whispered.

"What are they riding?"

"I think they're bears."

Shivers shot across Mischa's skin. Rogue warriors could tear their company apart. They had been marching for weeks. They were hungry, exhausted, and not equipped for battle. The two held very still, praying they hadn't been noticed. The host was riding in their direction, the shapes slowly growing larger. But suddenly, the wind picked up, stirring up whirlwinds of snow that filled the plains beyond. Dark clouds pressed in around the rogues, and the riders disappeared in the storm.

Wind and snow cut at Mischa's face, making her eyes water. She grabbed Tori's hand and they hurried back to camp. While the Alyut prepared for one of the legendary squalls of the North, Alyk assured them that it was very unlikely the rogue clans would have wandered this close to Iqala. They were within a couple days' march of the center of Alyut civilization. It might have even been Bear Rider scouts from the city. But Mischa did not fully believe him. Despite his assurances, Alyk increased the guard detail that night.

The wind howled throughout the night and the yurt shook as the fierce northern tempest descended upon them. Mischa did not sleep through a moment of the storm.

———

MISCHA SMELLED THE SEA ONE DAY BEFORE THEY REACHED THE ICE City. It was not as sweet as the islands, where fragrances were accented by flowers and ripening fruit—the scents of living things. This smell reminded her of the fish markets of the Trium'vel, but it lifted her spirits all the same. The last night of their journey, Mischa slept soundly and dreamed of the beaches of Melanesia. Ala came to her in the night, and the salt on her lips was sweet as sugar. It felt so good to be held close again. To be loved. But Mischa woke up cold and alone.

The furs beside her were empty. Everyone was already awake. Mischa did not hurry to leave. The dream had been good. Usually her dreams of Ala ended in tragedy, but this one never turned dark, and Mischa wanted to crawl back into the dream and return to the islands. That beach had been like a secret world she and Ala escaped to every night that summer. A world of midnight swims and nervous laughter, without social strata and honor and customs and… arranged marriages.

Her fourteenth summer was the last calm before the ensuing storm that had been Mischa's life ever since she and Ala were discovered.

You are a disgrace to this family! Her father's words still stung, but what he'd done after was unforgivable. Yet she still thought fondly of that summer, that first love.

Her thoughts soon turned to the loves that had followed. Zaya Shalvar. Mischa's feelings had been torn at the end, but her death at the Watchtower haunted Mischa's thoughts. Zaya had been lost in the devastation of the Rulaqs, after Tori stirred them to a rage of violence, and Mischa's guilt was increased by the fact that she had broken things off with Zaya hours before her death. And then there was Vashti Burodai. Her betrayal still stung deeply. Mischa had to believe that it was not permanent, that the Yan Avii princess would choose differently when this revolution came to Osha. She had to believe that none of the Watchers who had joined the chancellor were lost. She couldn't bear the thought of fighting people who had once been close as family.

Mischa was jolted from her thoughts when Tes came hurrying in, nearly tumbling on her crutch. "We've reached the Ice City! You can see it from the top of the hill. Come look!"

Mischa followed after, glad for a distraction. Even on a crutch, Tes flew across the ice. Her leg was healing quickly. They reached the top of the hardened drift of snow and looked out across the expanse of white, but white was all Mischa saw. Though the scent of the sea was stronger than ever.

"I don't see it," Mischa said.

Tes pointed north. "Look, there, near the horizon, where the ice shimmers."

"I see the shimmers."

"That's the Ice City! Alyk says we'll be there by supper."

The company was nearly finished packing up camp by the time they descended the drifts. Everyone's spirits were high as they set out on the last leg of their long journey from the Crooked Teeth.

Mischa joined Tori and Alyk at the front of the company as they neared, and spires of ice began to take form on the horizon. There were four distinct spires that rose from the ice sheets like giant spears.

"For the four clans," said Alyk. "The *Nuq'vana*—the Bear Riders. The *Tu'va*—the people of the forest. The *Iqu'vara*—the hunters upon the ice. And the *Karu'va*—the people of the caverns below the world."

"Which are you?" said Tori.

"Shamans have no clan. We serve everyone. But before I was a shaman, I was an ice hunter. They fish the ice shores and hunt whales and seals from their qayaqs. You've met the forest folk of Uluq. They send hunting expeditions to the Crooked Teeth every summer, and they supply what little timber we use here in Iqala. The Bear Riders tame the northbears like warhorses. And the cave folk mine firestone, the only source of heat in the North. We work together to provide for our people."

The four spires, Mischa soon discovered, were at least five hundred feet high, rising from a mountain of obsidian star rock. Four villages encircled the mountain, the buildings crafted from blocks of ice, and enclosing them all within one city was a wall of ice thirty feet high.

When they were a mile from the city, a young woman rode out to meet them, accompanied by a dozen warriors on the backs of shaggy white northbears. The girl was darkly beautiful. In the afternoon sun, she left her hood down, letting her dark hair fly. The left side of her head was shaved to the skin, revealing a vibrant tattoo of red and blue markings that were strange to Mischa.

"That is Skya," said Alyk.

"Your war chief?" asked Mischa.

"My sister." His tone betrayed an air of disdain. Alyk murmured something, and then Tori held up her hand for the company to stop. Skya dul Baruk and her Bear Riders did not slow until they were nearly upon them. Mischa noted that all the riders were women. Skya's eyes went wide and passed from Alyk to the two strange young women at his side.

"You were sent on a hunting party, *Baru*. Instead, you bring outsiders to our sacred city," Skya said. Mischa did not like the girl's tone.

"*Saru,* I bring refugees from the Teeth," said Alyk, dipping his head in a sort of bow. "We have long traded with the Crooked folk."

"Trade, yes. But we have never escorted them straight to the heart of our people. To our only stronghold. Our *madru* is far from pleased, Alyk. And the shamans sense more than Crooked folk in your company." Her eyes narrowed at Tori and Mischa.

"This is the Gallows Saint of Osha, Astoria Burodai, and her companion, Mischa Sufai…"

Mischa felt as though the warrior's eyes might bore a hole straight through her.

"They are our allies," Alyk said. "There's no need to fear their gifts."

"Our people have always feared magic," said Skya. "Or have you forgotten why you were trained since boyhood to render it useless in the North?"

"Our people once knew beautiful magic. Or have *you* forgotten what lies in our temple? Have you forgotten what our Great Shaman foresaw of the Restoration of our people?"

"They are darklings," Skya hissed. "That is all I need to remember."

"Their magic saved us from frost giants in the Mouth of the Gods."

Skya's eyes went dark, and her expression hardened. "Yes… frost giants and Rulaqs wander the North once more. And our traders return from their summer voyages with one ship lost, bearing tidings of sea dragons in the Channel Sea. To hear the tales, your darkling is the one to blame for this new threat to our people." Skya pointed a long, tattooed finger at Tori.

"Tales told by our adversary," said Alyk. "The chancellor bleeds lies. Tori is our ally."

"The High Elder will determine both their loyalties. Tell me, how many died during your journey through the Mouth, *Baru?*"

Alyk's face went tight. "Nineteen."

Skya motioned to her riders. "Bind them."

A pair of fierce-looking women dismounted and approached. Each wore a necklace of long teeth and shared Skya's shaved head and strange markings.

Alyk went pale, but he whispered quickly, "Don't, Mischa!"

It was then Mischa realized she'd lost all sense of her magic. *Was it Alyk? Or another shaman?* Mischa did not know. But there was no use resisting. The warriors seized Tori and Mischa by the arms.

"No," cried Mischa. "This is a mistake! Please."

But Tori shook her head. "Play along," she whispered. "That is all we can do."

Skya's eyes went wide as she addressed them. "Astoria Burodai, the Gallows Girl of Osha, you are to be put on trial for the deaths of nineteen of the Alyut people in the Mouth of the Gods. For the destruction of one of our trading vessels in the Channel Sea, along with all its cargo, and the lives of the forty-three Alyut crew members aboard."

Tori did not argue against the woman's claims. She merely nodded in submission. Mischa was furious. *How can they do this? None of this is Tori's fault!*

But Mischa knew she was fooling herself.

Whatever had happened, Tori was at the exact center of all the chaos in the New World.

Skya motioned to her warriors. "Take them to the caves. The trial will be held at the sign of the Empty Moons. May the gods judge the Gallows Girl justly."

The Alyut warriors bound Tori's and Mischa's hands behind their backs and led them into the Ice City. It was not the welcome Mischa had envisioned at all.

PART FOUR
BATTLE OF GODS & MONSTERS

Looking back now, I see it clearly. This was when the world changed. This was when the earth began to break apart at its seams.

—the Last Commander of the Metamorphi
as quoted in *Dawn of the Third World*

CHAPTER NINE

When he was a boy, Darien Redvar saw his future in the mountains, sowing crops and tending to the alkine herds his people had domesticated. He saw a life of peace, and if he would have fought, it would have been in defense of the Klavash mountains of his boyhood, like his ancestors before him. Never could he have imagined that one day he would be sitting on the chancellor's war council as the commander of the Sky Guard. Yet here he was, at a great round table in the Chamber of the High Council, a map of Osha spread wide before them. The council consisted entirely of highborn lords and ladies: Lord Fedra, Lady Dragonis, Lord Wallis, Lord Barra, Lady Tindeir, Lord Reath, and Lord Zamel—commander of all the Night Legions…

And then, there was Darien Redvar, a lowborn Klavash boy raised in the mountains. A few months ago, he was but a common soldier in the Legions. He was conscious that he was the only council member who did not descend from ancient Oshan bloodlines. In this room, he was nothing. The families represented here had ruled Osha since the dawn of the New World.

Darien had heard it said that the chancellors of the past had been little more than puppets in the hands of the Oshan nobles. The chancellors functioned as a face of absolute power that was manipulated by invisible strings. But things were changing, and if anyone resented Darien's rise to power or his lowborn Klavash presence in the room, they were careful not to let it show. Rulaqs had a way of minimizing the importance of racial tensions.

The great two-headed monsters from the Old World had left the Crooked Teeth fifty leagues north of the city, and were marching south. All of Maro'El was preparing for battle, and Darien's *Sky Guard* might well be their best chance at survival. Even so, Darien let the nobles speak first.

"The beasts will reach the city by tomorrow night," Commander Zamel said. "An army two hundred strong. The northern hold of Griswal fell this morning."

"They're destroying farmlands up north," said Lady Tindeir. "The ore fields as well."

"*My* ore fields," said Lady Dragonis coolly.

"What effect will our cannons render on the bastards?" said Lord Wallis.

"The beasts stand four stories tall..." said Commander Zamel.

Darien grimly recalled his own encounter with the Rulaqs at the Watchtower only a few short weeks ago. The beasts had first served the chancellor's scheme to destroy the fortress of the Shadow Watch, but in the mayhem, the monsters had worked themselves into a frenzy. The Legions had been forced to flee underground, and the Rulaqs went on to devastate the entire North. And all of it had been enabled by the chancellor's godstones. But the members of the High Council did not know this.

"They could decimate our city walls with a twitch of just one of their great necks," said Zamel. "Their skin is scaled beneath their fur, thick as the length of your hand. Even a well-aimed cannon shot at one of their heads would only incapacitate half the creature. A mere three beasts fell at Griswal."

"What about those Morgathian bombs?" said Lord Barra. His son had led a company beside Darien's at the Battle of Fire and Fury, which had ended the Morgathian rebellion.

Zamel shook his head. "The Morgathians left only five of them in Goran'El. The bloody heathens made sure they did not go quietly. They and their bloody god. Their alchemists slit their own throats before the end."

"Five bombs could still wreak some carnage," said Barra. His son—a Legion general—had been killed by a firebomb at Goran'El. Barra's face tensed with subdued rage, as though killing the Rulaqs with firebombs might somehow avenge his son's death.

"Two were lost in the catacombs beneath the Crooked Teeth," said Zamel. "One is being examined by our own alchemists, though they've not unraveled what substances render the bombs so explosive. That leaves only two remaining. The bombs wreak carnage, yes. They might kill five or six beasts, maybe even a dozen if well aimed. But the bombs will not save us any more than they did their Morgathian creators."

"Gods save us," murmured Lord Fedra.

"Gods?" At this, the chancellor stood, scowling.

Medea Lorzarre rose beside him, and she seemed to match his mood. Since revealing his sorcery to the empire, the chancellor had kept the woman very close. Before, she had only joined him when it suited his purpose, but now the chancellor did not seem to feel the need to hide the sorceress who had helped him gain so much power. The lords and ladies had taken to calling her the Darkling Witch, though not in the chancellor's presence.

The ghostly woman still struck a chord of fear in Darien, though he could not precisely say why. There was something unnatural about her. She was powerful, yes, but not nearly so much as the chancellor.

But Medea could see into his mind, if she wished. She had probed there once, before Darien had been turned into a Morph. He had proved his loyalty then. But that was before his mind had become haunted by nightmares. Ol' Merri still came to him in his dreams, as much as he wished to forget her. What might Medea find buried, should she decide to probe the depths of his mind again?

Medea touched the chancellor's arm, calming his rising anger at Lord Fedra's mention of the old gods.

"No gods will be coming to save you, Fedra," the chancellor said coldly. "But my Sky Guard just might!"

"*Your* Guard?" Lady Dragonis laughed shrilly. She was a fiercely beautiful woman. Her form-fitting satin gown tapered past a slender waist to curvaceous hips, and firm breasts teased from a strapless design that she had popularized amongst the nobles. Full, pursed lips formed an insidious expression as she looked the chancellor in the eyes. She was a woman who got her way. Darien had heard rumors that the lady had murdered two husbands in their sleep. One had been found with a nightling. The other had merely proved inept. With her house's standing, both men had married into *her* name. "Your Grace, as best I can tell, your little Sky Guard are the ones responsible for our plight."

"M-my lady!" said Lord Wallis, shocked at her forthrightness.

"Am I wrong?" said Lady Dragonis, her eyes still fixed unwaveringly upon Cyrus Maro. "Why do we need saving? That is the question we should be asking."

"Surely, it is an important question," said Lord Wallis. "But now we must focus on surviving this devilish horde."

"No," said Fedra. "The lady is right. Why do we need saving, indeed, Your Grace?"

Lord Barra and Lady Tindeir nodded their agreed sentiment.

"It was the Gallows Girl," growled the chancellor. "As you already know!"

It was strange to see the chancellor so rattled by these nobles. Cyrus Maro seemed so fierce in the company of soldiers, but with the nobles, Darien had the sense they were nearly equals. The chancellor was fighting for control of this council.

"Rulaqs rise out of myth," hissed Lady Dragonis. "And we are to believe some vague notion that the Gallows Girl conjured them up out of nowhere to escape the clutches of your Morphs? A situation, I might add, that was due to your own neglect in killing her the first time."

The chancellor's revelation of magic power had rendered the lowborns awestruck, but in several of the nobles, it had merely aroused more anger and suspicion. Their puppet strings were beginning to fray.

Darien finally spoke up, standing to face the fierce Oshan noble-woman. "I am responsible for the Gallows Girl's escape, my lady. Not His Grace."

"Yes," said Lady Dragonis. Her intoxicating eyes seemed to draw him closer. "We heard. Because you were raided by gods-damned Nosferati. And where did *they* come from?"

The chancellor had not publicly revealed the power of the godstones, and he looked on with evident horror as Medea stood, holding out the vibrant green stones in her palm.

"The Gallows Girl used these, my lady," Medea said softly. Her purring voice seemed to ride upon the air, permeating the room.

All were shocked at the words. Medea never spoke to anyone, but at the chancellor's bidding. Cyrus Maro nodded.

"A pair of gems?" said Dragonis haughtily.

"The Gallows Girl used the same stones the First Chancellor used to lock the beasts away," said Medea, her expression hardening. "The godstones."

The other lords and ladies showed fear, but not Lady Dragonis. "Pah!" she cried. "You mean for me to believe some Old World myth?"

Medea did not answer. She gritted her teeth, crossed the room, and took hold of the lady's wrist. The two vanished in a rush of mist.

The rest in the room looked on in horror. The chancellor regained his cool composure and forced a thin smile.

Did he intend for this to happen? Darien wondered.

"W-what has that witch done with her?" said Fedra tremulously.

The others stood silent, mouths agape. The chancellor answered with a continued smile.

Moments later, the mists swirled again, and Medea returned with Lady Dragonis in tow. The lady cried out in pain. The stones were in her trembling hand, glowing with searing magic.

Medea peeled the stones from the lady's blistering skin and stowed them in her black cloak. Dragonis clutched her hand to herself and moaned in agony. Darien noted that Medea kept her own hand hidden in her cloak, her face tensed in a slight grimace. It was not painless for her to use the stones either. It was Watcher blood that sustained her passage between worlds.

"What did you see?" Lord Wallis said to Dragonis, helping her to her feet.

"I-it was t-terrible," Dragonis said, groaning. "I... I saw... the Old World."

The nobles gasped, but Darien and Zamel nodded knowingly. They understood the cost of its passage. Without Regenero blood, not even Medea or the chancellor could survive the journey.

"Pray you never see it again," Medea whispered to the whimpering lady.

The chancellor stood tall, his dominance restored in the Chamber of the High Council. "The Gallows Girl unearthed a dark secret, lost to our world long ago," Cyrus Maro said. "Thankfully, I secured the godstones before she could unleash more carnage than she already did. Dajha!" he cried, turning to the chamber doors.

The Parjhan guard, who stood watch outside, hurried into the chamber, his long dreadlocks swaying from the motion.

"Take Lady Dragonis to see Sahra—your healer. But let her skin scar over. I want her to forever remember her passage between the worlds."

"Aye, milord," said the Parjhan, taking hold of the lady's uninjured arm nonchalantly.

The Oshan woman regarded Dajha with a momentary air of contempt, but quickly conceded and followed the Parjhan out the door.

"Do not forget who presides over this council, my gentle lords and ladies," said the chancellor. "This is no longer the same world you ruled with my ancestors of old. The New World is different now. We are entering a new era. A Third World."

The remaining council members hid their displeasure at this revelation. Their expressions were as carefully molded as statues.

"Commander Redvar," said the chancellor, turning to Darien. "Now that we've heard the lords' and ladies'… counsel… do you have a strategy in mind for defeating this oncoming horde?"

Darien stood and all eyes rushed to him. It felt good to have the undivided attention of lords and ladies, and he forgot his dreams of Merri and his fears of Medea. War was what he was made for. He hadn't felt so confident since he'd joined the Night Legions. To have remained among the peaceful mountains of his youth would have been to never know his true capacities, his true gifts. He deserved to be here on this council more than any other person in this room, save the chancellor, and perhaps Commander Zamel. He had not been born to this position. He had earned it.

And besides, his plan was brilliant.

"I do have a strategy, milord." Darien paused a moment. The idea had come to him as he surveyed the city the past few days, though he had not been sure whether he should dare utter it before the council. But now that the godstones were no secret, he felt at ease to speak. Another demonstration of power might have *all* the Oshan lords and ladies on their knees before the end.

"Tell us," said Cyrus Maro mockingly, "will *firebombs* be our salvation?" There was a flash in his eyes as they met Darien's, as though they held a great secret, known only between them. Darien swelled with pride. The chancellor had been confident all along in his commander of the Sky Guard.

"No, milord, not bombs," Darien said. He looked around the room. The lords and ladies regarded him with trepidation. A lowly Klavash boy now commanded the respect of the greatest lords and ladies of Osha.

"Our salvation lies in the Sky Guard. In magic. Though, I will need the aid of your… Darkling Witch."

Darien smiled as he said the name the lords and ladies secretly used for Medea, and he looked each of the nobles in the eyes as he spoke it. He enjoyed watching them glance away nervously.

They were afraid of *him* too.

CHAPTER TEN

Rhaena was not the only nightling in the White Citadel, but she was the chancellor's favorite. A Faerish girl, she had the black eyes and copper skin that signified the remnant race of the Ruined Empire.

The ancient Faere dynasty was destroyed in the Old World, when the fair-skinned conquerors from what was now known only as the Lost Continent arrived. The Elyans. First, they took the Southern Isles, then they crossed the Channel Sea and expanded their dominion. Their descendants eventually formed the peoples of Osha, Morgath, and the Southern Isles.

Since their conquest, Faerish history was a tale of blood and hardship, the land passing through many kingdoms over the past two thousand years, most recently the rule of Osha. Cyrus Maro's grandfather had lost Faere to a rebellion sixty years previous, but even freedom had been written in blood for the Faerish. The realm seemed to pass on to another lord with each passing year, the Faerish clans in a near-constant state of war and upheaval. Rhaena claimed she'd been an attendant to one of the many men who'd claimed lordship over the southern subcontinent during the War of Nine Towers. Before she ran away from the capital city of Run Khaen and sold herself to a nighthouse in Maro'El.

The chancellor knew Rhaena had lied about her past. But it was this boldness that the chancellor liked about her, along with her effervescent beauty. Her skin was without blemish—which made Cyrus Maro doubt she'd ever been a servant in the Ruined Empire—her body slender and strong, and whether it was genuine or not, her smile and laughter made him feel something akin to passion.

Or perhaps Rhaena simply kindled old memories of passion. Since Elara was stolen from him, about the only time he did not feel alone in the world was when he was with Rhaena. For a few hours, he would forget all the things that haunted him, and in her arms, he could even capture elusive sleep.

But not tonight.

Rhaena lay naked, wrapped in a tangle of sheets, dozing peacefully, but Cyrus Maro could not find sleep any more than he had found comfort with Rhaena tonight. He rose from the bed and wrapped himself in a fine-spun woolen robe. The short summer had slipped away into an even shorter autumn season, and his chambers were growing cold, even with the fire simmering in the hearth across the room. He would need to layer his walls with furs once this damned Rulaq horde was taken care of.

The nightling muttered unintelligibly in her sleep. The chancellor did not carouse with nightlings often, but he'd hardly slept since the terrors of the catacombs. It was the first time he'd ever been so aware of his own mortality. Despite all his power, it would have taken but one bite from the Nosferati, and he would have joined their demonic clan below the Crooked Teeth—never truly living nor dying. One creature had landed upon him, teeth bared. If not for Vashti, he might have been bitten. And the undead monster had looked so much like him. It was *that* face that haunted his sleep.

The Nosferati had looked just like his brother, Loras.

If there are gods, they are mocking me, Cyrus Maro thought as he paced his chambers.

Of course, he knew it was impossible that the creature had been the reincarnation of his dead brother. Loras was utterly dead, along with Elara, and both his parents. All of them, thoroughly dead.

And then, there was the Gallows Girl.

Ever since the chancellor had made an example of the traitorous servant boy, he had been paranoid. A traitor, right here in the White Citadel. How many more might be passing that bitch's symbol around his city?

It could be anyone, Medea had cautioned him often.

Soon, Cyrus found himself searching through Rhaena's cloak and nightling gown for hidden bits of parchment with a treasonous symbol. She had been thoroughly searched by his own guard before she came anywhere near the upper reaches of the citadel, but he couldn't help himself.

Yes, Rhaena swore loyalty to his reign. She was treated well for her station, the chancellor had made sure of that. Her services were reserved only for him. She was given fine quarters in the central citadel, where she enjoyed the amenities of nobles: fine clothes, delectable foods, and rare working hours. There were times the chancellor even swore she felt some care for him, taking interest beyond the expectations of her role.

It could be anyone…

Even Rhaena.

The Gallows Girl had ruined the one thing that still brought him pleasure. All night, he could not shake the suspicion. Even the throes of passion had offered him little respite tonight. He replaced Rhaena's clothes and stood before the fire. It was dwindling, so he stoked it himself. He did not like sending for servants in the night. Not anymore.

Everywhere he went, his suspicion was growing. Even the nobles of this very city were not above suspicion. If there was one thing he'd learned from watching his father and his father before him, it was that the nobles only loved their ruler so much as he was convenient for them. Aleksander Maro had bent constantly to their will, and even then, there were some who had all too easily aided Cyrus's own schemes.

Among them, Ren Andovier and Commander Ruben Scelero.

Now, the chancellor knew, *he* was becoming inconvenient as well. Ilyana Dragonis might have been dealt with for the moment, but once the Rulaqs were dispatched, it would only be a matter of time before another noble grew bold. *Maybe I'll have them ALL taken to the Old World,* he thought with satisfaction.

But it was not that simple. The nobles were the backbone of the Oshan empire. Their slaves mined ore and salt. Their smiths built cannons and muskets and sabers. Their merchants traded with the companies of the Trium'vel. Their fisheries, farms, and slaughterhouses supplied the city with sustenance. To replace them all in one fell stroke would be chaotic for the empire, even disastrous. He needed to build alliances, find those he could trust. It had always been this way. Even with magic, things were not simple. A truth that he loathed.

Nevertheless, the chancellor had loved seeing Dragonis's face when she returned from the Old World. Her scar would not soon be forgotten. It was surely being whispered of throughout the city. Medea's brilliant act had secured the compliance of the nobles—at least until the war against the Rulaqs was over. But inwardly, Cyrus Maro feared that act would have repercussions.

There was a knock at his chamber doors. Was it early morning, or late night? He could not tell. The night sky had not yet begun to turn grey with the coming light. "The Lady Medea to see you, milord," announced the Morph outside the room.

Rhaena stirred. "Tell that witch to bugger off," she moaned sleepily. "And come back to bed. It's cold in here alone—milord," she added pointedly, with a drowsy giggle.

The chancellor smiled. "Sleep on, my dear. I won't be gone long."

Almost immediately, Rhaena was sleeping again. The chancellor dressed himself quickly and withdrew. Medea was waiting in the antechamber, impatient arms crossed.

"It is time, Your Grace," Medea said. "The horde will be upon us in two days."

"Can't it wait until morning?"

"Do you want the entire citadel to know you are harvesting your own fiancee's blood?"

The chancellor nodded. "Very well, then. Let's be done with it."

They slipped into the night and made for Vashti Burodai's bedchambers.

Cyrus Maro had been dreading this moment, though he knew it was only a matter of time. He hoped Lady Vashti would join him willingly on journeys with the godstones. Her Regenero gifts were essential to surviving the trek. But Medea would need to travel many times between worlds in the coming battle, and the stores of Tori's blood were spent. *Salla will be furious when he finds out.*

The alliance with the Yan Avii was fragile, especially until the wedding was official. And that matter was complicated enough as it was. The nobles were not at all pleased with an alliance with the barbaric herdsmen of the Steppe. It had been necessary to avoid an attack while the Legions were exhausted from the war against the rebel Morgathians, but the nobles took the news begrudgingly. The fact that their chancellor meant to wed a bronze-skinned sand girl only exacerbated the problem. He could not please everyone at once.

Power is a game in which you please the right people at the right time, Cyrus Maro thought. *Nothing more.*

Harvesting Vashti's blood might strain the alliance with Salla, not to mention his coming marriage. But right now, there was an army of Rulaqs two days' march from the city. There was no getting around the matter.

Medea led the way to Vashti's chambers. The marriage had not yet been announced outside the Chamber of the High Council. To the rest of the city, the Yan Avii princess was seen as an ambassador from the Red City. But Cyrus Maro had restricted her to her chambers until this madness with the Rulaqs was over, giving the lords and ladies the impression she was withdrawn and valued her privacy. Vashti was displeased, but he could not risk the uproar that would inevitably occur when the rest of the nobles found out their ruler planned to wed a girl of the Red City. At least, not until his favor was restored.

"When your union is announced," said Medea, "your nightling will have to disappear, you know."

The chancellor nodded. Of course he knew.

Medea was growing bolder lately, and he was not sure that he liked it. When he had first found her, she was grateful to be spared, eager to serve him, and she had remained quiet about the dark taste of his methods.

But she was right. As she'd been right to use the godstones on Lady Dragonis today. He ought to have been the one to order it, though, no matter how brilliantly it had subdued the lords and ladies of the High Council. But then, he admired such brashness. It was what drew him to Medea. And Commander Redvar. Empires were not built by doing what you were told. His father had learned that lesson the hard way.

They found Vashti awake in her chambers. She'd been crying, he could tell, and amazingly, he felt a twinge of pity for her. The Yan Avii princess had helped him take the Watchtower. She had volunteered for her role in all this, but he of all people knew what it was like to feel alone in the world. He pushed the thought away.

"My dear, we've come—"

"Don't patronize me," Vashti said. "I know you've come for my blood. Just like all the rest of my kind."

"You are not like any other of your kind, my dear," he said, touching her cheek gently.

The Yan Avii princess pulled away. "Aren't I? Ren is locked away in the dungeons. And I'm locked away up here. We are both supplying you with blood. Tell me, what is the difference?"

"I assure you, when this war is over, I will announce our marriage, and you will be free to roam the citadel as you wish. You'll have streams of attendants. Anything you want."

Vashti was silent. She gazed out the window. It faced the southern peaks of the Crooked Teeth, and beyond, across many leagues of mountains and forest, lay the vast plains of the Steppe.

"I heard news from the Red City tonight," she said evenly. "I overheard the servants talking."

Damn the bloody servants. He thought of the boy Ren had killed and bit the inside of his cheek. He'd have whoever told her flayed. But he subdued his anger and nodded for his queen-to-be to go on.

"The Red City is no more," Vashti finished. "Thousands of my people are dead."

"I am… very sorry, my dear, truly, but your brother is alive. He and the other survivors journey to Pendra as we speak. And when these monsters have been dealt with, Osha will send further aid."

"Was it her?" Vashti demanded.

"Was what whom?" said the chancellor.

"You claim that the Gallows Girl is responsible for the unraveling of our world. But I know you let the Rulaqs through. She may have stirred them up, but you made it possible."

He nodded again.

"So tell me the truth. The Nosferati. The sea dragons the sailors speak of. Xa'Rila. Did Tori let these monsters through from the Old World?"

The chancellor knew his next words must be truthful. *I must please the right people at the right time.*

"I don't know anything with certainty, my queen. But I do know it was not I who did it. I believe the Gallows Girl let them through, though I don't know how she did it. She's far more powerful than I thought, and far more a threat than I ever dreamed."

Vashti came within inches of his face and looked him deeply in the eyes. "I believe you, my lord. And that means that little Gallows Whore has slaughtered my people."

"I fear it is so, my queen."

"You need my blood to save this city, and I will offer it willingly. But if I am to be your bride, you must promise me something more than aid for the surviving Yan Avii."

"I do not hold that alliance lightly. Anything for your people," said the chancellor, hoping he would not regret it.

"For my wedding gift, I want the Gallows Girl."

The chancellor nodded carefully. "As soon as these Rulaqs are vanquished, I will send my Sky Guard to hunt her down." It could not happen soon enough as far as Cyrus Maro was concerned.

Vashti's eyes narrowed, and her face drew taut with subdued rage. When she spoke, the chancellor could sense a tremor of anger. "I want it to be finished. I want Tori's head—served to me on a platter at our wedding feast."

The chancellor nearly smiled at this, though he held it back. He could not reveal just how pleased he was by her redirection of outrage. He remained solemn and took Vashti's hand. "For you, my queen, nothing would please me more."

"Good," said Vashti coldly. "Now, do what you've come to do."

And far better than even the chancellor could have hoped, Vashti Burodai gave up her blood with a fierce smile stretched across her face.

CHAPTER ELEVEN

Maro'El glowed peacefully with the light of ten thousand lanterns. Wisps of fog hung over vacant lanes, and the towers of the nobles jutted out like little daggers above the sprawling Oshan capital. Darien's own tower lay north of the White Citadel and rose above the city walls; from the perch of his bedchamber balcony, he could look out over the city to the plains beyond. The northern walls were weaker than the rest of the city. No invader had ever attacked from the north. But in a sense, it was better that the walls would come down easier.

Darien ran the stages of the battle through his head over and over, but so much would depend on the beasts. If there was one thing he'd learned, though, it was that the appearance of a sure victory could make the most cunning of enemies move foolishly. They could only hope that this would prove true with the Rulaqs.

A hand brushed his shoulder from behind, and he reached for his saber.

Valeria laughed.

Darien scowled. "You shouldn't be here. All the city can see this—"

The sight of her ended his complaints immediately. Valeria Sardona smiled, her seductive eyes glistening in the lamplight.

"What's one more nightling visiting a noble in his chambers?"

Darien's heartbeat quickened. Valeria—his closest comrade and the woman he had been suppressing feelings for since their victory at

Morgath—was dressed in a silken ebony gown with a shawl drawn over her head, concealing most of her face in shadows, though wisps of her silver hair teased from the darkness and fell past her fair shoulders. Darien had never seen her hair down. It was always pulled back in the fashion of the Night Legions. And he certainly had never seen so much of her ivory skin. The gown fastened about her neck with thin folds of fabric, and a near nonexistent back teased him with the skin he could see, and what he could not.

Valeria was right. No one would mistake her for a captain of the Sky Guard.

Her hand traveled from his shoulder and came to rest upon his bare forearm. His skin pricked with shivers, as though suddenly coming to life after months of hibernation. He saw her every day as they drilled the Sky Guard, but they could appear nothing more than comrades before the rest of the city, and he had been filled with longing that had been driving him mad ever since he'd first embraced his true feelings for her, after surviving the Nosferati attack in the catacombs of the Crooked Teeth. Darien reminded himself that these were improper feelings for a comrade. He pulled away. "I don't summon nightlings. My servants may get suspicious."

Valeria's periwinkle eyes glared from the depths of her hood. "I've wanted to do this before every battle we've faced. Every time, I wondered if I'd die and miss my chance. But not this time."

Valeria pulled him away from the balcony walls and into the shadows, and he let his inhibitions disintegrate as she pulled him in. Her lips tasted of mint and her neck smelled of sweet Trium spices. She had held nothing back in her nightling persona. His hands wandered into curls of soft silver hair, and her hood fell away.

Gods! He had wanted this for so long. Darien pulled her closer, her body searing through the thin fabric of her gown. His hands traveled to her shoulders and down to her waist. Every bit of her was taut muscle—a body fashioned for war, not gowns. Though, he did not mind seeing her this way.

When Valeria pulled back, he felt himself longing for more. Perhaps it was the nightling gown. But he knew it was for the best. "That was incredible," he murmured.

Valeria smiled, resting her hands on the stone balcony, and looked out at the city. "I wish we could just hide away. Pretend there is no war."

Darien wished it too. But there *was* a war, and it fell upon them to protect the city—two foreigners who had somehow earned the chancellor's favor. The Rulaqs would reach the city by daybreak. Now, it was the arduous stillness before all hell broke loose upon Maro'El, and they needed to be ready to fly at any moment. "We're soldiers. War is in our blood."

"I only wish it, Darien… In all honesty, I crave battle. I've lived this fight a dozen times already in my dreams."

"It's what we're made for, you and me. If there are gods, then that is why they brought us to life. To fight." He recited the mantra of the Shadow Camps, though his true thoughts were unsure.

"If there are gods, I think they are mocking us. Look, my hands are trembling, but it's not out of fear. It's anticipation. Desire. My knuckles long to feel blood running from the hilt of my saber. My eyes long to train a musket on some soldier's head. We've seen little rest from war, but ever since we returned to the citadel, I've longed for the day I would exchange city life for the battlefield once more… but sometimes, I wish I didn't. I wish I longed for rest and luxury. Families and trivial affairs."

Me too…

"Do you ever wonder what we would do if all this ended?" Valeria said. "If the wars were over?" She took hold of his hand.

At times like this, yes…

"There's always another war to fight," Darien said instead.

"That's why I wish we could pretend."

Darien wrapped his arm around her, and they stood for some time in silence. But even with her warmth beside him, his mind returned to the coming battle. It was true, he longed for it. It was the one thing he was good at.

In the past few days, he had memorized every street, every wall, every tower in Maro'El. He knew where the cannons would have the best angle for fire. He knew the weakest sections of wall, where the beasts were sure to break through first. He knew the Rulaqs would want to tear down the White Citadel most of all—the symbol of their oppression in the North since the days of the Old World.

"It will work," Valeria whispered, as though reading his mind. "Your plan."

It was her plan as much as his, but he was the commander of the Sky Guard, and she'd insisted he take the credit when he presented his strategy to the High Council.

"It has to," he said. "There are two hundred thousand people living in this city. And half a million across the Meridian, in the Fringes."

"Only slaves," she said. It was the sentiment he should share, he knew. "Your concern is the city."

"They're not just slaves, they're... comrades. I was a slave in the Fringes. I served in the workhouses. I..."

"You served in this estate," she finished.

Darien nodded, thinking back to the days he and Tori had served Commander Scelero in these halls, biding time until they were drafted into the Night Legions. Now, Scelero was a traitor lost somewhere in the catacombs, and Tori...

"It all brought me here," Darien said. "I was one of them. And now, I can save them."

"Your job is to protect the citadel. Protect the nobles."

"I don't give a damn about the nobles," he muttered darkly.

Valeria turned to him. "Careful, Darien. You speak treason."

"I speak the truth. All my years of servitude, I blamed the chancellor for the injustices I witnessed. I went to the gallows to resist him. But now, being in this city, sitting on their councils, I see I was resisting the wrong power. The chancellor has been nothing but good to me. The nobles are relics of an ancient system of corruption. The chancellor is building a different world. One where a Klavash boy and a girl of the Isles lead Osha's finest soldiers. Truth be told, I think the chancellor wants them dead more than I do."

Valeria's hand rested on his own, and it calmed him. "Osha is not the only land filled with injustice. My parents sold me into slavery in the Southern Isles. But I made the best of it, and now, I'm here. One day, maybe I'll make things better for people like me, but..." She turned and pointed at the looming crystal tower behind them. "The White Citadel is our only concern today. The chancellor *and* the nobles in that keep. We can't afford to consider anyone else."

Darien nodded. He never had a chance to say anything further. The night was split by the piercing clangor of bells from the towers upon the walls. The ringing spread as each tower responded to the sound and rang its own siren bell. The towers lit up with torches, forming a wall of fire around the city.

Valeria touched his face, turning him toward her. It lasted only a moment, and Darien wished it could last so much longer. This second kiss might be their last, and now, more than ever, he realized he longed for many more.

"To war," she said, pulling away. And then she morphed and disappeared into the night.

"To war," Darien muttered after her.

It was still hours from daybreak. The monsters had crossed the plains faster than expected. Darien knew they were building speed for the attack. *They hoped to surprise us in the night. But we are ready. More ready than those beasts could ever know.*

Darien cried out for his attendant, and the boy appeared with his armor moments later. The boy's name was Jann, a turned Watcher of the Fieri order, though Darien rather wished he was a Medici. A healer would be most valuable at his side today. But of course, Sahra and the few other Medici were needed on the battlefield.

Jann helped Commander Redvar don his thick leathern armor, though Darien knew it would help little if one of those monsters seized him with its fangs. Jann handed him his saber. The blade had cut through Morgathian heathens and undead devils, but it would barely scratch the thick hides of the Rulaqs. *This is my greatest foe yet.*

Jann was about to hand over his musket, but Darien stopped him. "You keep it." The boy seemed confused. "I need someone to cover my ass." The boy beamed with pride, and Darien knew he had chosen his attendant wisely. Jann longed to prove himself just as Darien had once longed to prove himself to General Thrain.

The ground rumbled, rattling the chandeliers within Darien's estate.

"To the wall?" Jann said.

"To the wall."

Together, they took flight, sailing over the city, Darien on thick black Morph wings, the boy on nothing but Watcher magic. Below them, the streets filled with Legions readying their positions within the city. Somewhere in the madness, Medea was preparing herself with Watcher blood.

To the Battle of Gods and Monsters, Darien thought.

CHAPTER TWELVE

Maro'El seethed with the throes of battle. Smoke shrouded the streets in a thick fog from cannon-fire and rubble, but the pillared necks of a dozen Rulaqs cut through it as the beasts moved into the city.

The northern walls held strong for less than an hour. It was enough time for the cannons to take out a handful of the beasts before the real plan fell into place. The two weakest points in the northern wall fell first, and just as Darien had hoped, the two-headed beasts began to pour through those two openings, forsaking their work on other ends of the wall soon to fall.

The Legions fixed cannons on those openings and let hell rain down on the first beasts to enter the city, taking several down. As the beasts fell, their comrades were fueled with rage and charged into the streets, swinging their mighty heads with fury.

Valeria had concocted the idea of stretching wire from the rooftops. Made from bound strands of forged steel and whittled down to a fine razor's edge, the wire was like a great scythe, decapitating the monsters as they surged into the streets with vengeful rage.

One beast attempted to wrench a wire free with its teeth, ripping out its own jaw in the process. The wires held the onslaught of one or two beasts before the force would rip them free of their holds. The Rulaqs surged forward to meet yet another wire at the next street. The beasts appeared to be overtaking the city, but with devastating losses. The grey cobblestone of Maro'El turned a strange purplish hue as Rulaq blood bathed the streets.

It was not long before the beasts figured out how to dislodge the wires by pummeling the towers that held them, but it was then the Shadows deployed bombs made of pitch, ignited by a pair of Fieri Watchers. Flaming pitch and the stench of burning hair melded with the fog of battle.

Valeria attacked next, leading a force of flying Morphs and turned Watchers, while Commander Zamel led his Shadows in the streets below. The lanes filled with even more musket- and cannon-fire, the winds bearing thick plumes west, enshrouding the far ends of the city.

Darien was forced to watch everything unfold from his perch atop the White Citadel—standing alongside the chancellor on his crystal balcony.

When the walls fell, Darien and Jann had retreated to a better vantage point. It pained him to be removed from battle so early, but it was the only way he could oversee everything, the only way he could direct his generals and adjust their strategy as the battle played out before him. More razor wires were being wrenched from their holds, and the beasts were surging forward, but so far things were going according to plan.

Valeria had intentionally set fewer wires and flaming bombs along certain paths, making it easier for the beasts to press toward the citadel, but only along the ways they intended. When these paths converged along Citadel Road, the troops thinned in the streets, and the Rulaqs roared forward, straight toward the center of the city.

It was a delicate balance. To leave that path wide open would make it too obvious that the beasts were being funneled through the city intentionally. It needed to appear as though they were forging this path on their own.

"The beasts will reach Maro Square shortly," said Darien. While the nobles cowered within, the chancellor had been watching the battle from the beginning. Perhaps longing for the action as much as Darien.

"Medea is ready in the square," said Cyrus Maro.

Medea stood below the citadel, where once—a lifetime ago, it seemed —Darien had been strung from the gallows at the chancellor's drafting ceremony. Medea was filled with Regenero blood, which would allow her to cross back and forth to the Old World and send these monsters back to the hell world where they belonged. Surrounding Medea was her company of Morphs and Watchers. The citadel's last defense.

"A brilliant plan, Commander," said the chancellor. "Your cunning may save us all."

"There is much battle left, milord."

The chancellor smiled and clapped him on the shoulder. "You have won my confidence, Commander. The beasts rage forward, just as you predicted. A human foe might retreat, regroup, attack from another vantage point. But these are beasts consumed with rage."

Darien nodded. "Rage makes man and beast alike move without caution, milord."

"We may have underestimated these beasts when they came through the portal, but the nobles overestimated their strength in the skirmishes further north. They did not have the Sky Guard. Nor you in command."

"Thank you, milord."

"When all is told, the nobles will bow before us, Commander, praising our magic army. The people will tell tales, the minstrels will write songs about how magic saved them in the Battle of Gods and Monsters."

Darien caught himself momentarily imagining Ilyana Dragonis kneeling at his feet in desperate thankfulness. With a victory, all would hail the Sky Guard as saviors. They would be the heroes of Osha. Nearly gods.

Jann tugged at his arm, and Darien was jarred back to reality. The boy pointed to the western ends of the city. "C-Commander…"

Darien followed his finger, through the billowing smoke to a place where the thick shroud was thinning as it spread across the west. *Oh gods…*

There was a breach in the western wall—an unplanned breach. In the madness and smoke, a small company of Rulaqs had circled around the city, unnoticed. They were entering streets that had been rigged with no razor wire and were lightly defended. From that vantage point, they could route the Legions and Watchers defending the streets in the north.

Below, it appeared Valeria had also noticed the breach, for her legion of Morphs and Watchers was already flying to the western end of the city. A host of Shadows followed after on the ground, but Darien feared it was not enough.

"I must go, milord," said Darien.

"I will not lose the commander of my Sky Guard. The Legions will hold them."

"I cannot stand by and see this plan fail, milord. We have two

Morgathian firebombs. We can seal off the streets and turn them toward the others."

"Those bombs are meant to seal off the square," said the chancellor.

"It won't matter if the beasts never reach the square. If they break free of our intended path, they can storm the citadel from all sides, and the city will fall."

The chancellor had lost his cool assurance of victory. He surveyed the mayhem below, tapped his ringed fingers on the wall, and then nodded. "Take Medea's legion as well."

"That will leave the square defenseless."

"As you said, Commander, none of it will matter if the beasts never reach the square. Take out those Rulaqs before they tear us apart on all sides. And be back before the horde reaches the square, or all is lost."

It amazed Darien how swiftly battles could turn from sure victory to such fear of defeat. But they could be turned back just as swiftly.

Darien clapped Jann on the back. The boy was trembling. "To war, comrade."

Jann nodded fearfully, but clutched his musket tight. Together, they took flight from the White Citadel and landed in the square below.

Medea stepped aside, and Darien stood upon the great stage where he'd nearly been hung for defection only a year and a half ago. But the chancellor had spared him, perhaps for this very moment, to do what he did best.

"To me, comrades of the Sky Guard!" Darien shouted, raising his hands. The Watchers and Morphs left their posts around the square and gathered around him.

"What news from the citadel, Commander?" Medea said. She wore a leathern cuirass over her usual dark gown.

"The western wall is breached, and there are a dozen Rulaqs tearing through the city unopposed," Darien said. "We must stop them, or die in the attempt. The fate of Osha lies in our hands now, comrades."

There was a momentary silence. This company was to be the last line of defense until the climax of the battle, when Medea would send the surviving Rulaqs back to the Abyss. They were not to be sent to battle except at last resort. *And we are the last resort.*

"Ooh, rah!" cried Dajha, the first Watcher to step forward. "We will not fail!"

"Ooh, rah!" cried another. "For death and glory."

"For the salvation of the New World!" cried Medea, floating into the air above her company. Darien took his Morph form, great black wings stretching out, his saber pointed to the sky, and he rose to join her.

The Morphs and Watchers cried out, "Ooh, rah! Ooh, rah!" and pounded their fists against their chests and clanged their sabers and readied their muskets.

The Watchers and winged Morphs took flight, and the wingless Morphs donned their giant warg-like forms, bounding through the streets —all following their commander into the heart of the battle.

Darien and his small band of soldiers broke through the thick of the smoke to find their comrades in a desperate state. The Rulaqs towered over Valeria's company. Their twin necks were thick as tree trunks, and their heads reached four stories into the sky.

Up close, the soldiers battling them seemed as absurd as a flock of sparrows against a dragon. They danced through the air, dodging, weaving about their heads like flies. Fieri launched balls of flame, and Conjuri launched rubble from the walls of Maro'El, which kept the beasts distracted, but it would not hold them off long. From below, a small company of Shadows fired their muskets to no avail.

Valeria Sardona and another Morph were frantically stretching razor wire above streets facing south. Darien knew it would not be enough to deter these monsters, but he breathed with relief to see Valeria still alive. Already a half dozen Morphs had fallen. Darien landed in a square a short distance from the fray.

"Dajha, Corryn," Darien shouted. "Take the firebombs to Captain Sardona. If we don't seal off the southern streets, we're doomed."

The two Watchers were both Enduro, and they would get the bombs set quicker than anyone else. They heaved the great sacks over their shoulders and flew away.

"The rest of you, when the bombs go, attack with everything you've got. Watchers, use your gifts. Push them together. Bring them to this square."

"Aye, sir!"

The Watchers and Morphs took flight.

"Medea, how much blood do you have?" Darien asked.

"The problem isn't the supply, I'm afraid. Vashti's blood gives me her Regenero power, but the travel takes its toll. It takes time to heal. I don't dare more than two passages now, or I'll never have the strength for the horde in Maro Square."

It won't matter if the beasts don't reach the square.

Darien clasped her shoulder. Her cloak fluttered in the wind, and he could see a line of vials at her belt. "Then we must make them both count!" he cried. "Stay close to me. Jann," he shouted, turning to his attendant. "You cover Medea, no matter what. Even if I'm dying, you cover her. She is the key to our victory." The boy nodded to him tremulously. Darien gripped the boy's shoulder. He had been afraid, too, at his first battle. "Be brave, Jann. War is our great test. And we must not fail."

The three of them flew to a tower overlooking the square below. There, they could see every piece of this haphazard plan, and all they could do was wait until their part in it came, and hope the others would not fail.

Everything that followed seemed a haze to Darien. The streets shuddered with the detonation of the Morgathian firebombs. Shards of stone the size of horses filled the air.

The two widest southern streets were sealed off in an explosion that brought down taverns and towers and shops alike, rendering the streets impassable.

One Rulaq was taken in the explosion, both its heads crushed by massive debris. Shaking away chunks of rubble, a second beast rose back up, swung its necks in fury, and charged a small street. Valeria's razor wire did its work, slicing through bone and sinew, and the Rulaq's necks flopped like felled trees, exploding with rushes of dark blood. A third Rulaq tore maniacally at the towers holding the wires. As the beast ripped at the stone, the soft tissue of its throats was exposed, and a Conjuri launched two spears with a flare of his power, lodging them deep into both skulls.

The other beasts veered from the explosion. Fire and debris filled the air, wielded by Conjuri and Fieri. Morphs flew around their heads and lashed out for their eyes with blade-like talons. The Conjuri with the spears took one more Rulaq down, but another took him from behind and rended him in two with its teeth. The soldiers could do little against such mighty beasts, but still, they managed to push them north.

Before Darien knew it, their time had come. Three of the beasts had entered the square, pushed forward by a pair of Fieri and a host of Morphs. With Medea able to manage only two passages, Darien had hoped for more. The other five monsters were nowhere close, but they could not let these beasts pass.

"Now, Medea, now!"

Medea and Jann flew to the ground. Darien flew straight at the three beasts. Six heads towered above the streets, and Darien had to keep them all distracted. He flew on thick black wings, weaving in and out, narrowly missing sets of spearhead-sized teeth. The other Morphs took the cue and did the same. Somewhere in the madness, he spotted Valeria. She swung her saber deftly, wounding the eye of one head, and managed to skirt away before the monster lashed out. The Fieri let balls of flame fly at the beasts from behind, pushing them forward. They built speed and charged for the open lane beyond the square.

But just then, Medea opened the portal. The square opened up, and suddenly, beyond the square, rather than a street, there was a dull grey meadow. The Rulaqs did not have time to slow their charge. The portal disappeared, and so, too, did the monsters.

A cheer rose up from the Sky Guard. The Watchers and Morphs landed in the empty square, a sudden burst of relief and confidence coming over them. Darien felt it as well. *We may win this battle yet.*

Valeria barked an order from the rooftops. "This is not over, comrades. In case you've forgotten, there are five more Rulaqs to be dispatched. Now, fly, and bring the last of them here!"

"Ooh, rah!" they roared. And Valeria and the others disappeared beyond the rooftops.

Moments later, there was a rift in the air, as though a giant invisible door had been opened. Medea staggered back from the Old World, and the opening disappeared. But something was wrong. Her face was riddled with pain—she was bleeding from a wound in her shoulder. Jann sprinted to her side and supported her, but still she crumpled to her knees.

Darien knelt beside her, morphing to his human form. "What happened?"

She grimaced. "Only grazed me. As they were coming through the portal. It'll heal."

Jann removed her cuirass. The leathern armor was tattered and shorn, drenched in blood. The wound beneath was deep, despite the Regenero blood coursing through her veins, and it was not healing quickly enough. Blood gushed like a fountain.

"Press it down, Jann," Darien ordered. Jann ripped a shred of cloth from his shirt and pressed it hard against her shoulder. The white cloth was soon crimson. *Gods, I wish he was a Medici.*

The wound closed slowly, the magic weakened by the passage to the Old World and back. Medea went pale with loss of blood before it was done.

The air filled with a cacophonous roar. Darien saw one, two, four heads rising above the streets beyond, and then more. The other beasts were being herded into the square, and there was no way Medea had the strength left to open another passage to the Old World. She needed time to heal, but they had to stop these beasts. Beyond this square the streets branched out, and the Rulaqs could wreak havoc on the citadel. That left Darien only one option.

"Jann, get her to safety."

"No, Commander," protested Medea. "I'll be all right. I can open the passage once more."

Darien had once feared the sorceress, but now, he felt a strange bond with her. Battle had a way of sifting out old differences. It was how he'd grown close to Valeria. In the Battle of Fire and Fury, something had changed, and they seemed to share something new, something that kept them alive. And with Medea, it was similar. The sorceress was brave, cunning, and unrelenting. A soldier he could proudly stand beside. And one he could not afford to lose.

He took her hand. Her fingers trembled with pain. "Regain your strength. You've a horde of your own to come in Maro Square."

"Commander, what do you—"

He already had the godstones. She'd dropped them while Jann was pressing her wound. He showed the emerald gems to her.

"Give me one of your vials," he commanded.

She nodded grimly and squeezed his hand shut around the stones. "I see what the chancellor sees in you, Commander." Medea drew a vial of Vashti's blood from her cloak. "When the time comes, close your hand over the stones, and open your mind to their power. Think of the Old World, and the stones will do the rest. I should warn you, Commander. It hurts like nothing you've ever felt."

Darien nodded. "Jann, get her safely to the citadel. Now!"

The first of the Rulaqs entered the square. Jann and Medea staggered away, leaving Darien alone to face the beasts.

CHAPTER THIRTEEN

The Yan Avii princess's blood tasted strangely sweet at first, then it went briny, and then sour. It made his stomach churn, but he held it down. In moments, Darien could feel something coursing through him. He felt warm all over, and he became more aware of his body than he'd ever felt. He had never noticed the warmth of blood in his veins, nor the relieving sensation of each breath as its life-giving air spread through him. Nor had he ever so sharply realized how the intensity of battle managed to mask pain.

Suddenly, he felt it, like the instant, agonizing chill from jumping in an icy pond. His neck rushed with pain. In the chaos, he had not even realized he'd been injured by one of the three Rulaqs they'd already sent back to the Old World, and now it hit him all at once—blood desperate to return to his body, skin desperate to be closed off from the world.

There was a tingling at his neck, blood seeped back to its rightful place, and then skin closed over, fibers weaving in and out until all was restored. There was a jarring pain in his back as a bit of shrapnel—an old wound from the war against Morgath—removed itself from his body.

Darien felt more whole than he'd ever felt before. More alive. More invincible. It was incredible. All from Watcher blood. And none too soon. The beasts were entering the square. First one, two, then three Rulaqs. All of it happened so quickly, Darien did not think through his actions. It was all instinct.

Valeria led the company, herding the last two Rulaqs into the square. Darien held out the stones for her to see, and their eyes locked for a moment, and he knew she understood what he was doing—without thinking, he cried out to Rivka, the god of his ancestors. *Let this work. Let me see her again.*

The beasts were charging for the opening to the city beyond. Darien was the only thing that stood between them, and the Rulaqs meant to trample him. He waited until the last possible moment. He closed his hand over the stones and their warmth spread through him, searching for a host.

Open your mind to the stones, Medea had said.

And he did.

Think of the Old World.

The warmth became a fierce burning sensation in his hand. His palm screamed, and his mouth nearly did the same. He could feel power leaving him, the stones doing their work.

The beasts were upon him.

A rush of energy. A gateway opened, and Darien found himself standing at the edge of two worlds. He stood aside as the beasts charged past him. Before they realized what had happened, or where they were, he released the stones and the gateway was gone. He was alone with the beasts in a great dismal world.

Darien stood in a vast meadow. The grass was a dull grey. In fact, the entire world seemed to consist of shades of grey, as though all the color had been drained from it. He had been there once before, to help the chancellor escape when Tori had resisted him at the Watchtower, but that had only been a momentary glimpse of the horror of the Old World.

Realizing where they were, the Rulaqs went into a frenzy, rearing up and thrashing their mighty heads around. When one caught sight of him, it lashed out with its neck, and Darien threw himself into the tall grass, narrowly avoiding the attack.

His hand was searing with pain, and it wasn't going away. *Magic doesn't work here.*

The ground thudded nearby as the beast attempted to crush him. Even Medea had not escaped their wrath. He clutched his fingers tight. But the stones were gone. Somehow, instinctively, he had released them as soon as he entered the world, his body seeking relief.

Gods! He combed through the thick grey grass, looking desperately for the emerald stones. A great fanged head came bearing down, and he dove aside, wishing he had his Morph wings.

He crawled his way back to where he'd first entered the world. Another attack, and he dove ahead, then scrambled back. There was a subtle glow a few yards off. A slightly lighter shade in the dark grey grass. Another head swung into view, and he ducked.

Of course! In here, the stones would be grey like everything else. He dove for the glow, his palm closing over the stones. Warmth spread over him. A portal opened, and he dove back into the world of color and life.

He landed in the square upon cold stone. There was a blaring noise ringing in his ears. This world was pain and confusion. His entire body seized. He felt like he was on fire. But he wasn't. Vaguely, he understood. *I'm dying.*

And death was chaos.

Motion swirled around him. Bodies. Sabers. The sky filled with blurs, and he didn't understand what was happening. Had there been more Rulaqs than they'd thought? Had the battle lines fallen in the northern ends of Maro'El?

He felt himself slipping away and was unable to resist, as though the grey world was pulling him back. Was he still holding the stones? He didn't know. He closed his eyes to the chaos. His mind numbed his body to the pain that coursed through him. It was a glorious relief. He could still hear the blaring noise.

War horns, he thought vaguely. But the noise was fading.

His body was nothing.

His mind was nothing.

And then, there was everything.

His eyes spread wide. The pain returned with fury, and he was back in the square. Someone knelt over him, and he was shaking in her arms.

"No! Darien! Gods damn you! Don't you dare!"

His vision focused on one thing amidst the world of blurs and pain and chaos. A face—smooth pale skin and hair the color of mist, eyes that shone like sapphires against a cloudy sky.

Valeria!

Darien shot back to life at the sight of her. Valeria was peeling something from his hand. The stones. Slowly, relief spread through him.

"Oh, thank the gods," Valeria muttered so only he could hear.

The pain dulled again, but this time not at the expense of his consciousness. His mind sharpened, and he realized that the blurs were soldiers rushing past them, Watchers and Morphs taking to the sky. *Rushing to battle.*

"What's happening?"

"The beasts have reached the citadel!"

Darien felt as though he'd been stabbed in the gut. He was too late. He'd failed. They'd taken too long in sending the beasts to the Old World, and now, the battle was lost.

Darien was not strong enough to fly. Not yet. But there was no time to wait. His body slowly healed, his skin pricking with sharp pangs, as he and Valeria staggered through the shambles of streets and toppled buildings. Maro'El seemed more like a graveyard than the capital of the greatest nation in the New World. The bodies of comrades littered the streets. Good men and women, chosen by the chancellor to defend the realm. Darien had been chosen to lead them all. And he had failed.

His side was on fire from running. The godstones had left him weak, and his lungs ached with each breath. He had never felt so tired before. The cries of the dying and the roars of the triumphant beasts hung over the city, as though they were echoing off the face of the heavens.

"We're too late," Darien moaned, clutching his side, staggering across a ruined marketplace. Citadel Road led straight to Maro Square. The White Citadel was visible from the very end of the road, but now the streets were enveloped in thick plumes of smoke. A smoldering corpse lay in a puddle of pitch, tiny flames lapping at the blackened remains. The sight made him thirsty for no good reason.

Valeria wrapped her arm around him, supporting him beneath the shoulder. "The battle isn't over so long as we're breathing."

Darien laughed darkly. "Look around you. Hundreds are dead. Thousands." The streets shuddered. "The city is lost, Valeria!"

Valeria slapped him across the face. "Those are not the words of the man who attacked the Rebel King at the Battle of Fire and Fury."

His skin ignited with pain, but this time it didn't last long. The pain in his lungs subsided, and he looked at his hand. The wound from the stones had closed over. Vashti's Regenero blood had done its work at last. Strength and adrenaline returned to him.

Valeria gripped him by the back of the neck and pulled him close. "We're still breathing, Darien."

The streets around them were empty of monsters. The beasts might not have followed the intended path, but one thing was certain: they were all clustered in one place—Maro Square.

Darien pressed his hand against the stones in his pocket. He nodded to Valeria and drew close. "The Rulaqs are all in the square. We have to get the stones to Medea."

"Can you fly?"

"I have to!" His body was tingling with energy now that he'd healed. It was strange, as though his body were playing tricks with his mind. Moments ago, he'd been staggering. Now, he morphed and took flight with relative ease. Darien and Valeria became two dark forms in the haze of smoke, flying straight down Citadel Road.

Maro Square was a roiling, seething mass of blood, smoke, and chaos. The Rulaqs filled the square, their immense necks swinging around like the tentacles of a giant sea dragon. There were dozens of them thrashing and tearing at the base of the White Citadel. The Legions attacked from the entrances to the square, but their musket-fire did little. The surviving Morphs and Watchers attacked from the air, but their numbers were thinning, and all of them were tired and weak from battle. High atop the citadel, Darien spotted Medea at the chancellor's side. Below, several of the beasts took turns charging at the palace. The largest of the Rulaqs, a beast with dark grey fur who seemed to be their leader, roared and led the charge. Each attack echoed across the city. They backed up and charged again.

Crystal shattered.

Stone crumbled.

Darien held the godstones high and caught Medea's gaze. She took flight. He knew it was a long shot, but Medea was their only chance. Valeria split off to rally the Sky Guard, to drive the beasts forward one last time. Darien and Medea met in midair, hovering. He handed her the stones, but she only took one.

"This gateway will require us both." Medea took hold of his hand, and they descended.

The leader of the Rulaqs led a charge of four others. They backed up, then galloped forward, ready to slam into the side of the tower with their massive bodies. All the Legions, Morphs, and Watchers attacked at once. The horde pressed closer to the citadel.

Darien and Medea landed directly in front of the attacking beasts. The portal opened, and pain shot through Darien's hand anew. The gateway stretched out in front of the entire palace, and Darien and Medea stood at the edge of it. Four of the Rulaqs stopped, but the leader did not. He surged forward at full speed, swinging his massive necks.

The impact launched Darien from his feet, and Medea's hand was wrenched from his grasp. He landed twenty yards away. Instantly, the gateway disappeared, and the only thing standing between the Rulaq and the citadel was Medea. The beast backed up for another attack, but she did not move.

Medea stood tall, facing the Rulaq. Clenching the godstone with one hand, she fearlessly reached toward the beast with the other. The beast lowered its heads and charged.

Medea did not move. Her fingers remained outstretched. Her eyes were closed in concentration, and the godstone glowed fiercely.

The stone in Darien's hand glowed as well. His skin stung as the stone surged with power.

Suddenly, the Rulaq leader eased its charge.

It slowed to a walk, and then stopped altogether, lowering its heads toward Medea. Her eyes were still closed, her hand held out before her, the godstone glowing with a fierce emerald light. Darien did not want to watch the woman be devoured, but he could not turn away.

The Rulaq did not open its jaws to rend her in two.

It stood still.

Medea opened her eyes, her chest heaving as though she'd run many miles. She stepped closer. She touched each of the beast's heads, carefully, as one might a stallion that was first being broke. The beast did not move. Its breaths slowed. The monsters behind it stood immobile, watching their leader.

Darien did not understand at first what was happening. Somehow, Medea was alive. She brushed the fibrous fur of the Rulaq, and the monster held still. A low moaning sound uttered. It was the only sound in Maro Square. The streets echoed with a nightmarish purr.

Medea released contact, and the Rulaq leader's eyes opened wide again. They were as settled as a mountain lake. The leader turned to the other monsters and released a strange growling sound, speaking to its soldiers.

It was then, Darien realized the battle had ceased. The Rulaqs were all watching their leader, and the Legions were all watching Medea. The Darkling Witch walked silently past the leader, and all around, the Rulaqs lowered their heads to her. One by one, she reached out and touched their grey noses with her long fingers. She never said an audible word, but somehow, Darien knew she was communicating with the beasts through her sorcerous mind and the power of the godstones.

PART FIVE
TRIAL OF FIRE & ICE

There is no place more deadly than the Great White North. For centuries, the survival of the Alyut was an unnerving mystery to the Southern folk. The Alyut must have been blessed by their gods in some special way. Perhaps that is why no one ventured into their domain. They feared the power of the Northern gods.

—from *Dawn of the Third World*

CHAPTER FOURTEEN

Time bled slowly beneath the Ice City of Iqala. The cells where Astoria and Mischa were taken were unlike any dungeons Tori had ever heard of. First of all, they were warm. Beyond anything she might have expected this far north—where the harsh world above was composed of thick ice sheets, layer upon layer of snowfall, and fierce peaks of obsidian star rock. The porous stone beneath the city emanated a soft, seeping heat. Though they were given thick furs under which to sleep, Tori often lay on top of them, basking in the warmth of the cavernous cell.

It was a stark contrast to the last cell she had called home, beneath the White Citadel, where Tori had endured the chancellor's bloodletting for over a year.

And it was a testament to the civility of the so-called savages of the Great White North. Tori supposed the notion had been perpetuated by the ancient Elyan invaders to justify their conquests, which had forced the Alyut to become people of the mountains and ice of the North. The caricature of the savage Northmen was sustained even by the Yan Avii, who were wild by any Oshan standard—nomads who spent much of the year wandering the vast Steppe, living off their herds and the land.

Tori remembered tales told around village fires during her childhood amongst her people, tales of Northmen pillaging the tribes who ventured too far north, stealing horses and women and disappearing into the blizzards that raged across the northern Steppe in winter.

None of this eased her mind about her predicament. The fact remained that she was to be tried for crimes she had not committed. Alyk dul Baruk may have been nothing like the Northmen Tori had been told about in her youth, but it mattered little.

He had still betrayed her…

Tori lay awake upon her furs, tossing and turning. She swore it was hotter than any other night in their cell. Or perhaps it was all her pent-up frustration. She stripped off her woolen tunic and trousers and lay in her undergarments.

Did Alyk know all along? she wondered. *Did he bring me all this way under the illusion of revolution? Or was he really that much of a fool?* The Alyut soldiers who had greeted her had not seemed the least bit enticed by the thought of revolution, if Skya dul Baruk's reaction was any indication.

And Alyk had, once again, separated Tori from her connection with the forces behind the world. Her magic was useless in the North from the moment Skya had greeted them outside the Ice City. And who else but Alyk could have rendered her so helpless?

Mischa sat up beside her and lit the lantern that had been given to them when they arrived. "Can't sleep either?" She chuckled as she took in Tori's lack of garb. "Rough night?"

"It's like an oven in here," said Tori. "And of course I can't sleep. We've been waiting for weeks."

"Skya said the trial would be at the Empty Moons. Should be soon."

"And not a single person has come to see us this entire time. No one's come to hear our side of these accusations. The only living soul we've seen is that guard who brings our food."

"She's been pleasant enough," said Mischa optimistically. "And the food is decent."

"Where in the Abyss is Alyk? What is going on up there?"

Mischa sighed. They had been through this before. "I trust him, Tori. You should too. He saved you once."

"After he tried to kill me."

"From the way his sister spoke, he risked much just by bringing you here. We have to wait, and trust he is on our side."

Tori sat up, suddenly chilled. She drew the furs over her bare legs. "He cut off our magic, Misch. We could have escaped. Why would he do that?"

"Perhaps there are others, like him, who can obliviate magic."

Tori heaved a sigh.

"Or maybe," said Mischa, "Alyk feared what would happen if we fought back."

Tori had considered this. She had been furious when she realized that Skya dul Baruk had not come to welcome the Gallows Girl but to imprison her. A dark rage had filled her. She had fought hard not to let it show. Even Mischa hadn't realized it until Tori admitted it later. Tori had reached for her magic, desperate to lash out and flee, but it had been as though grasping for vapor. And all because of Alyk. "Then he was a fool! And a liar! He told us there was a gods-damned army up here!"

Mischa smiled.

"What?" said Tori, annoyed.

"Your fire is coming back. No more of that *shenzah* about all this being your fault."

She'd had much time to think on it. She had been a fool, a puppet in the chancellor's hands, and she wished she could go back and prevent the deaths of Zaya and the others. But the devastation of the beasts was not her fault.

The chancellor had made all this possible. He had tampered with power he did not understand, and he had forced her to use it as well. Nineteen innocent people had died in the Mouth of the Gods. Who knew how many more had died elsewhere?

And that blood was on the chancellor's hands, just like the blood of lowborn slaves and soldiers of Osha. Tori would not take it upon herself any longer, and the longer she waited beneath the Ice City, the more determined she was to destroy Cyrus Maro and free their friends. *And that possibility is dwindling the longer we sit in this damn cave!*

Tori gritted her teeth. "It doesn't matter if it's *shenzah* or not. What matters is that we are down here useless, while things get worse all over the New World."

Mischa smiled again.

"What?"

"We'll need that fire when we get out of here."

Tori glared. "If we get out of here."

There was a creak as an immense iron door opened across the room. Tori and Mischa shot to their feet. Two Alyut guards escorted Alyk dul Baruk into the room.

The shaman looked more regal now. He had donned fine white furs and dark breeches. His stubble from their journey north had been shaved smooth and his dark hair was pulled back. Tori pushed away the fleeting thought that he looked handsome.

"Well, it's about time!" Tori said.

Alyk stopped a short distance from them, both guardswomen remaining close to his sides, hands at the ready on upright spears. The shaman met her glare, then glanced away sheepishly. "Er, would you mind dressing yourself, Tori?"

Tori glanced down at her exposed legs and thin undershirt. She quickly pulled on her trousers and woolen tunic.

Alyk smiled, still blushing. "Thank you. It was a little... distracting."

Tori nearly smiled back. She hated how easily he could disarm her. That she had to remind herself she was furious at him. "Where have you been?"

Alyk remained calm. "You've been treated well?"

"Y-yes, but—"

"You've been warm and fed? The guards have not harmed you?"

Tori huffed. "Yes, they've been fine."

"Good," he said steadily. "By your tone, I was worried that something—"

"My tone is like this because I'm bloody pissed at you, Alyk dul Baruk! You brought us all this way, only to throw us in prison?"

Alyk scowled. The guardswomen stood expressionless beside him, but their fingers tightened around their spears. "That was my sister's doing, Tori, and yes, this is more complicated than I'd hoped. But I have been working hard to defend you in the preliminary discussions before your trial."

"Preliminary discussions? You said your people were raising an army. You said they were ready for their Restoration."

"I did!" Alyk raised his voice, and it made Tori glad. She wanted to rile him. "I was not lying, Tori. Restoration has been prophesied for many years amongst the shamans. But many others... are not as ready to seize it as we are."

"I think they're more than not ready," Tori shot back. "I think you're an idealistic idiot."

Alyk was quiet for a moment. He sighed, and his eyes met hers. They were a warm brown and glowed in the lantern light. "Perhaps I am. Tomorrow will tell. But Tori..." Alyk drew near and took hold of her hands. His fingers were warm. And sweaty. He was nervous. "I... I need you to trust me."

Tori pulled away and crossed her arms. "Did you do it?" she demanded. "Did you take away our magic?"

Alyk's eyes fell. "I am not the only shaman with this ability... but yes, I did."

At least he's honest, Tori thought, but she scowled all the more.

"I'm not here to apologize."

"Then why are you here?" said Tori.

"I have news from Osha."

Tori's stomach felt queasy. Mischa squeezed her hand.

"The others?" Mischa asked.

Alyk nodded. "Many survived your encounter with the Nosferati, it seems. Including your Captain. Ren, was it?"

Tori and Mischa nodded.

"But I'm afraid that's the only good news. While we were traveling north, that horde of Rulaqs from the Crooked Teeth made its way to Osha. They attacked Maro'El in an attempt to take back their realm."

"Good," said Tori. "I hope they ruined that city."

Alyk shook his head. "I'm afraid it gets worse. Magic is no longer forbidden in Osha. The chancellor revealed his power, and he has formed his own magical army. He calls it the Sky Guard. They are led by your friend, the Gallows Boy."

"Darien?" Tori whispered, barely able to utter his name. She had been a fool to entertain Merri's hope for him.

Alyk nodded. "He led the defense of the city. The Sky Guard and the Night Legions fought valiantly against the Rulaqs under Darien's leadership, but... it was a hopeless resistance. The Rulaqs broke through the city walls and were prepared to raze the White Citadel. But that is when she intervened."

"Who?" said Tori.

"They call her the Darkling Witch, but her true name is Medea Lorzarre. She subdued the Rulaqs. She saved the city."

Tori remembered her well from the Watchtower. The last she had known, the woman was lost when the Legions fled to the catacombs. *That would have been too convenient.*

"Subdued," said Tori. "You mean she sent them back to the Old World?"

Alyk was silent for a moment. "No, she... communicated with

them… Word of it is spreading all across the New World. The Rulaqs withdrew their assault on Osha. They made peace with the chancellor."

Tori could not believe it. The thought made her sick. After all the chancellors of old had done to the beasts of the Old World…

"How?" Tori finally said. "How did she do it?"

Alyk shrugged. "They say she spoke to their minds. It was an unparalleled demonstration of power for any age of the world. Medea is being hailed the Savior of the North. People everywhere are spreading tales of the chancellor and his Darkling Witch."

"Gods," said Mischa. "The chancellor unleashed hell upon the New World, and has managed to set himself up as the bloody savior from that very same hell."

"He claims you're the cause of all this, Tori," said Alyk. "And… and the people of Osha believe him. There were rumors of lowborns stirring, calling themselves the Saints of the North. But this has lessened since the battle."

Tori felt squeamish. This would not help her case before the Alyut elders. Her innocence rested on the claim that the chancellor was the one who had unleashed the mayhem of the Old World beasts. But with the attack on Maro'El, and the chancellor's miraculous victory, her claims would seem all the more unfounded.

"You've come to tell me it's hopeless, then," said Tori.

Alyk's eyes betrayed his uncertainty, though his words claimed otherwise. "Nothing's hopeless… but things are not going well. The elders are skeptical as ever, and my *madru* is chief among them."

"Who is your mother exactly?" said Tori. *Why didn't you ever tell me about her, or any of this? We would have avoided the North altogether.*

Alyk glanced at the guardswomen, and Tori realized they had been sent to watch him as much as the two young Watchers. "My *madru* is Fara dul Baruk, elder of the *Nuq'vana*, the Bear Rider clan. She is also the High Elder among the four clans. And I'm afraid she will be the hardest of them all to convince. Her lover was the captain of the trading vessel that was lost in the Channel Sea."

Tori wondered if things could possibly get any worse.

"And even if, somehow, the others should decide to believe us, with this news from Osha, they are even more wary of any notions of Restoration or war. And we have no allies."

"You have the Crooked folk," said Mischa. "More would join us, I'm sure of it."

"You spoke of the Witch Queen of the Southern Isles," said Tori. "Or was that more of your idealistic *shenzah*?"

"It's not." Alyk's face tensed. "I saw the queen in a vision, not long before I left for the Crooked Teeth. Not long before I found you. I believe she will play a part in all this. But all of those futures depend on convincing the elders of your innocence." Alyk would not meet her gaze.

"Look at me," said Tori. Alyk did. "What will happen if they find me guilty?"

Alyk gulped, but he held her gaze as he answered. "If the elders find you guilty, you will be tried by fire and ice. And unless the gods intervene on your behalf, you will die."

Mischa gripped her hand. Tori felt weak. Had she really come all this way only to be sentenced to death in the one place where her Regenero abilities could be rendered useless?

"Then, let me speak to them," Tori said, more irritated than ever about being left helpless underground.

Alyk sighed. "You will have your chance to defend yourself at the trial. But you should know, our elders do not highly value the testimony of those wishing to defend themselves. It is, by its very nature, self-serving. That is the other reason I've come. The trial will be held tonight, at the rise of the Empty Moons. But before that time, they wish to speak with *you*, Mischa."

Mischa nodded, but she did not hide her grim expression. The guardswomen lowered their spears and stepped forward. Mischa squeezed Tori's hand. "I'll convince them, Tori."

Alyk managed a smile in Tori's direction. The guards took Mischa by the arms and led her out. Alyk followed. And Tori was left alone in the dungeons beneath the Ice City.

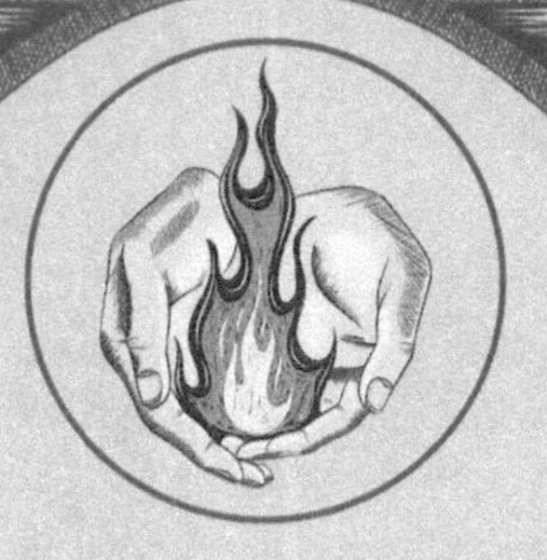

CHAPTER FIFTEEN

Alyk dul Baruk led Mischa through winding passages and narrow stairways cut straight into the star rock foundations of the Ice City. Their path was lit by pale blue crystals, which glowed with a warm luminescence. Mischa had not noticed the strange light the last time she had journeyed down these halls, for she and Tori both had been bound and blindfolded. The guards followed close behind, but Mischa was not bound this time, which she hoped was a good omen.

"These stones are incredible," said Mischa, gesturing at the curious sources of light. "What are they?"

The crystals were the size of her fist, held by iron clasps fixed to the cavern walls. Alyk paused and, with a gloved hand, retrieved one of the glowing stones from its hold and handed it to her. Mischa flinched as it touched her skin, expecting it to be hot, but it did not burn her.

"It's cold," she observed. The stone glowed brighter against her skin. "Where does the light come from?"

Alyk's lips parted in a smile. "We call it icefire. Its light comes from within. Rather like glow worms."

"Glow worms?" said Mischa, perplexed.

Alyk laughed. He gestured down the hall, and they carried on. Mischa marveled at how light the stone was, as though it were hollow.

"My friend, you have not lived until you've walked through a cavern by the light of glow worms. They give off their own light and shine on cave walls like the night sky. Icefire, however, is more of a mystery. We do not understand the source of its light. It may be the crystal itself, or perhaps some tiny luminous creature that feeds off the minerals within, or perhaps it is fueled by a strange magic. But it is our main source of light here in the Ice City. Fuel is scarce for fires, and we use what little wood can be found this far north for shelters and building ships and qayaqs. Icefire was a blessing from the gods when it was discovered shortly after our arrival in the Icelands. It gives light to the North in the long, dark winters, much like the Lights of Anora."

Alyk handed the crystal to one of the guards and ordered her to restore it to its rightful place behind them, which she did with evident irritation. Mischa swore the other guard drew even closer during the brief time her partner was missing.

"Icefire," said Mischa as they pressed on.

"And the trial of fire and ice," Alyk finished for her. It would determine the future of their plight in the North. The future of their revolution. The future of Tori's life. "There is a reason the trial of the gods was given that name. Icefire is one of our most beloved gifts from Anora."

"Where does it come from?"

"The crystals form deep below Iqala in ancient caverns. We believe Anora once lived here, long ago, when the gods still walked the earth. We send hunters into the depths to harvest them."

"Do they burn out? The crystals?"

"So long as they remain connected to their *madru*, the earth, they shine without end. Up here, they last a few weeks."

They continued on in silence, and Mischa tried to steel herself for the interrogation to come. She felt a weight on her mind she had not felt since her fourteenth summer with Ala. Tori's life might rest on her words, on the answers she chose for the elders' questions, just as Ala's life had once rested on her answers to her father's questions. Mischa pushed the dark memory away.

She would not fail this time.

But what was she to say? Tori *had* opened up the portal to the Old World, as the chancellor claimed. She had stirred them up when she resisted the chancellor. And Alyk's mother wanted to believe the claims after the death of her lover by sea dragons. Tori herself feared she had let in those other monsters.

The truth was Mischa did not know what to believe. Had the chancellor done this, intending to turn the world against the Gallows Girl all along? Or was it some catastrophic accident?

Either way, there was no denying one thing: Tori was involved in this devastation.

Should she lie, then? Or would Alyk's mother see right through her?

When the stone tunnels turned to a massive hall made of ice, the guards lingered behind, standing watch at the iron door to the dungeons below. The halls of the palace were massive, supported by thick pillars that towered at least fifty feet to the arched roof, all made of intricately carved ice. The halls were filled with Alyut dressed in thick white furs, much like the giant furs lining the icy walls. Mischa wondered what animals the furs had belonged to. Mammuts, northbears, shadowcats?

Mischa's breath misted in front of her face now that they were aboveground, and she pulled her fur cloak tighter.

"Most of our dwellings are belowground," said Alyk as they walked.

Mischa wondered if he was telling her all this to distract himself. If so, she was glad for it. "It was so warm in our cell."

"The rock gives off heat from the world below, throughout the city's foundations. The ice insulates the walls of the palace well enough, but the comfort of the underworld is unmatched this far north, so most endure the darkness for the sake of warmth."

"I can't imagine why," said Mischa sardonically. She had never longed more for the warmth of the islands of her childhood than here in the North.

They crossed several similar halls, filled with warriors and fishermen and children and hunters. The palace seemed to be the hub of the city aboveground. Traders hauled carts filled with fish, lamp oil, and furs, but the busiest carts were those dealing in goods from the South: grain, fruits, spices, even jewelry. Many people watched them pass, their eyes settling on Mischa, which made her uncomfortable. She supposed that few of them had ever seen outsiders, let alone an island girl from the southern reaches of the continent.

The crowds dwindled as they reached a narrower passage with a guarded entrance. The throne room doors were decorated with icefire crystals, and glowed with a beautiful luminescence that reminded Mischa of moonlight on the beaches of her homeland. She paused outside the doors and touched Alyk's arm. The guards stood watch with one hand at their spears.

"Your mother," said Mischa. "She sounds like a fierce woman. What can I say to convince her?"

Alyk shook his head with a sigh. "My *madru* is a hard woman, but she loves her people. Her duty is to the well-being of the Alyut, first and foremost. You must convince her that letting the Gallows Girl live will be to the advantage of my people, that it will not bring more pain and suffering to the North."

"Haven't you already told her that? Tori could bring Restoration for your people."

Alyk grimaced. "Unfortunately, my *madru* and I do not see things with the same eyes. Where I see opportunity, she sees needless suffering for our people. She has heard my pleas, but she hardened her heart to me long ago. I should warn you, though, the elders will see through any lie."

"Then what do I say?" Mischa felt helpless, as though the verdict had already been determined.

"Speak wisely and speak the truth. But be cautious what truths you choose to share." Alyk nodded to the guards, and they pushed open the doors.

Mischa fought back the urge to retch with nervousness. The throne room was bordered by immense ice pillars, and between the pillars stood rows of guards, lining the hall all the way to the four icefire thrones set upon the dais. One throne for each elder, Mischa assumed.

A woman sat erect upon one of the glowing thrones, her fingers forming a tower near her chin, as though deep in thought. The room was silent as Alyk and Mischa approached, but as they neared, Mischa realized that the throne was not occupied by the High Elder. It was occupied by her daughter, Skya dul Baruk.

Mischa glanced around, but there was no one else in the throne room. None of the elders had come to hear her plea for Tori's life.

The fierce-looking young Bear Rider leaned forward as Mischa and Alyk approached the Alyut thrones. Alyk cursed under his breath. "Where's *Madru*?"

Skya's expression betrayed a hint of bemusement. "She was taken away by tribal matters. I'm sure you can imagine our High Elder is a busy woman. A host of refugees have joined our already teeming city. Hunting is growing sparse as winter descends, and much of our supply for the Long Night was lost at sea, thanks to your Gallows Girl."

Alyk threw back his head with exasperation. "The trial is hours away, and Mischa's testimony is vital to our case!"

Skya's brow rose. "Which is why our *madru* asked me to hear the island girl's testimony in her stead."

"You?" said Alyk, his hands running through his long hair.

Skya rose to her feet and descended from the throne. "I am a captain of the *Nuq'vana*, daughter of the High Elder. I've killed more rogues than most of my kin. Why not me?" She and Alyk stood eye to eye for a moment, and then they clasped shoulders in a formal greeting.

The Alyut siblings were nearly identical in height, but that was where the similarities ended as far as Mischa could tell. Alyk was a shaman, while his sister was a warrior and a hunter. Alyk was lanky, even beneath his thick cloak and long leather sleeves. Skya's muscular arms were bare beneath her fur cloak, despite the chill. Tattoos wove around her left arm in red and blue cyclical patterns identical to those on the side of her head, where her long dark hair was shaved. Alyk's face was soft and kind, while Skya's was stern and fierce. But her expression softened as she released her brother's grip.

"Your fight is not with me, *Baru*. You know that, don't you?"

Alyk nodded, though Mischa was not convinced.

"We may have our differences," Skya went on. "You whisper prayers, while I prefer the way of the spear, but I harbor no ill will toward you."

"I wish I could say the same for our *madru*. And she is the one I must convince of Tori's innocence. And where in the Abyss is she?" Mischa could tell Alyk cared for Tori, but there was a desperation in Alyk's voice that worried her.

Skya's expression turned grim. "You know as well as I, our High Elder does not heed the counsel of shamans, least of all, you."

Alyk nodded, though Mischa noted a sad mistiness in his eyes. "Then, it's already been decided?"

Skya shook her head. "I did not say that."

The warrior turned to Mischa, looking her up and down. Mischa was conscious of the fact that she had been wearing the same clothes ever since she had left the Watchtower. Though she had been able to wash herself in their cell underground, she was relieved it was cool in the world above, so the stench of her garments was subdued.

"Convince me, my lady."

Mischa could not decide if Skya was mocking her or simply attempting courtesy. Mischa had not been addressed so formally since her childhood. "My name is Mischa Sufai of Melanesia."

Mischa held the warrior's gaze. Her features appeared perpetually hardened, perhaps due to her station as a captain, but Skya managed a hint of a smile.

"Defend your Gallows Girl, then, Mischa. What are we to make of the chancellor's claims?" Skya returned to her seat upon the throne, leaned back in a slight slouch, and crossed one leg over the other. Her smile faded, and Mischa felt naked under the girl's scrutinizing gaze.

Mischa knew there was no way she could lie. She straightened up and began. "The chancellor blames Astoria Burodai for the havoc that is being wreaked throughout the New World. And he is… not fully wrong."

Skya's eyebrows rose.

"But he is a master at disguising truths within lies, Captain. It is true that Tori brought back the beasts of the Old World. I was there when the chancellor took her there and forced her to bring them back."

"Took her to the Old World…" said Skya querulously.

"With godstones."

Skya sat up straight. "So they're real."

Mischa hoped this was a good sign. "The chancellors of old, the descendants of the conquerors who drove *your* people out of Osha, used the stones to create this other world where they banished the creatures of the Old World." Mischa hoped that bit of ancient history might register an emotional effect, but Skya's expression had resumed its mildly interested appearance.

Mischa went on. "That is how all these beasts have returned, seemingly out of myth. Cyrus Maro used Tori's magic to open a portal between the worlds. He wanted to unleash the Rulaqs to destroy our fortress in the Crooked Teeth. We were mounting a rebellion against him."

"Hmmm." Skya drummed her fingers on the icy arms of the glowing throne. She looked fiercely captivating in the blue light. The glow softened her smooth skin, and Mischa wondered how old she was. Likely little older than herself.

"So you saw the chancellor take her to this other world?" asked Skya.

"Well…" In fact, Mischa had only heard the account from Tori. She had remained with Zaya and the other Watcher prisoners while the chancellor dealt with Tori. "Well, er, no, I did not witness it, Captain."

"But you *saw* her come back with the Rulaqs, then?"

Mischa shook her head, fear beginning to penetrate her resolve. "I… heard only the accounts of others who witnessed the attack. I was imprisoned inside the Watchtower after the chancellor invaded our fortress."

Skya nodded. "Because you were rebelling… So you did not see who, in fact, let in the beasts from this other world. Nor how it was accomplished?"

"No."

"I see." Skya remained expressionless.

Mischa clenched her fists in frustration. "No, I did not see it. But I heard the story from Tori. She is my friend, and I trust her. She did not willingly let the Rulaqs in. The chancellor forced her hand. She was trying to save the rest of us. The chancellor threatened to kill us all, to exterminate our kind just like his forefathers. She had no choice. She had no idea the devastation the monsters would cause, and she deeply regrets that choice."

"You're saying the chancellor used the Gallows Girl to let in the beasts that attacked his own capital only weeks ago?"

"The beasts got out of his control. But it was *his* scheme. Tori was a pawn in his plot to dominate the North."

Skya thought for a minute. "Believe me, Mischa, we in the North hold no love for the chancellor, nor Osha. But you must admit, the chancellor's subduing of the Rulaqs in Maro'El does not help your case."

"That was his witch, Medea, who was there when the Watchtower was attacked."

"And what of these other beasts? The frost giants who attacked my people in the Mouth of the Gods. The sea dragons that attacked our traders in the Channel Sea. What are we to make of them? How did they return to haunt our world? Was it Tori who let *them* in as well?"

"I… I don't know."

Skya nodded grimly. "Well, what do you think?"

Mischa threw up her hands. "What difference does it make what I think? Your mind is already made up, so why are we even speaking?"

Alyk tried to cut her off. "Mischa, you—"

But Mischa was through with this political game. "You want to know what I think, Skya dul Baruk? I think you and your elders *want* to believe the chancellor's lies. I think you want an excuse not to seek your Restoration. You've found comfort in exile. You keep warm underground with your firestones and your pretty icefire lights. No one in the world cares what you do in the North, and you've come to enjoy that isolation. You fear bringing attention to the North by harboring the Gallows Girl, and so you believe the chancellor's words, because they are convenient. But you do not know the injustices of the southern world, Captain."

"You think we do not know of their cruelty?" Skya's eyes grew wide. "Need I remind you it was they who drove my people from the land they call Osha?"

Mischa fought back a smile. She had hit her mark, but she did not hold back. "The chancellors still rule your homeland with cruelty and blood, and you fear the cost of leaving this place and taking back your home. You fear the unknown enough to sacrifice my friend to save your own skins."

Skya glared down from the throne, and Mischa swore the icefire light grew darker. "You dishonor my people with such words, Mischa Sufai."

Alyk stood beside Mischa, shaking his head at her brazenness. Skya dul Baruk's eyes were alight, and Mischa felt as though the captain's gaze might cut straight through her.

But Mischa did not quit. "You dishonor yourselves if you think killing Tori will save you from the same fate as those in the South. One day, the chancellor's wrath will turn to the North, and you will regret killing the one true hope the New World had."

Skya stood, towering over her now. "That is what you think, little island girl?" Skya descended the steps and stood over her. The guards drew closer. Mischa could feel the Bear Rider's hot breath on her face, and she worried the young warrior was going to pummel her.

Skya was trying to show her dominance, like curs did among packs of wild dogs in the poor districts of the Trium'vel, but Mischa held the warrior's gaze. "Yes, that's what I think. And if you and your mother ignore this opportunity, if you kill her, you'll be no better than the slave traders and highborns of the southern world. Looking the other way for your own comfort."

The captain of the Bear Riders reached for her, and Mischa winced, but to her amazement, Skya did not strike her. She clasped her shoulder in a firm but comradely fashion. "Few are bold enough to speak that way to me, Mischa Sufai. You presume much about me, and my people, but… I can sense your sincerity."

Mischa was not sure what to say, so she nodded.

"You truly believe the Gallows Girl is the hope of the New World?"

"I have seen the way the Crooked refugees, and some of your own people, responded to her on our journey here. I think people across the world will rally behind her. I think Astoria Burodai might just be able to change this dark world."

"With magic," said Skya. "We do not trust magic in the North, you know. It was used against us, once. So we learned to dismantle its hold on us."

"Magic has returned to the world, whether you like it or not. And if it is left to the chancellor, it will mean the end of the New World as we know it. But with Tori, magic might just save us all."

Skya managed a hint of a smile, and she squeezed Mischa's shoulder. Her touch was remarkably warm. "I like your spirit, Mischa Sufai. And you have said what I hoped to hear."

Alyk looked up with surprise. "She did?"

Mischa's body relaxed a little at the words.

"Yes, *Baru,* and I am not the only one."

Another young woman stepped from behind a pillar, where she had been listening to their conversation. Her silver hair fell in waves over her shoulders. She was dressed in a regal sapphire gown with sparkling sleeves that reached her wrists. The finery immediately betrayed her otherness in this place. No Alyut or Crooked refugee dressed so finely, or without furs. She wore only a thin shawl over her gown. Her breath did not mist the way Mischa's did, and her eyes shone like icefire.

"Who're you?" said Alyk, his hand flying to the hunting blade at his belt.

The woman smiled nonchalantly. "Don't you know my face, Alyk dul Baruk? I remember yours."

"W-what?"

"From our visions, of course."

"Our... our visions?"

"They work both ways, you know." The woman smiled, and Mischa was struck by the way her presence seemed to dominate the room. Mischa could not take her eyes off the stately young woman. It reminded her of the time one of the princes of Malai had come to Melanesia. There had been a parade and young Mischa had watched the young boy until he completely disappeared from sight, marveling at his attire, his procession, his noble air. She felt the same presence from this woman now.

Alyk's eyes spread wide with amazement, and his hand relaxed at his blade. "My visions... incredible. You mean, you've seen *me* as well?"

"Of course I have, Alyk dul Baruk. Where did you think the visions came from? The gods?" The young woman chuckled.

"Well, yes, actually," said Alyk. "I've had other visions, in fact... er, apart from the ones of you."

The woman's eyes sparkled with fascination. "Really?"

"For those of us who were not involved in these visions, would you all mind explaining what in the Abyss is going on?" asked Mischa.

Alyk pulled himself together, his eyes leaving the woman for the first time since she appeared. He straightened himself. "This is Seren lè Tal."

Mischa did not recognize the name. "And?"

"She's the Witch Queen of the Southern Isles."

Now, Mischa was intrigued. The infamous sorceress of the southern world had come here?

"But how?" Alyk said, turning to the queen.

Skya interjected. "You told me of your visions of the queen before you left for the Crooked Teeth."

"And you thought them ridiculous," said Alyk.

"I did. Until we heard word from Uluq of the events in the Mouth of the Gods, and the Gallows Girl who was journeying with you. While our High Elder prepared to seize her upon your arrival, I sent word to the Southern Isles."

"I have very much wanted to meet your friend, Mischa," said the Witch Queen, who struck Mischa as far more relaxed than any dignitary Mischa had ever heard of. Her voice was soft and wispy. Her presence was strong and demanded attention, but not in a harsh way like the chancellor's. No one had even bowed when she revealed herself.

"But how did you arrive so quickly?" said Alyk.

"Sorcery," said Seren lè Tal. "And after hearing your words, Mischa, I am glad I came as fast as I did. There is much I wish to discuss with your Gallows Girl."

"She will testify before the elders tonight," said Skya. "On Astoria Burodai's behalf."

Alyk shook his head in disbelief. "I… I am sorry I doubted you, *Saru.*" He embraced his sister, and though a little stiffly, she returned it.

For the first time since arriving in the North, Mischa felt relief. With Skya and the Witch Queen on their side, surely the elders could not argue for Tori's execution.

But her relief was short-lived. The icefire doors spread wide with a groan, and a young soldier crossed the room. When he reached them, he bowed to Skya and then to Alyk.

"Captain—Shaman—the elders have requested your audience in the assembly."

"The assembly?" said Alyk incredulously.

"Now?" said Skya, a dark look crossing her face. The soldier nodded. "The trial is not until moonrise."

Mischa's stomach knotted beneath her skin as she realized what had happened.

The soldier shook his head. "The trial is over. That is why your *madru* asked you to handle the throne in her stead."

CHAPTER SIXTEEN

The trial was a farce, and Tori knew it the moment she was taken from her cell beneath the Ice City. Alyk's mother came to take her from her cell only minutes after Alyk and Mischa left. Fara dul Baruk did not bother to explain herself as two guards led Tori down the blue-lit passage, while the High Elder led the way to the city above. Tori knew what was happening. And it was confirmed the moment she reached the round assembly chamber of the Ice City. The room was filled with Alyut of all ages, and even a few Crooked folk, but Alyk and Mischa were nowhere to be seen.

It was clear the elders had never intended that Tori might go free. The trial was swift and pointless, the witnesses cleverly chosen, the questions of the elders worded to work against her. Most had already testified before Tori even arrived to hear their scapegoat accusations.

According to one young impressionable witness, Tori had *let* the frost giant wreak havoc on their company in the Mouth of the Gods, failing, or perhaps intending to fail, in her attempt to fight the Old World monster. And if it hadn't been for Tesleh, they all might have died.

It was truth shrouded by lies.

So the entire trial went.

Crooked refugees were brought forward, and their regard for the Gallows Girl changed drastically the moment the tribal elders informed them that Tori had been the one who had unleashed the Rulaqs upon their villages.

It was a truth Tori could not deny, and though distorted against her, she could not reason her way out of the blame. She had pressed her hand against the portal, alongside the chancellor, the godstone searing her palm. It had been her blood that worked the stones to bring that devastation upon the Crooked Teeth.

One Alyut sailor even proposed the absurd notion that he had seen the Gallows Girl's sorcerous face in the mists moments before the sea dragons attacked the trading fleet in the Channel Sea.

The four tribal elders devoured the *shenzah* like pigs to slop. The entire charade seemed to take only minutes. Tori kept glancing at the doors, hoping that any moment Mischa and Alyk would come to defend her. Surely the elders would allow someone to defend her side of things.

But no one came. The accusations mounted, and the assembly began to grow angry, goaded by the elders and their predetermined case.

When it was clear the verdict was all but decided, Fara dul Baruk finally addressed Tori before the assembly.

"You have heard the charges made against you, Gallows Girl." Fara dul Baruk's face was cold with unabashed hatred. "By your own admission, with the use of dark sorcery, you let the Rulaqs that destroyed the homes of these poor Crooked folk through this demonic portal. You stand accused, not only of the slaughter of hundreds of Crooked folk, but of nineteen of my kinsmen in the Mouth of the Gods, as well as the forty-three brave souls lost in the Channel Sea. I shudder to think how many more have died across the New World from your actions. What say you to these accusations?"

Tori stood before the assembly. She had no connection to her magic; it had not returned to her once since she'd arrived in Iqala. She had no help from Mischa or Alyk or anyone else. She had nothing but words, so Tori held her head high and addressed the assembly, holding on to the fading hope that she could convince these people she was their ally, not their enemy.

"Good people of the North. You mourn your dead, and you long for justice. And I do not blame you for that desire. Crooked folk, you have lost many innocent lives. Alyut, you have lost as well. I mourned those we lost in the Mouth of the Gods, alongside many of you, as we marched across the Icelands. Mothers and fathers, sons and daughters. Good people who did not deserve to die in such a terrible way. But you are not alone in your suffering. The whole world is suffering. It is true that I had a hand in their deaths, though I am afraid, not in the way you would like. I was forced to choose, and I resisted the chancellor. This act stirred up the Rulaqs. They destroyed our fortress as well. All these deaths. The Watchers, the Crooked folk, the Alyut, they were all at the hand of a common enemy."

"Yes," said the High Elder, waving her hands in mockery. "You would have us believe that the Chancellor of Osha unleashed the very creatures who devastated his own city."

Tori fought back the urge to lash out. She unclenched her fists and spoke evenly. "With all due respect, Elder Baruk, it is clear your beliefs are set regardless of what I could ever say to convince you, or anyone else. You have taken my only witnesses from me and ensured that no voice but my own can defend me. My own testimony is self-serving, and so you will likely disregard it, no matter what I say."

The High Elder huffed and crossed her arms, but the elder of the *Karu'va* clan gestured for her to go on.

"You should know that killing me will not keep you safe forever. I fear the losses in the Mouth and the Channel Sea are only the beginning. The Old World has returned to us with all its curses. Whether you will believe me or not, it is true. The chancellor did this. Like all the chancellors before him, Cyrus Maro's only goal is to spread his dominion across the world. And if he has truly subdued the Rulaqs as the tales say, then I fear that soon he will use these monsters from the Old World to rule the New. Killing me is exactly what he wants."

Elder Baruk laughed darkly. Tori noted that the other three elders did not share her sardonic mirth. "If this is your attempt to persuade us, you have a curious way of doing it. It seems to me that appeasing the chancellor is the one thing that might spare us this dark tide in the South. Why shouldn't we do as he wants?"

Tori stood tall. She looked out upon the faces of those in the assembly. She could sense their fear. "For centuries, you have lived apart from the world, and though it has required much sacrifice, you have grown strong in this isolation. And for centuries, the world has been content to ignore what happens here in the White North. But that age is over."

Fara dul Baruk approached her, but Tori did not stop. She focused on the people of the assembly. This was her last chance.

"Magic and monsters have returned to the world, and they will shape it, one way or another. People of the North, you have seen it. You have seen Rulaqs and frost giants and sea dragons returned. If you kill me, you may appease the chancellor for a while. But how long until more monsters slaughter your people? How long until the chancellor decides to subdue the peoples of the North? The time will come when no one can fight because all are spread too far across the world. Now is the opportunity your shamans have foreseen. I know you long for Restoration. So join us and fight Osha. Take back your—"

The High Elder's backhand ended her plea, and Tori crumpled to the ground. The taste of blood filled her mouth. Her jaw ached, and it did not heal. The shamans made sure of it.

"Enough!" cried Fara dul Baruk, standing over her, veins surging at her temples. "Do not pretend you know anything about my people, darkling. You know nothing of the North." The High Elder turned to the other elders. "We have heard enough of this sorcerer's lies! The girl has confessed to the crimes of which she has been accused. What shall our verdict be?"

The elders circled up, and the assembly went silent. A pair of guards seized Tori by the shoulders and jerked her to her feet. Tori did not fight the guards. She knew it was no use. She had no power over them with magic, any more than she had through words.

Blood poured from the corners of her lips. Rage surged inside her as she watched the High Elder's vehement whispers. Tori longed for her connection to the energy behind the world. It had become such a part of her, the truest part of her, and if she was going to die, she wished to feel fully alive one more time.

The other three elders nodded their heads submissively at Elder Baruk. Tori could tell that her words had worried them, but she feared it did not matter. The elders conferred amongst themselves for only a few moments before they turned to the assembly. Fara dul Baruk was the first to speak. "The *Nuq'vana* find Astoria Burodai, this darkling known as the Gallows Girl, guilty of murder."

The elder of the *Tu'va* spoke next. "Guilty."

And then the elder of the *Iqu'vara*. "Guilty."

And finally, the elder of the *Karu'va*. The man held her gaze for a moment, and Tori thought there might be the slightest chance he would dissent. But then he spoke. "Guilty."

The assembly began to chant. "Guilty, guilty, guilty!"

"And how do we deal with murderers in the North?" cried Fara dul Baruk over the din.

The chant morphed, then. At first it was muddled, and hard to distinguish, but then Tori pieced together the words. The chorus unified into a dark cadence. "Fire and ice, fire and ice, fire and ice!"

The High Elder raised her hands and the crowd quieted. "Take her to the pyre!"

The crowd roared.

Before the guards dragged her away, Fara dul Baruk leaned close, a wicked smile on her lips. "Let's see the Gallows Girl rise from death in the North."

CHAPTER SEVENTEEN

As Tori was led to the stake, she was shoved and cursed. Children threw rocks. Their parents volleyed insults. But little Tesleh threw herself in front of the procession.

"No! You can't do this! She's good!" Tes was shoved aside by one of the guards, and the poor young Watcher was slow to rise, her leg still weak from her encounter with the frost giant. Her brother Jordie helped her up, and Tori met their gazes as the guards shoved her on down the main thoroughfare of the Ice City.

"Don't you listen to them, Tes. Your gifts are good. Mischa will help you learn them."

Tes choked back a sob. "O-okay."

"You take care of your sister, Jordie."

The young Crooked boy nodded to her, but his eyes were not filled with the sorrow his sister's were. He was expressionless, and Tori felt sure he'd been swayed by the High Elder's words. Like all the other Crooked folk. She had let the Rulaqs through that destroyed their homeland, and no one but Tes protested as the Gallows Girl was led to the pyre. The guards shoved her onward, poking her back with the butt-ends of their spears.

No one was coming to save her. Alyk and Mischa were nowhere to be found. The Crooked folk had turned against her, and the Alyut were growing more furious the longer the procession went on.

Did Alyk play a part in this scheme? Is that why he's disappeared? Tori wanted to think not. She wanted to believe in him. But it didn't matter. Either he was a traitor or a fool, and regardless, she was going to die, and no one was going to come. Fara dul Baruk had made sure of that.

Tori had never before wondered what it would be like to burn to death, but she hoped it would end quickly.

In her last moments, she thought strangely of her nemesis at the Watchtower. Years ago, Vashti Burodai had endured this same fate at her father's hand. But her budding Regenero gifts had kept her alive. Ren and Kale had rescued her, brought her to the Watchtower, all so she could betray the Shadow Watch.

In a way, Vashti's own burning at the stake had led to Tori's, to this moment. She pushed away the hollow bitterness she felt. It seemed pointless, considering the circumstances. Vashti had had her reasons, and Tori supposed Elder Baruk had her reasons as well. Perhaps the chancellor had his reasons, just as Ren had back at the Watchtower. And all their reasons had mounted into a death sentence that Tori was weary of running from. She had been dancing with death since the day of the Gallows, and death had finally matched her steps.

They reached their destination at the center of the city, where a great pyre of pale snowpine had been set up in an open square. Fara dul Baruk stood before the pyre. The other three clan elders stood beside her, holding lanterns made of blue icefire. Tori realized that no one carried torches here in the Ice City. Alyut light seemed to center around the mysterious crystals.

When Tori had been chained securely to the lone pole standing from the base of logs, the High Elder raised her hands for silence.

"My kinsmen," Elder Baruk said, addressing the hundreds of people gathered to watch the Gallows Girl die. "Centuries ago, invaders arrived on the shores of our world, bearing fair countenances and dark magic. They drove our people from our homeland, and we fled here, to the Great White North, cursing the darklings and their sorcery. Thanks to the blessings of Shalam and Anora, our shamans learned sacred arts to render that darkness useless here in the North. We have lived in peace ever since. We have made a new home, safe from the curses of the southern world. But now, this darkling has brought those curses upon us anew. At the hands of this Gallows Girl, monsters have been brought back to haunt our world, and as is common of such things, *our* people have suffered at the whims of darklings.

"Astoria Burodai, you have been found guilty before the elders, before the people of the Great White North, and before the gods. You shall be executed according to the customs of the North, a punishment reserved only for those who delve into the darkness behind the world. The trial of fire and ice."

Fara dul Baruk held up a glowing blue stone. Its veiny markings made it seem like some sort of living thing. It reminded Tori vaguely of the chancellor's godstones. A serene feeling of acceptance came over her as the High Elder brandished the crystal.

Her end had come.

"Anora gifted our people with her lights, in the sky and in the earth below, so that we might see in a dark world." The icefire stone pulsed in the elder's hands. "May Anora bring justice to the North."

The crowd cried out with a guttural roar. It transformed into a chant. The people swayed to the rhythm, and Tori realized it was a sort of ritualistic prayer.

Then, the world went silent.

The High Elder cried out in the tongue of the North, holding the icefire crystal high, and then she cast the stone into the pyre. To Tori's amazement, the crystal shattered with a flash of blue flame. The kindling wedged between the logs was the first to ignite.

The elder of the *Tu'va* cast the next stone, and more kindling caught fire.

When the elders were finished, a large flame had caught at the base of the pyre. The clansmen and -women proceeded to cast more stones, handed to them by the elders. A procession passed by, old men and young children, warriors and mothers bearing infants. All were part of this dark ceremony. Icefire shattered upon the wood and the glowing blue flames grew larger and larger, rushing from log to log. Tori steeled herself for the pain to come. She resisted tears. She thought of the way Darien had once bravely faced a martyr's death. He had been so strong. Tori had stolen that death from him, but she knew there could be power in her own death now. The realization seemed to come from outside her.

"Do not forget those who suffer in the southern world!" Tori shouted. "Do not forget your Restoration! Your time is near!"

At these words, the faces of many of the Alyut people changed, and Tori thought that perhaps there was hope. But then, the flames grew darker, until they reached a violent hue, lapping at Tori's feet, and then her legs.

Tori kept expecting to feel searing, agonizing heat, but instead she only felt colder. A sharp chill cut through her woolen garments and her fur-lined cloak.

The icefire consumed the wood, crackling and hissing, like any fire. But this fire felt utterly different. The larger the flames, the more she shivered.

Tori's boots disintegrated and her feet grew numb. The flames lapped at her legs, up to her fingers. She could not feel them any longer.

And then, with fury, the pain came.

Tori screamed, only once. She clenched her teeth and held in the agony. She would not give the elders the satisfaction of her torture. She pictured Darien on the day of the Gallows, and she straightened herself. She would die bravely.

Her exposed toes cracked and peeled with the searing cold. She clenched her fists so that her nails tore into her palms. Sharp pangs shot up her raw and aching legs. She bit down on her tongue and held in a shriek. Her spine felt like it might shatter inside her. Her chest felt heavy as the flames rose higher and higher.

Her mind was fading. Elder Baruk was saying something. People were jeering. And poor Tes was crying, down on her knees, her brother holding on to her hand.

The flames grew higher, singeing Tori's hair. Her clothes began to burn and fall away. Her skin was blue, and she could not move her body any longer.

Tori's mind drifted away. The numbness returned, the terrible pain faded, and in the flames, Tori saw a strange face. Ugly, but smiling.

It welcomed her to the world beyond.

And she felt… at peace.

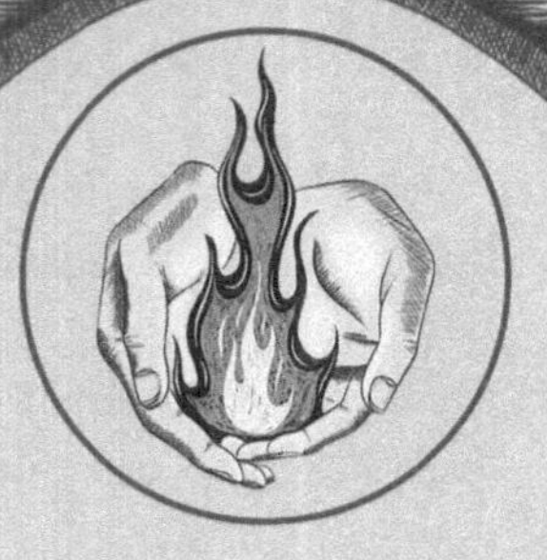

CHAPTER EIGHTEEN

Alyk and Skya sprinted from the throne room, and Mischa ran after them, joined by Seren lè Tal. The main halls of the palace were empty, and so was the assembly chamber. They soon realized why. The entire city was herding down the main thoroughfare of Iqala, chanting a dark mantra in the ancient language of the Alyut.

"They're taking her to the pyre!" said Skya, her eyes lit with rage.

Mischa's heart filled with dread. *How can this be possible? How could Alyk's mother be so ruthless? They can't kill her, they can't!*

Alyk cursed and pressed into the crowd. Skya followed, shoving her way violently. Mischa wished she had access to her Watcher gifts. She wished she could fly over this teeming mass and find Tori. They could still escape, if only the barrier could be removed from her magic. But there was no time. Mischa lowered her shoulder, ready to shove her way through or be trampled in the process, but a hand held her back.

It was the Witch Queen.

"What are you doing?" Mischa shouted, jerking her arm away.

"Saving your friend."

Mischa stepped away from the crowd. "What are you saying?"

"It is clear the Gallows Girl has already been condemned. Even if you make it to her before she is consumed by fire and ice, what will you do?"

"I'll free her, or I'll die trying."

"I know a way that may not require your death."

"What way?" Mischa demanded.

"You must follow me."

"Where?"

"To the outskirts of the city."

"But they're taking her to the heart of the city!"

"We'll never make it in time that way. The crowds are too thick." The queen gripped Mischa's hand. "You must trust me. It is Tori's only hope."

The queen sprinted back through the empty palace, the way they'd come, and Mischa raced after her. She had never felt so slow, despite the fact Mischa and the queen were sprinting through the Ice City. Seren lè Tal flew down the halls on light feet that barely seemed to touch the ground. When they reached the northern entrance to the palace, they emerged on a dark abandoned lane. The queen did not hesitate. She raced down the street, turning corners with sheer confidence. The din of the procession ebbed into a dull roar, like distant waves on a pebbled shore. Seren led them farther and farther from the place Tori was being executed.

Mischa cursed herself. She was a fool to trust this strange sorceress, yet Seren lè Tal might be Tori's only hope. The queen had arrived by magic, and Mischa hoped desperately it was something the gods-damned shamans couldn't render useless.

They reached the rolling hills of ice and star rock that surrounded Iqala. The wind whipped across the ice and stung Mischa's face as they ran. She worried she would lose her footing on the slick surface. They crested another hill, and Mischa noticed a glow beyond a great mound ahead. The queen raced over the steep hillside, and Mischa saw a schooner sitting upon the ice.

It was one of the strangest sights Mischa had ever beheld. It looked as though the ship had been capsized during a storm. What other explanation was there? Except the ship was not smattered upon the ice, though it must have been thrown several leagues inland.

It sat upon an icy plain, glowing with a soft golden luminescence. Specks of light were fixed upon the rigging, the deck, and the taffrail. It was majestic, and it made no sense why such a thing would be out here beyond the city. Was there a frozen lake beneath the ice?

The queen sprinted across the snow. "Lir'ghe!" she shouted. "Ready the sails!"

The golden light grew fiercer, and as she neared, Mischa realized it was not the light of lanterns that created the ship's glow. It emanated from tiny creatures. At the queen's voice, they flitted around the ship on tiny golden wings. Strange markings slowly lit up along the sides of the ship. Glyphs written in a language unknown to Mischa. The characters were not rooted in the Common Tongue, nor the ancient tongues of the southern world.

Mischa sprinted after Seren lè Tal up the gangplank. The ship trembled beneath them as they reached the stern. The queen pulled a lever. The sails unfurled, but not only the ones fixed to the mast. Two great expanses of sail stretched from either side like white wings. One of the tiny golden creatures shot over to them, a thousand others swarming all around. Mischa had heard tales of faeries in the Old World. They were said to be among the loveliest creatures of the ancient days, though their seductions led many to their demise.

But this faerie was not seductive in the least. Up close, the creature was abhorrent. Its face was twisted and dark horns protruded from its skull. It hovered before the queen, bowing in the air, its wings vibrating with the speed of a hummingbird's. "Leaving so soon, my queen? What is being wrong? The trial goes so poorly?"

Mischa had expected a high voice, but the faerie's was low and grave.

"No time, Lir'ghe. Get us airborne!" The queen gripped the helm.

Airborne? Mischa shivered.

Lir'ghe let out a screeching cry in a strange language, but it must have been an order, for at his voice, the world filled with the shrill buzzing of the demon faeries. Seren gripped the helm tightly. More luminescent glyphs appeared on the deck, and then the sails. The ship lurched beneath her feet, and Mischa fell to her knees.

"Where to?" cried Lir'ghe in a shout that was uncanny for his small size.

"The center of the Ice City," said Seren lè Tal.

The ship arched back, the snow and ice groaning beneath the weight of the immense craft, and then it eased into the air. Mischa scrambled to her feet, gripping the ship's rail, watching with wonder as the ship rose ten, then twenty feet, then higher. Mischa could see the blue glow of Iqala looming beyond. "How is this possible?"

Seren lè Tal grinned, the wind whipping through her silver hair. "Those shamans can't stop the magic of the Kroqala. We're going to save the Gallows Girl."

The Kroqala flitted all around the ship, shifting the sails, and then, the ship's wings caught a gust of wind, and they veered sharply. At the center of the Ice City, a great burst of blue light shot into the sky, and Mischa prayed that they would not be too late.

CHAPTER NINETEEN

A face appeared in the blue flames, but it was not who Astoria expected to meet at the moment of her death.

It was small and twisted, like something from a nightmare.

The world was swirling chaos. A roaring cacophony filled her ears. Flashes of blue and golden light swelled around her in madness. Tori thought she had died and been sent to the Abyss to atone for all the suffering she had brought upon the world. She had heard tales of the wretched souls who lived in darkness, pleading desperately for aid from anything that crossed their path. The horrid cries grew louder and louder. The shrieks of the undying.

A hellish face shot past her, and then, Tori felt her hands again. She could move her fingers.

They were free. Her chains had fallen away.

But that was foolishness.

Tori was chained to a pole of snowpine. Blue flames engulfed her with the cruel fire of the North. These were hallucinations of her dying mind. Her thoughts began to grow foggy again, and she knew she was near death. She closed her eyes.

Pain returned in fury, and the numbness that had overtaken her fraught body vanished. Tori cried out, thinking the flames had reached her face, overtaking her entire being at last. Her eyes shot open.

The strange, fearsome face reappeared right before her eyes, glowing in a golden light like the fires of the southern world. Its light seemed to cast away the blue glow of the icefire.

The face belonged to some sort of fiery creature with tiny horns. It hovered in front of her, long nails glistening from its slender fingers like talons. It had stung her face, or perhaps stabbed her, and she had felt the pain. By some miracle, Tori could still feel it, and she emerged from the deathly fog in an instant.

The creature shot toward her.

She cringed. *Is this the last stage of my execution? A delusion of the dying?*

But the thing did not sting her again. It pulled desperately at her cloak, which hung in shreds from her frozen shoulders. And then there were more golden creatures, glowing like the floating lanterns of the Trium'vel. They tugged on her body, and their tiny hands felt warm on her frigid skin. These things were not attacking her at all. They were trying to help her.

Something stirred within Tori's mind, and with the last fragments of strength she possessed, she took a step forward, then another, and another.

Tori stumbled free of the blue hell and collapsed in the snow, gazing up at the sky. Glowing specks flickered in the heavens, and there was something more. Something out of place.

Massive golden sails filled her vision, floating in the sky.

But it couldn't be…

Alyk's face flitted in and out of focus, blocking the light, but Tori's mind was fading once more. His face seemed to be glowing and flickering as well. The world was blurs of color and light. Voices called to her from some distant place. The roar had been replaced by soft whispers.

The last thing Tori recalled was searing pain crashing over her body in violent waves. But the blue flames were gone, and she knew that pain was a sign of glorious life.

———

TORI DREAMED OF THE SOUTHERN WORLD, OF THE HOT, HUMID merch houses of the Trium'vel, like the one she had labored in as a child. The work had been easier there. The Southern merchers were not as harsh as the masters of the northern world. Her labor had been softer, as many other things had been during her years in the Trium. Tori strolled the streets of Vel'Kerren, the floating lanterns hovering over the city during one of the many festivals. Her mum was there, and they strolled together, and they did not have to hide their magic.

She dreamed of the beaches of Melanesia as Mischa had so often described them during their journey north. Soft sand squished between Tori's toes, and gentle waves lapped at her ankles, and the Sisters shone like the eyes of the gods upon her. She felt light and happy. Darien was there too, walking down the beach, and Tori did not fear him. He turned to her, standing in his human form, smiling, the way he had when they served Scelero, back in another life-time. And yet, it was not the same smile. It was warm and safe and free, in a way it never could have been in Maro'El when they had lived to serve others. He called out to her and his voice was light and serene. Tori ran to him and he pulled her into an embrace, and they both cried. But they were happy tears.

"We made it," Darien whispered. "We survived."

Tori didn't speak. She just held him, grateful he was alive, grateful they were together and free. The southern world was beautiful. Insects chirped from gigantic leafy trees. Colorful birds soared across the sky in the moonlight. Everything was so full of life.

But it did not last…

Tori swam out of the dream world and woke in a blue light that pierced the beauty and filled her with fear. She sat up with a start, terrified that she was still in the fire, that her escape had been a delusion.

She found herself not in a world of flames, but rather in a bed of soft white furs in a room beneath the ice, illuminated by the light of icefire crystals set inside a lantern so it filled the room with a soft glow. Her sudden movement sent waves of pain crashing up her spine.

I'm alive! she thought, never more grateful to feel pain.

Judging by the number of bandages that had been wrapped around her body, she was just barely alive. Her skin felt like it was boiling. She was about to examine what was hidden beneath the linen wraps, when a voice interrupted her.

"Alyk said you can't touch those." It was Tesleh. The Crooked girl was smiling at her. She stood up from a chair made of what Tori guessed was whale bone. The room was carved out of obsidian stone, so smooth it reflected the light in shimmers.

"I can't believe you're alive," Tes said.

The young Watcher touched her hand, and Tori squeezed it, grateful to be able to perform such a simple task. "Me too, Tes."

"Guess you showed them, didn't you?"

"Showed them what?" Her voice croaked. Her throat felt dry and grainy.

"That you can't kill a god."

Tori smiled. It hurt to smile, like her skin was stretched too tight over her jaw. She felt nothing like a god, but she did not argue with the girl. Tes fetched her some water, and Tori drank it greedily. "What happened, Tes? How *did* I survive?"

The memory was hazy and made no sense. It must have been part of her death visions.

Tes was beaming. "The gods saved you."

"The gods?"

"Faeries actually." It was Mischa. Her friend rushed to the side of the bed and sat, clasping her hand tenderly.

Tori recalled the ugly face in the flames. "Faeries. But they were so hideous!"

Mischa laughed. "Better not tell *them* that. They're Kroqala. Demon faeries. But they seem a bit self-conscious about their looks, if you ask me."

"They're still here?"

"They're with the Witch Queen," said Tes ecstatically.

"What?" Tori's head was beginning to hurt.

Mischa nodded. "It's true. The faeries serve the Witch Queen of the Southern Isles. She came north to see you."

"And not a minute too soon, either." Alyk entered the room, accompanied by his sister, Skya. Her presence was met with no animosity from Mischa or Alyk, which confused Tori.

"How did I survive?" said Tori. "I mean, I'm healing, aren't I?"

Alyk nodded. "When you stepped from the pyre, it was seen as a sign from the gods. According to the laws of fire and ice, if the gods intervene in an execution, it means the defendant was innocent in their eyes. I commanded the shamans to withdraw the barrier from your magic, and your body began to heal."

Alyk carefully unraveled one of the wraps around Tori's arms, revealing swollen red skin that was moist and oozed a yellowish liquid. The unwrapping felt like it might peel all her skin away as Alyk unraveled past her wrist. Tori felt sick at the sight. The very air stung her arm. Her head ached. Her whole body ached for that matter.

Skya handed her brother a jar, and he lathered a salve on the skin.

"Our medicines helped as well. You were barely recognizable when we brought you here, but your wounds are nearly recovered."

Tori did not feel like it. She shuddered at the thought that her entire body looked like her arm. "Where are we?"

"Beneath the Ice City," said Skya. "My bedroom, as a matter of fact."

"Yours?" Tori thought Skya was the enemy.

"After all my *madru* put you through, I thought it was the least I could do. I'm sorry about our first meeting. But I hope you understand I had to put up a good act to fool her."

Alyk gripped his sister's shoulder. "She sent word to the Witch Queen. If not for Skya, my *madru* would have succeeded in her mummer's trial."

"Where is she?" Tori demanded.

"Don't worry, Tori," said Alyk. "The elders must heed the will of the gods like all others. You are safe now. You have been for three days."

I slept that long? Tori was overwhelmed. Her head hurt, and she lay back down. The act stung her all over, but she was relieved to be here, amongst friends, alive.

"You should rest," Alyk said. "We'll talk more when…"

But Tori was already fading into the dream world again.

———

TORI DID NOT WAKE AGAIN FOR TWO MORE DAYS. ALYK WAS dressing her wounds, and she woke to sharp stings in her legs. A young Alyut girl spread the salve while Alyk wrapped the linens gently around her knee, all the way to her ankles on both legs. Once wrapped, though, the pain eased. Minus the wraps, Tori wore only a cotton shift.

"Don't see you blushing now at seeing me undressed," Tori managed. Her lips stung and her voice cracked. It felt like years since Alyk had come to see her before the trial, before his mother rigged the entire charade.

Alyk smiled, but did not speak until he was finished. He handed the young shaman the remaining linen wraps. "Thank you, Behla." The girl nodded and left the room, taking the old bandages with her.

"I'm sorry, Tori," Alyk said. "Perhaps I should have had another dress your wounds. I had Behla apply the—"

"No," said Tori, a slight smile rising at Alyk's modesty. "I'm glad it was you… How does it feel to have seen the Gallows Girl without any of her mysteries?"

Now, Alyk did blush. "Believe me, there are still plenty of, er, mysteries."

Tori chuckled, then tried to stop herself because it hurt. She squeezed his hand, which hurt less. "I'm teasing."

"I know. Anyway, it was not exactly the first time. For Behla or me. Your clothes were nearly burned off in the pyre. The, er, whole city saw you."

"I'll bet that was a sight."

Alyk frowned. "It was horrible, Tori. I am so sorry this happened. I should have seen through my *madru*'s schemes."

Tori didn't want to think of it. She changed the subject. "I didn't realize you were a healer as well as a shaman."

"They are one and the same in the North."

"How are my wounds?" Tori grimaced as she tried to raise herself to a seated position. It hurt, but it was not agony. Alyk helped her, propping a pillow behind her back.

"Your legs took the worst of it. Your face is healed, and your upper body is getting close. We removed the bandages yesterday, though the skin may be tender for a few days. But your body recovers incredibly fast, much quicker than I ever might have guessed. I've never seen anything like it. You should be dead, Tori. Many times over."

"That wasn't my doing. Is it true about the Witch Queen? Did she really save me? Or was that only part of my fever dreams?"

"Not a dream. Seren lè Tal has been waiting for you to recover."

"What is she doing here at all?"

"I'll let her answer that."

Behla returned with a tray of flatbread and strange purple fruits shaped like tiny hearts. Tori tried one. The texture was strangely pasty, but it was sweet. "I've never had these before. Are they from the Trium?"

Alyk shook his head. "Gemstars. The only fruit that grows in the North. We harvest them from the world below. They grow only where icefire abounds."

Tori was amazed at how much life was able to survive in the Great White North. It was as though, just like the Alyut people, nature had managed to adapt to whatever surroundings it found itself in. Still, she doubted she would ever behold that strange blue crystal with positive feelings. Though it seemed to be the source of most life in the North, including the Alyut, the very light in the room made her feel uneasy.

Tesleh poked her head through the door. "Alyk, the queen is here."

"Let her in."

Tes smiled at Tori before she hurried off to fetch the Witch Queen. Seren lè Tal walked with a regal gait, but Tori could tell it did not come naturally to her. It was practiced formality. It reminded her of the way she held herself when she was attempting to appear more proper than she was, back almost too straight to compensate for years of labor. True nobles moved more fluidly. The queen took a seat in a chair by the bedside and her shoulders relaxed. A golden blur hovered near her shoulder and then alighted upon the armrest. Tori recognized the face from the pyre.

Tori gestured to the grotesque faerie. "You pulled me from the fire."

The Kroqala's features seemed to be hardened in a permanent scowl, but it nodded to her.

The queen giggled. She was captivating, without doubt. Her porcelain face shimmered in the blue light, and her silver hair was smooth as silk. Her sapphire gown hugged her body. She wore long dark sleeves that left only her palms bare. She looked Tori up and down, then shook her head. "Incredible. You have not disappointed, Gallows Girl."

"Thank you, milady."

"Seren, please. You are not one of my subjects, and if your rapid recovery is any indication, we are equals, you and I."

"I owe you my life," said Tori.

"A life I was eager to save."

"Why?"

Seren lè Tal leaned forward in her seat, a sparkle flashing in her eyes. "Well, if we believe your shaman boyfriend here—"

Alyk blushed. "Oh, er, we're not—"

Tori enjoyed watching him stumble over his words. The queen giggled again, almost childishly, and Tori wondered how old she was. Seren lè Tal waved her hand dismissively. "Well, whatever he is, Alyk seems to think our fates are entwined. I don't believe much in fate. I've seen too much hardship in my homeland. But Alyk may convince me yet. I've been searching for you since the day you escaped the White Citadel. But my spies lost track of you when the Watchtower fell."

"Valeria," said Tori, remembering how the Southern Islander had whispered words of hope shortly before she and Mischa escaped.

"She was one of mine, yes. Though I've not heard from her since. Which is more worrisome than you might think."

"Why?" Tori asked. "She helped us escape the chancellor. I'm sure she wouldn't—"

"She ought to have come with you. Instead, she returned to the White Citadel and helped lead the defense of Maro'El against the Rulaqs. Alongside the Gallows Boy. I fear her loyalties waver. But I won't burden you with my troubles."

But they weren't Seren's alone. If Valeria's loyalties wavered, what might that mean for Darien? Tori had seen the way he looked to her.

Seren went on. "At any rate, I've hoped this day would come for some time. I've had my own battles to fight with the return of the sea dragons in the Isles, and I had lost hope of ever finding you, after communication ended from Valeria. Then, I received a raven from Skya dul Baruk. And here I am."

"But why have you been looking for me?"

"Osha has been gaining power in the world. With the fall of Morgath and the alliance with the Yan Avii, the chancellor is nearly uncontested in the western world. And now, with monsters bending to his will, I fear he will soon set his sights on the Isles. While you've been recovering, Alyk and I have been conspiring. You came to the North to raise an army, yes?"

Tori nodded. "My fellow Watchers are locked in the citadel. I seek justice for all the chancellor has done to my kind."

Seren smiled. "Good. But I am sure you know that a few spears, and even Bear Riders, will be little match for Osha's forces. My people have been free for less than a century, and that time has been turbulent. We have warred with each other as much as the Oshans or the Faerish. We are not a unified nation, just rivaling island kingdoms whose allegiance moves with the wind. But that is changing. Under my rule, most of the Isles sail under one banner for the first time in centuries, and with the right show of strength, that alliance may last centuries."

"Show of strength?" said Tori. "That's where I come in?"

"Where we all come in," said Alyk.

"I want to wage war against Osha," said Seren lè Tal. "Unite my people against a common enemy while the time is ripe. Bring the chancellor to his knees. And I want the peoples of the North to join us. With you leading them alongside me."

Tori shook her head with frustration. "In case you didn't notice, the Alyut very recently tried to execute me."

Alyk squeezed her hand. "Your return from death has swayed them. The elders have declared you innocent before the gods. And with Skya's support, the Bear Riders would follow you into battle. I know that my people have done a terrible wrong—"

"They tried to kill me!"

"I… I know. And I know that we do not deserve your aid, Tori. But they *will* follow you. Your last words in the flames were *Do not forget your Restoration*. And with your miraculous survival, they are ready to believe you. They are ready to seize their Restoration. They are ready to follow you into battle. And besides… it is the best chance your friends in the citadel may have."

Tori breathed for a moment, trying to take in all the information. She could not even get out of bed yet, and she was supposed to lead an army into war?

But she knew Alyk was right.

Even from the flames, Tori had not cursed the Alyut. Their actions were stirred by the injustices rained upon them by the chancellor. She thought of Ren and the other Watchers. More than ever, she wanted to see Cyrus Maro dead.

Finally, she spoke. She looked from the Witch Queen to Alyk dul Baruk. "I will lead the Alyut against the White Citadel alongside you."

"Then it is to war," said Seren lè Tal solemnly.

The words filled Tori with an unquenchable flame. This was what she and Mischa had wanted since they'd escaped from the chancellor's clutches in the catacombs. Now, they had an army.

"To war."

PART SIX
THE FORBIDDEN SYMBOL

There were legends in the Old World of beings more ancient and mysterious than the Watchers. Some claimed they were as old as the world itself. Some claimed they were the last of a failed generation, gifted with powers beyond all else in existence. Powers they could not handle. Even the power to overcome death. If not gods, what else would you call them?

—from *New Histories of the Old World*

CHAPTER TWENTY

I t was late evening when the company of Yan Avii entered the Oshan city of Pendra, yet the festivities showed no sign of waning. The main thoroughfares of the trade city thrummed with the beating of drums and the chanting of old victory ballads. Kale recognized the rollicking verse of "The Great Bear of Galahan," the rousing cadence of "The Ride of the Raven King," and the bawdy chorus of "The Milkmaid in the Hay" as Ashi led them through the city in search of a tavern.

They had ridden hard for two weeks from Vlyanii, and finally they reached the edge of Greater Osha. Kale had been dreading the return to his old homeland, and all that lay in store for him there. They were heading to Maro'El, where Ren and all the other Watchers he had betrayed were in captivity. Except, of course, for the ones who had joined the chancellor's Sky Guard. And Kirra, for reasons Kale could not quite ascertain, wanted to join them.

Is Kirra truly willing to do this in exchange for her sight? Kale had often wondered during their journey. *Or is there an ulterior motive? If so, what?*

He could not figure it out, but it felt like some sort of cosmic justice that Kale should have to face his brother, and in doing so, he would be betraying him again, by joining the Sky Guard. Why in the Abyss would Kirra want to go to Maro'El?

Before their party left the Red City, Kirra and Salla held a brief private exchange. It was all Kale could do not to use his Cerebro gifts.

But he knew he had lost all right to question Kirra's motives, and she had, thus far, shown no desire to share her plans with him. He had asked once, and she had swiftly changed the subject, and Kale knew she still did not trust him.

All his life, Kale had made a habit of running from his problems. It was why he was called the Exiled Lord. But Kirra was one to be in the middle of everything. It was what had gotten her captured by the Meta-morphi—off searching for answers to ancient mysteries, godstones and mythic wells of magic. It was how she had gotten them both caught up in Salla Burodai's schemes in the Red City to begin with. It was a trait he simultaneously admired and despised.

After all these years, Kirra was still a mystery to him.

Ashi checked with half a dozen inns, but they were all full. Kale had never been one to long for beds or roofs, but Ashi had been adamant they rest the steeds a full day before they set north for Maro'El, and the five Ilya men who accompanied them had been more than eager for a warm meal. Women traditionally prepared the food in Yan Avii culture, but Ashi was no typical Yan Avii woman. She led the expedition, and had no intentions of bothering with food preparations, nor the extraneous baggage of bringing a kitchen wench and provisions. They had lived off kela jerky and dried dates for the past two weeks. Even so, with the chaotic frivolities surrounding them, Kale detested their choice to stay in the city more than ever.

"It would seem your Legions did not lose their war against the beasts of the Old World," Ashi muttered sardonically as they passed through the city center. Here, the crowd and mayhem were even thicker. The place pulsed with energy.

My Legions? Kale almost said, but held back. Ashi knew little of Osha, but she knew enough to know Kale bore no love for the empire. She was only antagonizing him, a habit that strangely endeared her to him. Kirra was speaking to him on occasion, but she remained cool and distant. She had spent much of the ride brooding silently, and so Kale endured Ashi's gibes without complaint.

Laughter and cheers collided into a joyous cacophony all around. The very air Kale breathed seemed to be alive with celebration. Dancers twirled through the cobbled thoroughfares, troubadours belted their tunes, and nightlings hung on the arms of nobles, who watched the festiv-ities in the city center from their balconies. But the nobles were not alone in their sultry indulgences. A trio of street wenches rushed their small company. Two latched onto a pair of Yan Avii men, and the third wrapped her slender fingers around Kale's arm. Ashi was guiding Kirra's steps through the crowd, and Kale thought he felt a twinge in Kirra's mind, but it was hard to discern amidst the hive of minds that swarmed around him.

"Ah, a party from the rollin' hills!" the wench on Kale's arm cooed. "Had a long journey, have yeh? Only a copper fer a warm bed an' all the frills." She stroked his arm.

Kale nearly choked on the young girl's cheap perfume. Her skimpy blue gown left little to the imagination, her eyes were caked with dark cosmetics, and her skin was caked in oil. *Or is it sweat? Gods!*

Kale's stomach lurched at the thought, but she pressed closer to him. He tried to shake free of her grasp and move on, but the wench held fast.

"No need for your beds tonight," Kale said, pressing through the crowd, but she followed along gleefully.

"Come now, rest yer weary legs awhile. I don't mind doin' all the work." She giggled, and her warm cleavage pressed against his chest. Her breath tasted of cheap ale and *hessa,* a pipe tobacco from the Trium'vel. Her hand gripped his traveling cloak and pulled him even closer.

Kirra stepped in, suddenly, and despite her blindness, wrested the wench's hands free of his arm. "Keep your hands away from my husband, wench, if you know what's good for you."

Husband? Kale thought. Of course, he knew it was simply the quickest way to be rid of the wench so their company might find rest.

"Yeh can join, too, if yeh like." The wench chortled. "Don't mean ter leave no one out. It's a day o' celebration, don't yeh know." She flung her arms out extravagantly. "The Battle o' Gods and Monsters is won. And the empire remains stronger than ever. Aha!"

Ashi tossed the wench a copper coin, taking hold of Kirra's arm to steady her. "Off with you. There're plenty of other patrons for your ilk in these streets."

The wench caught the coin and left with a glint in her eyes, though her gaze lingered on Kale longer than he liked as she disappeared into the crowd.

Ashi drove off the other wenches in a similar manner, to the apparent dismay of Olevar Rajii, one of the Ilya, who grumbled about the overwhelming ratio of men on their expedition. Ashi looked like she wanted to slap him, but she held back and pressed on.

Kirra said nothing else, but she held onto Kale's arm for guidance the rest of the way to the tavern, an act that forced Kale to fight a bemused smile.

They were accosted by no more street wenches, and they soon arrived at their final destination—the Raging Boar.

The inn, too, was filled with raucous festivities. Kale, Kirra, Ashi, and the five Ilya all squeezed around a small table in the corner of the room.

The innkeeper came by after some time. A portly Faerish woman with greying dark hair and dark eyes, she glanced at their company with amusement. "It's been a time since I saw an Oshan, a Jurkan, and a herd o' Yan Avii in the same company. But if today be any proof, the gods're yet performin' miracles. What'll it be?" She glanced around as though trying to determine who their leader was. Her eyes widened when Ashi spoke.

"Dinner, and rooms, if you have any," said Ashi.

"Aye, we've a room or two ter spare." The innkeeper eyed Ashi with suspicion. "If you have coin."

Ashi huffed and produced a satchel from her cloak. It jingled to the innkeeper's satisfaction.

"What's for dinner?" asked an Ilya named Kesh.

The innkeeper guffawed. "Boar, o' course! The girls'll be out in a minute." The woman bustled away, close to hysterics.

The boar was cooked to a crisp, and was nearly as tough as jerky, but it was warm and fresh, and no one in the company complained. The ale was better, though a little sour, but it relaxed Kale's senses after the second mug. He was able to tune out the ringing of minds in his Cerebro sense and listen in on conversations.

The Battle of Gods and Monsters, as the attack of the Rulaqs on Maro'El had come to be called, had been a near slaughter. From what Kale overheard, the Legions and the Sky Guard had fought valiantly, but still, the beasts razed much of the city to the ground, killing thousands. It was the final moments of the battle that particularly caught Kale's attention. He kept catching bits and pieces, but it didn't quite make sense. Everyone was praising some Darkling Witch.

Kale caught the arm of a serving girl as she came to replenish their drinks. "We've been traveling for some time, and have not heard all the details of the cause of this celebration. How exactly was the battle won?"

The serving girl's hazel eyes went wide. "You en't heard? A bloody miracle it was. The Darkling Witch stopped the whole horde o' beasts at the base o' the White Citadel."

"Who's this Darkling Witch?" said Kale, a fearful realization teasing his mind.

"No one knows exactly. She's been close in the chancellor's company for months now, they say. One o' the sorcerers from his Sky Guard. Some say she's the one who turned him from the ancient ways o' the chancellors. Her name is Medea Lorzarre. The Darkling Witch saved the whole bloody city. The whole empire, more like."

At Medea's name, Kale's stomach knotted, his suspicions confirmed. "How exactly did she save the city?"

"She calmed the bloody beasts!" said the girl, with evident reverence. "Spoke to 'em inside their minds, they say. The Rulaqs quit their onslaught and bowed before the citadel. They say the beasts do her bidding now." The girl shook her head. "Can't believe you en't heard!" She ran off to tend to other patrons.

Kale turned to Kirra and Ashi. They shook their heads.

"Medea…" said Kale, shuddering as he recalled his last encounter with the Darkling Witch, when she invaded his mind and uncovered the location of the Watchtower. The thought made his fists clench.

"She subdued a whole herd of Rulaqs," said Ashi in disbelief. "What does that mean?" She did not sound as pleased as she ought to have been, considering the Yan Avii were the chancellor's allies.

Kirra shook her head, her blind eyes closed. Medea's name brought back memories for her as well. Memories of Kale's betrayal. He resisted the temptation to sense her true feelings about those memories.

"It means," said Kirra slowly, "if there was any doubt about the chancellor's might in the New World among the lowborns, it's gone now. Any thoughts of rebellion in the name of the Gallows Girl have vanished."

Ashi grimaced. "Look at these people. Faerish, Morgathians, Oshans… all celebrating the chancellor as some savior."

A bard struck up a new song about the victory called "The Chancellor and his Darkling Witch," and the tavern soon rollicked with a chorus celebrating the return of magic to the empire.

"Looks like we've made the right choice in joining them," Kirra muttered.

Kale did not know what to say. He soon excused himself, and left the inn for some fresh air to clear his mind.

The air was far from fresh in Pendra that night, filled with tobacco smoke and the mixed aromas of roast meat, spilled ale, and cheap perfume. Kale wandered the streets alone. He left the main thoroughfares and soon found himself in narrow side streets that were, to his relief, relatively quiet.

What in the Abyss are we doing? he wondered. The chancellor was growing more powerful than ever, and he and Kirra were heading into the heart of it all. And if Kirra truly wanted to join the chancellor…

A cold breeze gusted through the streets, and Kale pulled his cloak close to his chest. He thrust his hands in his pockets, and his fingers brushed against a strange bit of parchment that he hadn't put there.

Where did it come from? he thought, pulling it from his cloak.

A chill rushed through him as he unraveled the paper.

Scrawled upon it in black ink was the image of a gallows with a broken beam.

The infamous sign of the Gallows Saint.

Written upon the faded parchment, below the symbol, were three words: *The Viper's Lair.*

Kale's heart thundered in his chest as he pulled the hood of his cloak tight, swiftly crumpled the damning piece of parchment, and kept moving.

Pendra was the inland trading center of Greater Osha, a bridge between the east and west of the New World. Traders came all the way from Jurka and the Trium'vel to deal their spices, dyes, stallions, and slaves. The main thoroughfares were wide and straight, and contained many open market squares, but beyond the city center, the place was a wending disarray of progressively dingier lanes and more decrepit buildings. The Oshan lords and upstanding merchants kept their estates near the center of commerce.

Kale wandered into a notably poorer district. The masonry was ancient and crumbling, and the streets composed of nothing but dirt.

How had the symbol wound up in Kale's pocket? And why would someone deliver it to *him*, specifically? It made little sense. He was but a traveler in a company of Yan Avii traders to the eyes of anyone in Pendra. *The crowd was thick,* he thought. *It might have been anyone, but…*

He recalled the wench's hands at his cloak, the way her gaze had lingered with him even after she had disappeared into the celebratory masses. He had thought the wench was simply trying to seduce him, maybe even pick his pockets, which contained no money, anyway.

Kale might have spent the past couple months largely in the underworld of the Red City, but he knew what that gallows symbolized: the lowborn resistance against the chancellor was perhaps not as dead as Kirra suspected.

But with Cyrus Maro's revelation of his Sky Guard and Medea's miraculous demonstration of power in the Battle of Gods and Monsters, Kale doubted what hold the so-called Saints might find.

But it seemed that some of them remained in Pendra.

And they were trying to contact him. But why?

At his first opportunity, Kale cast the parchment into a small rubbish fire at the corner of a hardpan street. He was near the outskirts of the city, a desolate district clearly populated by lowborns. A small group of shabbily clad men and women were gathered around the fire, warming their hands, and Kale joined them briefly, so as not to seem too eager to be on his way. Lowborns rarely had a reason to hurry anywhere in such places.

His cloak was dusty and weathered from two weeks on the Steppe, and his face was masked by even more weeks' worth of beard. Despite his Oshan features, he could easily pass for an unassuming servant. The lowborns around the fire passed around a pipe of *hessa* and chatted about the strange times, though their fascination with the chancellor's Darkling Witch seemed more subdued than that of the crowds in the city center. He reached out for more with his senses, but found nothing of substance. No unspoken animosity or thoughts of revolution. They seemed amazed, if dubiously, at the tidings, but nothing more.

No resistance could possibly be gaining followers, Kale thought. *I should ignore it. Besides, I owe it to Kirra to help her regain her sight.*

Still, the wench lingered in his mind. Was the parchment from her? And why was he so curious to find out? He did not want to join any resistance. If anything, he wanted to flee the western world altogether.

"Who yeh serve?" a man with a greying beard asked Kale. He passed him the pipe, and Kale drew in a long breath. It was laced with something that gave it a slightly tangy flavor. Smoke filled his lungs, he exhaled, and a warm relief followed. He took another pull then passed it on.

"House Barra," said Kale without hesitation.

"En't seen yeh here before," said a woman missing two front teeth.

"Serve milord's merchers," said Kale, donning a lowborn flair to his speech. "Used ter tend a warehouse in Barra'El. First time in Pendra. Me master is joining the festivities with all the lordlings, so I came out ter see the city."

"Yer master?" said the woman. "Yeh don't serve Barra himself?" Her tone conveyed the answer she sought. To serve a lord directly would be cause for mistrust, even if he *was* lowborn.

"Far from it," said Kale. "Me master is but a low mercher. Small goods. Sealskins mostly. Trium folk love sealskins." Kale could have sworn the fire folk were eying him suspiciously, but he told himself it was his own paranoia.

"Well, yeh've found about the worst part o' the city ter visit," said the bearded man with a laugh.

"Aye," chorused another.

Kale shared a laugh and a thin smile. "I've served me master in the Fringes. This place is a lordling's estate compared with the best o' that hellhole."

The lowborns seemed to appreciate the compliment. They passed him the pipe again.

"Is it true?" asked the toothless woman. "What they're sayin' about them Rulaqs?"

Kale nodded. "En't seen 'em meself, but heard as much ter believe it's true."

"Gods," said the bearded man. "Rulaqs. Never would've believed it in my lifetime."

"And that witch," said a hunchbacked man. "She bloody calmed 'em."

Kale swiftly changed the subject. "Say, I'm looking fer a place called the Viper's Lair. Yeh heard of it?"

The bearded man guffawed. "Aye, I heard o' it. Lookin' fer a bit o' fun, are yeh?" His eyes narrowed. "The Viper's Lair is a nighthouse near the city center. Modest place, but I reckon the price is o'er yer coin purse if yeh serve but a low mercher."

"Ah, likely true. Story of my life." Kale made to leave before the interrogation grew antagonistic. *A nighthouse,* thought Kale with strange satisfaction. *So it was that wench.*

"Ey," said the woman as he backed away from the fire. "Why yeh lookin' fer the Viper's Lair if yeh don't even know what it is? There's plenty o' nighthouses yeh might've landed in."

Kale hesitated for a moment. His pulse quickened. "Ah, o'erheard a mercher mention it. Just in passing. Said the Viper's Lair was the best part of Pendra."

The woman shrugged, apparently satisfied, but the lowborns eyed him warily as he turned away. When he had turned the corner, he sprinted down the next street. He left the lowborn district as quickly as he could, glancing often over his shoulder to be sure no one was following him.

He made a direct path for the city center of Pendra. He knew it was folly, but he felt an uncanny need to find out why the parchment had been given to him.

This want made him fearfully excited.

CHAPTER TWENTY-ONE

Kale had only ever been to one nighthouse in his life. His uncle took him to one of the finest in Maro'El when he was barely fourteen. It was his cousin's birthday, and Kale's uncle thought it best they both earn their manhood for the first time to commemorate the occasion. The establishment, called the Scarlet Lace, had been luminated by red-tinted lanterns, and thin scarlet draperies lined the entrances to bedrooms where the exotic nightlings took their lordlings after seducing them over fine wine and conversation. Kale's cousin, Tylen, had reveled in the evening and bragged about his conquests for weeks afterward, but Kale had been relieved when the entire ordeal was over.

It was not until he met Kirra that he fully realized why the place had not brought him the same satisfaction it did other lordlings. As a young girl, Kirra was one of the *halcya* of Jurka, slaves forced to attend their masters in whatever way suited them, much like Ashi had in the Red Palace. When Kale had first fallen for Kirra on the Isle of Jallaa, she had been slow to warm up to the idea of romance. All her understanding of intimacy had been in the context of slavery. The thought that others had used her in such a way, against her will, enraged Kale. And he understood why the practice had not appealed to him in his youth. Though the nightlings appeared as though they reveled in their profession, Kale knew it was all a facade. At best, the nightlings were a product of their environment, forced to take the job for lack of better opportunity, and at worst, they were slaves forced to do their master's bidding no matter how shameful.

The Viper's Lair was a modest tavern by any standard, and Kale doubted such a place would find any business from the lordlings of Maro'El. This was a house for soldiers and traders. Within, the main room looked much like any other inn. The tables were poorly crafted and packed with patrons, a bard strummed his lyre in the corner, and serving girls bustled about. These serving girls donned far more risque attire than the servants of the Raging Boar, and there were other girls bustling about. Girls with oiled skin and dark cosmetics and slitted gowns revealing long, smooth legs that teased at what was hidden beyond their silken shields. There were no curtained doorways as in Maro'El, but Kale made note when a sun-specked Morgathian girl led a staggering member of the city watch up the staircase to a line of closed doors above the balcony.

Kale did not see the wench anywhere. He took a seat at a long table, ordered an ale, and waited, wondering if all of this was a grave mistake.

The bard struck up "The Chancellor and his Darkling Witch," and the patrons sang along. The song was growing popular, it seemed, though this bard spun new verses of his own. Nightlings sat on the laps of guards and common merchers, male and female alike, swaying to the music. But still, no sign of the street wench.

How had anyone known he was coming to Pendra? How could they know he was associated with the Gallows Girl? Was there a Watcher in this city? Another Cerebro?

He jumped when the wench from the street brushed his shoulder.

"Rest easy, traveler," she cooed sweetly. "It's only me."

Kale spun swiftly, then calmed himself. The wench took an immediate seat on his lap. He felt awkward with her bosoms in his face and her perfume stifling his breath. He thought guiltily of Kirra, though he wasn't entirely sure why anymore.

"What do you—"

The wench touched his lips gently with her finger and *shhhed* him. He flinched, but she smiled. "I said, *rest easy.*" She leaned in close, her lips brushing his ear as she whispered, "No patron runs upstairs right away. The nightling arts are slow and… seductive." She giggled. Kale realized her lowborn accent from the street was now lost. She spoke well for a street wench. "Play along, Kale. I'm Nyla, and never fear, you'll have your answers."

How does she know my name?

Kale's nerves were on fire, but he obeyed. He placed his hands at the wench's hips, as he'd noted the other patrons doing. Nyla sipped from his flagon of ale and leaned into his chest, bantering seductively.

"Are yeh weary?" she said, louder now, her lowborn accent returning.

"Ah, er, yes," Kale said. "It's been a long ride, indeed."

"Where do yeh hail from, handsome?"

Kale tried to recall his tale from the rubbish fire. It was best he did not draw attention to his party of Yan Avii. "A merching company from Barra'El."

"Ah," she said. "A coastling. And what brings yeh to the Viper's Lair, little mercher?" She poked his chest and arched her back, and Kale felt even more uncomfortable.

"I've heard tales of the exotic nightlings of Pendra, and I knew I must see them with my own eyes." He tried to sound as though he was attempting to woo her. Kale wanted to leave this place as soon as possible, but he needed to know why this wench had given him the message. And the more he played into the role, the quicker she would take him to one of the upstairs rooms.

Nyla draped her arm around his shoulder, leaned back, and laughed. "The loveliest nightlings in the empire are here at the Lair! But I'm afraid I am not one of them. A proper dirty girl from the streets, I am." The wench howled with sensuous laughter, and a nearby patron caught Kale's eye.

"Yeh caught a good one, then," the greasy man bellowed.

Kale managed an awkward smile in return.

Nyla shrugged flirtatiously, then downed the remainder of his ale and slid from his lap, holding onto his hand. "Come, little coastling. Let me show yeh the true reason the nightlings of Pendra are renowned across the land."

Kale followed. Nyla's entire gait was a practiced seduction. Her hips swayed with each step. Her fingers traced over his hands as she led him up to the door at the end of the long line of rooms along the balcony. She closed the door slowly.

Nyla leapt upon the bed and sat, crossing her legs beneath her, leaving Kale standing in the middle of the room. The space was sparsely decorated, and the bed was dressed with plain linens. Kale supposed the matron of the house did not see the need to splurge on needless niceties. *No one stays long in these rooms.*

Nyla giggled. It came so easily. Kale wondered if this was the woman's real laughter. There was no one to perform for any longer.

"You're a terrible actor, you know," Nyla said, her proper speech returning. "A coastling? Gods, please. Your voice has no lilt."

Kale scowled. He had known plenty of coastal lords during his youth in Maro'El. "What do you know of the coast? Have you ever been?"

Nyla raised her eyebrows and leaned forward, a grin teasing her lips. It struck Kale how young she seemed up close. She was barely a woman grown. "I am close with folk from all over the New World. They whisper all night in my ears. Coastlings speak lightly, Kale, like the ebb and flow of the waves."

The wench was well-spoken, indeed. Strange for a nightling. "How did you find me? Do I know you?" Kale had been trying to figure out how she knew his name, but he couldn't place it.

Nyla laughed. "I think not. I never forget a face."

"Why did you give me the sign of the—"

"Shhh… not so loud, Kale." She glanced at the door cautiously.

"How do you know me?" he demanded.

She lowered her voice. "We share a… mutual friend, who asked me to find you when you arrived in the city."

His thoughts went straight to the chancellor. All this was a trap. Kale's senses flared. His nails dug into his palms. He nearly ran straight from the room, but he had to know for certain.

Nyla leaned forward, resting her chin on her hands. She blinked. Even her blinks had a calming, seductive nature. Her long lashes drew in his gaze.

"Who asked you to find me?" Kale said at last.

"Lazarus Delahi."

Kale took a sharp breath. His fists clenched. "What?"

It couldn't be possible. Lazarus was dead. He had died on the Isle of Jallaa, along with all the other Watchers. Kale had seen their leader's body. The man who had recruited him and Kirra and all the others. He had held Lazarus's wrist and checked for a pulse after the Morphs attacked their small community.

"That's impossible." Kale slumped back against the door, feeling uneasy.

Nyla jumped up and helped him over to the bed to sit. "So, you saw him die, then?" Nyla spoke the words so nonchalantly.

Kale nodded. It made no sense. Dead was dead. There could be no coming back from that, could there? "How do you know him? How is he alive? What does he want from me?"

"Shhh… rest easy, traveler." Nyla smiled, reverence evident in her voice when she spoke. "Lazarus is the one who showed me my gifts. Just as he showed you yours."

"Your gifts?" said Kale.

Nyla pointed to her head.

"A Cerebro," said Kale.

She nodded. "That's how I convinced you to come here. I marked you the moment I felt your mind in the city center."

"Marked me?" Of course, why else would he have come here so foolishly? It was not his nature to be so curious. "I… I didn't even feel your effect on my mind." The thought was incredibly unnerving.

Nyla smiled and brushed his cheek. "Your old master trained me well."

"Why the gallows?"

"Please," Nyla cooed. "Haven't you figured it out by now? Lazarus Delahi is the one organizing these lowborn uprisings. Your old master is the leader of the Saints of the North."

Kale felt queasy again. "What does he want with me?"

"Why do you think, Kale?" Nyla said, drawing nearer. "He wants you to join him."

CHAPTER TWENTY-TWO

Kale pulled up the hood of his cloak, shielding his face, and left the nighthouse unsure what to do or what to believe. His mind told him it was impossible that his old master was still alive, but his instinct told him there was no way Nyla could have lied. She had not tried to guard her mind from him, and he had sensed the sincerity of what she'd said.

Was it possible that his old master had incited the uprisings of the past year, ever since the day of the Gallows? Uprisings which had all but ceased since the attack of the Rulaqs. The lowborns' hope in the Gallows Girl was waning. After all, she had not saved them from an attack by Old World monsters. The chancellor had. Which was why Lazarus Delahi needed Kale's help when he arrived in Maro'El.

It was all too much to take in. Kale longed to talk with Kirra, but he did not even know if he could trust her. And if Ashi knew of it, then who knew what she would do? They had promised to look after Vashti. And joining a rebellion against the chancellor was exactly the opposite of that.

Furthermore, Kale did not know what he wanted. He felt helpless. As though the gods had deigned to forever place him in no-man's-land, torn between two impossible destinies.

He had made some terrible mistakes. And those mistakes had come at great cost. He longed to right what he had wronged in the world. He had not realized just how much until they set out for Maro'El. The closer they got, the more he feared Kirra had made a terrible choice.

But what was the greater good? Was there any good in the world, or only lesser evils?

Kale cursed and darted through the streets of Pendra. The festivities were finally dying down; it was the depths of the night, and the lanes were clear, save for the occasional drunkard. The central room of the Raging Boar contained a few tables of patrons, and a bard strummed a drunken ballad in the corner, but otherwise, the place had quieted down considerably since he left.

Gods, how long was I gone? he wondered.

He hadn't thought of the others, nor the effect of his sudden departure. He had left in a fit of irritation, and the others had surely missed him by now. After getting directions from the innkeeper, he hurried to their room. Kirra and Ashi were standing outside the door, and he tensed. He could sense their anger, even without delving into their minds.

"Where have you been?" Ashi hissed as he neared. "I sent Olevar looking for you two hours ago. I thought you were just stepping outside!"

What could he say? He shrugged. "Went for a walk. What does it matter? The city is in celebration."

Kirra spoke with an even tone. "We were followed through the city today, Kale."

Kale's stomach twisted. Did she know about the wench?

"Someone knows we are here, and they are keeping tabs on us," said Ashi.

"Who? The chancellor?" said Kale. "What reason would he have to track us? We're coming to join his Sky Guard."

Unless the chancellor suspected something. Perhaps Cyrus Maro had been tracking Nyla or another of the Saints. Perhaps this was all another of his schemes. Perhaps Kale had been wrong about Nyla.

"I don't know who it was," said Ashi. "But I don't want you disappearing like that again. You swore an oath to Salla to remain with us and to protect Vashti. Why did you run off?"

Kale was about to lie, but Kirra cut him off.

"I know why." Her tone was cold. "Your cloak reeks of cheap perfume. You were at a nighthouse."

Kale gulped, but he could not deny it. Nor could he explain himself. Not in front of Ashi. "I... I..."

At the mention of a nighthouse, Ashi glared at him. "You can't be serious."

Kale did not know what to say.

Kirra's voice was like ice. "Well, we can only hope your… pleasures… did not put us all in mortal danger." She did not say another word, but her grimace told all for Kale.

She'll never forgive me, he thought.

Kirra's movements were slow and calculated. She retreated to the room, carefully closing the door behind her, leaving Kale alone with Ashi.

The Ilya woman shook her head. "I've got to hand it to you, Sky Blood. You're the biggest horse's ass I've ever met… A nighthouse, really?"

Kale glared at her. "Enough."

"You didn't draw attention to yourself, I hope?"

Kale shook his head. "I gave an alias everywhere I went in the city."

"Then you knew we were followed as well?"

"I sensed them… but I could not tell who they were or what they wanted." Kale hoped his lie was convincing. He had not suspected Nyla until he discovered the gallows symbol. And he had sensed no one else.

Ashi eyed him for a moment, then gestured at the door. "We're all sharing one room. It's all they had available. I took the first watch. I think you may as well take the next until Kirra is asleep."

Ashi left him, and Kale stood in the hall, leaning back against the doorframe. Within, he could hear whispers, but Kirra's mind was more walled off to him than ever.

Kale cursed. It was all a stupid misunderstanding. But could he explain to Kirra what had really happened? Would she believe him? What did she want from this journey?

Kale had trouble believing Kirra would join the Sky Guard in order to restore her sight. She was up to something, but he did not know what.

One thing was certain—she did not trust him.

And he was not sure he was trustworthy.

PART SEVEN
ARMY OF THE NORTH

They were a silent sleeping threat. The world had all but forgotten about them. But an army in the North could change the world forever.

—from *Dawn of the Third World*

CHAPTER TWENTY-THREE

storia spent several days recovering from wounds sustained during her execution. She slept for most of it. The rest she spent with Alyk, Mischa, Tes, and Jordie. The young Crooked boy had given up his cold feelings toward her from the trial. Jordie apologized repeatedly. As had all the others she had come into contact with since the trial. But the memory of their swift turn would not be easily forgotten.

She did not fault the people for this. They had believed a lie.

Fara dul Baruk had brought about the whole ordeal. Over the past few days, the other elders had visited her, offering their own deepest apologies for their errant judgment. They saw her rise as a sign from the gods. If Tori would have them, they would follow her into war. Fara dul Baruk, however, did not show her face in Tori's chambers, and Tori feared she had not seen the last of the High Elder's schemes.

The day that Tori's bandages were removed, Seren lè Tal came to visit her. The faerie, Lir'ghe, hovered above her right shoulder. The creature did not seem to speak much. When Tori had thanked him for saving her life, he'd merely grunted and said, "It was nothing."

It was more than she had heard him say to anyone but his queen.

Seren lè Tal had come yesterday to discuss war strategies with Tori, Skya, and the Alyut elders. Skya and her *Nuq'vana* were already training a large volunteer force of Alyut and Crooked folk. The Witch Queen sought to act quickly. Combined with the fleets of the Isles, they would soon have a force to be reckoned with.

Today, the queen came only with Lir'ghe. She wore an obsidian gown that covered her arms to her palms and a collar that reached her chin. The material was thin and shimmered like it was covered in tiny stars. The queen wore no cloaks or furs that Tori had seen. Just her long-sleeved gowns. Tori smiled at her arrival. Already, she was growing fond of the queen and felt she could relate to her in a way she could with few others. Someone else young who bore great responsibility. "Don't you get cold?" she asked.

Seren lè Tal smiled and shook her head. "I have not felt cold in some time, nor heat."

"I'm jealous."

The queen shrugged. "It is not as wonderful as you might think. The senses are a gift, so we may feel life in all its glory, as well as its misery."

"You were not always this way?"

Seren lè Tal shook her head. "Magic comes at a price. I think you know this more than anyone. And that is all I will say on the matter. I do not expect you to reveal the secrets behind your own magic, so I ask that you grant me the same courtesy. My father taught me to keep friends close, but not so close they know the scent of your stench."

Tori laughed. "Sound advice."

"My father was an ambitious bastard." The queen smirked. "But in that, he was not wrong."

Tori knew it was wise they keep their secrets. If things did not go well, the chancellor would not hesitate to exploit them in whatever way he could. He had done just that with Kale in Vlyanii, and with Vashti and the other turned Watchers. Tori feared for Ren and the others, but knew she must move wisely, and without emotion.

The Watchers were not their first priority. After all, infiltrating the White Citadel would not likely happen until late into the invasion. If they reached it at all.

"I am always cautious, but I hope you know that I trust you, Astoria," said Seren lè Tal, touching her arm kindly. Her hands were neither warm nor cool.

"And I trust you," said Tori. She leaned forward in her bed, and for once, the act did not come with pain.

The queen smiled. "I'm glad, because I am afraid I must ask you to trust me even more than you already have."

"What do you mean?"

"I am leaving. We have much to accomplish and little time to do so. I've already sent ravens to the kings and queens of the Isles, calling for a war conclave. But I cannot go alone. If I make claims that Watchers and Northmen are going to war, I must bring emissaries."

Tori knew where this was going.

"I've already spoken to Mischa," said Seren. "She has agreed to journey with me, along with Geryn dul Narsuk, elder of the *Iqu'vara*."

Tori hated the idea of losing her friend on the eve of war. Mischa had become her closest confidant over the past few months, and the thought of moving forward with this war, not to mention being stranded in the North without her, made Tori feel uneasy.

"If all goes well, in a few weeks, we will all be reunited in battle."

Tori nodded. "I would have no one else go as emissary. Mischa is my most trusted ally."

"I've noticed. I know well the cost of losing dear allies, and so out of good faith, I will be leaving one of my own. Lir'ghe is a prince among the Kroqala, and a dear friend. He will remain with you until I return." Lir'ghe made no comment nor showed any expression on the matter. He hovered above his queen's shoulder and merely nodded to Tori.

There was a knock. Mischa, Alyk, and Skya entered.

"I'll leave you to your farewells," said Seren lè Tal. "Mischa, we fly in an hour."

And with that the queen left them. Lir'ghe darted after her on soft golden wings.

Mischa hurried over and hugged her. Then, remembering herself, she pulled away. "Gods, I'm sorry, does it still hurt?"

"It's all right." Tori hugged Mischa again tightly. Though it stung, she didn't care.

"I won't be gone long."

"The Southern Isles," said Tori. "I've known nothing but tales. I can't wait to hear about them. I want to know what the Floating Mountains look like."

"Aren't those myths?"

Tori smiled and shook her head. "There are many things we've found are not myths that I wish were, but islands in the sky are a sight I hope is real."

Mischa squeezed her hand. "We're going to save them, Tori. We're going to kill Cyrus Maro and rescue them all."

Tori hoped it was true. She knew it would not be so simple, especially considering Vashti and the others who had joined the chancellor. She feared that many more of her friends would likely die before all this was done. But she did not voice these fears. "Yes, we are."

Skya drew near. "Mischa, you should get ready. I'll help with your things." There was a twinkle in her eyes that Tori did not miss. She had noted the way Mischa stole glances at the Alyut warrior over the past few days. Skya brushed her shoulder, and Mischa smiled in a way Tori had never seen before.

"I'll meet you in the square for the send off," said Alyk.

"We both will," said Tori.

Mischa and Skya left.

Alyk shook his head. "I am not sure that walking is such a good—"

Tori shifted her legs to the edge of the bed. "Just… help me, will you?" She grabbed on to his shoulder, and he held on to her waist. The pressure was uncomfortable, but she ignored it.

"You planned this all along," said Alyk, noting her woolen breeches emerging from beneath the bed of furs.

Tori had intended to walk today the minute Behla removed the last of her bandages. She had quickly asked the Alyut girl to help her into real clothes again. She'd felt like a child lying around all day in a cotton shift.

It took more energy to stand than Tori expected, but she managed. Each step was slow and deliberate, and sent slight tremors up her thighs, but she was relieved she could still move. Alyk helped her into layers of wool and a thick fur cloak.

Tori gripped Alyk's shoulder tightly as he guided her through Skya's sitting room and out another door, which led to a wide passage carved straight out of the star rock. The ground was warm beneath her feet.

They followed the passage to an immense cavern. It was like a giant dome beneath the earth. The ceiling rose well over fifty feet and people bustled about like it was a market square in Maro'El.

"The Under Realm. Most of my people live down here below the surface once winter descends. It is too cold to hunt, or do much of anything in the World Above. But down here, it is warm and livable."

"It's incredible." Tori marveled at the way the Alyut managed to adapt to the harsh conditions of the North.

The more Tori walked, the more her strength increased. The barriers were gone from her magic, and she was healing. Mischa and Skya met them near the end of the thoroughfare beneath the earth. Mischa wore clothes of the North that Skya must have given her after the trial. Mischa kept by Skya's side, and they shared sweet smiles as they crossed the underground dome. It made Tori glad to see her friend happy again. They had been through so much darkness, there were times Tori had wondered if they would ever feel happy or safe again. But now, Mischa was filled with glorious hope, and it helped Tori find that hope as well.

Skya led the way up a narrow staircase carved straight into the rock, and they emerged in one of the immense receiving halls of the ice palace. Tes bombarded them as they entered the streets of Iqala, giving Tori a warm hug and Mischa a cold glare.

"What's wrong?" said Mischa, patting her shoulder.

"Benja says you're leaving."

The old Crooked man was panting as he arrived from chasing after the spritely girl. "Apologies, my saint. I tried to stop her from bothering you."

Tori waved her hand dismissively. "Tes is never a bother."

"Is it true?" Tes demanded, glaring up at Mischa.

Mischa stooped down to one knee. "I'll only be gone a few weeks."

Tes crossed her arms. "You're supposed to help me train. We've only had two lessons."

Mischa smiled. "There'll be plenty of time for more lessons."

"Not before the war!"

Mischa brushed the girl's messy hair out of her eyes. "Tes, you won't be fighting in this war."

"I want to fight!"

"Your day will come," Tori said. "But for now, Mischa is right. You're too young for war. But I promise to train you while Mischa is away."

Tes did not argue, but she stormed away, Benja hurrying after, hollering back over his shoulder, "Apologies again, my saint."

"She has every right to want to fight," Tori said.

"She's a child," said Mischa.

"Tes has seen more than many see in a lifetime."

"You're not thinking of letting her fight?"

Tori shook her head. "No, but she'll make a fine warrior someday."

"I hope she never sees war," said Mischa. "I wish I never had."

Tori said little else, but she feared that this war was only beginning. They would do well to look to the future, and Tes's gifts would be an asset for that future.

A crowd was gathered in the same square where they had come to watch Tori's execution only days before. But rather than a pyre, an immense ship sat at the center of the crowd. Strange runes glowed along the sides and thick sails of the vessel. Tori had thought the flying ship part of her death dreams, but the sight of it now was even more magnificent than she remembered. The skyship floated a few feet above the ground, and a long plank stretched up to the deck. Alyut men and women hauled crates of supplies, and Seren lè Tal stood upon the aft deck, watching as they approached. The Witch Queen looked god-like at the glowing helm of the skyship.

It struck Tori how coincidental it was that at the same time in history that the Watchers were regaining strength, another form of magic would also rise up in the world. She did not truly believe in fate, but moments such as now made her wonder. Skya dul Baruk had sent for her, and if not, Tori would be dead. And Alyk had seen visions of them both. What was she to make of that?

The last of the supply crates were boarded, and Seren lè Tal motioned for Mischa to come aboard. Mischa hugged Skya, then Alyk, and finally Tori.

"See you soon," said Mischa, squeezing her tight.

"See you in war." It was a dark thought, but one that brought smiles to both their faces. They were going to save their friends. They were going to fight the chancellor. And that was reason to be glad.

Mischa kissed Tori's cheek, and then she ascended the gangway. Alyk supported Tori as they watched the ship lift into the sky. Geryn dul Narsuk waved as the skyship soared over the city, and the Alyut clans cheered. It was a marked difference from the death cadence they had chanted in this square only days ago. It amazed Tori how quickly and easily people's minds could be swayed.

As she made her way back through the crowd, her arm around Alyk dul Baruk's shoulders for support, the people smiled and waved and tried to catch a brief word with her. The Alyut saw her as a god once more, or at least someone sent by the gods. *But will that sentiment remain?* Tori wondered.

Tori had still not seen Fara dul Baruk since her execution.

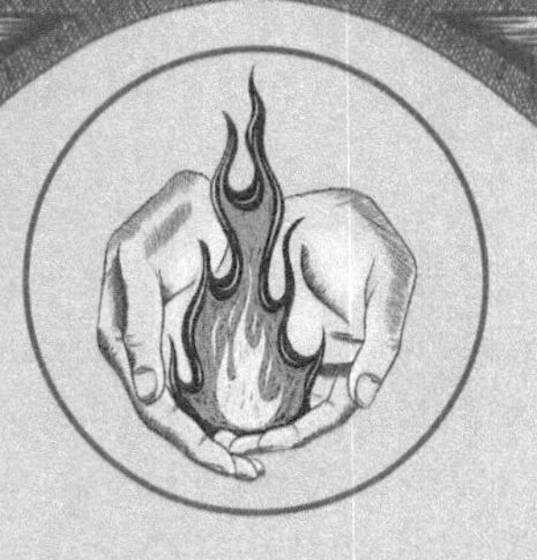

CHAPTER TWENTY-FOUR

The world was breathtaking from the skies. It was almost painful how quickly Iqala and the Icelands faded into the distance as the skyship soared. It had taken Mischa weeks to reach the Ice City. Many had died on the journey, and now she was leaving it behind in a matter of hours.

Soon the smooth plains of ice were displaced by the jagged peaks of the northern Teeth. According to the Witch Queen, they would fly over the Boundless Sea for most of the journey to avoid notice from the continent. They would pass Osha in a matter of days, returning to the seas below at night so Seren and the Kroqala could rest. They would reach Elya, the port capital of the Southern Isles, in less than a week.

The air was sharp on Mischa's skin, despite her thick furs. Geryn dul Narsuk soon retreated to the cabin belowdecks, but Mischa remained on the foredeck for several hours, taking in the sights. The northern sky was clear, but she could see large plumes of clouds on the hazy horizon.

"It's amazing, isn't it?" said Seren lè Tal. The queen leaned against the rail, the wind rushing through her silver hair magnificently. She still wore only her thin long-sleeved gown.

"Why does the world look so skewed from up here?" asked Mischa, gesturing to the southern horizon. "Is it an effect of the air?"

"I believe it is because the world itself is curved. It's only a theory. But the *scholai* who taught me in my youth was an ardent student of the stars.

He built a powerful looking glass, like a sailor's but much larger, to magnify their appearance. I spent many hours studying the strange bodies beyond our world. All of them appear to be spherical, just like the Sisters in our night sky. Why shouldn't *our* world be just so? Perhaps the stars themselves are merely other spheres beyond our reach."

Mischa thought it hard to comprehend. She had always been taught the world was like a great plate of glass. If you traveled far enough, you would fall off the edge into the Abyss and share the fate of all those on the Lost Continent who disappeared without a trace so many years ago. But then, she had been taught many false things in her life. She liked the idea of other worlds, though. It reminded her of the ancient teachings of the Watchers regarding the afterlife.

"It's a beautiful idea," said Mischa, watching as the horizon began to bleed with brilliant colors. "You said the *scholai* of your youth. But you look so young. Surely it hasn't been that long since you were a student."

The queen giggled, the sunlight dancing over her smooth face. "I suppose I am still a youth. I began talking that way to make myself seem less of a child as I gained power in the Isles. My nineteenth summer just passed."

So young, thought Mischa, *and yet so formidable. Like Tori.*

But the queen seemed to shoulder the weight of her station in a way Tori had not yet mastered. She had the stature of someone far older.

"You think me a child?" said Seren.

Mischa shook her head and smiled. "Not at all. Age means little, I think. I've met merchers and privateers who act like children, and I've met children who are braver than most seasoned soldiers."

She was thinking of Tes. Mischa wished she could have stayed back to train the girl. Tes had a spirit she would miss while she was separated from the others.

"You speak wisely," said Seren. "I suspect you were forced to grow up at a young age as well."

Mischa nodded. She was forced to grow up the day she fled Melanesia. *No, even before that. Ever since Ala…*

The Witch Queen touched her shoulder kindly. "My *scholai* once told me to never let anyone look down on me for my age. He said that the hope of the world lies in young folk."

"Your *scholai* sounds like a good man."

"Yes, indeed." Seren's face twitched. Like there was more she wanted to say.

"Your house must not have been as lowly as I've heard to afford such a brilliant teacher."

Seren smiled, but shook her head. "He should have been the most expensive one in the Isles. But like most people ahead of their time, he was an outcast amongst the Southern *scholerat*. And on top of that, he was blind. No one wanted him. He was the only teacher my family could afford."

"Blind, yet he built a looking glass for the stars?" said Mischa, bewildered.

"He could work better with his hands than most can, even with their sight. He used to say that losing his eyes helped him discover everything there is to see without them. But he was always saddened he could no longer see the night sky. I described everything I saw through his night-glass. In exchange for my assistance with his studies, along with his daily household tasks, he taught me everything he knew. Which turned out to be far more than my parents ever could have dreamed."

Mischa detected a tremble in her voice the more she spoke of the *scholai*. "Does he still teach you?"

Seren gazed out at the stunning sunset. "He died. For teaching me about the Old World. About magic."

"Morphs?" asked Mischa.

Seren lè Tal shook her head. "Osha is not the only place where magic comes at a cost." Her jaw clenched. "But things are changing, aren't they?"

"I hope so."

The Witch Queen said no more and soon returned to the helm. Once the sun had set, Mischa retreated to the cabin. Her room was small, but then, Mischa had never required much space. She had brought only a rucksack with a change of clothes and a small trunk with extra furs, which she was glad for. Though they were traveling south, it was still frigid up in the sky, even in her cabin.

Mischa sat on the bed and dug in her pack, retrieving a small blade that Skya dul Baruk had given her. It was no ordinary knife, however. It was a small shank made of icefire.

"I hope you won't need it," Skya had said, "but this will kill anyone you stab in seconds. The crystal shatters and poisons their blood."

"You don't trust the queen?"

Skya gripped her shoulder. "I trust her, but I've never seen a transition of power that went uncontested. And the Southern Isles, of all places, is not known for peaceful conclaves. I doubt the queen is bringing you along only as proof of our alliance. And I'd personally like to see you come *back* to the North."

Mischa held on to the memory and smiled. She could nearly feel the warmth of the Bear Rider's fingers. Skya was nothing like Vashti or Ala or Zaya.

Vashti had been fierce, but had never been one to share much affection. Ala had been too soft for this world, and the world had overcome her. And Zaya… the Medici had always been a mistake. A feeble attempt to move past Vashti. Now Zaya was dead too. Another tragedy left in Mischa's wake to haunt her dreams. She pushed the thought away.

Skya was different, and Mischa liked this about her. She shared Vashti's fierceness, but she had a soft side as well. However, Mischa's feelings were torn about even considering such a thing right now. And not just because they were going to war.

Despite the betrayal, despite all the horrible things Vashti had done, Mischa still cared for her. It was not the same. It could never be the same. But as much as Mischa longed to finally move on, she was unsure she was ready.

She toyed with the icefire blade in her hands. The handle was made of whalebone wrapped with sealskin, and it glowed softly when she removed it from its sheath. The same strange stone that had nearly killed Tori might very well save her life. Mischa hoped she would not need it.

A chilly draft coursed through the room. Mischa stowed the blade away and went to her trunk to grab her kendrak furs, but when she undid the latch, she found no furs. Instead, a small head of bushy dark hair popped out of the trunk. Mischa instinctively struck the flints at her wrists, forming a swift flame. But she let it die just as quickly when she realized who was in her trunk. "Tes?"

The girl smiled sheepishly as she crawled out of the cramped space.

"What are you doing here?"

"I… I had to come!" Tes protested.

"Gods, I'm glad I found you. There may still be time to turn back." Mischa made for the door.

"Wait!" Tes hollered, running after her. "Please!"

Mischa stopped and turned. "Tes, you can't come, do you hear me? It's too dangerous. And you need to train back in Iqala."

Tes crossed her arms over her chest. "I don't want to learn from Tori."

"What are you talking about?"

"She's the Gallows Girl. She doesn't have time to train me to fight."

"You're a child, Tes. Children should not go to war."

"The chancellor killed *my* mum and pa!" The girl's voice was shrill, and she shook with anger as tears streaked down her cheeks. "He ruined my home! You don't understand. I have to fight!"

Mischa stooped to a knee and placed her hand on the girl's shoulder, meeting her gaze. Tes's eyes were alight. "I do understand."

"I want to learn from *you*. And I want to help at the war meeting."

"How will you help?" said Mischa. "You can't control your gift."

"I could hear what you and the queen were talking about on deck." Tes hopped up on the bed, and Mischa sat beside her with a resigned sigh.

"You could?"

Tes nodded. "She was talking about her star teacher or something."

Mischa raised an eyebrow. "When did you realize you could do that?"

"At Tori's trial. I listened in from outside because they wouldn't let me in."

Mischa was always amazed at the astonishing way Watcher abilities revealed themselves in times of need. Not only could Tes manipulate sound like a shrill weapon, as she had when she killed the frost giant, but she also had highly sensitive hearing.

"Please, don't take me back to the Ice City," Tes pleaded.

"What about your brother?"

"Benja will take care of him. I want to help. I know I can't fight in some big battle, but I can help now."

"What do you expect we'll need to hear at the conclave?"

"The Isles have lots of kings and queens, right?"

"One rules each isle," said Mischa.

"Well, I was thinking the others probably don't all like that the Witch Queen is getting so powerful."

"That is likely."

"Maybe one of them is plotting something. And if they are, maybe I can find out."

Mischa smiled and patted the girl on the knee. Tes had a point. Her ears might very well prove invaluable if something were to happen. "All right, you can stay. But you stay with me at all times, unless I say otherwise. Clear?"

"Clear."

Mischa got up and made for the door. "Then, let's start your training."

"Where are we going?"

"The mess hall. The Kroqala are the rowdiest bunch I've ever seen during mealtimes."

"How will that help?" Tes asked as she followed after. "Don't I want it quiet? I could barely hear you and the queen, and there were hardly any other sounds, then."

"You need to learn to tune out the noise."

The din of buzzing demon faeries was cacophonous before Mischa even opened the door. And despite the likely discomfort in her Watcher sense, the little Crooked girl was beaming as they entered.

CHAPTER TWENTY-FIVE

Tori and Alyk watched from the side of a large training arena at the edge of the Ice City as Skya and her *Nuq'vana* led the Northern recruits in spear drills. The Alyut were skilled hunters, and Tori marveled at their ability to hit targets, both while standing still and from the backs of mighty northbears. Their skills with bows and the few muskets that had found their way this far north also proved encouraging to watch. Their hunting prowess would prove invaluable in the war to come.

The Crooked folk were untrained, but many had some experience in close combat from their ruthless cage fights. Most of the Alyut had very little training in proper combat. The Northmen had few human enemies. There were small rogue clans farther north, like the ones Tori and Mischa were sure they'd glimpsed during their journey across the Icelands, but according to Alyk, the Bear Riders dealt with them in swift order when they ventured too close, and they did not often dare attack the larger organized clans of Iqala.

This was the one thing that made Tori nervous about marching these people to war. Both groups were filled with strong and resilient people, but other than the Bear Riders, they were not warriors. The Night Legions would outmatch them in close quarters any day.

Tori's soldiers were eager to learn, however, and they were filled with a hunger that no Legion Shadow could possess. They had known only tales of their homeland. For centuries, they had known only injustice because of the sins of the chancellors long ago. What they lacked in experience, they might just make up for in fierce determination. Skya drilled them for hours on end, and none complained. They were improving noticeably each day.

Skya and Alyk paired off to demonstrate a sparring routine, leaving Tori to observe alone. Lir'ghe hovered nearby, watching the regimen with interest, though he kept enough distance not to speak. The faerie was not social, but he always kept close. He seemed to unnerve many of the Alyut, but Tori appreciated his silent presence. She'd had few moments for reflection since her body healed. There was too much to do, but there was much yet to consider. And despite Lir'ghe's hideous features, he had a reassuring effect on Tori, in a way that few other people in the North did. After all, it was the demon faerie who had saved her life, and he had sworn to serve her just as he served his queen. And with Mischa gone, and Tes stowed away after her, Tori liked having him near.

The training arena filled with the song of clashing spear points. Alyk and his sister whipped their weapons around quicker than most could wield a saber. Tori loved the paradox between Alyk's peaceful spirituality and his impressive martial skill. Skya taught the new recruits how to make use of the entire spear, including the whalebone shaft, to block an attacking spear or saber. The soldiers observed closely, then paired off to practice the maneuver.

Next, the soldiers perfected lethal thrusts on dummies made of wood and sealskin.

Tera dul Hesak, elder of the *Tu'va* forest clan, and Lyren dul Vanuk of the *Karu'va* had been observing the drills for some time from a distance. For a short while, their High Elder had joined them, but Fara dul Baruk did not watch long. Tera approached as Tori took stock of her new army. Tori had been waiting for one of them to disturb her ever since the High Elder left, as the two elders seemed to be making a point to talk to Tori when given the opportunity, as though trying to prove themselves. Lir'ghe hovered closer as Tera dul Hesak neared.

"What do you think of them, my saint?" the elder asked, leaning against the ice wall surrounding the arena.

Tori could not explain why, but something felt forced about the question, and so she did not reveal her true thoughts. "They are coming along well. Their hearts are filled with hope, and they are very skilled. I will be proud to lead them into battle."

The woman nodded calculatedly. "And we will be proud to march with you."

"But not all of you," said Tori evenly. She met the elder's gaze. "Elder Baruk did not observe her soldiers long."

"I assure you, my saint, the High Elder will not provoke you. We have allied ourselves with you and the Witch Queen."

"Yes, and we march south in a matter of weeks, and I have yet to meet with the eldest of the four clan leaders. Will Elder Baruk be marching to war with us?"

Elder Hesak eyed Lir'ghe, who hovered in place with rapid wings. "I... cannot speak for her, my saint."

It was as good as a *no*.

"Well, I am glad to have your support, Elder Hesak," said Tori, gripping the woman's arm in a comradely fashion. Her tone conveyed the necessity of that continued allegiance.

The elder managed a smile. "You bear the support of my people. That is all that matters, my saint. A good chieftain heeds the will of her clan."

But does Fara dul Baruk feel the same?

Tori forced a smile, then returned to observing her soldiers. Elder Hesak soon took the hint and moved on. It was strange to think how only a few days before, the elder had stood by while Fara dul Baruk rigged the trial of fire and ice against her. While Tori was grateful for the support of the other three elders, she did not trust them. She had seen the way they had bent to their High Elder's will once before. And *she* had clearly not thrown her lot in with this war.

Alyk returned to her side, having finished his demonstrations. He was grinning, and Tori's mood brightened. He stood close to her, so their arms brushed. Tori was grateful to still have him with her. She felt so alone and set apart in her role as the Gallows Saint, and with Mischa gone, this feeling had only intensified. She missed the days at the Watchtower, when she had been one of many Watchers bent on revolution. Sure, she had still borne the weight of being the Gallows Girl, but she'd had Ren to look to for leadership and guidance. Now, with even Tes gone, Tori was the lone Watcher in the Great White North, and the Alyut were all looking to her. She wished desperately for the simplicity of days on Orran's Mountain with Ren.

She could hardly find time to practice her own gifts. Since her recovery from the trial of fire and ice, she had begun waking early to focus on her magic, which had hardly been used since the chancellor's attack on the Watchtower. Her Conjuri skills were strong when she had time to focus on the objects she manipulated. But that was not how battles worked. She needed to be reactionary. The frost giant had defeated her because she couldn't control her gifts without thinking, and she could not afford to let that happen again when they marched against Osha.

The Northern soldiers stowed their weapons away. Skya led them on a conditioning exercise into the deep snow beyond the city, shouting orders from her northbear while the soldiers trudged along at a swift pace in only their fur boots and *muqbluqs*.

Alyk and Tori walked back through the city. "What did Elder Hesak want?" Alyk asked as they neared the central square.

"She asked what I thought of the army."

"And?"

"Their hearts are strong," said Tori.

"But..." Alyk offered a thin smile.

"But I wish we had more time."

Alyk sighed. "Autumn is nearly over. If we wait any longer, the ice will set in, and we will be forced underground."

"And if we wait through the winter, the opportunity will pass," said Tori. "I know it. Queen Seren will not be able to muster the Isles for some distant future war."

What made matters worse was the latest news that had arrived by raven that morning. The chancellor had issued an incredible reward for any information leading to the Gallows Girl's whereabouts. The queen-to-be wanted her dead, for a wedding gift, and the chancellor meant to oblige. Considering the chancellor's victory over the Rulaqs, and the fact that Osha blamed Tori for the return of the beasts, things were looking bleak.

"Rumors tell that Morphs are scouring the Teeth for signs of my whereabouts ever since Vashti's... wedding request. It is only a matter of time before they come to the North. Now is the time to strike." She was trying to convince herself.

Alyk stopped and looked her in the eyes. "It *is* the time, Tori."

"You know what the chancellor is capable of. How can you be so confident?"

"I have faith."

"How can you put so much faith in some vision? What if this is a mistake? What if your *madru* is right, and I am leading your people to their destruction?"

Alyk took her hand. He wore fur-lined gloves, just like Tori, but she wished, fleetingly, she could feel the warmth of his hands on her bare skin. "Come with me. I want to show you why I believe."

Tori followed him through the city. They entered the Under Realm through the central palace, but they did not stop when they arrived in the main underground chamber. Alyk led the way through a narrow passage and then down a winding staircase carved straight out of the stone.

The passage wended deep beneath Iqala, and the deeper they went, the warmer Tori became. At the end of the passage stood a lone iron door. Beside the door were several hooks made of long, white northbear claws. Alyk removed his cloak and hung it up. Tori did the same. He removed his boots and woolen layers, until he wore only a pair of linen pants. No shirt. Tori did not mind seeing him this way. Though he had no warrior's build, he was lean and his muscles were strong and defined.

"You'll want to… wear less. It's very warm beyond the door."

"What's in there?" said Tori, as she too removed her many layers. She stripped down to her small shorts and undershirt.

Alyk smiled. "Do you remember where my visions of Restoration first came from?"

"You said your grandmother saw a vision of a winter lily, which you believed was me. But I've never met your grandmother."

Alyk nodded. "It would be difficult considering my *madram*'s been dead since I was a young boy."

"But you said she was the High Shaman."

"She is."

"I don't understand. How could a dead woman serve your people's religion?"

"Who better to teach us of what is beyond ourselves than someone who has been beyond the boundaries of our first existence?"

Alyk pushed the door open. Steam gushed from the room within, and Tori was struck with an intense heat. Blue icefire crystals lined the walls, illuminating the strange room in a soft sapphire glow. At the center of the space, a small pool of water bubbled and gushed with steam. Tori instantly began to sweat. The pool glowed with a different light. It was silver. Small streams glowed on the floor like silver veins leading from the heart of the earth, all of them converging in the pool.

"This is the inner temple of the Alyut, where the High Shaman resides to offer guidance until one of her followers is chosen to take her place."

"Where is she?" asked Tori, glancing around the room.

Alyk pointed at the pool and stepped in. He held on to Tori's hand. "It's hot, but it will not burn you."

The pool was waist deep. As they entered, steam rushed and water churned violently. The air grew so thick Tori could not see a thing. For a moment, it was hard to breathe, the air was so heavy. But as she inhaled, the sensation went away, and soon, Tori felt as though the steam were filling her, like wind in a sail. Alyk held tight to her hand, and she was consumed by warmth, but it was not from Alyk, nor even the pool itself. It was a strange presence pressing all around her.

The room disappeared, and Tori stifled a scream.

Tori no longer felt the water or the heat. She felt disconnected from the world, as though she were in a dream, except she was aware it was a dream. It reminded her of the feeling of her nightmares in the Forest of Ghen. The only constant was Alyk's hand on hers.

A face appeared in the mist.

An elderly Alyut woman with stark-white hair.

Mala dul Baruk, Tori thought, *the High Shaman.*

Her face was not fully present. It came and went, wafting in and out of focus like driftwood on the tide. But her voice was steady and seemed to come from all around the room.

"You've brought a visitor," the shaman said.

"A good friend, *Madram,*" said Alyk.

"Only a friend?" the shaman said with a chuckle. Her face dissipated, and the mists swirled around, but Tori could have sworn she felt a hand brush her face. It startled her, but she was not afraid. She wished the touch had lasted longer. "I recognize your face, Astoria Burodai… that is your name, isn't it?"

"Yes. It's an honor to meet you, Shaman."

"Call me Mala." The shaman's face drifted back with the mists. She was smiling, and Tori felt warm all over.

"You've seen me before," said Tori.

"Aye," said Mala. "The Aether is full of eyes, and many of them have been watching you with much interest."

"Alyk said you knew I would come to the North. You knew Queen Seren would come too."

The face disappeared, and Tori was engulfed in mist, as though she were being consumed by a mystical warmth. The air echoed with faint laughter. "Nothing is known, child. There are many eyes, and they see many things. Though I am pleased you *did* decide to come to the North."

"But Alyk said you saw the Restoration of the Alyut."

Mala's face reappeared and nodded. "Years ago, I envisioned a dream built on hope. Not sight. You want me to tell you whether you are doing the right thing, whether you will win this war. And I am afraid I cannot give you the answers you seek, Astoria."

"Well, what are we doing then?" Tori instantly regretted her demand. "I'm sorry, I've never spoken with the dead."

Mala chuckled. "That's not what the dead say. They remember you."

Suddenly, Tori was taken back to the forest where many ghosts had tormented her. "The Forest of Ghen, it's like this room, isn't it?"

"The veil between worlds is thin in Ghen, as it is here."

"Our temple is far more... controlled than the Haunted Forest," said Alyk reassuringly.

"How can you bring back the dead?" said Tori.

"There is no such thing," said Mala.

"As death?"

Mala laughed. "Death is an idea invented by those who've not experienced what lies beyond the corporeal world."

"What does lie beyond?"

"That knowledge is reserved only for those who lie there. Some things must remain a mystery. It is the way of things."

"Can you see anyone from this temple?" Tori asked. "Or is it only for you, Mala?"

"This temple is merely a looking glass. But it was not made for me. Nor my people, for that matter. We discovered this veil, as we discovered the veils in Ghen before the Elyan races stole that place from us and let the ghosts run free. Only the gods know the limits of this veil... There is someone you wish to see?"

Tori nodded.

"Your *madru*," said the High Shaman. "Hmmm... I am not sure that would be wise, my dear."

"Please, Mala."

"You've seen her before."

"In Ghen."

"That memory haunts you," said Mala. "I can sense it. What makes you think this time will be different?"

"This place is different."

"Aye, child. It is. But the dead are best left to their own schemes."

"Says the dead shaman who shares visions of the future."

The mists swirled, and the room rumbled with laughter. Mala's face drew near. "If you are sure."

Alyk gripped her hand tight, but Tori held Mala dul Baruk's gaze. "I'm sure."

Mala did not respond. The mists swirled as though they were the eye of a storm, sparking and singing with a strange energy.

And then, a face appeared. A face Tori had not seen in eleven years. The air felt warm all around her. Tears filled her eyes. She could hardly believe it.

"Mum!" Tori was engulfed in a phantom embrace.

"My little love." It was her. Really her. Her mum's voice sounded like the most beautiful melody.

"Mum!" Tori reached up to touch the face in the mists, but her hand passed right through the vapor.

"It's only a looking glass, remember," said Alyk, still holding her tightly.

"Yes, it's me," said Celene Burodai. "I've been watching you, little love. I knew you would remember your gifts when the time was right. I'm so proud of you."

Tori choked back a sob. "Mum, you… you died because of me."

"Don't waste your sorrow on the dead. I died because Aleksander Maro ordered it. And now, you fight his heir. You bring hope to many, my love. Watchers, lowborns. It was well worth the sacrifice."

"Gods, I miss you, Mum. I'm so sorry." Tori felt tense all over. She was so angry at Osha's long legacy of oppression. Her mum had been murdered for possessing gifts the current chancellor now manipulated for his own gain. A buried rage kindled within her. "I'm going to get revenge. For you. For all the Watchers and lowborns who have suffered. I am going to end the Maro reign with the chancellor and his traitor of a queen."

Her mum's face disappeared, and the mists swirled.

"Mum?" Tori reached into the mists. They were colder now. Then, the face returned and Tori was filled with relief.

"You have been through much, my love. I do not blame you for your anger and hatred. But please… don't take it out on Vashti Burodai."

Tori started at the name. Her mum knew who the Yan Avii princess was?

Her fists clenched. It had been bad enough that Vashti had betrayed the Shadow Watch, but now she wanted Tori's head as a wedding gift.

"What do you mean? How can you say that? Vashti is a traitor. She's my enemy. The enemy of our revolution. She wants me dead!"

Tori was engulfed again in mists, and she felt like she might suffocate.

"She may be your enemy… but she is also… your sister."

A sinking feeling dragged at Tori's gut, jerking her from the mists. "Mum…"

But Celene Burodai was already gone. The mists faded, and Tori and Alyk stood again in the looking glass pool. The water had calmed.

But Tori had not. She felt nothing but rage.

Alyk wrenched his hand away. It had gone white from her furious grip.

Tori felt power rise up in her like water from a breached dam. She screamed. The icefire crystals that lit the temple flickered and then exploded, and the room plunged into darkness.

PART EIGHT
THE HANGMAN

Elesa volonai [The gods move through us]
Menassa elonai [We are the gods]
Utlesa sheshonash [From them we were begotten]
*Alesa renonash [To them we shall return]**

—a lost mantra of the Watcher orders
(translated from Old Elyan by Aldon Taldona)

**Annotation: "While popularized by the Watchers to justify their deeds, the poem's syntax and structure predates the Watcher orders. Some scholai believe it is a remnant of the Ancient Men. Which begs the question: Who believed themselves to be gods?"*

CHAPTER TWENTY-SIX

Darien and Valeria danced the dance they knew better than any other—the dance of sabers. In the sky above the great training square of Maro'El, they spun through the air on black wings. Valeria Sardona swooped in from his right. Darien shifted his wings, catching a stream of air from the west, and he arched his body. His saber met hers with a clang that sent shivers through him. A sly grin stretched Valeria's face as she flashed by, and Darien thought that she had never looked more alluring.

Even in her Morph form, Darien found her taut militant figure utterly captivating. He banked in the air and gave chase. She weaved amongst a series of ruined spires beyond the training grounds, but he did not follow. She disappeared from sight for a moment, and Darien raced ahead, adrenaline pumping, predicting where she would appear next. He grew hot with sweat and excitement.

He shifted his wings and rode a current of the wind to find a higher vantage point.

Valeria shot from behind a tower below. Darien turned hard and plummeted to attack. But amazingly, Valeria had anticipated the maneuver. They had become so in sync with one another, it might have been frustrating, if Darien were not so electrified by her cunning.

She parried his attack, the world consumed by the sharp clanging of their sabers. They weaved in the air, exchanging blow after blow. As they plunged toward the earth, the training field loomed larger and larger. They were both grinning as they sought for the victorious blow. The earth rose to swallow them, and Darien slowed his descent ever so slightly.

At the last possible moment, Valeria extended her wings to recover, and that was when Darien struck out with his saber, clipping her left wing. Just in time, Darien swooped upward, morphed forms, and landed on his human feet. Valeria landed off-balance from his blow, and Darien leapt forward, knocking her on her back. He resisted the urge to join her there, and instead held his blade at her throat.

She grimaced as she morphed back into her human form, sweat dripping from her silver hair. She shook her head with annoyance, but conceded.

The members of the Sky Guard, who had been watching them all the while, applauded as Darien helped Valeria to her feet. Her skin was hot to the touch, and he longed to feel her touch for longer. Since the night before the Battle of Gods and Monsters, when she had first kissed him, his desire had only increased, and it was driving him mad. He longed to find a secluded place, the weaponry or a narrow stairwell, and steal another momentary taste of their forbidden, intoxicating romance.

Instead, Commander Redvar turned to his soldiers and sheathed his sword. Valeria left his side and joined the others. Darien turned off his emotions, as he so often found himself required to do, and became a stern military leader. "Why was I able to defeat Captain Sardona?" he said, addressing his Sky Guard.

A Conjuri named Lesa spoke up. "She was the first to recover her descent, Commander. You dared it longer."

"That's part of it," said Darien. Lesa was from his own homeland, and she was showing much promise.

"She didn't anticipate your attack," said Jann, Darien's young protege. "We must always be anticipating our opponent's next move."

"True, but that is not the heart of it."

"Captain Sardona put herself in a position where she was not in control." The answer came from beyond the group. Dressed in a wispy cream-colored gown, Vashti Burodai crossed the field to join the soldiers.

"We are honored to have you join us, my queen," said Darien, crossing his right arm across his chest in salute.

Vashti drew to the front of the crowd and nodded to him in greeting. "Don't be hasty, Commander. My wedding is not for several weeks."

"Of course not. To what do we owe this honor, milady?"

"I was watching your demonstration for some time," said the queen-to-be. "Captain Sardona fought beautifully. She matched your every move. But you let up slightly in your final descent. The captain was put in a situation where she was forced to make the first move, and you seized that moment."

"A soldier's observation, milady," said Darien.

Vashti hinted a smile. "It is a good lesson to teach them, Commander. Even magic can become a crutch."

"The queen speaks wise words," Darien said to his soldiers. "Remember them well. Flight can be a great advantage in battle, but only if you do not let it rule you. Be careful not to depend on your magic. Use it as a tool, not a necessity. Now, pair up for sparring drills."

The Morphs donned their human forms, and the Watchers refrained from using their magical gifts. Darien thought it best they not associate their battle skills with magic. He had seen the weakness of the Watchers without their powers. They were little more than cattle as the Legions had herded them through the catacombs beneath the Crooked Teeth, but here, under his tutelage, they would become true warriors.

The training grounds filled with the beautiful clash of swords, and Darien watched his soldiers intently, walking amongst them, observing their form, offering suggestions for improvement, as General Thrain had once done for him, not so long ago. It was several minutes before Darien realized that Vashti Burodai had not left them. She stood at the edge of the field with arms crossed.

Darien commanded his soldiers to take to the air. They formed two groups and began practicing attack maneuvers, this time without swords. They weaved through the air, assuming battle formations, attacking the opposing group, and then banking to miss their opponents by the mere breadth of a hand. They were coming along well. The Sky Guard had been thrust, too soon, into battle against the Rulaqs, but it had worked for the best. The Morphs and Watchers had been forced to work together, despite their bitter pasts, and they had been unified by a common enemy. The Rulaqs were subdued, and Osha was more unified than ever.

As Darien observed his soldiers from below, Vashti Burodai made her way to his side.

"My queen."

"I hope you don't mind me watching, Commander."

"Milady, you are welcome on these grounds any time you like. In a few weeks, your word will command them. We are honored to have you."

"I never thought I'd see the day that Watchers and Morphs would fight side by side."

Darien nodded. "It is an age of many surprises in the New World."

Vashti mused for a moment, watching her former comrades train. "They look good, Commander. You are training them well."

"You're too kind, milady."

Though she tried to hide it, Darien could tell the queen-to-be enjoyed his formal pleasantries. Vashti retrieved a dull sparring blade from the ground and shifted it between her hands.

"You may join them in their drills, if you wish," Darien said. "You have the mind of a soldier. I'd wager it pairs with a soldier's skill."

Vashti's lips creased with a subdued smile. She toyed with the blade, and Darien could tell by her grip that she knew her way with sabers. She tossed it upon the ground. "Perhaps another day. I am sorry for stealing your time, Commander. I should not distract your training."

"A queen is never a distraction."

"Yes, well, thank you, Commander." She turned and began to cross the field, her gown fluttering in the wind.

Darien was not sure what compelled him, but he called after her. "You made the right decision, my queen." She turned to him. "At the Watchtower. You saved them. Your old comrades know it too."

Vashti paused for a moment, then turned back and nodded to him. "Thank you, Commander Redvar."

And Vashti left them.

The Sky Guard soon returned to the earth, and Darien dismissed them to wash and prepare for supper. As his sorcerers retreated to their bathhouses in the guardtower, Darien made his way to his own private room. He ascended the steps slowly, his thoughts now able to unravel. A few weeks of peace, and he was already anticipating when they would begin their hunt for the Gallows Girl. Now that the Rulaqs had been overcome, he suspected it would be any day. He had already sent out scouts, so far without luck. He considered returning to the Teeth, trying to locate where Tori had emerged from the catacombs, though all tracks would certainly be long lost now in autumn snows. But there might be other signs.

It would have to be a Morph hunting party, he knew that much. He did not trust the turned Watchers enough yet. Especially not since the queen had asked for Tori's death as a wedding present. He pushed the thought away. Thoughts of Tori were confusing and only filled him with anger and regret.

As he reached for the door to his quarters, it flew open, and he was accosted from the other side.

A woman pulled him in and shoved him up against the wall, a blade at his mouth. Then, she replaced the blade with her lips, and Darien forgot all thoughts of Tori.

Valeria's kiss was soft and warm, and she tasted of sweat, which was an oddly alluring taste. Her body pressed against him, still clad in her leathern armor. How had she managed to beat him up here? It did not matter. He savored the moment, letting his mind fall into the abyss of her presence. But as with all their moments, this one did not last long.

Since the Battle of Gods and Monsters, she had not again come to his estate. Of course, Darien saw Valeria in the citadel regularly, and daily in the training fields, but he could appear as nothing but a comrade. He was her superior, after all. It pained him to be so close, and yet to feel such distance between them. His skin tingled as she pulled away from him.

"You're not falling for the queen, I hope," Valeria said with a sly smile.

Darien laughed. "Hardly."

"Good," said Valeria, pulling off her leathern armor. "I don't want to be tried for regicide."

Darien kissed her again. She bit his bottom lip playfully. "We can't have that. I don't want to have to hunt you down for regicide."

Valeria pulled away. "Ever my honorable comrade. What did the queen want?"

"I think she missed training for war."

"Don't blame her. I would go crazy locked up in a palace all day."

"I offered for her to join the exercises."

"Really?"

"The chancellor goes to war. Why not his queen?"

"If she does train with us, let me spar with her." There was a sparkle in Valeria's eyes that Darien wished he could enjoy for hours rather than such brief moments.

Gods, she is breathtaking. But Darien felt a twinge of guilt again. She was a comrade. "She might beat you," he teased. "She saw through my maneuver."

"Please," said Valeria. "I let you win."

Darien grinned and kissed her again.

There was a sudden shuffling from the stairs beyond, and Darien quickly moved behind his desk, where maps of Osha were spread, and he and Valeria feigned studying them as the intruder entered. Even in their lies, they were in sync. Captain Sardona was pointing to a spot on the coast of Greater Osha, commenting on the terrain and logistical advantages for a new tower, when young Jann appeared at the door.

"Er, my apologies, Commander, if I am interrupting."

Darien waved nonchalantly. "Not at all, lad. What is it?"

Jann eyed Valeria with a querulous look, only briefly, and then locked eyes with his commander. "Er, the chancellor has summoned you, sir. Some Watchers just arrived from Vlyanii. They want to join the Sky Guard."

———

DARIEN AND VALERIA LEFT HIS CHAMBERS. HE ORDERED DAJHA AND a Morph named Sade to join them in welcoming the new recruits. Sade had served beneath Commander Scelero for years. He was a veteran from the magic-hunting days of the Metamorphi, before Cyrus Maro ascended the Oshan throne. Dajha Bhati had shown more potential than any other Watcher. He was talented and motivated, and the other Watchers looked to him for guidance as they navigated this new world in Maro'El. Valeria joined as well, for she was his right hand in the Guard.

They donned their formal uniforms and, together, marched from the training grounds and reached the White Citadel before the autumn sun began its early descent. The nights would be growing longer by the day, and come winter, they would have only a few hours of daylight in which to train.

The chancellor welcomed them in his throne room. The shimmering crystal palace was not empty, as was usual for Darien's meetings with the chancellor. Cyrus Maro sat his throne and Vashti stood at his side. Medea stood below the throne, at the base of the steps, wearing her customary dark silks. Several members of the High Council were seated at the front of the hall: Wallis, Dragonis, Fedra, and the others. The Morphs on palace duty for the evening lined the halls and quietly stood at the ready. This was apparently no private matter of the Sky Guard.

Darien and his comrades bowed before the crystal throne, and the chancellor bade them rise.

"These new Yan Avii recruits," said Darien, glancing around the room and spying no new faces. "Who are they?"

The chancellor smiled. "Salla Burodai sent a company of Ilya to see to Vashti's wedding preparations. Or perhaps I should say, Sheva Zora." The chancellor made light of the feigned name.

At this, he took his bride-to-be's hand, and she smiled. But Darien sensed it was slightly forced. He supposed most marriages amongst nobles were for power and influence, rather than love or attraction. But Darien knew the smile of desire. Valeria's smile lingered in his mind as he lay in bed, even in his dreams. He doubted that Vashti's smile had a similar effect on the chancellor.

"Since the princess was technically executed by her father, years ago," said the chancellor, "Salla has asked that his sister be known by another name. It would not do for her to apparently rise from the dead. Superstitious nonsense, if you ask me."

He seemed to say this for the benefit of the council, for Darien noted the way he glanced in their direction as he spoke. Several council members had been displeased when the chancellor announced his bride after the victory over the Rulaqs. There had never been a non-Oshan queen in the White Citadel, let alone a Yan Avii one. Darien thought it more likely they were angry their own daughters had lost their chance at seducing him.

But Cyrus Maro was favored amongst the people after his Darkling Witch saved the city, and so Darien only heard of the council members' qualms through rumors. Still, the chancellor seemed to be trying to please them.

Vashti remained stoic, despite her fiancee's insult to her people's beliefs.

The chancellor went on. "So it seems I am marrying the daughter of another chieftain, by name. But it is no matter. It seals Salla's loyalties. And I get to marry my lovely desert flower."

Vashti smiled at this and whispered sweetly, "You are most gracious, Chancellor Maro." It was clear she knew her way around the pleasantries of court as well as she did sabers.

"As for the new recruits, I will not spoil the surprise." The chancellor gestured to the guards standing at the immense crystal doors. "Now that the commander has arrived, the High Council is ready to receive the emissaries from the Steppe."

Four guards slowly pushed the great doors open, and the company from Vlyanii entered. Darien's interest was piqued when he realized who followed Ashi Burodai, the Great Soltayne's head servant, into the room.

He recognized them both immediately. A couple months ago, Valeria had assumed Kirra Fehn's likeness in the Red City while Salla concocted his devious ascent to the Yan Avii throne, and the other Watcher was Kale Andovier, former lordling of Maro'El and brother of the Watcher captain currently locked beneath the citadel.

Darien and his comrades stood at the base of the chancellor's dais to receive the new recruits. Four Yan Avii tribesmen accompanied Ashi and her Watchers. Salla's devoted Ilya assassins, Darien presumed. All seven of the company bowed before the throne.

The chancellor bade them rise. "Friends of Soltayne Burodai, welcome to Maro'El."

Ashi was the first to speak. "Thank you for receiving us, milord. We come with dark tidings from the Red City."

"It was with sorrow that we heard that the bane of your people has returned," said the chancellor evenly.

"Our city lies in ruins, Chancellor Maro, and our winter stores with it. My people seek aid from our ally."

"You are not alone in this devastation," said the chancellor, who caught the furtive glances of the council members in the room. "My city is in disrepair as well."

"Milord, with respect, your empire still stands. My people are without a home. Half our herds were in Vlyanii, and more than half our stores. Thousands of souls were lost. If you do not help us, thousands more will die this winter. I ask that you remember my chief's loyalty. Remember how he ended a war before it began, while you were yet weary from your own war with the Morgathians. Remember his aid in your own endeavors."

"I remember well Salla's loyalty. He is an ally Osha wishes to keep." The chancellor spoke these words more to his council than to Ashi, his eyes stern and his voice firm. "The High Lords will send aid to Pendra, where your people will be offered sanctuary until such time as you are able to rebuild your city."

Ashi bowed, a grim smile on her face. "Thank you, milord. You are most gracious. I will send word to my chief. My tribesmen and I, however, wish to stay and assist our princess's preparations for the great union of our peoples."

"You are most welcome in Maro'El. I will have quarters arranged for you all here in the White Citadel," said the chancellor with a wave of his hand. "But you bring two who are not your tribesmen, I believe. What of them?"

Kirra and Kale stepped forward. "We have come to bow the knee," said Kirra, who Darien noted moved a little unsteadily as she reached for the floor to kneel. He remembered well the injuries she had sustained from the chancellor's manipulation of her Lumeni power. The scars were still fresh on her face. Her eyes flitted about but did not settle on the chancellor as she spoke.

Blind, Darien realized.

The chancellor smiled and gestured to Darien, who stepped forward.

Kale and Kirra stood once more, remaining silent as Darien looked them over.

"Milady, you do not look well since our last encounter," said Darien. "Your partner had a little more sense, then, as I recall."

Kirra grimaced, her fists tightening, but she caught herself and remained silent. Darien made note of the reaction.

"We have both learned our lesson well, Commander," said Kale. "We regret our rebellion against the empire. We have aided Osha before, and we would do it again."

"We have come to offer our services in your Sky Guard," said Kirra.

"And what good do you suppose a blind wielder of light would do for my Guard?" said Darien coldly.

Kirra tensed again, but this time she did not remain silent. "It is true my gift is useless now, but I have gained another."

Darien's brows rose at this. "Really?"

Ashi interjected. "It is true, milord. Her Sonora magic was what saved my people from complete annihilation in the Red City. Kirra heard Xa'Rila approaching, allowing our Great Soltayne and many others to escape before the beasts consumed the city."

"Interesting," said Darien.

"Salla has personally vouched for their loyalty," said Ashi. "In exchange for their Watcher gifts, Salla asks that you consider restoring Kirra's sight."

Darien looked to the chancellor, but an idea had already come to him. "It is true that one of the Watcher healers might be able to accomplish this, though your wounds are far along in healing."

Kirra nodded. "All I ask is that they try, Commander."

"Sonora have their uses, but your Lumeni gift is an incredible one," said Darien. "It is one I would value greatly in the Guard. I would like to see your gift restored as well, but first, I must have proof of your loyalties."

Kale Andovier crossed his arm against his chest in salute. "We will be yours to command, sir."

"I am glad to hear it," said Darien. "Because you're the one who will be demonstrating your loyalties. I have a task for you, Lord Andovier. Should you complete it satisfactorily, I will have Kirra's sight restored, and you will both serve the empire as the chancellor sees fit."

Kale did not answer at once. He and Kirra conferred briefly, but Darien could tell that, though they were joining his Guard together, there was tension between them. Kirra's face tightened whenever Kale spoke.

Finally Kirra turned to him. She faced him directly, despite her lack of sight. "We are yours to command."

CHAPTER TWENTY-SEVEN

Kale Andovier hated Maro'El. He hated the people with their haughty expressions and finely woven garb. He hated the slender, curved architecture, the way the towers of the nobles' estates glowed all across the city at night, and the imposing magnificence of the White Citadel. But mostly he hated the memories, and himself.

He had not set foot in Maro'El since his youth, since he fled for his life and took the path of the Exiled Lord, abandoning his mother in order to save his own skin. Of course, he could not have saved her. If he had stayed in Osha, they both would have perished, but he hated himself all the same.

It was in the grand city of his boyhood that he discovered his Watcher abilities. And it was his own indiscretions using them that inevitably led to his mother's execution, and to the eventual demise of House Andovier.

Kale stood on a balcony halfway up the towering citadel and looked out over the city, letting the memories plague him.

Kirra's quarters were next door, and he wished he could talk to her, but they had barely spoken a word since they'd left the city of Pendra. He did not know what to do. She had pledged their allegiance to the chancellor, and Kale longed to tell her this was madness. He longed to tell her of Lazarus Delahi and the Saints of the North. Somewhere in this city, the old sorcerer was secretly directing a rebellion that needed their help. And he did not know what to do.

He feared they had walked straight into a mire. This city would be the death of them both. The more they tangled themselves in the schemes of the players in this game, the more harm they might cause.

But what else could they do?

All the Watchers were here. Ren and Vonn and a few others remained in the dungeons beneath the White Citadel. Meanwhile, Dajha Bhati was one of the rising leaders amongst the Sky Guard, and many of the others had joined as well. Perhaps they were sincere in their treachery, or perhaps they were biding their time. It didn't matter. The chancellor was bending them all slowly to his will, and the thought made Kale sick.

But Kirra did not trust him. For he had been the one who had begun this progression. And until he knew what was truly going on with the Saints of the North, he could not risk telling her, or anyone. He was not sure it was worth the risk at all.

If he went down the path of rebellion, he would put an end to any hope Kirra had of regaining her sight. And he might very well get them both killed, maybe the others as well. Including his brother.

And for what? The chancellor was stronger than ever. Magic had returned to the world without the Shadow Watch, and any hope stirred up previously by the Gallows Girl had surely been quenched after the chancellor used magic to save the city. Astoria Burodai was said to be to blame, and from what he had gathered during the past week traveling across Osha, the people were happy to believe that *shenzah*.

According to Nyla, before the war with the Rulaqs, the Saints of the North had been gaining influence amongst the lowborns. Uprisings had stirred up across the empire, but there had been no activity since the Battle of Gods and Monsters.

If he joined them, he might kill everyone he loved for nothing. Still, something about the idea tugged at him. *What is Lazarus up to in this wretched city? And how in the Abyss is he the one leading this rebellion? How is he even alive?*

The old sorcerer had once taught him that, despite his mother's tragic death, his gifts were not a curse. Kale had discovered the beauty of his magic under the man's tutelage. Kale had believed, then, that he had been given his gifts for the purpose of bringing magic back to the world. He had helped Lazarus gather the Watchers that formed the commune on the Isle of Jallaa, and Lazarus had led him to Kirra.

And somehow, the man had returned from the dead. According to the nightling, he had truly risen from the dead, which made no sense. But nevertheless, he wanted to see Kale. Nyla had said that Lazarus would find him once they were in Maro'El, but there was little time now.

The Gallows Boy had plans for Kale to show his loyalty. He would report to Commander Redvar tomorrow, and Kale feared that once they stepped into the world of the Sky Guard, there might be no going back. Their fates, and the fates of all the Watchers, might be ensnared in the chancellor's schemes.

Kale made his decision. He leapt from the window and landed softly, with a flare of magic, in the courtyard hundreds of feet below. The Morphs no longer hunted sorcerers, and Kale was a member of the Sky Guard now, so why shouldn't he use his gifts?

He set out into the heart of the city, unsure exactly where to go. Everywhere he went, memories plagued him, particularly near the central sectors of the Oshan capital. The estates of nobles towered over the streets near the White Citadel, homes of lordlings with whom he had grown up, attended noble academies, played the courtier. It had only been eight years, but it felt like many lifetimes ago.

Kale wandered past the mansions, through the central square, and beyond to the lesser markets in the western parts of the city. Maro'El was in disrepair, but it would soon be grander than ever, Kale had no doubt. Slave crews were laboring by the light of immense fires to rebuild the ruined streets and buildings. In mere weeks since the devastation, the districts surrounding the citadel were already in remarkable shape.

Near the western walls, though, the city was largely in shambles. The walls themselves bore giant crevasses where the Rulaqs had broken into the city. The buildings in the old West Wall trading district were in ruins. But there was one nighthouse that lit up the night like a beacon drawing lost sea vessels to a better place. Patrons' laughter echoed from within, the minds of bawdy men and women filled Kale's sense, and a ramshackle sign hung over the curtained front door: The Tamed Beast.

It was no match for the Scarlet Lace of Kale's youth, and likely had never been so fine, even before the devastation of the Rulaqs, but a pair of beautiful nightlings in emerald gowns stood at the steps and ushered people into the run-down building. Kale nodded to them as he entered.

A minstrel played jovially within. Nightlings danced seductively in scanty clothing from a stage at the center of the room, and patrons howled in drunken pleasure. Kale found a seat near the back of the room, ordered an ale, and waited.

He hated these establishments, but he supposed a run-down joint like this would be the best place to look for someone connected to Lazarus Delahi. He reached out with his mind for thoughts directed at him, but the room was a muddle of lust and drunken stupors. He kept expecting someone to approach him, to notice who he was, maybe even sneak him another slip of paper with that treacherous gallows symbol.

But the nightlings hardly paid him any mind. When it became clear he was not looking for a journey to the upstairs rooms, the nightlings began avoiding his corner completely. He noted their scathing glances from afar. He was taking a seat away from a more profitable patron.

An hour passed, and no one came. The frivolities increased. The dancers reached greater degrees of undress as the night went on.

Another hour, and still no one approached Kale.

It was near midnight, and the tavern was filled to the brim with men and women, merchers and small house lordlings, even a few lowborns—estate managers and guards, most likely. People pressed into all corners of the place, and their minds became a weight on Kale's sense, but still, no one came. More than a few eyed his table, which bore nothing but an empty mug, but he kept his hood up, glared, and they moved on.

At last, a beautiful Oshan woman in a fine, and not quite as revealing gown—who Kale suspected was the mistress of the establishment—approached from across the room. Kale had noted her gaze on more than one occasion. Perhaps this was the informant he was looking for.

Her sardonic voice informed him she was not. "Look here, lordling. We don't cater to loiterers. You been here for hours, and you've not bought company nor a bed."

"I bought a drink," said Kale.

"Aye, and your mug's been warm and empty for two hours. My girls say you rejected their advances as well as their offers for another mug. You're making them nervous."

"I'm a paying customer. What's it matter?"

"You're a waste of space, lordling. This is the only nighthouse in the West Wall that survived the war, and in a few weeks, more taverns will be popping back up, and it will be business as usual. Far as I'm concerned, this is our chance to roll in this opportunity. And you're hurting my gods-damned business. Four gents could sit in this corner, and you're back here making my patrons wary, just by your brooding face. Now, you can make a choice. You can purchase a tumble in the sheets, and keep the drinks coming, or you can find someone else's tavern to mope around in."

A pair of immense guards came and joined the mistress, and Kale took the hint. "All right, all right. I'm leaving."

Kale cursed and exited the Tamed Beast. He left the West Wall and was wending his way south toward the more refined Merching district, sticking to narrower, less traveled lanes, when a sudden hand grabbed his cloak and pulled him into the shadows.

It was Nyla.

"What in the Abyss were you thinking showing your face in a place like that?"

Kale was impressed with her strength for someone so small. Lazarus was training her well. "What are *you* doing in Maro'El?"

Nyla grinned slyly. "I followed you here. Lazarus owns most of the establishments along the South Road, so we're able to travel easily between Oshan cities. You were supposed to wait until he's ready to see you. It's all over the city that a company of Yan Avii arrived with recruits for the Sky Guard. And with a long-lost member of the Cursed House of Andovier."

"Really?"

"You've been away from court a long time, haven't you, lordling?"

Kale rolled his eyes. "I need to see Lazarus, now."

"Can't happen. The Hangman doesn't show his face on demand. It's too risky."

Kale cursed. "If he wants anything from me, it will have to be now. I report to Commander Redvar tomorrow morning for a special mission."

Nyla was silent a moment. She blocked him from her mind, but her silence was enough. "So soon?"

"He wants me to prove my loyalty. I've a feeling the chancellor plans to use my Cerebro abilities for his schemes again."

"The queen's wedding gift," Nyla mused. "They're going to use you to find the Gallows Girl."

Kale nodded. "The commander never said it outright, but I suspect that is his intention. So now would be an excellent time for Lazarus to tell me what he wants."

"Gods damn it," Nyla muttered. Then, without another word, she turned and walked away, making for the end of the lane.

"What are you doing?"

Nyla turned, her movements soft and fluid. "Come along, Kale. Keep close and shut up. I'll take you to see your old master."

The nightling led Kale to the edge of the Merching district. Though it was not a district for high nobles, outwardly there was little difference. The higher merchers lived like nobles. Some were from lower houses, but many were foreigners and lowborns who struck fortune in trade. Kale guessed the most successful were those who dealt in human fare.

The high estates of the district sat on a hill, which was walled off from the lesser parts of the city. The area appeared to have been untouched in the recent war. The estates were made of marble, with high towers and windows made of magnificent stained glass.

"Thought you'd find Laz in the back of a nighthouse, did you?" Nyla said bemusedly. She giggled to herself, and again, Kale was struck with how young the girl was.

"How old are you?"

"What's it matter?"

"Have it your way."

"You're no fun. You give up too easily." She giggled again. "If I were a noble, I'd have just come of age."

"Gods."

"What?" Nyla asked disdainfully. "Do I look younger?"

"Er, no, I just… you've been through much for your age."

The nightling shrugged. "Who hasn't?"

They approached one of the finest mansions in the district. A wall hid most of it from view. Nyla led them around the back of the estate, and they slipped in through a small gate, which required a key Nyla kept round her neck. They crossed a vast lawn, which was still green despite the cooling weather. They entered by a servant's passage.

In the great room, a bald Jurkan man was seated in a large chair beside an intricately crafted stone hearth. He was unfamiliar, but seemed to recognize Kale, for he jumped to his feet upon their entrance, a smile stretching wide. "Welcome, my friend."

Kale eyed the man warily. "Do I know you?"

"Ah, my apologies. I sometimes forget that I once bore a different body back on the Isle of Jallaa."

"A different…" The voice possessed a different timbre, but Kale recognized it all the same. "Lazarus?"

The old man nodded. Though he did not appear old any longer. His olive skin showed a few wrinkles, but otherwise, he had the lean body of a middle-aged Jurkan man. He laughed, and Kale knew the bubbling brook sound anywhere. He had heard that laugh for three years during his days in the Far East.

Kale and Lazarus clasped shoulders in greeting. "I… saw you die," Kale said.

Lazarus laughed. "So you did. So you did."

"How are you here? Was that even you who died when the Morphs attacked?" There was an edge to his voice. He felt like a fool. He had beaten himself up for years over the events on the Isle of Jallaa, all the innocent young Watchers who died, and here was the most prominent of them, back from the dead.

Nyla came to stand by the man's side, and Lazarus smiled. "Of course it was me, Kale."

"What of the others?" he said hopefully.

Lazarus's smile waned. "I am sorry, Kale. All were lost but me. And you and Kirra, it seems."

"How… I don't understand."

"I barely understand it myself, so I would not expect you to, my son."

There was a time when being called this by Lazarus Delahi would have filled Kale with a sort of pride. But he had been young and naïve when the old Watcher first recruited him. Kale was not that same impressionable young man. "Try me."

"All right… As I said, I do not fully understand it. But I will tell you what I know. Long ago, I received a strange gift. I did not realize it until I died the first time. Firsts are always the most memorable, and that goes for resurrections too."

Lazarus paused, perhaps waiting for a laugh from Kale. He did not laugh.

"It was before the Watchers first formed their orders. I was killed by a vile man bent on resurrecting a ruined empire. He betrayed me. I remember the hate in his eyes as he slit my throat. His image faded as my mind went black. I woke up sometime later, with no pain. I did not realize I had woken in a new body until my mother came to wake me. My mother had been dead for some years. And this woman looked nothing like her, and yet I knew she was my mother.

"Every time I die, I awake in a new life. Sometimes as a child, sometimes as an old man, sometimes as a young woman, even. I carry my old memories, and I gain those of my host. When I died on Jallaa, I woke as the slave of an Oshan lord."

"You've come far from that, haven't you?" said Kale, gesturing about the fine room.

"Indeed, I have," said Lazarus. "But all this, you should know, is but a facade."

"They call you the Hangman. Leader of the Saints of the Gallows Girl."

"That is what they call me, yes."

"Your little rebellion seems to be in shambles, from what I hear." The man's calm spirit annoyed him, and Kale sought to stir a rise from him. But without luck.

"And what do you hear?" Lazarus said without emotion.

"The people, even the lowborns, blame the Gallows Girl for the Rulaq attack, and for all these other foul beasts who've returned to haunt our world."

"And do you believe them?"

"No," said Kale evenly. "But it doesn't matter."

"It's all that matters. You believe the truth. And as long as there are some that do, there is hope."

"The people once put their hope in Astoria Burodai. But she has not been seen in months. The chancellor and his Darkling Witch, however, are fixed firmly in their memory."

Lazarus sighed and nodded. "You speak truth, Kale. You have never been one for foolish talk. It is a trait I have always admired in you."

"You wish to recruit my help. But it seems to me, I would be signing my own death warrant, and for what?"

Lazarus turned to Nyla. "My dear, would you have Harl and Juri ready my carriage?"

The nightling smiled sweetly at him and left. It was clear that she admired him a great deal. Kale had too, once.

"That's it?" said Kale. "You're not going to try to persuade me?"

Lazarus shook his head. "It seems your mind is already made."

Kale grimaced. It ought to be made, but there was still a part of him that wanted to know what Lazarus had planned.

Lazarus walked toward the door. "But if there is any part of you that wonders whether there is still hope for revolution, I would invite you to accompany me on a brief expedition. There is something I'd like to show you."

"I report to the Sky Guard in the morning."

"Well, it will only take a few hours. And as I recall, you have never been one for beauty rest."

Kale cracked a smile. "All right. Show me."

CHAPTER TWENTY-EIGHT

Kale and Lazarus rode through the dark streets of Maro'El in an ebony coach made of sleek balak wood from the southern world. The plush seats were extraordinarily comfortable, and the ride was smooth. Kale marveled at the finery his old master had accrued while being a revolutionary. This fact did not make him feel better about this revolution. While Lazarus Delahi lived in a mansion and rode carriages pulled by finely bred horses, his revolution was crumbling.

But Kale's judgment was softened shortly. They only rode a few blocks before they switched coaches beneath a bridge at the edge of the Merching district. This coach was run-down and rattled terribly as they left the city and crossed the Meridian bridge east of the capital.

"The Fringes?" said Kale as they ventured south, then west along Citadel Road.

"If you spend all your time with highborns, you will see the world only as highborns see it," said Lazarus. "Though I have strategically climbed the social strata of Maro'El, as much as any non-Oshan is able to climb, I have never forgotten where I came from. When I died on Jallaa, I woke a slave here. I spent two years in the Fringes, and I never go a week without returning for fear I might grow comfortable amongst the highborns."

"Comfortable?"

"It is how the system works in Osha. It is the reason the Legion indoctrination works so well. Soldiers are given glory and prestige beyond anything they have received as a slave. But rather than using that position to institute change, they become mindless servants, pacified by pleasures that ought to be granted to all people. It is the reason so few servants in Maro'El rise up. They come from this hellhole. Even servitude seems a mercy in the city."

Lazarus pulled back the curtains so Kale could see the grimy streets and ramshackle buildings as they rumbled past.

"I've seen the Fringes before," said Kale.

"Yes, but have you seen the people of the Fringes?"

Kale had last been here the day he and Ren had rescued Astoria from the Metamorphi. He had only come one other time in his life—the day he fled Maro'El for good. Of course, he had heard tales of the wretched lowborns while growing up in Maro'El. They swarmed at the edges of civilization like flies over rotten meat. He had been taught to believe they were a sort of necessary evil. Some could still serve the empire. Some might even rise above their station. But they were not Oshan. They could never contribute the way a noble could. During his years in exile, he'd forgotten most of the *shenzah* he was taught in his youth, but in truth, he had never given the Fringe rats much thought.

Kale gazed out at the bleak shantytown illuminated by the pale light of the Sisters. Few people wandered the streets at night for fear of being mugged or worse over coppers or stale food. "I see them."

"What do you see?" Lazarus asked him.

"People downtrodden and mistreated by the rich. Worked and starved to death serving an empire that rules over them with an iron fist and an inescapable hierarchy."

Lazarus smiled, but shook his head. "Then you have not seen the Fringe rats at all, my son."

Kale raised a brow. The carriage came to a stop, and Lazarus stepped out. Kale followed. The dark street was empty, save for the rubbish and excrement that lined most Fringe lanes. Lazarus pulled up his hood and led the way. They wended between shanties and jagged stone walls, lined with shattered glass to keep thieves from climbing over into the Fringe factories and storehouses. They approached a small square, but Lazarus paused midstep and shoved Kale up against a wall, covering his mouth. He held his finger over his lips as he released him, then pointed behind them. Fear crept into Kale's gut. He could not afford to be spotted with a revolutionary. This was a grave mistake, just as he'd feared.

They remained perfectly still, clinging to the shadows cast by the moonlight. After a minute or two, Kale heard soft footsteps. It was not a soldier, but rather a cloaked figure who moved slowly and methodically down the lanes from the direction they had come, keeping close to the walls. Lazarus pressed his hand against Kale's chest, and he held his breath.

The figure was slender and stepped lightly. A woman. She came within ten yards and froze, turning her head back and forth. She was almost certainly following them, but had they been spotted?

Kale reached out with his sense, but the mind was closed to him. *No one but a Morph or one of the Ilya has such training.* Kale shuddered to think what might happen if either the chancellor or Salla discovered him with the Hangman.

He reached for his blade.

The figure crept forward again.

It would have to be quick.

Kale tensed, anticipation rushing through him. The stalker did not seem to sense them, continuing her path along the wall. Ten feet. Five feet.

Kale and Lazarus rushed forward, seizing the stalker unaware. Kale pinned his arm around her neck, and Laz pressed his blade against her temple. She cried out, and that was when Kale recognized her.

"Ashi?"

Kale spun her around so he could see her face in the moonlight. She opened her mind to Kale, and he knew she was no Morph in disguise. He eased his hold, but Lazarus kept his blade at the ready.

"Ashi, what are you doing here?" Kale demanded. "You've been watching me?"

The Ilya woman nodded, shrugging away his grip annoyedly. "Since we left Pendra."

"Why?"

"Because I asked her to," said an unmistakable voice.

Kirra moved toward them, her hand tracing the walls lining the lane for guidance. "When you went to the nighthouse, something felt wrong. You've changed much since the days we first met, but I could not believe you would consort with nightlings for pleasure."

"I feared you were meeting with the chancellor's spies," said Ashi.

"So we watched you. What are you doing in the Fringes, Kale?"

"I brought him here, Kirra," said Lazarus.

"I… I know that voice."

"I would hope so. You would not have met Kale without me."

"Lazarus? How is that possible?"

Lazarus explained it for her. Ashi listened in silence. Kirra listened with the amazement expected when an old friend returns from the dead. When Lazarus had finished, he turned to Kale and whispered, "The Yan Avii woman, can she be trusted?"

Kale eyed the Ilya woman. The obvious answer was "no," but there had always been something different about Ashi.

"And if I cannot be trusted?" Ashi interjected. "What then? Will your Saints dispose of me?"

Lazarus chuckled with dark amusement. "Should we dispose of you?"

Ashi drew near, holding the revolutionary's gaze. "You're here to show Kale the hope of a revolution. Well, as far as I can see, the truth of that hope affects me as much as him or Kirra. I hold no love for the chancellor either."

"Your Great Soltayne is pledged to Cyrus Maro," said Kale.

"So are you," said Ashi. "Do not underestimate Salla, Sky Blood. Convince me of a better alliance, if you believe it exists. I do what is best for my people, and thus far, this alliance with Osha has only brought destruction."

Lazarus scowled. He had still not sheathed his blade.

"I trust her," said Kirra.

Lazarus looked to Kale. He did not speak immediately. Much could ride on this decision. But since he'd first met Ashi, Kale had sensed something about her. She was a slave, and he could sense a buried anger surfacing at what had been done to her people. "She can be trusted," Kale said at last.

Lazarus stowed his blade and nodded. "Very well. Follow me. It's not much farther."

They wended down several run-down lanes. Kirra held on to Kale's forearm for support, and it felt good to be near her again, but he was still wary of Ashi. Kirra gripped his hand, and she opened her mind to him.

I trust her, Kale.

They reached a large square in the southern Fringes and froze. Kale could sense the rage welling up in Ashi's mind.

"What is that smell?" Kirra whispered.

Kale described the sight. At the center of the square, three tall poles of snowpine jutted into the air, each sharpened to a spear-like point.

Impaled upon them were two men and a woman, stripped naked, their skin pocked and eye sockets vacant from the feasting of crows. The poles pierced their rectums and emerged at the neck or skull. The corpses were swollen and gruesome, coated in grime and dried blood.

Lazarus led them closer, and Kale recognized a familiar symbol etched upon their bare chests. The same gallows that had been scrawled on the parchment Nyla had given him in Pendra.

Lazarus looked up at the bodies, staring at their expressions of agony, which had been frozen with their deaths. A stake emerged from the woman's mouth like a striking serpent. The rotting stench filled the square. Lazarus's expression turned deeply solemn as he gazed up.

Kale swallowed back bile.

Ashi covered her mouth, her entire body tense. "W-what did they do?"

Lazarus did not answer right away. He looked up at the boy on the right stake. He was Jurkan, barely a man grown.

"They resisted," Lazarus whispered. "These poor souls were not starving beggars. They were not weak. They were not desperate. They were fierce warriors, braver than most found on any battlefield in the New World. They were Saints. While those living in comfort sang the praises of the chancellor and his Darkling Witch, they clung to hope."

Lazarus stepped closer. "There are still Saints remaining in Osha. There is still hope."

Ashi shook her head. "You call this hope?"

Lazarus grimaced, but said nothing. He touched the foot of the boy on the stake, only briefly, then stepped back.

Ashi had spoken true. Kale did not see hope when he looked at the poor corpses. He saw the futility of resistance. He saw the scars on Kirra's face. He saw Dajha and the others who had joined the Sky Guard, rather than face such a horrific fate.

Was this all Lazarus had to show them? A few executed rebels? This was no inspiration. This was a needless slaughter. It was just as Kale had imagined. There had been many reported uprisings since the day of the Gallows, and they had all been crushed. And those had all contained much greater threats than these three.

Kale shook his head, irritated that he had risked his and Kirra's lives to come see how fruitless this resistance was. Ashi would never trust them after this. "Lazarus, three dead revolutionaries means nothing."

Lazarus's gaze turned cold. Kale felt as though the light had dimmed.

Lazarus looked back up at the dead boy. "Three died today for the sake of all the others."

"The others?" said Ashi.

"I hear them approaching," said Kirra.

Chills shot up Kale's spine. They were not alone in the Fringe square.

Kale's heart raced as his senses filled with angry minds. From the shadows emerged a pair of dark figures. Three more followed. A dozen others. And more. The square slowly filled with people in ragged cloaks drawn to hide their faces. Fifty at least. Maybe one hundred. They gathered around the impaled corpses in silence. Kirra gripped his hand tight.

Lazarus gazed up at the boy on the spike. He did not turn to them as he spoke. "We Saints have not yet begun to rise."

The Saints silently removed the stakes from the ground, then carefully, almost tenderly, removed them from the bodies of their fallen comrades. The rotting stench grew worse, but the people seemed unfazed. The corpses were wrapped in dark cloths. The emptied stakes were replaced at the center of the square, but not before a young boy attached to each one a black banner emblazoned with a crudely painted gallows symbol.

Cloaked figures bore the martyrs upon their shoulders, and they stole back into the shadows of the Fringes. Within a few minutes, the square was empty, and Kale, Kirra, and Ashi followed Lazarus through the narrow streets.

The Saints took different paths, wending through the Fringes, making their way to a factory at the southern edge of the shanty city. They were among the last to enter.

"What is this place?" Ashi asked.

The expansive room was filled with immense furnaces. Three of them were being stoked with coal and burned brightly. There were no windows. The only evidence of this meeting were the three stacks emitting smoke from the roof, and Kale doubted it was uncommon for factories to run through the night. He had not thought twice about the sight until he saw the gathering within.

"You own this forge?" Kale asked, turning to his old master.

Lazarus shook his head. "This is not just a forge." Lazarus drew his attention to a space at the end. It was lined with sabers and helmets and shields. "Most armories are owned by high nobles. It helps keep weapons out of the hands of the lowborns who craft them. This one happens to belong to a certain noble sympathetic to our cause."

The last of the Saints had arrived. There were even more hooded figures in the room than had been in the square. They gathered around the lit forges, and Lazarus stood upon an anvil to speak.

"Friends, we are here to set to rest three Saints who paid the ultimate price for our revolution. They volunteered for this mission, and through their sacrifice, others were able to seize the precious Morgathian cargo before it reached the capital. So, it is to these three we offer a great debt of gratitude as we return them to the Other."

The crowd uttered a soft prayer. "*Elesa volonai. Menassa elonai. Utlesa sheshonash. Alesa renonash.*"

"What are they saying?" Ashi whispered.

"I've never heard the language before," said Kale. His mother had taught him prayers to the old gods, but this was something different entirely. It was an ancient tongue.

"I think it's from the Old World," Kirra murmured.

"Doesn't sound like any Old Tongue I've ever heard," said Ashi.

Lazarus raised his hands and gazed up to the sky. "May the Other grant our brothers and sister safe passage to the World Beyond. May they be hailed for their bravery, for their hope, for their sacrifice."

There was a second strange utterance. The cadence was reminiscent of the death rituals of the southern world, but this particular burial rite was not from any culture Kale knew. *What is this Other he speaks of? A new god?*

Kale had never heard Lazarus speak of it during his years in Jallaa. But the foreign nature of the ritual did not unnerve him. There was beauty in it. A trio of young girls drew back their hoods and danced an aggressive step around the bodies. All the other Saints chanted softly, like a collective whisper, but the girls moved to the rhythm as though it were a thunderous drum beat.

"*Elesa volonai. Menassa elonai. Utlesa sheshonash. Alesa renonash.*"

Cloaked figures bearing small sacks sprinkled dirt upon the wrapped corpses, then they lifted the bodies and pushed them into the fiery furnaces. The chant grew more intense. The bodies ignited with a quick flash. *The dirt must have been gunpowder.*

The room went silent, everyone watching as the bodies were consumed. No one cried. No one looked away.

When it was done, Lazarus spoke. "Julen, Kevron, and Hesa died in the most honorable way possible. As martyrs. As Saints. And they have been welcomed with honor and glory by the Other into the World Beyond. Tonight, they ride flying steeds in crimson skies. They eat fruits sweeter than any in our own world. They stroll in halls of silver and wear garments made of angel silk. Let us be sure they did not die in vain. The Hellfire Plot has only begun. And soon, the freedom of Saints will be won."

"The freedom of Saints will be won," the Saints echoed softly.

The people dispersed from the place as quickly and as quietly as they'd arrived. Soon, Kale was alone with Lazarus. The fires in the furnaces burned low, but Lazarus stood before one of them in particular. Kale sensed it was the fire that had burned the boy from the stake, the one Lazarus had touched in the square.

"You cared for the boy," said Kale.

"You're in my head," said Lazarus. "Good."

"Who was he?" said Kirra.

"Julen was my son."

"I'm sorry."

"Rather, he was the son of my host. I fathered him only in the years since I left Jallaa. I brought him up, showed him the truth about this world, showed him his potential. Similar to the way I guided you and Kirra and all the others. In a way, I suppose he helped me mourn their deaths. He was a fine boy."

Ashi watched the fire closely. She had not said a word.

"He died well," Kale said.

"Yes, he did… Kale, I cannot tell you how relieved I was when I heard you were not dead. And I am glad to see you, too, Kirra. It saddens me to see what the chancellor has done to you. So tragic for one with your incredible gifts. Even more for the guilt you both carry."

Kirra held on to Kale's arm, and her grip tensed.

"Guilt?" said Kirra.

"For what happened to the others on Jallaa. For what happened to the Watchers in the Crooked Teeth."

Neither of them responded.

"I sense guilt in you as well," said Lazarus, turning to Ashi. She still gazed at the fire. "For what has happened to the Red City."

Ashi merely nodded.

"The First Chancellor rose to power, thinking he was saving the world by putting an end to magic. But the reign of the chancellors has brought nothing but suffering and injustice. And it is time for us to rise up. So, I ask you, do you still believe?"

"In what?" said Kale.

"In hope."

Kirra was the first to speak. "I hope to free the Watchers we failed. They are imprisoned in the White Citadel. If we join your Saints, we may very well condemn them."

"My brother is among them," said Kale.

Lazarus nodded. "And does the fear of what will happen to them sway you as well, Kale?"

"I am swayed by many fears. I regret much that I've done in my life. But more than anything, I wish to right my wrongs."

"For your friends?" Lazarus asked.

"For as many as I can."

"And you, Ashi?"

Ashi turned to him. "I do what is best for my people."

Lazarus looked at the flames that had now consumed his son's body. "Sometimes, a few must be lost so that many may go free."

"Sounds like *shenzah*," Ashi muttered.

Lazarus chuckled. "Most truths do at first, because truth makes us uncomfortable. It is too absolute. Like death."

"I have seen much death in Osha," said Ashi. "I fear what may come of my Soltayne's alliance with the White Citadel. For my people… and for the slaves who labor here as well."

Kale looked his old master in the eyes. "You truly believe your resistance stands a chance?"

"I do. You have seen but a fraction. Our networks are extensive. There are Saints in every city and village in Osha. There are Saints on the chancellor's own High Council."

"Who?" Kale asked.

Lazarus smiled. "Few even in our highest ranks know that."

Kale looked to Kirra. The scars on her face saddened him, but he could sense her desire, and he knew what they must do. He looked to Ashi, and she nodded solemnly.

"What is the Hellfire Plot?" said Kirra.

"And who is this Other?" Ashi asked.

"I'm afraid I won't be giving away all our secrets at once. You must earn such information. You will have to choose, I'm afraid. I cannot heal Kirra's eyes. Few Medicis could. I expect the only one able is the one they have serving the chancellor. The one you came to Maro'El to see. I have no Medicis to offer you."

Kirra gripped Kale's hand. "There are worse things than losing sight."

"I cannot promise the freedom of your friends either," Lazarus said. "If the opportunity arises, I will do what I can. But I have greater priorities."

Kale and Kirra nodded. Ashi scowled. "And the Yan Avii?"

"The Saints fight for all people, the Yan Avii included. But no one receives special treatment. And no one wins until the chancellor is brought low."

Kirra grabbed Ashi's hand, and the Yan Avii slave nodded her agreement. "What can we do?"

"Your new position in the White Citadel offers a true advantage to our plot."

"In what way?" said Kale. "The chancellor wants me to track down the Gallows Girl."

"Yes, word has spread of the new queen's request for her head at their wedding feast."

"And when I refuse, we will be forced to flee," Kale said.

Lazarus shook his head with a dark laugh. "Not at all, my son. I don't want you to refuse. I want you to find Astoria just as the chancellor requests. I want you to bring the Gallows Girl to Maro'El for the wedding. How else can her Saints be expected to rise?"

CHAPTER TWENTY-NINE

Tension that rivaled wartime strife filled the chambers of the High Council. A series of small uprisings had occurred in the night, and to make matters worse, the chancellor had invited his queen-to-be to the council meeting. Though the nobles did not voice their outrage at having an outsider in their inner circle during such sensitive circumstances, Cyrus Maro could feel it dripping from their breaths.

But he had won the Battle of Gods and Monsters. He had won the love of the people, and the high nobles needed to be reminded that it was he who ruled in the White Citadel.

And he needed to keep Vashti Burodai happy for the time being, especially since her brother's spies had arrived in Maro'El. Though he would never speak it to the council, nor anyone else, he knew his empire stood at the edge of a great precipice. The alliance with Salla Burodai was of paramount importance, especially with the latest whispers of the Witch Queen's suspicious activities. *There are so many pieces to this gods-damned game.*

When Cyrus and his brother, Loras, were children, they used to play a war game called *stratagem*. Two sides began with equal pieces—archers, foot soldiers, trebuchets, even giants. Each of them had to keep their citadel from toppling. Loras had taken to the game quickly. He had a knack for battle tactics. For years, his brother lauded over his triumphs at the game. At first, Cyrus got flustered with early setbacks, and he made foolish reactionary maneuvers. But in time, he learned to harness his aggression into strategy and manipulation. He learned to lure his brother into situations of false security, and then, he would sweep in for the unlikely victory. After a string of defeats, Cyrus's brother refused to play again. But Cyrus learned much from the game.

Most importantly, he learned that the game never ended.

A lesson Loras Maro had learned too late. *The poor fool.*

All the lords and ladies in the council chamber were game pieces, some more aware of this than others. Medea and Darien stood at either side of the chancellor and his queen-to-be, while the treasurer went on about the costs of reconstruction and the lords and ladies complained about the increase in taxes during such fraught times.

Ilyana Dragonis had become more tranquil since the day Medea took her to the Old World. She still bore the scar on her hand. Though she had lost two grainhouses in the slave uprisings, Dragonis did not air this grievance before the council, nor did she complain about the new tax.

However, Lord Barra and Lady Tindeir were growing more antagonistic. The chancellor intentionally neglected to mention the slave uprisings that had occurred in their cities, but finally the lord and lady stepped onto the game board.

"How can we afford this tax?" cried Salyse Tindeir bitterly. "These bloody Saints are still wreaking havoc amongst the lowborns!"

"How so?" said Cyrus Maro evenly. "The city is in repair and songs of our victory fill the streets. Spirits have not been this high in many years."

"Yes," said Tindeir, "they sing here in the capital. But elsewhere…"

"You speak of a few missing corpses in the Fringes?"

Lady Tindeir was clearly unsure whether she dared to mention the real reason for her outrage. She glanced around the table, then nodded. "Rebels are rebels, my lord."

"The Fringes has always been its own lawless beast," said the chancellor. "You have seen the place, haven't you?"

"Lady Tindeir speaks true," said Barra. "My slaves are growing more bold as well."

The chancellor drummed his fingers on the table. "Sounds to me like you don't know how to manage your household, Marcus."

"Don't know how to—" Marcus Barra pounded the table. "My *household* runs trading fleets all the way from Elya to Malai! My city rivals the prosperity of any city in the empire."

Cyrus Maro smiled. It was just the reaction he was hoping for. "And yet, there was an uprising in your precious city last night, wasn't there? That is what this is really about, though you won't say it."

Barra was flustered. "Well, uprising is perhaps too strong a—"

"And *you*, Salyse, you are far from worried about a few missing corpses in the Fringes. You are angry about your missing caravan from Morgath."

Lady Tindeir crossed her arms, but she did not deny it.

"Train better guards," said Cyrus Maro. "Or better yet, pay them a decent wage so they can't be bought by the first rogue mercher who offers them a handout from her thick purse."

"I lost three ships in that uprising!" cried Barra.

The chancellor resisted the urge to laugh. "Your slaves are not my concern. I have an empire to rule. Figure out how to make your slaves happy and be done with it. You could take a note from how they behave here in the capital."

Lord Barra pounded the table again. "As long as the damned Gallows Girl lives, these Saints will keep rising up. The empire is in danger."

"You're right, Marcus. Perhaps I should have left the city to you during the Rulaq attack, while I scoured the world for her."

"You created this… problem, my lord," said Lady Tindeir. She would not quite look him in the eye, which pleased him.

Barra pressed on. "Why should our households suffer because you did not dispose of her the first time?"

Both Barra and Tindeir tensed, their eyes passing from Cyrus Maro to his Darkling Witch. The chancellor was glad to see they feared suffering the same fate as Ilyana Dragonis. Her silence had surely heightened the tension for all in the room.

But Cyrus Maro knew that sometimes, it was best to show mercy and admit past failures. "For the first time in your tirade, you are correct. I will not take the fault for your slaves, but it is true, the Gallows Girl is a monster I created. And now that the empire has been saved from the horde, it is time to slay one more monster." He noted the way Vashti's eyes lit up at these words.

The chancellor turned to Commander Redvar. "Bring in your tracker."

Redvar went to the door and was quickly back in the room with Captain Sardona and the Sky Guard's newest recruits, Kale Andovier and Kirra Fehn. They walked with their heads high. The chancellor noted the ease with which the blind Watcher moved. She held on to Kale's elbow lightly, but her feet fell with surprising precision.

They knelt before the chancellor, and he bid them rise. "Lord Andovier, under the old rule, your House was put asunder because of their adherence to the Old Ways, because of their affinity for magic. My father's act, though, like the acts of his fathers before him, is in my mind an abomination. A tragic waste. But things are different now in the White Citadel. Commander Redvar sees this act as a sign of loyalty. Upon the successful capture of the Gallows Girl, he plans to return your lady's sight and offer you both a place in the Sky Guard."

"We will both be honored to serve you in this capacity, my lord," said Kale.

The chancellor smiled. "An honor, indeed. But I wish to offer you something even greater. You come from noble birth, Andovier. You deserve a place in this Third World we are creating. The greatest threat to that world is the Gallows Girl. If you succeed in bringing her back, I would like to extend an even greater honor than the Sky Guard. I would see the return of the Andovier estate. I would see you raised back to your rightful station, as high lord of House Andovier."

The chancellor felt a twinge in his mind, and he knew the Watcher was trying to determine his authenticity, and he let Kale see it. The young lordling smiled.

"I would be honored, my lord." Kale bowed.

Medea moved to the front of the room, a giant window that over-looked the city. Commander Redvar stood at her side and addressed the council. "Lords and ladies, the Gallows Girl has eluded our scouts for two months. But now, we have a tracker who can detect Watchers across great distances. Amplifying his skills with the godstones, Medea will be able to sense Astoria's gifts, and we will know where to find her."

Kale Andovier knelt before the window. He looked nothing like the desperate little boy who had bent to the chancellor's will in the Red City. He held his head high and faced his fate without trepidation.

Medea gently grasped his head with her long fingers. Kale closed his eyes and arched his neck back. There was a stunning invisible energy that enveloped the two. Medea's eyes went wide and appeared to mist over.

The search did not take long.

After less than a minute, Kale's body relaxed, and Medea released her grip. She turned to the council. "The Gallows Girl has fled to the Great White North. To Iqala."

Kale Andovier did not rise at once. His body was spent from Medea's intrusion into his mind. The chancellor strode over and helped him to his feet.

"I applaud your willing contribution to this mission. Not long ago, I was given no choice but to force your hand. Now, you come willingly. That good faith will not be forgotten, Lord Andovier."

Kale bowed his head. "Thank you, my lord."

"To ensure your full cooperation, Kirra will be joining Commander Redvar on this hunt in the North, while you serve here in Maro'El."

It was Kirra's turn to bow. "I would be honored to serve in whatever capacity you require, my lord."

"Very good," said Cyrus Maro. "I see you also have learned your lesson since the Red City. It is a lesson I had hoped your brother would learn, Kale."

"My lord?" said Kale.

The chamber doors flew open, and Dajha Bhati entered, escorting Ren Andovier in chains. He had aged much in a short time. His beard was greying despite his youth. His dark hair was growing thin and patchy. His skin was blotched with malnutrition. He staggered into the room, his chains rattling, and the noble men and ladies gasped at the stench that permeated the room. The sight of the captain of the Watchers did not please Cyrus Maro, but he smiled nonetheless.

"B-Brother…" Ren murmured, his eyes narrowing at Kale. "You *skazha!*" The curse was strong, but his voice was barely a whisper.

Kale held his brother's gaze only briefly, then looked away.

The chancellor laughed. "Kale, I offered your brother the same opportunity, but he did not receive it with the same gratitude. He has not learned his lesson, I'm afraid."

"Why have you brought this traitor?" asked Lady Tindeir, covering her nose with a handkerchief. "He smells like horseshit."

Cyrus Maro made a show of his amusement. "I believe that is actually his own excrement."

Ren said nothing. His head slumped forward. His muscles were fading quickly. He could not regenerate the way Tori had when she'd endured the chancellor's bloodletting. Ren would not last much longer under such harsh conditions.

"My gentle lords and ladies, Ren Andovier betrayed me once, many years ago. Many of you may remember how he served in my inner circle in my early days as chancellor of Osha. But he sought to use his station for his own gains. He fled the capital and hid in the mountains plotting his pathetic little rebellion. And despite all this, I offered him redemption. An offer he refused."

Ren spat on the floor. It was equal parts blood and spittle. "Why don't you kill me and be done with it?"

The chancellor forced a laugh. "Because you're still a pawn in this game. Tori cares for you, as she cares for the other Watchers bleeding out in my dungeons. And I suspect she may require some convincing to come quietly to my wedding. At the Watchtower, I promised her I would keep you safe, so long as she did as she was bid. But if she did not… I made another promise. A promise I intend to keep."

"So, you *are* going to kill me," Ren murmured.

Was that relief in his voice? Cyrus Maro noted that Kale Andovier betrayed no reaction. "Shocking as that might be," the chancellor said, "it wouldn't exactly convince her that there is hope for you, now would it? You see, I need Astoria to hope. I need her to feel desperate. So, no, I am not going to kill you… yet. For now, I only need a token. Something that will show her without doubt the gravity of her decision. Sergeant Bhati, chain Ren to the table."

There was a flurry of murmurs amongst the High Council, which gave Cyrus Maro the utmost pleasure.

Dajha hesitated for only a fraction of a moment, but it did not go unnoticed, and then, the Parjhan guard shoved his old captain to his knees and fixed the chains to the table with a mallet that a servant provided him with. The nails held Ren's shackles in place so both his hands stretched out in front of him, flat against the ornate woodwork, palms down.

Kale and Kirra stood silently in the corner, but the chancellor could sense their tension. The entire room was brimming with it.

"Lord Andovier," said the chancellor evenly, "which of your brother's hands does he favor?"

Kale blinked hard, but did not hesitate. "The left, my lord."

Commander Redvar stepped forward to do the deed, a large dagger in his hand.

In a way, Cyrus Maro admired the Watcher captain. Ren did not protest, did not plead. His only words were for his brother. "If I live to be free of these chains, I will kill you, brother."

Kirra was gripping Kale's arm now.

Lord Barra groaned and spluttered. "S-surely, you do not mean to subject high nobles to this savagery!"

The chancellor shook his head. "You sensitive lot are the reason this empire is in shambles. You let others do your dirty work. You sit in vast estates and turn a blind eye to all that transpires around you. I mean to remedy that. Commander, give Lord Barra your blade. I would have *him* do the deed."

"Y-you can't be serious!" Barra exploded.

"Would you deny your chancellor?"

The room was silent, save for Marcus Barra's splutterings. Commander Redvar shoved the dagger into the lord's hands. The chancellor doubted that Barra had wielded a blade since his days in the academy, which were far behind him.

Barra fumbled with the large blade, but when no other nobles offered any protest, he reluctantly oriented himself to the task. He took hold of Ren's left wrist. Barra's hand was shaking.

"Hold it steady, Marcus."

Lord Barra pressed the blade against Ren's skin. He closed his eyes briefly, then focused.

"You must choose," said the chancellor. "Chop it with one swift stroke? Or saw it off with smaller ones?"

Barra looked like he might throw up.

Ren gritted his teeth. "Get it over with, Barra, you spineless worm!"

Lord Barra breathed for a moment. Every eye in the room was on Barra, and this pleased Cyrus Maro most of all, for he had not commanded their attention. They knew what was expected. No one would look away.

Finally, Lord Barra hefted the dagger above his head. It shimmered in the light pouring in from the window. Barra brought it down with a cry.

The first hack did not sever Ren's hand completely. Lord Barra's strength had waned since his academy days, along with his dexterity with a blade. Blood splattered across the council table from the jagged wound, a shard of bone protruding from the mess of sinew and muscle. Ren grunted with pain, gritting his teeth tighter.

Barra brought the blade down a second time, and then a third, and finally the hand came free, and Ren's left arm fell limp from the shackle that had bound it.

Blood gushed onto the floor. It coated Lord Barra's fine garb like a butcher's apron. Blood specked the faces of Lady Tindeir and many of the other nobles, including the chancellor.

But Cyrus Maro did not wince at the sight the way his feeble lords and ladies did. He plucked up the severed hand by the fingers and held it up for all to see. The skin was still warm, and blood dripped all over his robes.

He addressed Darien. "When you find the Gallows Girl, give her this... token. If she resists, I will continue to send Ren to her piece by piece. And then, I will start in on all the other Watchers who have refused to turn from their rebellion. If she does not surrender, it will not stop until they are all dead."

Darien nodded and stowed the severed hand in a satchel. Blood quickly soaked through the leather. Ren slumped against the table in a heap, his stump oozing with blood.

"Lady Tindeir," said the chancellor, "would you be so kind as to stop the captain's bleeding? I don't want him to die just yet."

Lady Tindeir eyed Ren with disgust, but she retrieved a handkerchief from her pocket and stepped forward.

The chancellor held her back by the arm with a laugh. "I'm afraid you'll need more than cloth for such a wound." He pointed at the fire roaring in the hearth. Captain Sardona retrieved an iron that had been sitting in the coals the entire time, unnoticed by any but the chancellor. "You'll need to sear it."

Ren had made little sound during the severing, but his shrieks filled the room when the iron touched the raw nerve endings where his left hand had once been.

PART NINE
THE LONG NIGHT

The Alyut were once many tribes. Before the Elyan invaders displaced them. The survivors fled to the North and formed a new tribe, united in their suffering. But by the end of the New World, those ties had begun to dissolve.

—from Dawn of the Third World

CHAPTER THIRTY

Tori staggered from the darkness of the Alyut temple with Alyk chasing after her. But she did not want to talk to him about what her mum had revealed. She did not want to even think of it. Her greatest nemesis, the traitorous whore who had asked for her head as a wedding gift, was her sister?

She raced down the corridors beneath the Ice City, forgetting completely that she was wearing only her undergarments. When she opened the door from the passage to the temple, she nearly ran into the High Elder of the Alyut. Fara dul Baruk scowled, her hands crossed over her chest.

"What were you doing down there?" the woman asked coldly.

"I don't answer to you," said Tori, pushing her way past.

The woman had been avoiding her all this time, and now she wanted to talk? Of course.

Fara dul Baruk seized her arm. "Yes, that's right, you are the Gallows Girl. You answer to no one. You string us all along, and we must bend to your will. Anyone you can use to your own advantage. You may have fooled my son, but you have not fooled me with your little savior act. And I must say, that *was* one damned impressive act at your execution."

"Let me pass." Tori jerked her arm away.

The door flew open behind her, and Alyk emerged from the passage, bearing a heap of her clothes and furs. "What are you doing here, *Madru?*"

Fara dul Baruk's eyes lit up with anger. "You let an outsider into our temple? Both of you practically naked?"

Alyk, still bare-chested, quickly lost his defiance.

"You have defiled our most sacred place."

"You speak of defilement?" said Alyk. "The gods have much to say about feigning justice in their names."

Fara dul Baruk slapped her son across the face. "No son of mine will question my loyalty to the gods. They called me to serve my people. And I did just that. I cannot believe you are so blinded by youthful desire that you do not see how this Gallows Girl will lead our people to ruin."

Alyk shook his head. "If we head toward ruin, at least we can say we tried. You would have us hide with our heads in the snow for the rest of our existence!"

"I would have my people survive. Now, if you'll excuse me, I have come to pray. You will not see the truth. I pray the gods you claim to serve will show it to you."

Fara dul Baruk left them alone in the passage.

Without a word, Tori took her garments and furs from Alyk, and despite her dampness, she slipped quickly into them. Her skin stung with the heat, and she only then realized how cold she was in these underground chambers of stone. Her feet had gone numb.

"Tori, I'm sorry," Alyk murmured as he donned his own clothes.

Tori shook her head. "Your *madru* is the least of my worries." She headed off in silence, alone, passing through the main thoroughfare of the Under Realm, weaving her way between crowds of people. Skya had insisted Tori continue to stay in her chambers as long as they were in the North, and Tori headed straight there.

She sat in an immense chair draped in thick furs beside the hearth of firestone, wishing it held flaming logs instead of strange stones that convected heat from the depths of the earth. The stones were a marvel, but Tori loved the way you could lose yourself in the dance of flames. It reminded her of simpler times, when she was a young girl on the Steppe.

But all that life had been a lie.

Her mum had lied to her.

About her magic. About her father.

According to her, he'd run off and abandoned them. Celene Burodai had been a servant of the *soltaya*, a mere slave. But thinking back, they'd had their own tent, which was uncommon for a woman of such humble status. Her mum had assisted a *thrasii,* a gentler form of servitude.

If Vashti was Tori's sister, then that meant that Vashti's father, the Great Soltayne, had been Tori's father. The man who had burned his sorcerous daughter at the stake. *I'm a chief's bastard,* Tori thought. *All these years I thought he was just some tribesman…*

It wasn't until Tori was much older that she'd understood the darker side to her people, the injustices, the way a man of high status could take any lesser woman for his pleasure. *Is that how I came to be born? Why would Mum want me to spare Vashti? She's the daughter of the chieftain who took Mum like some courtesan of the pleasure barges!*

Tori was growing hot, and she felt uncomfortable in her damp clothes. She changed into a lighter pair of pants and a thin shirt and sat for a long time on the floor, with her back against the chair.

There was a knock from outside. Tori sighed. She did not want to talk, but she did not really want to be alone either.

Finally, she said, "Come in."

Alyk entered softly, bearing a flask and a pair of whalebone goblets. "Thought you could use a drink."

Tori managed a slight smile. "Might need a few."

"There's more where this came from. Skya has a soft spot for the Southern vintages. And the traders returned with a fresh shipment shortly before we arrived."

Tori chuckled at this and took the goblet once he'd filled it. She drank it down quick.

"Easy there," Alyk said.

Tori filled the goblet again. "I told you I needed a few."

Alyk sat on the arm of the chair, but Tori pulled him down beside her, thigh against thigh, on the floor. The skin of his forearm brushed against her own, and warmth rushed through her. He looked handsome in the soft blue glow of the icefire crystals lining the walls, and Tori thought briefly of kissing him. She'd thought of it before, and it would be the perfect distraction.

But Tori didn't want it to happen like that. She'd tried using a boy to forget her troubles before, and the last time, it had been the trick of a Morph. Tori pushed the dark memory away and set her goblet down. She stared at the dark firestones, which glowed ever so subtly with whatever fueled their heat.

Alyk said nothing for some time, and Tori was grateful. He could read her, and she liked this about him. She was glad she had him to help her lead the people of the North. She was glad he was here now, by her side. His skin against hers.

But he would never make the first move. He was rather reserved that way. Tori slipped her hand into his, and they sat in silence, fingers intertwined.

Finally, Tori voiced what was tormenting her. "Do you think that was really her?"

"Really your *madru?*"

Tori nodded. "The ghosts of Ghen were liars. They played off my fears."

Alyk shook his head. "I… wish I could say it might be true, but the temple does not work that way."

"So she must have been telling the truth."

"I'm afraid so."

"Well… that complicates things."

Alyk laughed softly. "Family always does, I think."

Tori leaned closer, her head against his shoulder.

Just then, the door flew open, and Tori and Alyk quickly moved apart. It was Skya. The warrior's expression was serious, but she still smirked at the sight of them. "I'd tell you to get a room, but we've got to go." Her voice was stern, worried.

"What's wrong?" said Tori.

"The ice," said Skya, grimacing. "The Long Night is setting in early. The sea passage is closing over. In a few days, the Frozen Sea will be impassable."

Alyk cursed, jumping to his feet. "So soon?"

"I've already given the order to gather in the palace. Come on. The people will need to hear from our saint."

Tori's stomach twisted as they hurried from the room. "We were supposed to have weeks left." Weeks to train, to strategize, to deal with any resistance the High Elder might pose, to wait for Queen Seren to gather her fleets in the South. "What do we do?"

Skya shook her head. Alyk said nothing.

None of them knew.

———

There were hundreds gathered in the great halls of the palace of ice. Tori stood upon the steps outside the throne room, Alyk and Skya dul Baruk on either side of her. The two remaining Alyut elders —for Fara dul Baruk was not present and Geryn dul Narsuk had flown south with Seren lè Tal—stood at the base of the steps, their faces betraying their concern about this dark turn of events. On their way to the palace, Tera dul Hesak had implored Tori to stay in the North.

"It is a sign from the gods, my saint. Surely you must see this. We must heed this warning."

"Thank you for your counsel," was all Tori had said, hurrying past the elder.

But the thought plagued her. Was this truly some foul omen? She had never considered herself superstitious, and despite the influence of Alyk's firm shaman's faith, Tori still had doubts about the very existence of the gods. But nevertheless, she wondered: *Is something trying to warn us against rushing to this war?*

Or was it simply one more obstacle to be overcome? If not now, then when would they march against the White Citadel? If they waited out the long northern winter, the chancellor would have recovered from the Battle of Gods and Monsters. Maro'El would be rebuilt. Armies would be replenished. And the kingdoms of the Southern Isles might be fractured once more. Seren lè Tal thought she could unify them for an attack against Osha, but not in the distant future. Now was the time.

"What do you think?" Tori had asked Alyk as they'd hurried through the tunnels beneath the city.

"I trust the gods. I trust in my saint."

"Your saint is a bloody symbol, Alyk. You know this more than anyone."

"Now is the time for that symbol to be known. I am sure of that."

Alyk nodded his reassurance now, but Tori did not share his confidence. She felt queasy as she stood before the people of the North. Her followers. Some of them had followed her all the way from the Crooked Teeth. And though they had all watched her burn, their devotion was undaunted now. After her failed execution, the people saw her at the very least as their leader chosen by the gods, and to many, she was a god come down in the flesh.

Tori knew they would follow her if she commanded it. But would they follow her to their deaths?

All eyes were upon her. Hundreds of expectant eyes. Children and old men. Warriors and midwives. Crooked folk and Alyut. After centuries of prophecies, prayers, and failed hopes, all of them now put their trust in the Gallows Girl. It was their time of Restoration.

"People of the North," Tori began. Not for the first time, Tori felt the gravity of her words, and the necessary ones came forth, as though they were being spoken through her. Or perhaps she was simply getting used to this.

"The time has come for our faith to be tested. I hoped that day would not come for a few more weeks, but we knew this revolution would not be easy. When you chose to follow me, you knew there was a risk. But you believed. And so, I must ask you to put your faith in me, in this cause, in this Restoration, even more."

The elders were shaking their heads, but Tori continued.

"The ice is setting in across the channels from Iqala. Every hour we wait, the greater risk it will be to sail south. And that is our greatest chance at surprising the chancellor. He does not know what lies here in the North. He does not know of our alliance with the Southern Isles. Our numbers will not match those of the Legions. That surprise is our advantage. An attack from land would prove too slow, and the passes of the Teeth are too treacherous to take such a large company. If we wait until spring, the opportunity may be lost. And so time is of the utmost importance. But I must confess to you, if we go, the result may very well be the deaths of many of the brave folk gathered here tonight.

"In the past, such grave choices have been made by elders and kings, chiefs and dictators. Throughout the world and throughout history, lowborns have been ordered by their betters to risk their lives, even for causes as noble as ours. But it is time for that sort of leadership to end."

The elders' eyes widened with hope.

"I cannot ask that of you, good people of the North. So I leave the decision up to you. If you decide it, we will sail, and I will lead you to war. And if you decide that the risk is too great, then we will stay."

A flurry of murmurs rose up among the people. The halls of ice resounded with cacophony. Lyren dul Vanuk raised his hands and the people quieted. "You heard our saint. The risk is great. I say we stay."

Tori scowled and raised her voice, trying to subdue her anger. "Step down, Elder Vanuk. This choice is not *yours* to make, nor to sway in your favor."

"M-my saint," Elder Vanuk spluttered. "I am merely looking out for my people as all elders have done for centuries."

Tori felt her senses rising up with bitterness. "Yes, I recall the last time you looked out for them very well. You elders pushed your justice once before, and it is only thanks to the gods that I am here to tell of it. I have seen the way your kind lead. And the North has seen enough of it. This choice belongs to the people. Crooked folk—*Iqu'vara, Karu'va, Nuq'vana,* and *Tu'va*—gather amongst yourselves, and when you've decided, we'll have a vote."

The crowds were already grouped according to clans, as was typical for such gatherings. The people huddled up and the room filled with thoughts, fears, and hopes.

Tera dul Hesak watched from the outskirts as the clan of the forest voiced their thoughts, but Lyren dul Vanuk stormed out of the room, an act that did not go unnoticed by his *Karu'va,* nor the other Alyut clans. Tori feared the elder's voice might still have its desired effect.

"He's gone to find *Madru,*" said Alyk. "I'd wager all the icefire in the North."

Alyk and Skya remained at Tori's side while the clans convened. Lir'ghe the Kroqala hovered nearby, but Tori could not hear the buzzing of his wings over the din of the gathering.

Skya nodded. "Her absence is not helping them either. Tori, you should have let us speak. We could persuade them, I'm sure of it."

"I could have spoken of the prophecies," said Alyk.

Tori shook her head. "They know where you stand. You're here by my side. That's enough."

"But Tori…" Skya whispered. "They may choose foolishly. They believe in omens. And this is a terrible one. They could ruin our chances."

"This war is only as strong as these people," said Tori. Of that she was sure. "The choice must be theirs. If their hearts are not in this, then we would fail from the start."

"Have faith, *Saru.* Our people are stronger and wiser than you give them credit for." Alyk gripped Tori's hand, and she was glad he was not voicing his sister's doubts, though she was sure he felt them. For she felt them as well.

Benja Starzen had assumed a leadership role amongst the Crooked folk, and Tori felt confident that they would choose to sail south. The fact that Tera dul Hesak had remained was promising for the *Tu'va,* but the Bear Riders were led by Elder Baruk, and Lyren dul Vanuk's cave folk would be doubtful as well. Meanwhile, the *Iqu'vara* were without their leader. And if they chose to stay? What then? Was this revolution over before it began?

Finally, the clans finished and representatives from each clan stepped forward. Tori hoped that Benja would be the first to speak. He might begin on a note of confidence, but instead a Bear Rider named Lysa stepped forward. She was a respected member of the *Nuq'vana*, and she had trained alongside the others for the past week, but Tori noted the faint sigh that Skya failed to suppress when the young woman stepped forward.

"My kinsmen, the *Nuq'vana* do not take this matter lightly. We understand, more than many of you, the gravity of this choice for the coming war. It is clear there is a great risk for us all if we leave now. The ice may cut us off. The storms are legendary along the Oshan coast this time of year."

Tori's heart sank at the woman's words.

"But…" Lysa paused for a moment. "But we have put our hope in our saint. We believe the gods brought her to us to bring Restoration for the peoples of the North. So we vote that we should sail."

A cheer rose up from the Bear Riders. Benja stepped forward, and as Tori hoped, the Crooked folk also voted to sail. The *Tu'va* echoed the others, as did the *Iqu'vara*. Tori's spirits soared at the overwhelming support. *Perhaps the gods are with us after all.*

Last came Lyren dul Vanuk's cave folk. The *Karu'va* representative was a young man named Jorn dul Kesak. He looked back to an elderly woman before he spoke. "We are not swayed by the whims of the Land Dwellers. We dig and mine beneath this land, and we spend much time separated from the other clans. But we, too, have been moved by this Gallows Saint. We, too, have longed for Restoration to the lands our ancestors knew. The lands they told us tales about as children. We have not forgotten those tales. Now is the time the gods have given us, and we would risk our lives to see our Restoration come."

Tori could not hide her smile. A tear streaked her cheek as she raised her hands for silence. "The people have spoken. We set sail tomorrow."

CHAPTER THIRTY-ONE

Tori should have been sleeping. She needed it terribly. The entire day had been emotionally exhausting, but her mind would not let up. Like one of the textile mills in the Fringes, cogs turning and turning, weaving and weaving.

They sailed in a matter of hours. Ravens had been sent to warn Queen Seren of their hastened departure from the North. They were about to go to war against the chancellor, and there were so many things to think through. But Tori's mind was avoiding the great unknowns of the war.

She lay in bed, staring up at the dark ceiling of rock in Skya dul Baruk's chambers. Skya and Alyk slept on furs in the adjacent room. A fact that made the empty space in Skya's large bed all the more apparent.

Tonight of all nights, Tori hated sleeping alone. It reminded her too much of her cell in the White Citadel. It had been half a year since that hellish existence, but it seemed like a lifetime. And she had spent little of that time alone. At the Watchtower, she had shared a room with Vashti and Mischa, and had spent all her waking hours training with Ren and the other Watchers. Since the fall of the Watchtower, she and Mischa had hardly spent a moment apart, and they had been surrounded by Alyut and Crooked folk. The few days that had passed since Mischa embarked for the South had left Tori lonelier than she'd felt in some time.

She wondered what it would be like to feel Alyk's rhythmic breathing beside her. Would it calm her to feel his nearness? His warmth? The touch of his skin on her own? The press of his lips?

Ren came to her mind suddenly. It had not been so long ago that she had imagined the same things of the Watcher captain. But he had never felt that way about her. Looking back now, she wondered if that hadn't been for the best. Maybe that was why Ren had held back. Tori longed to free him from the chancellor's torturous cells in the White Citadel. She missed his training, his leadership, his lightheartedness. But she did not feel the same stirrings at the thought of him now. Not like before.

Alyk was different, and in a good way. He did not long for glory or thrones, yet he was not afraid to fight or lead. He was good, in a way that few people were in this world. Good, like Darien had been when they'd served Scelero. Only less angry.

Thoughts of Darien only brought about bitter hatred. Before she died, Merri had sworn he was still in there somewhere. The real Darien. But Tori feared it was idealistic *shenzah*. Over the past month, she had often envisioned what she would do when they met again. Her hope had weakened in their last encounter. She could not let him weaken her resolve. If he was lost, then she must be prepared to do anything. Even kill him, if he stood in the way of their revolution.

But what were they fighting for, if not hope that the evil the chancellor had caused could be undone? That those he had manipulated might not be lost.

Darien, Dajha, maybe even Vashti…

But the thought of the Yan Avii princess made her utterly sick. *My skazha of a sister! How is that even possible?*

Had her mum been a whore of the *soltaya*, and Tori had simply been too young to understand? What other explanation was there? And why in the Abyss had her mum asked her not to be too hard on her sister?

She wants my gods-damned head! Tori nearly screamed.

The thoughts tumbled around in her mind like a great storm rolling in from the sea. Finally, she could take it no longer.

Tori wrapped herself in her cloak of mammut fur and left Skya's chambers. To her surprise, Skya and Alyk were not sleeping. They were not in the next chamber at all. From another room, she heard whispers.

With an icefire lantern in hand, Tori stole out into the tunnels beneath the Ice City. The underground thoroughfare was more crowded than she'd expected. Porters were hauling crates of weapons and provisions to the world above. She kept her hood up to avoid any attention. She did not want word to reach the High Elder of where she was going.

Within minutes, she was stripping her clothes outside the temple again. The door groaned as she entered. The humid air was nearly suffocating it was so thick. The ancestral pool churned softly with white water as she stepped in. The mists swirled.

And then, the room disappeared.

The world filled with grey vapor. Tori felt like she was floating somewhere far above the world. But there was nothing to see. Nothing but greyness and emptiness. There was no one there. Perhaps she'd done something wrong. Perhaps she needed a shaman to work the pool.

The depth of her loneliness sunk in further and further.

She was about to step out of the roiling water, when suddenly there was a pulse of light from the strange veins that bled into the pool from deep within the earth. And then a warmth enveloped her.

"Mum?"

The mists swirled, and her mum's face emerged, fluttering like a reflection in water.

"I had a feeling you'd come back," Celene Burodai said. Her voice was too casual, too bright.

Tori shook her head, clenching her fists until it hurt. "Well, I saw my dead mum for the first time in eleven years, and she left me with some pretty damn big questions."

The mists churned, and Tori felt like her mum's presence was somehow passing through her. "I'm sorry for that, little love."

"Are you going to tell me how that's possible? Or is that another mystery only for dead people?"

Her mum chuckled. "I always loved your spirit, Astoria. I knew you would accomplish great things, one day. I can't tell you how it broke me to leave you."

Tori ought to have been heart-broken. Her mum had died saving her life. But the anger overpowered her. "How is a Yan Avii princess my sister?"

Her mum reached out a hand formed of mist. "Let me show you."

The mists shifted, turning from grey to many colors, finally settling upon a deep sandy red. The colors came into focus, and Tori realized it was the walls of Vlyanii. Tori remembered the great city from her childhood.

A young woman ran through tall grass outside the Red City. A Yan Avii man on a bay steed rode down a steep hill toward her. It was dusk, and the city glowed behind them with the setting sun. The girl's fair skin reflected the warm light. She was Oshan.

"That's you?" Tori asked.

"Yes, I fled to the Steppe when I was no older than you are now. I came from a mercher's house, and when I realized what I could do, what I was, I knew it was the only way I would survive. Perhaps if I had been born into a greater house, it would have been different. High lords and ladies with the curse often lived, so long as they did not practice their innate sorcery. My brother caught wind that the Morphs were coming and managed to barter passage out of the city with a trader. That trader was a bastard, and he sold me to a slaver the first chance he got. That was how I ended up serving the chieftain of the Burodai tribe."

Tori was no longer aware of her own body. The scene outside Vlyanii played out before her while her mum spoke. The man leapt from his horse. At first, Tori thought he was going to attack her mum, but instead, he swept her in his arms and they fell into the grass together, smiling and laughing.

"It turned out that trader's treachery was the best thing that could have happened to me. I served the *soltayne's* son, Prince Aron Burodai. And he was kind to me. His young wife had died giving birth to their second child, Vashti. I tended to his children. I grew to love them as my own. And I grew to love their father."

The Yan Avii man ran his hand through Celene Burodai's hair, tenderly, and she kissed him. This was Tori's father? The same man who had ordered Vashti to be burned to death for her sorcery?

"I thought you served a *thrasii*," said Tori. "I don't remember ever being close to the *soltaya*."

"Our affair lasted only a few months, but I loved him. And he loved me. But when I became pregnant with you... It was not Aron's choice to send me away. He wanted me to continue to serve his household. It was not uncommon, after all, for a servant to bear a bastard, so long as no one knew who it belonged to. But another prince from a rival tribe discovered us."

Her mum lay on the grass. Her belly had begun to swell, and Aron Burodai brushed his fingers over the small bump. Her mum and father whispered inaudibly, but she could see the love in their eyes. Was this real? Or had her mum glossed over this memory? Turned it into something she wanted to remember. Even in Osha, it was known that Soltayne Burodai had been a heartless ruler.

Tori started at a distant shape. There was a cloaked figure, hiding behind the trunk of a tree. The man ran away, unnoticed by the lovers, back toward the city.

"That is Xander Mynah," said Celene. "He was always envious of Aron's charisma. They were rivals from boyhood, and their tribes for many years before that. Mynah used the information about our affair against Aron's father. Noble bastards are slaughtered among the Yan Avii, along with their mothers, in order to keep the bloodlines clean. Aron came unhinged when his father passed the sentence. He nearly killed him. But in the end, the family had to abide by the traditions of their tribesmen."

"But we lived."

"Your grandfather, the *soltayne* of the Burodai, was a fierce leader. He had to save face, so he ordered our execution. But unbeknownst to anyone, even your father, the *soltayne* had mercy and sent me into the household of a trusted *thrasii*, who gave me decent wages and easy labor. We were well taken care of until the end."

Tori could hardly believe it. They had lived in the same Burodai tent city for seven years. And she had never seen her father. He had thought her dead, just like her mum.

The sun had now set, and the two lovers rose from the grass. They kissed one last time and then returned to the city separately.

The colors of memory blurred, and then the mists swirled and Tori was back with her mum in the ancestral pool.

"He changed since you knew him," said Tori. "My father."

Celene's voice betrayed invisible tears. Tori could not even see her face in the mists.

"I know. I saw it from a distance. After we were ripped away from him, he turned cold and bitter... and ambitious. He was powerless against his father and against the Mynah. It broke me to see him change. He might have been so much more."

"Why didn't you tell him you were alive?"

"It would have gotten out. It would have destroyed him and his family. His children."

Her mum reappeared, her face filled with sorrow and regret. "You can't let his daughter follow the same path, Astoria. Do you understand?" Her mum's voice was pleading.

"I'm afraid she's too far gone," said Tori. "She serves the chancellor now. She wants my head for her wedding present." This fact seemed more tragic now.

"No one's too far gone. You must keep believing that."

"The way you believed in my father?" Tori began backing away from the mists. "Those were fool's hopes, Mum. I can't believe in that. I'm sorry. But I have a war to win."

The mists swirled violently and then disappeared, and Tori staggered out of the pool. She slumped onto the wet stone and cried.

———

It was some time before Tori was startled by a strange voice. It was wispy and did not seem fully comfortable with the Common Tongue. "You waste time with crying, you know."

Lir'ghe. The Kroqala hovered in the air, his dark face glowing strangely in the icefire light.

"What do you know?" said Tori, growing angry. She had previously appreciated the faerie's quiet presence.

"I know that we sail in few hours, and you cry here over things long past."

"How long were you watching?"

"I follow you here."

"You saw me with my mum?"

Lir'ghe nodded, hovering in front of her. "People do not notice me most times. I see much. Past is sad, yes. But we are at war. It is waste. Better things to worry about."

"And you're not wasting time following me in the middle of the night?"

Lir'ghe crossed his arms. His skin was marbled with something akin to fire. "My queen asks me to protect you, Gallows Girl. I watch you at all times. Night or day. These things I see worry me."

"And what have you seen?" said Tori, sitting on the edge of the pool in her undergarments. A fact that did not discomfort her in the faerie's presence, strangely enough.

"I see girl who leads thousands, but still is not believing in herself. Still caring what people think. Still afraid."

"This is war. There is much to fear."

"Yes. Much fear. But not for things that cannot change. Like who is girl's sister."

"Then what should I fear?"

"High Elder is showing face little these past days. Do you know where she goes?"

Tori scowled. "Her home? To meet with her elders?"

Lir'ghe shook his head, an act that shook his whole body as he hovered. "She leaves city two times since my queen flies away. Riding on bear."

Tori's gut twisted. "Out of the city? W-where does she go?"

"That is what you should be fearing, I think. I do not know where. She goes again this night, riding east and north. This time, she takes other elder."

"Which elder?" said Tori, beginning to fear.

"One called Lyren."

"*Shenzah!* Why didn't you say anything?" Tori said, rising to her feet.

"First time, I do not know if worth telling. Second time, I am telling now."

Oh gods, thought Tori. *Fara dul Baruk is planning something before we leave. She's going to try to stop us.*

The door flew open and Alyk and Skya appeared.

"What's wrong?" said Tori.

Alyk looked concerned. "Nothing, Tori. It's morning. And time to board the ships. Should there be something wrong?"

Tori quickly dressed, and told them what Lir'ghe had said.

"She wouldn't," said Skya. "This is the will of her people. She wouldn't defy that."

Alyk shook his head, cursing, as they hurried back through the tunnels. "Are you sure about that, *Saru?*"

They emerged into the bright morning light. The air was surprisingly warm, which was great fortune, as it would decrease the amount of ice they would be navigating through. The captains had already expressed worry that they might not make it through the Frozen Sea in time. It was a good omen, if not for Tori, then at least for the people. The Alyut and Crooked folk streamed through the city with possessions and weapons borne upon backs and in carts.

Skya and her Bear Riders would be leading a company along the shore, through the westernmost Teeth, where the peaks were lower and the weather was relatively mild, and the bears and mammuts could move swiftly through the snow. As they crossed the mountains, they would join forces with a company of Crooked refugees in the village of Ynasa.

Their target would be the northernmost coastal tower of Stormfall. If they could seize that tower swiftly, before any rider could inform the citadel of their attack, then they could find an Oshan foothold from which to base their assault on the empire. Then, hopefully, by the time the Legions began pressing north, Seren and her Southern Islanders would attack from the sea. It was a risk now that they were forced to leave early, but it was still possible. Stormfall was an ancient fortress. It was well fortified, but loosely held, as no force had attacked that far north since the Old World.

Tori was on edge as they walked through the streets of the Ice City, but she tried not to let it show. The people were brimming with nervous excitement. It had been their choice to sail to war, and though it might mean their deaths, it might lead to their long-awaited Restoration. Tori had to believe in it more than they did, at least outwardly.

They descended a hill toward the harbor, where their ships were being loaded with cargo and people. They might not be seasoned soldiers, but they had something that the Legions did not have.

Something worth fighting for.

So long as Fara dul Baruk did not interfere.

Tori scanned the eastern edge of the city—where the endless plains of ice extended for hundreds of leagues into the uncharted Great White North, populated by nothing but wild northbears and scattered rogue clans—but she saw nothing. *What could Fara possibly be doing out there? Why would she and Lyren ride out in the night? Are they abandoning us?*

Dark clouds loomed on the eastern horizon, and Tori knew they needed to be swift in their departure. If they were delayed by a storm, it might end this war before it began.

Tera dul Hesak greeted Tori at the gangway of the largest vessel, *The Whaler's Queen.* The elder bowed her head, but Tori grasped her shoulder in solidarity. "You serve your people well, Elder Hesak."

The grim woman nodded. "I truly hope so."

"And what of the remaining elders?"

The woman shook her head. "The people have chosen to follow you, my saint. I promise you that I shall honor their decision, to whatever end it may require. But all my people do not sail to war. Someone must remain with the children, the old men, the young *madrus.*"

Tori nodded. As much as she distrusted Fara dul Baruk, she knew her absence would be felt. But this, at least, was better than outright defiance of her people's will. Tori had to be grateful for that. Perhaps it was for the best. Without her questioning the Gallows Girl at every turn, the people might be better served anyway.

Elder Hesak gripped her hand. "The weather is good, but a storm approaches, and either way, the seas may prove treacherous before we reach the warmer waters of the Boundless Sea. The people need reassurance. You should speak to them, my saint."

When Tori stood upon the stern of *The Whaler's Queen*, the great crowd fell silent. Many were gathered upon the docks, but most had already boarded one of the Alyut vessels.

Less than two thousand strong, Tori thought, looking at the sight of the crowd. All bunched together on the decks of the Alyut vessels, they looked like a great number. But Tori knew they would stand no chance against the Legions in open combat. They might take Stormfall, but what then? They had heard nothing still from Seren. What if something went wrong?

The people of the North looked to her with expectant smiles. *Have faith,* she told herself. *Seren and Mischa will come through. These people will come through.*

"People of the North!" Tori cried. "This harsh world was thrust upon you by ancient tyrants. Forced from the lands of your ancestors, you made this world your home. And the gods blessed you, provided for you, preserved you. Now, the gods have blessed us with clear weather and calm seas for the moment. But this war will not come easily. When strife comes, remember that the gods have been preparing you for this day. For centuries, you have grown strong and resilient in the North. These traits will be all too necessary in the weeks to come. I sail beside the bravest people I've ever known, and I will be proud to fight alongside you, even die. Any sacrifice, any hardship will be worthwhile if it brings justice. The day of Restoration is coming!"

At this, the crowd erupted in an incredible war cry.

The cheers went on for some time. It was so loud that Tori did not hear the whalehorns at first. But she saw the crowd forming in the streets descending from the Ice Palace.

Her heart sank.

It was no crowd.

It was an army.

Wild Northmen wearing ragged furs and armed with jagged spears marched down the wide thoroughfare toward the harbor. There were hundreds of them, and at the front, massive warriors clad in helms made of bone rode upon the most immense bears Tori had ever seen. And at the front of these warriors rode Fara dul Baruk.

The rogue clans of the White North. She has betrayed us all!

CHAPTER THIRTY-TWO

Tori seethed with a pulsing rage. Her senses flared. It was all she could do to not send spears flying with her Conjuri power. This was it. The moment she had been dreading since she'd first survived the execution. The entire hope of this war was now in her hands. How the Gallows Girl handled this moment could determine everything.

The waterfront filled with murmurs. All eyes were on her.

I've got to kill her, Tori thought fearfully, glancing at Alyk, whose eyes were wide with horror at the sight of his mother leading an army of rogue clans. *There's no other way. We cannot fight here in Iqala. It would ruin us. If these people even would fight against their High Elder.*

But if Tori was close and calculated, she could do it. She could end this, once and for all. She had to. Elder Baruk was defying the will of her own people. And that was the worst kind of treachery.

The crowd spread apart as Tori descended the gangway and approached the oncoming host. Alyk hurried after her. "I-I'll reason with her, Tori."

Tori shook her head. "There is no reasoning with your *madru.*"

Skya rode forward on her northbear, gripping her spear tight, looking darkly out at the approaching insurgents.

"Are you with me?" said Tori.

Skya nodded, her hair blowing in the icy wind. The dark clouds were coming closer on the horizon. "My riders are sworn to their people, not to their elders. We'll fight beside you, if it comes to it."

"And you?" Tori said, turning to Alyk.

"T-Tori…"

"Are you with me?"

Alyk nodded with an air of reluctance. "I'm with you. But Tori, we cannot afford a battle before we've even gone to war."

Tori gripped the handle of the blade at her belt. "Then, let's pray we can end this as quick as possible."

Alyk was about to protest, but Tori was done talking. She strode forward with determined steps. The Bear Riders formed up behind her to face the rogue clans of the North. Tori guessed there were five hundred of them. A few dozen rode bears, closely matching the Alyut numbers, but the majority of the rogue Northmen were on foot, and by sheer numbers, surely they would retreat once their leader was removed. Elder Baruk was clearly hoping that her people would be hesitant to resist her.

But Tori's heart warmed as she glanced back to see the Alyut forming up behind her, filling the waterfront. Her magic was a thrill inside her as she marched forward. She focused the energy, anticipating her moment. There would be no talk, no negotiation this time. She would get close to the High Elder, and she would strike.

The rogue host reached the bottom of the hill from the Ice Palace, only a few hundred yards away. They glanced back and forth, anger in their eyes. This would not come as easy as they hoped.

"Elder Baruk!" cried Tori, stepping forward.

"Tori, we can still reason with her," Alyk whispered beside her.

But Tori ignored him. Skya nodded to her without comment, and Tori strode to meet the elder. Fara dul Baruk signaled for her army to stop, and she rode out to meet the Gallows Girl.

Tori's hand went to the hilt of her blade, but in her sense, she focused on the spear in Skya's hands. She resisted the urge to attack too soon. But the closer she got, the harder it was to hold back. Fara dul Baruk's expression was dark, her eyes alight with hatred. She rode on her vicious-looking bear, but she drew no weapon.

Tori feared relying on her magic. All it would take was the right shaman to be on the High Elder's side, and Tori's powers could be rendered useless. And her saber was no match for a northbear. But Tori could feel her magic more than ever, like a dammed-up river begging to be unleashed.

"You have betrayed your people!" Tori cried.

Elder Baruk's eyes narrowed, and her voice was like slow ice forming in the Frozen Sea. "My people follow a fool, Gallows Girl."

"A fool they chose."

"Ah yes… the will of the people."

The bear was mere yards away. Fara dul Baruk's gaze stretched out to the masses behind Tori. *Now! Now is your chance!*

Her senses focused on Skya's spear. She drew her saber, diverting the elder's attention. Fara dul Baruk's eyes went wide.

But she did not attack.

Tori was about to leap forward, but the High Elder was chuckling. She climbed off her bear nonchalantly.

"Put your blade away, Gallows Girl."

"W-what?" Tori tensed, ready to seize Skya's spear and let it fly with her Conjuri power.

"You truly thought I would attack my own people?"

Tori hesitated, her magic dimming slightly. "You've proven ever since I arrived that you do not care for the will of your people, nor the hope that I bring them."

Fara dul Baruk shook her head, approaching slowly. "You assume much, considering you know nothing about me."

"Then what is this?" Tori said, gesturing out at the army behind the High Elder. The rogues gripped their weapons warily, but a grizzled man with a greying beard at the front held up his hand, signaling them to hold back.

"I do not like you, Gallows Girl. In that, you are correct. I do not like the hope you bring my people. I think it a fool's dream. But there is nothing I value more than their will, even if I believe it poorly founded. It has been a great deliberation for me these past days, as to how I should move forward after they so wholeheartedly supported you. It is why I was going down to the temple when we… ran into one another."

Tori let her magic subside completely, and she lowered her blade. "Then where did these rogues come from?"

"My people have chosen to follow you into war, to seek their Restoration. I wish it were not so. But if they should die in the attempt, I will die alongside them. And I will give them the best chance they have at victory."

Elder Baruk gestured at the rogues behind her. Their faces had softened now. The grizzled leader rode forward. He dismounted and stood by

Fara dul Baruk's side, clasping her hand in greeting, to the amazement of the Alyut people.

Fara dul Baruk addressed them. "The rogue clans were formed over petty squabbles long ago. But these people are Alyut. They long for the old lands and the old ways, just as we do. They also dream of Restoration. Let us put aside our past differences. If we are to win this war, we must be united as ever. If you will have them, they will ride with us, fight with us, die with us, if it will return our people to the lands of our ancestors. Will you accept their allegiance?"

A roar chorused through the streets, echoing off the buildings, carrying across the air and the icy seas.

"The people have spoken," the High Elder murmured to Tori. "Then, let us set off," Elder Baruk cried, raising her spear toward the sky. "A storm is coming, but victory is on the horizon. To war!"

The people shouted, "To war! To war!"

The rogue clans joined the cry. The icy streets trembled at the sound.

Fara dul Baruk led her new recruits through the streets, and the people returned to the ships. Alyk and Skya greeted their mother with warm embraces, uncharacteristic affection for their family, and they led the way back to the harbor.

The ships were soon brimming with brave warriors. The rogue riders would join Skya and the other Bear Riders as they rode through the mountains to rally the Crooked folk.

Tori watched, waiting until all were aboard *The Whaler's Queen*. The dark clouds had nearly reached the city, but still, Skya pulled Tori aside before she boarded.

"Do you trust her?" said Tori.

"For a moment, I doubted. But I see now that I should have trusted my instincts. My *madru* serves her people, first and foremost. She will not betray them."

"It was a close call," said Tori. "But I'm glad to be proven wrong."

"It was a very close call. Almost a terrible mistake," said Skya, gripping her spear and meeting Tori's gaze. "I felt your magic, Tori."

Tori's stomach tightened. It had very nearly been a catastrophic mistake. If she had attacked the High Elder, she would have undone everything.

Tori nodded to the warrior. "I'm sorry."

"I don't think Alyk realizes how close you came to murdering our *madru*. And I won't tell him. We avoided a tragedy, and our army is stronger than ever. And that is what matters. But from now on, we must trust one another."

"Your *madru* still hates the fact that your people follow me."

Skya gripped Tori's shoulder. "Then show her she's wrong. She's with us. She's proved that. Now prove you're worthy of being followed."

Tori managed a grim smile. "Be safe."

"Oh, I will," said Skya, grinning. "I'm not going to let cold or Rulaqs or war keep me from seeing your Watcher friend again. I'll see you in Stormfall."

Skya mounted her northbear and led the Bear Riders and rogues out of the city. They set off at a swift pace. Tori marveled at the speed with which the bears and mammuts could cross the snow. Tori smiled as she watched them leave.

A great crowd of Alyut waved and cheered from the docks as the others set sail. The seas were calm, and the ice was minimal, and the Ice City soon diminished to a faint point on the horizon.

Alyk stood alone on the foredeck of *The Whaler's Queen*. He would not meet Tori's gaze at first, and so she drew near and took his hand.

"I should have listened to you," she said. "I shouldn't have assumed the worst about your *madru*. You were right."

Alyk squeezed her hand. "I hope so. I hope I'm right about all of this."

Great bergs of ice drifted past them. They were like incredible mountains floating upon the sea. Alyk said they were normal this far north, shed by massive sheets of ice in the Great White North. Tori prayed the weather would hold and the ice would wait a few more days to set in. The storm clouds had shifted north and were disappearing on the horizon.

She hoped it was a good omen.

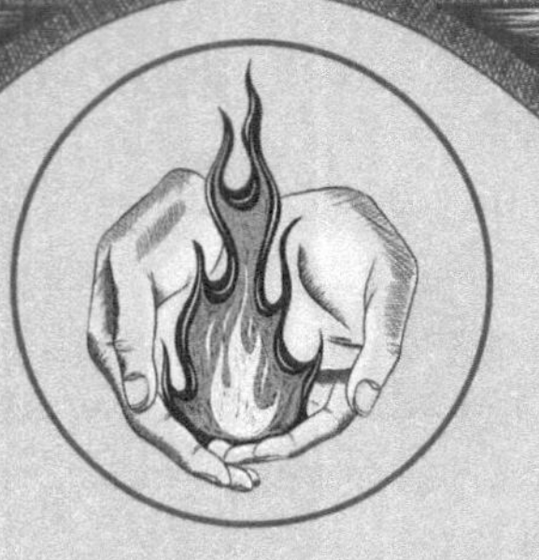

CHAPTER THIRTY-THREE

Mischa! You've got to come see!" Tes tugged on Mischa's arm and hurried them both up to the foredeck.

Mischa had been reading one of Seren lè Tal's books. A gift from her beloved *scholai* before he died. It was called *Lost Tales of the Old World*, and it was utterly fascinating. It consisted of only one volume, a thick tome of poorly bound parchment with a leather cover that was beginning to hang in threads from wear and poor craftsmanship. According to Seren, it was one of only a handful of copies that had survived the purgings of the Oshan Empire when it had ruled the entire New World. And for good reason. The book would have been treasonous.

It contained ancient tales of when the gods walked the earth and intervened in human affairs. These were typically brief, stories of miracles and years-long growing seasons and even longer droughts. There was one particular story that made Mischa chuckle out loud at its absurdity. An apocalyptic day when the gods got into a war amongst themselves, fighting with lightning and earthquakes and falling stars. The cataclysms supposedly formed such marvels as the Great Canyons of Dimh and the sharp peaks of the Southern Rim. It was said that, during the war, the sun stood still for days, and when night came the Sisters did not shine because of their grief for their fallen children.

The stories of the Watchers were more believable. For one, they were far more recent. The book had been written many years after the fall of the Old World, but Mischa knew the Order of the Watchers *had* existed, and their exploits were more within the realms of reason and her own understanding of magic. But the stories were forgotten when Mischa and Tes emerged on deck.

The Floating Mountains were the most incredible sight Mischa Sufai had ever seen in her seventeen years of life. And to see them while flying through the sky on a ship—whose wings glowed with magic runes that kept it airborne—was even more awe-inspiring. The massive hunks of rock were shrouded in mist, long vines descending the sides like living curtains. Beyond all reason, they hung thousands of feet above the sea. As the ship neared the mountains, Mischa noticed tiny waterfalls trickling down the sides, and she imagined that from the world below this place looked like nothing more than distant clouds drizzling with rain.

Seren lè Tal stood at the bow of the ship, taking in the view, the wind rushing through her silver hair, her gown flowing behind her with each gust of the breeze like a wave of the sea.

Birds flitted around the cliffs and dove down around the skyship as though inspecting the strange intruders. Many of the Kroqala flew around and joined them, dancing on the air. The amalgamation of birdsong and faerie buzzing filled the world with a beautifully chaotic symphony.

"Gods above!" cried Tes, running across the deck toward the queen, pointing at the magnificent mountains. "Seren, aren't they grand?"

Mischa was about to tell Tes not to disturb the queen. She often withdrew for solitude and meditation on deck, but Seren turned and smiled, messing Tes's hair when she reached her. Mischa joined them, her eyes rarely leaving the sight of the Floating Mountains, which grew larger and larger as they approached. They must have been a thousand feet tall or more.

"What do you think of them?" said Seren, patting Tes on the shoulder.

"Amazing!"

"According to tales, this was the home of the Order of the Watchers," said Mischa. She'd read about it yesterday in *Lost Tales of the Old World*.

"If Watchers ever lived here, it was long before the Orders were formed," said Seren lè Tal. "I've flown over the mountains several times, and there are no Old World ruins that I've seen. I'm afraid that was likely a myth."

"Maybe their houses were underground," said Tes.

Seren laughed. "You're a sharp one, Tes. I'm glad to have you along on this voyage. How's your training coming?"

Tes crossed her arms. "Makes my head hurt. The faeries make too much noise. I can't concentrate."

"Well, if it was easy, it wouldn't be training," said Seren. "Mischa is a wise teacher. Be sure to listen to her."

Tes nodded, though with a slight pout.

Geryn dul Narsuk came to join them briefly, his hands clinging to the railing, his mouth agape.

"Haven't seen you much, Elder Narsuk," said Seren, a slight smile teasing her lips.

"Rather prefer the confines of walls," said Geryn. "All this open air makes me… uneasy."

Uneasy was putting it mildly. Geryn dul Narsuk's face was noticeably discolored, and he had vomited on multiple occasions throughout the voyage. But the queen did not draw attention to his rosy portrayal of himself.

"Well, I'm glad you've come up for air. There are few sights that compare with this. But don't fear, we'll be descending shortly."

"So soon?" said Geryn, though the anticipation was clear in his voice. "We're some distance from the Isles yet."

Between bouts of airsickness, Elder Narsuk had spent much time poring over the queen's maps with a faerie named Ru'Khe, who was their navigator and had developed a curious bond with the Alyut elder, though they were only able to communicate through gestures. Few of the Kroqala spoke the Common Tongue, though they seemed to understand it well enough. Mischa thought it was something to do with their physical structure. Their tongues were split down the center, and their own language sounded to her more like a low whistle than words. She thought it must pose a challenge for them to speak like humans.

The Floating Mountains cast a dark shadow, blocking the sun as the ship came close.

"The mists form thick here," said Seren. "It's an ideal place to descend back to the world unseen. We'll spend the last two days of the journey on the sea."

"But what about the dragons plaguing the Channel Sea?" said Geryn.

"We'll sail well enough west of the channel."

"The beasts may have moved."

"There are many things that may happen in the world presently, Elder

Narsuk," said Seren sternly. "I'm afraid sea dragons may be the least of our worries in the coming weeks."

They passed below a pair of impressive hunks of rock, the distance between them forming a sort of airborne canyon. A chill shot up Mischa's arms. It was warmer now that they were in the South, and she had not worn even a light cloak in her hurry to see the mountains. But as they passed into the shadow and mists, the cold cut through her clothes and chilled her bones. Tes clutched Mischa's wrist, shivering.

Seren lè Tal shouted an order, and the faeries swarmed around the wings and sails of the ship. The whole vessel groaned as the Kroqala shifted their trajectory downward.

"Oh gods," said Elder Narsuk, clutching desperately at the railing.

Mischa stifled a laugh, pulling Tes closer. She was shaking, almost violently. The mountains had disappeared in the thick mist. Tes's eyes opened wide.

"It's all right, Tes. We'll be safe below soon," Mischa said.

Tes shook her head. A tear trickled down her cheek. "It's not the f-flying!" She held her ears, her chest heaving alarmingly. Tes fell to the deck and moaned.

Terror shot through Mischa as she knelt and held the girl. "Tes, what's wrong!"

"Don't you hear it?" the girl cried.

"Hear what, child?" said Seren, taking hold of her hand.

Tesleh rocked back and forth, trembling in Mischa's arms. She shook her head. "I don't know."

"What does it sound like?"

"Screaming!"

All Mischa heard was the wind rushing through the sails as they gained speed on their descent. She pulled Tes close and prayed that was all it was. Soon, they would be on the sea, sailing for Elya, the central port of the Southern Isles. *It's only the wind. Tes's hearing is just acute, and she hasn't learned to master harsh sounds.*

But then, Mischa thought she heard something else. It was distant and shrill and she could not place it. Her gut clenched.

Maybe it was her mind, filling in what she imagined Tes might be hearing.

But then it came again, louder this time. And the sound took Mischa back to one of the darkest nights of her life. The night the Watchtower fell. She'd heard that cry before.

The shriek grew louder and louder.

"What was that?" cried Geryn.

But Mischa knew, and it filled her with cold dread. She clutched Tes tighter. A shadow loomed above them, growing larger and larger in the mists, and it did not belong to the mountains. Another shadow appeared. And another.

"Morphs!" Mischa cried. "They've found us!"

"Dive! Dive!" shouted Seren.

The Kroqala shifted the sails, the shadows growing more threatening with every breath. Mischa held Tes's hand tight, envisioning the beasts snatching the young Watcher away from her like an eagle capturing its prey.

The vessel's nose dipped, and Mischa, Tes, and Geryn clutched the railing as they hastened their descent to the ocean below. The winds turned turbulent with the gathering speed, and Mischa wondered darkly at what speed the sea might turn into something like stone on impact.

"Sh-should I take the girl below?" asked Geryn tremulously.

"It's too late!" cried Mischa. "Hold tight!"

Seren was at the helm, barking orders to the Kroqala. Her face was deathly pale and her eyes were dark chasms.

An outline of black wings emerged from the mists, and the queen's eyes went wide. Tes screamed, holding her ears.

"*Ree!*" Seren shouted in a strange tongue Mischa guessed belonged to the Kroqala.

The demon faeries shifted the sails and the skyship banked hard to the left. A Morph shot past them, only clipping one of the sails.

"Do you think it's only the one?" shouted Geryn dul Narsuk.

As if in answer, another shadow appeared in the clouds. Mischa's teeth clenched. This beast descended even quicker, its wings tucked in a fierce dive, the claws of its feet stretching toward them.

Seren shouted, "*Kal!*"

The ship shifted again, and the second Morph shot past. Its claws missed them all, but there was a loud ripping sound as it passed. The ship jolted to the side, and Mischa could see light through a slit in one of the sails.

Two more shadows came in quick succession. Seren barked an order and the ship arced left again. The first beast missed entirely, but the second shot straight to the spot where the ship had moved, and its claws shredded two large holes in the main sail.

"Gods!" cried Seren. "They're trying to bring the whole ship down!"

"What do we do?" cried Geryn.

Mischa gripped Tes's hand and then let go of the railing. "We fight! If I can make it to the muskets down below, we might be able to ward them off."

Seren nodded and gripped the helm even tighter, bracing her feet as the ship gained speed.

There was a brief lull between attacks, and Mischa seized the opportunity. Without another word, she scrambled across the deck on all fours. She feared if she stood she would be swept away by the intense gusts of wind. She gripped the decking with mad determination.

Wind hissed in her ears, louder and louder, but finally she reached the stairs and leapt into the cabin. She sprinted as fast as she could down the hall belowdecks, bracing herself against the walls as the ship spun around her. The weapons were stowed in a locked cabinet in the navigation room. Mischa smashed the glass of the door and slung a pair of muskets over her shoulder, along with a bag of shot and a horn of powder. The ship rocked, and she fell to the floor. Blood splattered on the wood, but Mischa did not have time to worry about the injury. *Gods, how much longer before we hit the sea?*

Before she left, Mischa grabbed a saber and strapped it to her belt.

She flew back to the deck. The sails were in worse shape now, with several more gashes. Mischa shoved one of the muskets in Geryn's hands. "Can you shoot?"

The Alyut elder nodded, his eyes wide with fear.

Mischa handed Tes a small sheath from her belt. Despite the covering, the icefire still managed to glow. "If one of those beasts comes near, you stab them with this, you hear?"

Tes nodded, clenching her teeth, whether from fear or determination Mischa did not know.

"It'll kill them quick. You can do it!"

Tes clutched the blade tight.

"Incoming!" cried Seren.

A shadow materialized above them. Mischa planted her feet, aimed, and fired. But Tes's scream threw off her aim, and she missed.

Tes pointed a trembling finger behind Mischa's shoulder.

Mischa spun to find one of the Morphs climbing onto the deck from the clouds below, its claws reaching for her. She raised her musket, only to realize that she'd not reloaded. The creature's claws latched on to Mischa's cloak.

Elder Narsuk fired.

And the beast fell away.

But its claws were locked on Mischa's clothes, and Mischa was yanked from the deck and plummeted into the mists.

She wrestled with the falling beast for several seconds before she realized it was dead. Its fingers were stuck in the thick wool of her cloak. Together, they shot toward the earth. The clouds began to thin.

Mischa focused her senses, becoming aware of the forces behind the world. With determined clarity, she flicked the flints around her wrists and conjured a small spark, praying it would not simply be blown out in the wind.

She focused all her Fieri power on one sharp explosion of flame. Her cloak ignited in a quick burst. The fibers disintegrated. Her chest roared with pain. And the Morph slipped away.

The sea loomed below, but Mischa was free, and she caught a current of the wind with her magic and flew through the air, narrowly missing the roiling waves. Rain drenched her cloak.

They were landing in the midst of a storm.

There was a strike of lightning above, and Mischa caught a glimpse of the ship descending quickly toward the sea. Two beasts spun through the air, attacking from either side. It seemed Geryn had managed to fell another of the creatures. *He's a better shot than I gave him credit for.*

Mischa drew a dagger from her belt and flew with all her might. Back into the thick clouds above. The cold rain pelted her face like tiny bullets of ice, and she squinted to see through the tempest.

There was a gaping hole in the main sail. The ship weaved violently through the air, and Mischa did not think it was one of Seren's maneuvers. A loud cry echoed in the clouds as Mischa neared. The beasts had landed on deck, forcing Seren to release the wheel.

The ship jerked hard to the right, one of the wingmasts nearly clipping Mischa's head. She ducked, caught a sharp upward draft, and landed on deck. Seren drew her saber and faced off with the largest of the beasts, who had morphed into the form of an immense Oshan woman and wielded a massive broadsword.

A frantic shot fired. The other beast was taking on Tes and Geryn, and Geryn had missed. He scrambled to reload the musket, but the beast was upon them. Mischa did not have time to think. She flew through the air, her saber outstretched. The beast spun around just in time and blocked her attack. Mischa launched across the deck into the railing. The Morph transformed into its human form, and for a moment, Mischa froze.

It was Vashti.

But that made no sense.

Vashti couldn't be a Morph.

The Yan Avii princess strode toward her, and Mischa's resolve crumbled at the sight of the girl she had once loved. She couldn't kill her. She knew she couldn't.

"Why?" said Mischa as the princess drew her saber. Tears filled her eyes.

Vashti laughed. "I do what is best for my people, Mischa. I always have."

Mischa's fingers were trembling violently. She tried to grip her saber, but she could barely lift it. "Please, no!"

Vashti raised her saber high.

A violent scream. So loud that Vashti glanced back. Mischa shot forward, colliding with the girl, knocking her to the deck. Mischa threw away her sword. Her right fist connected with the princess's jaw. The left met her gut. But Mischa was so consumed with rage, she did not focus on her technique. She did not pin her down properly, and Vashti planted her feet against the railing and launched Mischa back. The princess stood.

And now, Mischa had no weapon.

"You can't kill me!" cried Vashti, her saber outstretched. "Even if you could, you don't have the guts."

"She doesn't have to!" cried a small voice.

It was Tes.

Vashti spun, but it was too late. Tes drove the glowing icefire blade into her side.

The poison worked immediately. Vashti dropped to the ground, her saber clattering onto the deck. She reached for Tes, but her fingers had lost their strength and only managed to knock the girl away.

Mischa hurried to Vashti's side. She didn't want her to die, as much as she hated her, but she knew there was nothing she could do to stop the poison. The princess's veins bulged, growing darker and darker. And she was laughing.

You bitch!

Vashti's body transformed again. But it was not into a beast. She shifted into a young Faerish girl with dark eyes and straight black hair.

It was not Vashti at all.

The Morph laughed some more, blood bubbling from her lips.

And then, she went still.

Mischa did not realize she was sobbing until it was over. She did not realize that Geryn had managed to kill the last Morph, nor that Seren had managed to steady the ship before they reached the sea.

Mischa sobbed as they descended from the storm into clear skies, and then her sorrow turned to rage. She beat the dead Morph over and over upon the chest until Geryn grasped her shoulder.

"What?" Mischa screamed.

Tes gripped her hand.

"We landed."

Mischa had not even felt the impact. Seren turned from the helm. The Kroqala darted through the air, working quickly to bring in the wings of the ship.

"We killed them," said Tes. "We're safe."

Mischa wordlessly stood to her feet. She felt numb all over.

"We survived," said Seren. "But I fear we are far from safe. Those Morphs were waiting for us. The chancellor knew we were coming."

PART TEN
STORMFALL

By necessity, the lines were blurred in those days. Between truth and lie. Friend and foe. Death and survival. We became what we hated. We became what was required in order to take one more breath. Allegiances could change with each gust of the wind.

—the Last Commander of the Metamorphi
as quoted in *Dawn of the Third World*

CHAPTER THIRTY-FOUR

Snow fell in lazy swirls as Darien rode ahead of his company, a host composed of Morphs and Legions. General Thuva rode beside him, and his company of Shadows stretched out, weaving through the highlands of northern Osha like a gargantuan grey serpent behind them. With the news that the Gallows Girl had fled north, the chancellor had commissioned greater forces to fortify the northern strongholds. War was coming to the North. The question was when and where.

Darien did not push away thoughts of Tori now. He could not be afraid. Fear had weakened his resolve before. If he had been entirely committed the first time, she never would have escaped. He would have seen through Merri's act. Perhaps he had even wanted Tori to escape, deep down. But he understood better now just how great a threat she posed to the empire, to the world. She had stirred up the Rulaqs. And now, she stirred a forgotten threat from slumber. The Alyut. That changed things. Even her former Watcher comrades understood this.

It was true, Darien found no pleasure in the task before him. But he could not let himself be weakened by his past. Yes, he and Tori had once been friends. But that was before her disastrous revolution. Before Darien bore the responsibilities of an officer, a commander. His duty was to the chancellor. To the people of Osha. To his soldiers.

But Darien was even more worried about another weakness. He pulled his horse to the side and watched the troops file past him.

Valeria brought up the rear, and the chancellor's final words echoed in Darien's mind as he watched her astride her grey-specked courser.

"I know you care for Captain Sardona," the chancellor had said before they'd marched from the White Citadel.

"As a comrade, certainly, milord."

The chancellor had laughed warmly. "Are you going to lie to your chancellor?"

Darien shook his head.

"I see the way you look to her. And the way she looks to you."

"Milord, I am sorry. It is not proper."

"No… and why do you think that is, Commander? Why is it improper for two comrades to be joined by more than duty?"

"We cannot be distracted."

The chancellor grasped his shoulder. "Redvar, if I were to ban distractions, the entire army would need to be reprimanded nightly. There is no law against a Shadow visiting the nighthouses. So why not be involved with comrades?"

"It would weaken us."

"Is that the case with you and Captain Sardona? I should think not. There is strength in the bond you share. When you fight, you become as one. Your minds, your blades, your skill combined. Together, you saved my life in the catacombs. You won the Battle of Morgath. And you led us to victory against the Rulaqs. You are an indefatigable pair. And believe me, you are hardly the first to lie with a comrade."

"Milord, we—"

"Of course not. You are a loyal commander."

Darien gulped. "I'll end things with her, milord."

"You may do as you please."

"Milord?"

"You're strong together, Commander Redvar. Any fool can see that. But even our greatest strengths can be held against us by our enemies. I should know, for I do not hesitate to exploit such weaknesses within my own adversaries."

Darien thought of the way he had manipulated Kale and Kirra.

"You are my chosen commander. I trust you'll ensure that nothing compromises your duty."

"Of course, milord."

"The Gallows Girl must die. I may not like it. Truth be told, I rather fancy young Astoria. You may laugh, Commander, but there was a time I entertained the thought she might make a fine queen when I brought magic back to the realm."

"Tori, milord?"

"She's a fierce young woman. But she is the world's greatest threat. You must bring her to Maro'El. And you must not let yourself be put in the awkward dilemma of choosing between your duty and the life of someone you love. Duty must always come first."

Valeria was the finest woman, the finest soldier, Darien had ever known, and he hated the idea of facing the Gallows Girl without her.

As they rode north, Darien watched her—her saber strapped to her hip, her silver hair blowing in the snowy air. His heart stirred, and he knew what he had to do. The Morphs and Legions crested a ridge ahead, and a horn echoed through the mountain pass.

Valeria galloped to meet him as the last of the troops passed by. "We've reached the fortress at last," she said, her eyes twinkling. "I'd forgotten how tedious it could be, riding to war. On horses. Funny how quickly we've become accustomed to Morph wings."

Darien smiled. It was strange to think how long ago it seemed since they had been nothing but human soldiers. The last of the Legions disappeared over the pass, and Darien was about to ride on, when Valeria touched his arm.

"Are you ready for this?" she said softly.

Darien shook his head, annoyed. "Of course I'm ready. I've hunted her before."

"She was your friend."

"Once," said Darien. "But she's changed. I've changed. The world has changed. It is my duty, and that is all that matters."

Valeria lowered her voice. "You're telling me you don't feel anything holding you back?"

"Should I?"

"Of course not. But you are human, Commander. Even in the catacombs, I could see it in your eyes. You did not like the idea of Tori being executed."

"What I like does not matter."

"Spoken like a true comrade."

"What is this about, Captain Sardona?"

"You loved the Gallows Girl. Once."

Did the chancellor ask her to do this? To question my resolve? Darien felt a rekindled ache of guilt in his stomach.

"That was another life…" Darien's thoughts drifted at this.

Tori had once whispered to him of another life, the night before he was drafted. A life when things might have been different. When they might have been born into a world where they could be together. Not as slaves. *Not on opposing sides of this war,* Darien thought darkly.

Merri had whispered of this world with her dying breath.

Tori still believes in you. And so do I…

But Merri hadn't known how great a threat Tori was. Thousands had died because of what she'd done to the Rulaqs. And now, more beasts were pillaging the world. Only the chancellor and his Darkling Witch could save them.

And instead of attempting to save anyone, Tori was stirring up war. Darien hated what Tori had become. It wasn't her fault, entirely. She had only been trying to save him. She hadn't tried to start a revolution. Not at first. It wasn't her magic that was her sin. It was the symbol she had become. The nations of the world hung by a thin rope, and if Tori Burodai continued to cause unrest, the world would be shorn in two.

"I love *you*, Valeria," said Darien at last. "And I serve the chancellor. That is where my allegiance lies."

And that is why I cannot face her with you…

Valeria held his gaze for several moments. Her periwinkle eyes pierced him, but he did not look away. She would sense his hesitation otherwise. "Good," she said. "I just needed to be sure where you stood."

Valeria rode off at a gallop, and Darien hurried after her. She returned to the rear of the troop as they rode out across the snowy plain. Darien rode to the front once more.

The commander of the Sky Guard led his soldiers toward the ancient fortress of Stormfall, the northernmost hold in all of Osha.

———

THE SNOW HAD TURNED TO A STEADY FALL BY THE TIME THEY WERE welcomed to Stormfall by Lord Byrn, a giant, fierce-looking noble with greying dark hair and a thick beard. A stark contrast to the sleek, clean look of the nobles in Maro'El. Lord Byrn's uncle tended to courtly matters in the capital, while Byrn and the rest of the family remained in the north.

Darien greeted the man in the Oshan fashion, crossing his right arm over his chest in salute, and the lord returned it.

"So you're the tribal boy my uncle has told me about."

Darien hated the way Oshans called attention to his race. What difference did it make? It was these sorts of interactions that reminded him why he admired the chancellor. Cyrus Maro had never batted an eye at his heritage. He was a fine soldier, and that was all that mattered. Cruel though it might have been to force Lord Barra and Lady Tindeir to mutilate the Watcher captain, it had given Darien a twisted pleasure watching the highborns squirm at the task. The chancellor had brought them low. And he had raised Darien up.

Darien stood tall despite the man's words. "I'm our chancellor's chosen commander, and a proud Oshan, milord."

"I don't give a bloody damn what you are, so long as you don't expect me to feed this lot out of my own stores like the last company the capital sent up here."

"We brought our own supplies, Lord Byrn."

The man slapped him on the shoulder a little roughly, but then cracked a thin smile. His cheeks were stiff, as though he did not do it often. "Good man! See, I like you already. My family en't like those prissies in the South. Living as close to the Crooked folk as we do, you develop a respect for different folks. I see the chancellor shares the same respect, if the tales I hear are true about you."

"They likely are," said Darien with little humility.

"The chancellor's right hand, sounds like to me. We Northern folk never did care for the Maros. I served Aleksander in the Trade Wars. And we all know how that sorry excuse for a war turned out."

"You were a sailor?"

"Aye," said Lord Byrn. "Not a good one, mind. But I could fight. My cannons could bring down any vessel in the five seas. But that piss-poor lout of a chancellor lost us the Channel Sea. And his father lost us the Southern Isles. These ruddy chancellors have been losing Oshan territories for three hundred years. This young one, though… I worried he was like the rest of them when Morgath rebelled, but he proved himself all right. And you too, it seems."

"Aye, milord."

"Nah, I don't give a bloody damn what they whisper about how Cyrus Maro got his throne. He's the ruthless sort we need. A true Northman!"

"Ooh, rah, milord!" Darien did not voice it, but he was caught off guard by the lord's comment. *Is there truth to the rumors? Did the chan-*

cellor really murder his family to take the throne away from his elder brother? Or do the nobles merely spread that story out of spite and jealousy?

Lord Byrn clapped Darien on the shoulder with a growling sort of laugh. "Har! Dine at my table tonight, Commander. I've got a fresh alkine bull just finished roasting and a good mead."

———

THE COMPANY FEASTED ON VENISON. STORES WERE SCANT AND expensive this far north, so the chancellor had provided ample supplies. Another reason they were slow in coming to Stormfall. Darien and General Thuva ate at Lord Byrn's private table at the head of the hall, and Byrn grew more rowdy as the night and the ale progressed. Darien felt a little guilty accepting Lord Byrn's offer. He preferred to dine with his soldiers. He'd always respected General Thrain for such actions. But it was an excuse to avoid Valeria. If she suspected what he planned to do, he feared he would lose his nerve.

More than once, she eyed him from across the great hall, and he feared she suspected his plans to leave her here. He had spoken with the Morphs he had chosen to take with him. They would leave in the night. It would be cold, but Darien thought it easier. She might talk him out of it if he told her himself.

Darien drank little of Lord Byrn's mead, but he devoured the roasted alkine. He would need the strength for the night's flight. After the meal was over, the majority of the soldiers were sent to the barracks, but the Legion officers remained to drink while Lord Byrn recounted tales of skirmishes with the Crooked folk, and his greatest feats during the Trade Wars.

And suddenly Valeria was sitting beside Darien again. Closer than he would have liked. He could feel his skin growing warm just being near her.

After a particularly rip-roaring story about a blundered attack on a nearby village, in which Lord Byrn had decapitated the Crooked leader, Lord Byrn suddenly grew serious. "The Crooked folk are on the move," he said, his tone growing somber. He took a long draw from his mug. The statement implied much more.

"Course they are," said General Thuva, refilling his own. "They're ruddy cowards. All they ever were. And I expect, seeing as the Darkling Witch sent the Rulaqs back on their way, the beasts are destructive as ever in the Teeth." Thuva deemed the likelihood of an attack from the North marginal at best, and he was none too pleased about being sent to Storm-fall on the eve of winter. Thuva was the epitome of why lordlings made piss-poor commanders, and he had made no complaints about eating and drinking while his soldiers set up their barracks.

"Aye, the Darkling Witch," said Byrn evenly.

"Bloody miracle, that was," said Thuva.

"A dark sort of miracle if you ask me."

Darien did not like these sorts of comments. Medea had an unnerving effect, it was true, but his feelings had changed much after fighting beside the sorceress. She was brave and cunning. And she was loyal to the empire.

"If that was dark magic," said Darien, suppressing his irritation, "then I say we need more of it."

"I'm only saying it was a… mystifying feat," said Byrn carefully. "You Morphs are a dark lot yourselves. Bloody brilliant, of course. But it's a strange thing what you can do. A vicious thing. I envy your magic, as a matter of fact."

"And you haven't even seen what we can do," said Valeria.

"Aye!" General Thuva laughed with more mirth than seemed appropriate.

"Aye," said Byrn. "Well, dark deeds aside, I'm inclined to agree with you, Commander. We need more of it. And soon. Now enough serious talk. How about more ale?"

The officers cheered, and General Thuva nearly spilled his mug.

Valeria's hand brushed Darien's arm as she reached for more ale. Her fingers lingered briefly on his thigh as she sat back down.

"Ah, I nearly forgot," said Lord Byrn, wiping ale from his beard. "We received a raven for you, Commander Redvar."

"What'd it say?"

"I don't make a practice of opening sealed parchments from the citadel. My attendant will fetch it for you." The Faerish man who had been serving them made to leave.

Valeria leaned close again, and Darien felt uncomfortable. He desired her touch, but not here. It was too bold, too public, even for drunken frivolity amongst comrades. The chancellor may have condoned their rela-tionship, but this was not acceptable, and the act itself was strange for her. *Is it the ale?*

"Captain Sardona, would you see to the message?" he said, glad for the excuse. His face felt flushed.

It's not the ale. She knows I'm hiding something from her.

His feelings were a mess. He wanted her by his side. But Tori had been willing to sacrifice her own friends when she resisted the chancellor the first time. He could not let Valeria be used against him. It was too great a risk.

Darien soon excused himself. "Well, it was a long march. And I've had too much ale already."

Of course, Darien had barely downed one mug, but he doubted anyone would have noticed. Lord Byrn, however, insisted on escorting Darien to his chambers in the tower above the barracks, along the northern wall of the fortress.

Lord Byrn laughed about how all Southern prissies were lightweights as they left, but his tone grew solemn once they'd reached the courtyard.

"Truth be told, I'm not as drunk as I appear either."

"Milord?"

"Barely drank a drop when I was a sailor. You never knew when some brigand would show up in the night. Only fools drink on the brink of war." He tossed the mug to the ground and it spilled a golden liquid. "Cider's all I drink these days."

"Why put on the show at all?" Darien asked. The snow had slowed again, and he felt an urge to hurry up the conversation and get ready to fly.

"Folks like a good laugh. And tales of a drunken lord give enemies a false confidence. Anyone who thinks of attacking Stormfall will have one bloody damn tougher of a fight in taking it than the tales of its lord might suggest."

"Crooked folk."

"Aye. And perhaps more where they came from."

"What do you know about the Alyut?" Darien asked, his interest piqued.

"I know there's more than Crooked folk that would bring these soldiers to my halls. And I know the commander of the Sky Guard en't here to bandy about war stories. Something is stirring in the Great White North. And it en't the bloody Rulaqs. That's what I know. My house's been saying for years that the wild folk won't be content to live on the fringes of civilization forever. Like I said, we have more contact with the

Northmen than anyone. And if the reason I suspect you're here is correct, then I wish you'd brought a couple thousand Shadows instead of five hundred. An army led by the Gallows Girl could ruin us this far north."

And I'm flying into the thick of it. But then, Darien had known as much all along. "I mean to end this before that can happen, Lord Byrn."

"I hope you do, Commander. I hope you do."

They reached the top of the stairs to the tower, and Byrn bid him good night. When Darien opened the door, his hand flew to his blade instinctively.

The room was dark, but he could sense someone's presence. The bed had been disturbed. He drew his saber and entered, his heart pounding.

Laughter filled the darkness.

The door closed with a slam.

Darien spun.

A lantern ignited. The sudden light illuminated Valeria's pale skin. His heart pounded, now for different reasons. She wore the nightling gown she had once worn to sneak into his estate in Maro'El. Her smile was calculated and seductive.

Darien stowed his blade. "What are you doing?"

"Waiting," she said, drawing near. Valeria gripped the collar of his uniform and pulled him close. So close he could feel the rise and fall of her chest against his own. Her breasts pressed against him, and he felt warm all over. He couldn't stop himself. He kissed her, but only once.

"You shouldn't be here," he whispered, his heart racing.

"You said you loved me," said Valeria. "On the ride in. Did you mean it?"

Darien had felt it for so long, he hadn't even realized he'd never told her so. "Yes."

"I love you too. I've loved you since the Shadow Camps. The other Shadows run off with nightlings as they please in the capital. And I'm tired of sneaking around. Settling for stolen kisses in dark corridors."

"This isn't sneaking around?"

"I thought this was what you wanted."

"Er... I mean, it is."

"Isn't that why you sent me away from Byrn's hall?" she said.

"I sent you to fetch a letter," he said, unable to hold back a smile. "What did it say?"

"Little of significance. Salla and his attendants have arrived in the citadel, and Chancellor Maro expressed every confidence you would succeed."

"Which is why this is a bad time for this to happen."

"It's the only time, and you know it."

"Valeria?"

"I know what the chancellor told you."

"What he told me?" said Darien.

"You intend to leave me at Stormfall while you hunt the Gallows Girl."

"How do you know?"

Valeria kissed his neck. "I'm a captain of the Sky Guard. Did you really think you could just run off in the middle of the night without me knowing it? We're here to prevent a war. Not wait for it to come to us. It's not the chancellor's way."

Gods, he loved how she could read him.

Sometimes it felt like they were one and the same person. And he could hardly resist her in her sleek gown. The sides were slit so he could see her long slender thighs when she moved. The back was open, and his hands ventured to her soft pale skin. She had let her silver hair down. He brushed it from her face and kissed her, longer this time.

"You should have just told me," she whispered, her hands lingering at the nape of his neck.

"I'm sorry."

"I'm not going to resist your orders."

"You won't?"

"I don't want to stay, but if you think it's best for the mission... I will." She ran her fingers into his hair.

Darien sighed. "You're the only thing the Gallows Girl could ever use against me, Valeria. I can't put myself in that situation."

"That's the sexiest thing you've ever said." She kissed him again and again. Her hands wandered down his back, sending shivers all through him. "You don't need to sneak away in the middle of the night. So give me tonight. Before you turn yourself over to the hands of wolves."

Her fingers reached beneath his uniform and touched bare skin, and there was no decision left for Darien to make. His world became her lips, her legs, her skin. A world he had desired for so many months.

As he lay entwined with Valeria and drifted into slumber, he wished the night would never end.

Outside, the snow returned. It fell harder and harder through the night, and when Darien pulled back the curtain in the morning, it was all he could see in any direction. Stormfall was in the heart of a blizzard.

He would not be able to fly north. Not for days.

CHAPTER THIRTY-FIVE

The sky had turned dark, though there were still hours of daylight left, as *The Whaler's Queen* led the Alyut fleet into a narrow channel off the northwestern coast of Osha. Massive cliffs towered hundreds of feet above them on either side. Snow drifted in the air lazily, and Tori hoped it would not worsen before they reached shore. But the darkness above them hinted that winter was setting in fast.

The voyage south had proven long and arduous. The Frozen Sea was a maze of massive sheets of floating ice. The small fleet had nearly been cut off when an ice shelf that stretched for many miles passed in front of them, colliding with the sheets forming in the shallow waters along the shoreline. If they had not had a Conjuri, they would have been forced to turn back. But with some of the greatest magic Tori had produced yet, she was able to force a channel through the surface-layer ice. The act had filled the warriors with even more hope.

The Gallows Saint had proved herself yet again, and more than ever, the people believed their Restoration was at hand. Even Tori's own belief had begun to require less acting. Stormfall would be the first step toward victory. There they could rally all the Alyut and Crooked folk and then launch a full-scale attack on Maro'El when Queen Seren returned with her army from the Southern Isles. And if they could take the ancient fortress swiftly and by surprise, they just might have a chance. Cyrus Maro's eyes would turn north, and Seren could attack from the south.

But Tori's hope was short-lived.

They had just received word from Seren lè Tal by raven, sent shortly before she arrived in the Southern Isles. They had survived a Morph attack. A fact that made the darkness seem to press around her. She only told Alyk. The last thing they needed was to spread unnecessary doubt and fear.

But fear was certainly warranted.

The chancellor had tried to kill Seren.

What else he knew was a mystery. Tori had the sick thought that they were sailing into a trap.

"Perhaps it will work to our advantage," Alyk said, returning the parchment.

His hand rested on her shoulder, and she leaned into his touch. "How?"

He pulled her closer. "If the chancellor's worried about the Southern Isles, then we just might pull this thing off by surprise." The snow specked his dark hair.

"You should be worrying of important things."

The voice made Tori jump and spin around.

It was Lir'ghe, hovering just above her. His dark eyes and fierce expression made him look sinister against the backdrop of clouds. A young soldier scowled from across the deck. The Alyut were still unnerved by the demon faerie even though he had proven incredibly useful in helping them navigate the Frozen Sea by scouting ahead for icebergs. Tori was not angered at his appearance, but at the creature's tendency for eavesdropping.

"You were listening in?" Tori said, moving away from Alyk.

"I hear you speak of my queen. You should be telling me anyway. But it is no matter."

"You're not worried about her? About things in the South?"

Lir'ghe crossed his arms. "What if, what if... worrying does nothing for my queen. She will do what needs done. We are on the brink of battle, Gallows Girl. We must be worrying about this only. The channel is growing narrow. We are nearly to shore."

They had been winding through cliff-lined channels for a full day. They seemed to be an endless maze with no shore. "These cliffs are just as high as ever."

"These channels are always being like this," said Lir'ghe. "But there is shore."

"How do you know?"

"I fly ahead and only now am returning." The demon faerie shook with something like laughter.

Tori shook her head with relief. These towering fjord walls reminded her of the narrow canyon that had led to the Watchtower. The last time she had been there, Ren had been about to bring the canyon walls down to block out the Rulaqs.

She pushed the thought away. Every time she thought of Ren, she was reminded of her failure the night the chancellor attacked. It pained her to think of what Ren and the other Watchers were suffering because of her failure.

She had agreed with Seren that freeing the Watchers could not be their first priority. They would be weakened from bloodletting and would provide little help in taking the citadel. But Tori was determined to free them. That, in and of itself, would be a victory. And time was of the essence. Ren and the others were not Regeneros. They would not last for months and months like she had. And she had great doubts the Alyut would be storming the citadel anytime soon.

A victory in Stormfall was one thing. But Maro'El? Even with a fleet from the Southern Isles, they would be fighting against the Legions, the most notorious and well-trained army in the New World.

"Well, if not for your queen, and the hope of her army, what important things should we be worrying about?" Tori asked, not bothering to mask her irritation.

Lir'ghe buzzed closer and hovered above her shoulder. He spoke so only she and Alyk could hear. "You should be worrying about why there is being no sign of Skya and her riding bears."

They had lost several days due to the heavy number of icebergs in the Frozen Sea, in addition to the ice shelf encounter.

Tori cursed. "They should be here by now!"

"It will be all right, Tori," said Alyk, glaring at the Kroqala.

"All right? What if there was a storm in the Teeth? What if the rogue clans turned? What if the Crooked folk—"

"What if, what if…" murmured Lir'ghe.

Alyk squeezed her hand. "Skya will make it. I am sure of it."

They rounded a corner in the narrowing channel, and Tori spotted the shore. Her heart swelled with relief. At least one thing was going well.

———

THE ALYUT FLEET CAME TO SHORE JUST IN TIME. NO SOONER HAD they weighed anchor than snow began to descend in thick streaks of white. The company quickly set up camp along a small stretch of rocky shoreline at the edge of the forest. Tori sent scouts up to the top of the fjord, led by Lir'ghe, who could travel the most inconspicuously.

After a supper of cured seal meat, Tori gathered the elders and warrior leaders in a tent coated with mammut fur to hear the scouts' report.

A gnawing anxiety picked at her insides. She had eaten nothing for supper. So much needed to go right. And there was still no sign of Skya.

"The fortress is near," said a young *Tu'va* boy named Renak. "Three miles south, at the top of a fjord. We could just see it before the snow picked up."

"It's larger than I thought it'd be," said Jorn of the *Karu'va*.

"Aye, and the fortress is strongly held, as well," said a speargirl named Dalla.

"What do you mean?" said Fara dul Baruk.

Dalla glanced at Lir'ghe, who hung in midair at the center of the group. "Lir'ghe saw 'em. He told us not to say so. But—"

"Say what, demon?" The High Elder's eyes were filled with spite.

The faerie held her fiery gaze and shrugged nonchalantly. "Numbers are no matter."

"Numbers are everything," said Fara dul Baruk. "We're missing much of our army. We thought this place would be loosely held. Without the Bear Riders, we will be no match. And if we wait, we risk being spotted by rangers from Stormfall. We've not even started and this is a fool's war."

"This is being subjective," said Lir'ghe.

"How many soldiers are there?" Tori asked, more gently, though she, too, was angry at the faerie's dismissive response.

"A thousand," said Lir'ghe.

"There were only supposed to be a few hundred!" said Lyren dul Vanuk.

"Aye, reckon there were," said Dalla. "Until the new troops arrived. Lir'ghe saw 'em when he flew ahead to scout out the terrain around Stormfall."

"New troops!" roared Elder Baruk.

Lir'ghe crossed his arms and scowled. "This is why I am not wanting to say. Now fear is taking over."

"Well-founded fear, I'd say," said Elder Vanuk.

"Gods," the High Elder murmured. "The chancellor already knows we're coming."

Alyk shook his head. "How large was this new regiment, Lir'ghe?"

"Five hundred. I count while I am scouting."

"And did you see the chancellor?"

"No."

Tori understood what Alyk was getting at. "If the chancellor knew, he would be with them. He would have sent far more troops."

"He is suspicious, at least," said Fara dul Baruk.

Why would he be? Tori thought of Seren's letter. How had the chancellor found her skyship?

The High Elder went on. "One thousand will leave us evenly matched considering they'll be behind that fortress. We'll lose many taking those walls."

Lir'ghe huffed and flew close to the High Elder. His voice grew hard and strangely upset. "Enough fearmongering! If elders are not believing, we will never win this battle. Besides, you are fearing for no reason."

"No reason?" Elder Baruk cried.

"This is why I ask scouts not to tell of numbers. Yes, it will be harder in taking walls. But we do not need to take them."

"What do you mean?" said Tori hopefully.

"I see many things in scouting, but most importantly, I am seeing a way in."

———

Lir'ghe explained his plan in detail, and with the storm beginning to thicken, now would be the only time it would work. Fara dul Baruk hated the idea of attacking before Skya and her Bear Riders arrived, but Tori agreed with Lir'ghe. There was a furious debate, but they all finally came to a compromise. They would wait for Skya for one day.

Tomorrow night, they would attack.

As Tori trudged through the snow to her tent, hoping to sleep a little, Lir'ghe buzzed along beside her. She stopped and gazed in the direction of the top of the fjord. She could see little now.

"You think this storm will last through tomorrow night?" she asked.

Lir'ghe nodded. "I am thinking the Northmen are knowing their storms better than me. If they believe, I will also."

Tori shivered, despite her thick layers and mammut fur cloak.

"Do not be fearing this," the faerie said.

"There's something more important, I take it."

Lir'ghe buzzed closer and perched on her shoulder. Tori had only ever seen him do this with Seren lè Tal. "There is more I see. But am not wanting to share in front of warriors. Only you."

"Why only me?"

"Because it matters only to you, I think. The one leading the new troops to Stormfall. It is not the chancellor. It is the one known as the Gallows Boy."

Darien is here.

At Stormfall…

Tori's gut twisted, and despite her exhaustion, she did not sleep all night. She thought through the coming battle over and over and over. She knew what she had to do. She envisioned it. Every scenario she could imagine. Every time she closed her eyes, she saw Darien. His dark eyes and brown skin. His muscled body in proper uniform. She saw the boy she knew from Scelero's estate.

And every time, she was killing him.

CHAPTER THIRTY-SIX

Darien was not sure he trusted the blind Watcher, Kirra Fehn. She had willfully joined the Sky Guard. She had stood by wordlessly while the chancellor took the severed hand that Darien had carried in a small satchel since they'd left Maro'El.

But Darien had been there when Kirra had tried to steal the godstones from the chancellor in the Red Palace of Vlyanii. It was for this act that she had received the wounds that scarred her face.

She was different now. And it was more than her scars or her blindness.

Then, she had been fierce and daring. Now, she kept her head down, her expression dismal. And the way her sightless head moved, as though she were searching for something, but with no eyes to search, unnerved him. Kirra was doing this when Darien discovered her at the parapet, staring off into the snowstorm that had consumed the fortress of Stormfall.

The wind howled. Snow swirled in the infinite void that stretched beyond the fortress walls.

Only one side of Kirra's head still bore hair, and this hair lashed about in the violent wind like a skiff in a hurricane. Yet she stood still, gazing out sightlessly into the abyss, her head turning back and forth.

What is she doing? Darien stood at a distance and watched her from the archway of one of the castle's towers. Darkness was approaching and the snow had still not let up. Lord Byrn claimed winter storms this far north could last days, sometimes weeks. A fact which made Darien increasingly nervous. It was too soon for such turbulent storms. Winter was descending early this year, and this felt like a dark omen.

Darien had spent the entire day pacing around. His room. The great hall. The barracks. And now the towers.

At supper, he could not eat. Valeria told him to relax. The storm would let up. His mission would be accomplished. She'd even teased that they might have another night together.

Darien had restrained himself and quietly left. He felt guilty about what they had done. The chancellor had cautioned him against letting his feelings be used against him. And he feared if he had only resisted the temptation to stay with Valeria, if he had only left last night before the storm arrived, as he had planned, he might be in the North right now.

Valeria would say that he couldn't have known. And even if he had, he would likely have been caught in the storm high in the Crooked Teeth, a prospect he did not like to think of. In a way, he was grateful to be trapped here. And he secretly longed for another night with Valeria.

Last night had been everything he'd hoped. All the passion and desire and tension that had been building inside him for months had finally been released. It had been glorious.

Until morning came.

Now, guilt plagued him, and another, darker feeling as well. He could not shake the sense that his mission was doomed. As though some... force was holding him back.

It's the gods... He could almost hear Ol' Merri's voice in his mind. *They still believe in you. An' so do I...*

Why did those dying words linger with him still?

"Gods, you are tense."

The voice made Darien jump. "W-what?"

Kirra did not turn away from the storm. "Your heart is pounding, Commander. I could've heard it from miles away."

"I... it's this storm," he said, trying to collect himself and forget treasonous thoughts. "What are you doing out here?"

Kirra did not respond at once. Her voice was soft. "Listening."

"What do you hear?"

"This storm is strong, but I think it will not last long. I expect it will clear by morning."

"How can you know this?"

"My new gift has taught me that everything tells if you listen closely enough."

"I hope you're right, comrade," said Darien. "Every delay brings us closer to an avoidable war. I meant to be in the White North by now. I meant to have delivered the chancellor's message."

"Yes, his message."

"You disapprove of the chancellor's treatment of your old captain?"

Kirra turned to face him. Her scars were still tender and swollen. "Not at all, Commander. But I wonder... do you really think the Gallows Girl will go willingly?"

"If she does not, then she condemns Ren Andovier to death. And any of the others who have not chosen the path you have."

"It is a high cost, yes," said Kirra. "But if the army that marched with us to Stormfall tells me anything, it is that the chancellor suspects the same thing I do."

Darien nodded, then realized she could not see him. "You're correct, comrade."

"He fears the Gallows Girl has formed new alliances in the North. Do you think she will forsake that for a few friends?"

Darien cringed. In truth, it was a doubt he bore as well. Tori had put her friends in danger before, at the Watchtower. Had she learned her lesson? Darien was not sure Tori would be so easily manipulated. But there were other ways...

"I don't know," Darien said. "Why are you asking about this?"

"You're a skilled commander. I just hope you have thought through your plan if the Gallows Girl does not surrender. If you are captured."

Darien nodded. "If I am not successful, you do not get your sight back."

Kirra nodded. "That is not the only reason I am concerned. But yes."

Darien could sense the sincerity in her voice. Yes, Kirra had changed much since the Red City. "How did it happen? This new gift of yours?"

"I lost one gift when I lost my sight in the Red City. And a new one awakened in its place."

"Yet you still seek your old gift."

"If you lost your leg, would you keep the peg replacement if you knew you could have the real thing again? I've lost a part of myself. And I will do whatever it takes to get it back."

"Is that the only reason you joined the Sky Guard?"

"Would you have brought me here, if you thought it was?"

Darien smiled. "No. I can tell you want this mission to succeed. But why?"

Kirra spoke carefully, as though weighing her words. "Most of my friends have already joined the Sky Guard. The others will soon, or else they will die. Because of the Gallows Girl. If she dies, the others will turn. That is what will save them. Your Sky Guard is not what Ren set out to create, but it has accomplished the same thing. My kind, our kind, are free to be ourselves. To use our gifts. That is what we longed for at the Watchtower. Why fight it?"

"Why indeed," Darien murmured.

"Ren and Tori are fighting an old fight. One that's already been lost. I've accepted that. The true enemy is not human. I witnessed the havoc the beasts wreaked on the Red City. You witnessed the devastation of the Rulaqs."

"They're no longer a threat, comrade. Medea dealt with them."

"For now, yes. But she gave them the Teeth. Do we give the Wandering Dunes to Xa'Rila? The Channel Sea to the dragons? Will the other beasts bend so easily if we try?"

The impending danger of the other beasts had weighed on his mind for some time. It was even more reason to end the unrest the Gallows Girl caused. The world was turning upside down. They could not afford to fight amongst themselves.

"I've had a lot of time to consider it, Commander. I fear we are children squabbling over trinkets while the real enemy bides its time."

"The Gallows Girl is that enemy," Darien said. "She unleashed the beasts."

"Do you truly know that?"

No, he did not. He had repeated the words because they were the chancellor's words. But he knew the chancellor feared another threat. One even greater than the Gallows Girl. However, he did not speak these thoughts to Kirra.

"Does anyone really know why these beasts are returning?" Kirra asked.

"If it's not the Gallows Girl, then the quicker she's dealt with, the quicker we can face the true enemy."

"And that is why I'm here. It's late, Commander. You should rest. I think you'll be able to set out in the morning."

"The storm tells you that?"

Kirra nodded.

"I think I *will* rest, comrade. Thank you." Darien believed her, and he was relieved to hear it. He was anxious to get this hunt over with. He returned to his chambers to find them disappointingly empty. Suddenly, he felt foolish for having abandoned Valeria at supper. He was acting as worrisome as a young mother, and he needn't.

His mission would succeed.

In the meantime, he desired to forget his worries for the night.

He left his room. In the distance, he could hear his soldiers laughing and hollering from the great hall. Lord Byrn had been generous with the wine and ale, considering the number Darien had brought with him. The frivolity grew louder as he neared.

He found Captain Brujha at the edge of the hall. Lord Byrn was recounting some martial escapade, and many of the soldiers were howling at his tale. Brujha sipped from her mug of ale. Her hair was dark and curly and her skin a dark brown, in her human form. In her Morph form she was Darien's kin, with bat-like wings and claws that could slice through skin as though it were paper.

She glanced over at Lord Byrn at the head of the hall and shook her head.

"Not your type of tale?" Darien asked.

"Ol' soldiers are all the same. Their tales o' war are as true as their nightling escapades. All a bloody pissing contest."

Darien smiled. He'd always liked Brujha's coarse honesty.

"Any word on the storm?" she said.

"We fly at dawn."

Brujha pushed the mug away. "Good. If I hear another one o' Byrn's stories, I may challenge him to a pissing contest myself. And wouldn't that be a sight? I'll tell the Morphs to switch to water." There was a devious glint in her eye.

"I'll see you at dawn."

"Ooh, rah, Commander."

Darien glanced about the room one last time, but he already knew Valeria was not there.

Brujha got up to leave, but before she left, she drew closer and whispered, "I believe the captain retired to her quarters a short while ago."

"Er, what?"

Brujha just shook her head and walked off, muttering something to herself and chuckling.

Darien left the great hall, drawing his hood up. Brujha might know, and maybe all of them did, but he felt uneasy about his soldiers seeing him openly involved with their captain.

But Stormfall was empty and no one saw him. He hurried to the next tower and knocked on Valeria's door. She had shed her uniform and wore only a thin shirt and woolen breeches. She pulled him in quickly.

"Gods, you'll let out all the warmth!" She smirked, her eyes alight in the flickering glow.

A fire blazed in the hearth, and Darien followed her over to the mantle, where a flask of wine had been opened.

"The storm should pass by morning," Darien said.

"Good," said Valeria. "Perhaps you had better rest tonight."

Darien did not answer verbally. But he had no intention of resting. He pulled her to him and kissed her. His whole body tingled with warmth and desire, and he slipped his hand beneath Valeria's shirt.

To his surprise, Valeria pushed his hand back and pulled away.

"W-what's wrong?" he said.

Valeria chuckled. "Too fast, Commander Redvar."

"What do you mean?"

Valeria rolled her eyes. "I may be a soldier, Darien, but I'm still a woman. Start slow." She reached for the flask and poured some into a mug. "Start with some wine."

Darien drank deeply. It was an old vintage, but it hadn't aged as well as wines did in Maro'El. But still, it warmed him.

"I'm glad you came around," Valeria said softly, drawing near again. Her fingers traced their way up his arms, and she removed his thick fur cloak. "I told you it would pass. Your mission will succeed. As it always does."

"I was foolish. I'm sorry." He held out the mug to her.

She shook her head and fetched her own. "I started before you arrived."

Valeria pulled him toward the bed. He took another long pull of wine. There was an odd taste to it. *Wine from the edge of the world,* he thought. *But it does the same job.*

Already, Darien felt warm all over. Valeria's hand touched his face, the side of his neck, and his skin tingled with shivers. She pulled him closer and kissed his neck. Her teeth nibbled at his skin, and this felt like a thousand sensations at once. He ran his hands through her soft silver hair, and she sighed. He closed his eyes and disappeared into the moment, his mind drifting. He could feel Valeria's hands running over him, and together, they fell back into the bed.

He felt light. As though they had disappeared into another realm.

But then, suddenly, Valeria disappeared too.

Darien opened his eyes, but his sight was hazy. Had the room filled with smoke? What was wrong? He tried to sit up, but his limbs felt like they weighed three times their normal weight and he fell back.

"Wh-whuz goinggg onnn?" he slurred. His tongue felt like a stone in his throat.

A blur passed before him.

"I'm sorry, Commander," Valeria said, though her soft voice felt like it was traveling a great distance. As though it were carried by the wind.

Darien could barely raise his head. Something passed in front of him. It was a mug.

The wine.

With horror, he realized what was happening.

"Whhhyyy?"

"I hated to do it, Darien. Truly." She tossed the mug of wine aside and came close. She kissed him one last time. "But it was the only way."

Darien was drifting farther and farther away from reality. The haze in his eyes thickened.

There was a great clamor. Something like thunder. And then another voice shouted from across a vast chasm.

The door opened and cold air rushed into the room. The chill wakened him slightly.

"Commander! Come quick! There's something in the storm. We're under attack!"

It was Kirra.

The last thing Darien saw was a flash of silver as Valeria approached the blind Watcher, her saber outstretched.

Darien tried to warn Kirra.

But his shouts were swallowed by an endless fog.

———

THE WORLD CHURNED LIKE A RAGING SEA AS DARIEN WOKE FROM the darkest nightmare he'd ever had. No, that was wrong. He woke in the darkest nightmare. His head throbbed, but the foggy effects of whatever

Valeria had laced the wine with had worn off, and he saw the nightmare with distinct clarity.

Blood streamed into the room from outside.

Kirra lay in the doorway, sprawled on her face, unmoving.

The blood was hers.

The sight made Darien sick. Frantically, he wrapped a cloth around the wound. The blood was warm, which meant she was alive for now.

The clamor of war echoed from the courtyard. *They've penetrated the fortress. How did they get in?*

But Darien already knew the answer. Valeria had betrayed him. Betrayed all her comrades to Tori's Northmen. Suddenly, Valeria's strange questions outside Stormfall rang true. She had been evaluating her next move. Had she known all along what would happen here? Had she been a traitor all these months? Since the Shadow Camps?

Darien staggered across the room, pulling on his leathern armor and grabbing a dirk from a belt draped over a chair. His fingers thrummed with rage as he gripped Valeria's blade. The screams of dying men and women filled his ears. When he reached the door, he nearly retched.

The courtyard was filled with bodies, most of them wearing Legion uniforms. Soldiers in thick white furs tore through them with jagged spears. Their form was like nothing he'd seen. The Northmen didn't move like trained regiments. They moved like wolves, working in groups to take down Shadow after Shadow. The Legions could not organize. Gunfire throttled the world in random bursts.

It was sick chaos.

Darien grieved as he watched his comrades fall.

Where are the Morphs? None of the creatures he'd brought from the citadel filled the air. There were no warg-like beasts taking down spearmen in the courtyard.

Darien changed his skin, dark wings spreading from his back, and he took flight. The Morphs slept in the adjacent tower, and the door was open. Darien tucked his wings and landed, morphing back to his human form as he shot through the doorway.

Inside was one of the most horrifying sights he had ever witnessed in battle.

For it was not an act of war, but betrayal.

The bodies of Morphs littered the floor, the beds. Four had slept there. All of them dead. Streams of thick fresh blood stained their necks.

Throats slit.

In their sleep.

Darien gripped his dirk and turned at the sound of footsteps. He nearly let his blade fly, but was glad he hesitated.

Captain Brujha appeared in the doorway. "Thank the gods, Commander. I thought you were dead." Blood streaked from a wound in her shoulder.

"What happened, Captain?" said Darien.

"She killed them all. Right before the attack."

"And not you?" Darien realized if Valeria had been part of this, anyone could have been. He readied the blade in his hands.

Brujha staggered away from the doorway. "The bitch came for me last. It was her mistake."

Darien felt the strangest tangle of emotions at the words. "Did you…"

"Nah, she lived."

"A damn shame."

"I didn't have my armor. But I still gave her a gods-damned fight. She flew when the Northmen reached the gates. I'd have followed, but I can't fly with this." She gripped her shoulder to stem the flow of blood.

Valeria killed the Morphs and then let the Northmen in to finish off the rest. He tasted bile.

Darien took hold of Brujha's other arm and helped her. An idea had come to him. "The great hall. We have to regroup or they'll tear us apart." She nodded, and together they staggered from the room.

But as soon as he stepped outside, a pair of Northwomen raced forward. Darien shoved Brujha aside. The first woman lunged with her spear. Darien dodged it. The walkway was narrow at the top of the tower. Only one could attack at a time. It was a risk. If he missed, it was over. But he waited until she lunged again, stepped aside, and let his blade fly.

It hit its mark in the woman's neck. As she slumped forward, he seized the shaft of her spear, whipped it around, and faced the other Northwoman.

Their pack tactics might work in open quarters, but up here in this narrow space, one-on-one, her lack of skill would be the death of her. She jabbed at his head, whipping her spear around with skill. But Darien was quick. He backed up, blocking another blow. She shot forward, farther this time, and Darien morphed so fast, the woman could not react. He flew to the side and whipped the spear around, slicing through her thick furs and splitting open her back. She screamed.

Darien landed behind her and drove the spear through her spine.

A cheer rose up at the sight of the commander in his Morph form. Brujha staggered, and Darien gripped her around the waist to steady her. The world below was a swarm of madness, smoke, and blood. "We'll get you to the hall." He motioned to the steps. But already another Northman was approaching.

Brujha shook her head. "I've got a better idea." She pointed to the dead Morphs' quarters. "Their muskets are still there. I'll cover you."

Darien squeezed her hand. "It's been an honor serving with you, Captain."

While Brujha loaded weapons, Darien dispatched the Northman. Brujha came out with four muskets. Now it was time for Darien to join the fray. He took flight.

Below the tower, Lord Byrn sparred with a giant beast of a man.

Darien swooped down and let his spear fly, skewering the man through the neck.

He landed in the courtyard, morphing back to his human form, and more Shadows formed up around him. He gripped Byrn's shoulder. "We must fall back to the great hall. We're too spread out here."

"Ooh, rah, Commander! Glad to see you survived the assassinations!"

Darien turned to the Shadows around him. "Stay together. Work in groups. When there's a way, make for the hall."

"Ooh, rah!"

A mass of warfare stood between them and the narrow lane that led to Lord Byrn's hall. General Thuva sparred with a pair of Northmen. He wasn't bad for a noble. Darien raced over to help, but before he reached them, a shot rang out. One Northman dropped, and Thuva made quick work of the other.

Darien found a saber on the ground and did what he did best.

Kill.

He kept close to Byrn and Thuva, and slowly more soldiers formed up around their leaders. They formed a circle of defense and slowly began to open a path toward the great hall. Brujha picked off several more Northern fighters, and soon they were able to begin pressing their way through the lane.

Brujha picked off two more Northmen and was reloading when the Gallows Girl appeared. Tori flew across the courtyard in the span of a fawn's breath and stabbed Brujha through the chest. Darien cringed as his comrade fell.

Another figure appeared at Tori's side.

Valeria. In her Morph form.

Darien did not have time to react. He screamed at his soldiers. "To the hall! Now!"

The Shadows sprinted through the narrow lane, cutting down the last of the invaders. If they could take back the hall, the narrow entrance might allow them to hold their own against this horde.

Darien did not follow. He stood to face Tori and Valeria, his face growing hot with rage.

CHAPTER THIRTY-SEVEN

The Morph sharpshooter gasped her last breaths with violent blood-filled coughs as Tori withdrew her blade. Darien's eyes were on fire as they locked on her.

Tori knew what she had to do.

There was no denying it now.

Even without Skya's Bear Riders, the Alyut and Crooked folk had infiltrated the fortress easily with Valeria's help. Tori had never been so glad to see a Morph in her life. Lir'ghe had flown ahead to warn Valeria. Tori marveled at the way the Witch Queen had been orchestrating rebellion against the chancellor for years.

Valeria had helped Mischa and Tori escape the chancellor's clutches in the catacombs beneath the Crooked Teeth. And she had been waiting for the ultimate moment to reveal her treachery against the White Citadel.

Valeria landed beside Tori. The Morph traitor gripped her hand. Nothing had held her back, and nothing could hold Tori back now.

Tori gripped her saber tight. *Where did he come from?*

Suddenly, Tori realized something.

"You spared him. All the other Morphs are dead."

"I couldn't do it," said Valeria. "I couldn't kill him. And this is my fault. The Legions are regrouping. But without Redvar, this is over. You have to kill him!"

The Legions were falling back. It must have been Darien's plan all along. If they regrouped beyond the courtyard, their smaller numbers might make little difference. They were better trained. *Gods, where in the Abyss are the Bear Riders?*

Darien strode forward in the courtyard below. A young Alyut warrior brazenly attacked, but Darien cut him down easily. The entire square was littered with bodies. Alyut. Oshan. Crooked folk. All of their blood mixed together in the snow.

Another warrior, a Crooked woman this time, and Darien slew her with a quick maneuver and a sweep of his blade. Tori tensed, marveling at his skill with a saber. He was a fine soldier, an incredible fighter. And a commander who could turn the tide of this battle.

Valeria was right. She had to kill him.

Tori was about to fly and attack, when Darien shouted, "Is this what you wanted, Tori?"

Darien killed one attacker, and then another. The Northmen began avoiding him, chasing after the others. The courtyard thinned as the Shadows retreated to the inner halls of the fortress, and a wide space opened up around Darien.

"All this blood is on your hands, Gallows Girl! And on yours, Captain Sardona!"

Valeria shook her head. "You chose the wrong side, Darien! I'm sorry!"

"If this is the wrong side, what do you have to be sorry for?"

A brash young Crooked girl attacked from behind, but Darien ducked and spun around, slicing open her stomach with a flourish. Her blood and entrails joined the growing pool in the snow.

Valeria gripped Tori's hand. She was trembling. Tori felt like she might retch.

"Is this your hope for the New World?" Darien bellowed. "These soldiers you've killed are like you and me, Tori. Do you remember how Legions get drafted?"

Darien was drawing closer and closer, and Tori's resolve was teetering. "I remember the monster who drafted them, Darien. I remember what you once were!"

"This is who I am." Darien exchanged blows with an Alyut man. In three moves, he had dealt the death blow. "And I am damn good at it! I protected the realm from the Rulaqs you stirred up. And I'll protect it from you again."

Now, Tori was angry. She dropped from the tower and landed in the courtyard, her saber extended. "I didn't open up that portal, Darien. That was your precious chancellor!"

"The chancellor is not what you want him to be. He raised me up, Tori. He took a scared mountain boy and turned him into a commander. Someone who can make a difference."

"This is your difference?" Tori shouted, stepping closer.

"You attacked *us*, remember? I came here for you. No one else." With that, Darien sprinted toward her.

At the last second, she took to the air. But Darien anticipated the maneuver. He morphed into his winged form and joined her there. Their sabers clashed. Tori spun around, exchanging blow after blow, but somehow, Darien seemed to see her moves before she'd begun. Their sabers danced a dark dance through the air.

But he wasn't ready for her magic.

As he moved on the offensive, she reached out with her senses. A large stone shot through the air. Darien saw it in the corner of his eye and ducked. Tori lunged with her sword and grazed his leg.

She shot past him and landed on a parapet overlooking the great hall. The Legions had regrouped inside. There were only two entrances at the top of a wide staircase, and the Shadows were cutting her Northern warriors down. The stairs filled with bodies. The tide of the battle was turning.

Darien landed farther down the rampart. He didn't even limp. The wound was barely a scratch. He took in the sight below and grimaced. *His army is gaining the upper hand. Why would he be upset?*

He stalked forward. Tori hated the sight of him in his Morph form. The monster the chancellor had put in Darien's body. But one person had believed in him. Before she died, Merri had sworn the real Darien was still in that monstrous form somewhere. A strange thought came to her after seeing him grimace at the sight of the carnage of war.

"Why didn't you kill her?" Tori let her sword down.

Darien came closer. "Who?"

"Ol' Merri," said Tori. "You knew her. You knew she'd never turn dark."

Darien grimaced again. "She played me. It was a mistake I won't make again."

"You chose to bring her to the Watchtower. You chose *her* to drain my blood. You let her get close."

"You don't know what you're talking about, Gallows Girl."

But the more she spoke, the more she understood what Merri had seen. "You're a brilliant commander. Anyone can see that. You're no fool. It's almost like you… wanted Merri to set me free."

Darien leapt into the air, and Tori barely raised her sword in time. She parried the blow and spun through the air. He struck again and again. She might not have possessed his skill with a blade, but she had learned much at the Watchtower. They swept over the battle below, swords flying, snow swirling around them. But Darien's strength began to wear on her. Tori reached out for her sense and sent a brick flying. It clipped his wing, but as he fell, he lashed out at her with his saber.

Tori's side ripped open.

She landed on a tower roof. Darien recovered and flew to her. His left wing was weakened, but not by much. They faced off, circling the angular surface. Tori groaned as her wound closed over. Thankfully it wasn't deep.

"There's still good in you, Darien."

Darien glared at her, his Morph eyes flashing in the early morning light. "Who are you to say what's good? Are you really naïve enough to think you bear no guilt for what's happened to our world? Look below. Do you see the cost of your rebellion?"

Tori clenched her teeth at the death. "You have no idea what guilt I bear."

Darien morphed back to his human form. His expression turned. It was not anger but sorrow. He looked out at the bloody chaos that had overtaken the fortress of Stormfall. "I do not revel in bloodshed, Tori. But I do my duty when it needs to be done. I mourn my comrades. But I grieve especially when they die for no purpose." He gestured at the carnage below. "Is this worth it? Alyut lives? Crooked lives? The lives of Legion boys and girls who never chose this?"

Tori saw so much blood. And suddenly, she felt the weight of Darien's words. Was she good? Was this any different than the blood that had once been drained from her body?

Was this her blood harvest?

She did not know what to say. She knew war would be like this, but she hadn't understood the cost. Not until she saw the blood and guts of men and women littering the snow, only their shells left behind.

"What about Ren's life?" Darien asked. "The other Watchers?"

"What are you talking about?"

"I did not come to the North seeking war. I came to bring you back. To end this."

"For Vashti's wedding gift?"

Darien nodded. "Everything has a cost, Tori. If you don't come, you damn Ren and all the others who refused the chancellor's mercy." Darien lowered his saber. "Call this off. Before more innocent people die. The chancellor wants this to end. He'll spare them if you turn yourself in."

Tori did not know what to do. The Alyut and Crooked folk were piling up outside the great hall. Could they even win? Was it worth losing every one of them?

Tori did not have a chance to answer.

She did not realize what was happening until it was too late.

A dark blur shot past her in the falling snow. It did not attack her, but Darien.

He could not react in time.

Valeria collided with him, her saber piercing him through the gut.

And together, they fell.

CHAPTER THIRTY-EIGHT

The world came to a halt. Moments stretched toward eternity. Tori's senses were a blazing fury. Darien and Valeria fought and twisted in the air as they fell from the tower. If the wound did not kill him, the fall certainly would.

Tori could not let him die.

She wanted to believe he was a monster.

A monster was easy to kill.

But whatever Darien was, it was more complicated than that. And despite what he had become, Tori cared for the man inside the Morph. The man who was still good, deep down. She had seen it.

Tori reached out with her senses. The world became infinitesimally small. She sensed Darien's body. Valeria's body. The energy that flowed between them. Between all things. She reached for it and slowed their descent.

They sprawled out in the snow. Valeria spun around to face Darien as he staggered to his feet. She gripped her blade tightly. It dripped with his blood. Darien's blade launched from his fingers in a flash.

But the blade froze in midair.

Tori released her magic and let it fall to the snow.

Darien clutched his stomach, blood pouring onto the snow. "Go on, Sardona!" he shouted, extending his arms vulnerably. "Finish it, you back-stabbing whore!"

Valeria stepped forward, crying, her saber outstretched. "Damn you, Darien Redvar!"

Tori shot to the ground, landing between them. "Nooo!"

"Don't be a fool!" Valeria shouted, tears streaming down her face. "It's the only way to end this, Tori."

Tori held out her hands, ready to let her magic flare if she needed to. "You're wrong."

Darien dropped to his knees, clutching his wound. He was turning pale, agony stretched across his face.

"It's over, Valeria!" Tori shouted.

"What are you talking about?"

"Listen."

It was barely audible over the clash of sabers and the thunder of musket-fire, but it echoed from the valley, building off the peaks of the Crooked Teeth, like the cry of an animal in the woods.

A war horn.

Bellowing from beyond the fortress.

"W-what is that?" Darien stammered, his entire body trembling. His face paled from blood loss.

"You underestimated our strength. Tell your Shadows to surrender, Commander," Tori said, relief sweeping over her. "Or let them all die at the hands of the Bear Riders and rogue clans of the Great White North."

The ground thundered as they reached the gates of Stormfall.

Tori knew what Darien would do. She had seen his eyes when he saw the carnage of this battle. He would not let his soldiers die needlessly.

Darien shouted the command moments before the Bear Riders stormed through the opened gates of the city.

The Battle of Stormfall was over.

———

THINGS BECAME A BLUR FOR TORI AS THE BATTLE CAME TO AN END. At the sight of the Bear Riders, the Legions quickly laid down their weapons, emerging from the great hall with hands behind their heads.

The leader of the rogue clans, Heldan dul Travak, bemoaned that they had missed all the glory of the battle. But Skya just shook her head with a smile and barked orders for the capture of their enemies. Those without mortal wounds were chained and guarded in the barracks of Stormfall. Tori ordered that the rest, along with Darien, be tended by the shamans.

This came at the protest of Fara dul Baruk. "You're making a grave mistake, Burodai. We should execute every one of them. Do you think for a minute that they would have done the same for us?"

Tori hoped they would have. But she did not say so. "We cannot become what we are fighting against, Elder Baruk."

"They showed no such mercy when they ripped our homelands from our ancestors. They showed no such mercy when they came for your kind. If we spare them, we give them another opportunity to stab us from behind."

But Tori knew where Legion soldiers came from. Darien had reminded her. Lowborn townships. The slaves of nobles. They were not the enemy. "They did not choose this war, Elder Baruk. Nor the side on which they must fight. They have never had a choice. I think it is time they were given one. But either way, we will not execute soldiers who have willingly surrendered."

"You would let them join us?" the chief exclaimed incredulously. "You would condemn us to death."

Thankfully, Alyk chimed in. "Our saint led us to victory, *Madru*."

"And you?" Fara asked her daughter.

Skya did not speak at once. She surveyed the battlefield as the Shadows were being led away. She measured her words carefully. "This is one victory. We now have a stronghold in Osha, but we've lost hundreds."

Fara scowled. "You brought many Crooked folk from the Teeth."

It was true. Skya had been delayed due to a war council among the Crooked villages. They had all agreed to band with the Alyut and the Southern Isles. The Northern host now housed at Stormfall was one to be proud of.

"Yes," said Skya. "They give us hundreds more hunters and townsfolk. But if we ever hope to storm Maro'El, we will need more than Alyut and Crooked folk. This revolution is meant to inspire the lowborn. Why shouldn't that include the Legions?"

Fara dul Baruk stormed away. "I've raised fools for children."

Skya saw to the war prisoners, ensuring they were well-fed and tended. Alone, Alyk and Tori embraced. The fog of leadership and duty faded for a moment, and relief washed over her. She pulled away but held onto his hand a moment longer. "I'm so glad you're all right."

Alyk's expression fell as he surveyed the carnage. It would be days of recovery. Tending to wounds. Burning the dead. "I'm not all right."

"War is hideous," Tori muttered.

Alyk merely nodded.

"Am I being a fool?"

Alyk sighed. "After all this bloodshed, I wonder if this entire thing is a fool's errand. But you are not a fool in this. We can't do things like the chancellors. We have to think about what comes after." Alyk let go of her hand. "I should tend to the wounded."

"I need you to see to the care of someone."

"Who?" said Alyk carefully.

"Commander Redvar."

"The Gallows Boy?"

Tori nodded. "His wounds are severe."

"I should be seeing to our own wounded first."

"He could die."

"He's the commander of our enemy," Alyk said, grimacing.

"Which makes him a valuable prisoner, Alyk."

Alyk sighed. "All right."

The great hall was transformed into a makeshift hospital, with Northmen and Shadows laid out on tables. Tori joined Alyk and the other shamans in seeing to the wounded. It was important she be seen by those who had nearly given their lives for her. She stopped by their bedsides and held their hands and offered words of encouragement. She spoke of hope and justice to warriors as their gaping wounds were cleaned and limbs were prepared for amputation. She helped where she could, but her Conjuri magic could not heal flesh and sinew. She could help set broken bones, but she could not fuse them back together as she could her own.

The Legions were housed on the other side of the room. A young boy was shrieking in pain. Several of the Northmen complained. "Gods, just put the bastard out of his misery!"

Tori frowned. "He's just a boy."

"He's the bloody enemy!" cried a thickset Crooked man.

This sentiment was not his alone. Tori had to make a statement. Both to the Northmen and the Shadows. She approached the boy's bedside. His leg was in shreds. A spear had nearly shorn it off. It was a jagged wound, and the lower half of his leg hung by exposed tendons and strips of flesh. The boy heaved with frantic breaths as a pair of shamans attempted to hold him down and shove a strip of cloth between his teeth, without success. At the sight of the Gallows Girl, the boy's eyes went wide, and he twisted and turned in bed.

"Use your sorcery and be done with me!" he shouted at her.

Tori's eyes filled with tears. This boy was Yan Avii. Her own blood. "I don't want to see you dead. But that leg will be the death of you. You've got to hold still."

The boy tensed all over. "I was there!" he screamed.

"Where?" she said softly.

"The Watchtower. The catacombs. I marched your friends in chains. I am your enemy! You want me dead, so just kill me!"

Tori bit the side of her lip, trying to keep her composure. "I don't want you to die. You're my tribesman."

"I am the blade in the chancellor's hand. A Shadow in his Legions."

"That is what you do. Not who you are. What tribe did you come from?"

The boy was crying with the pain, but he had stopped struggling. *Gods,* she thought. *He's younger than me.*

"I come from tribe Mynah."

"I am a Burodai."

The boy chuckled darkly, then winced. "You see? Even in the Red City we would be enemies."

"Why?" Tori said.

"It is the way of the world."

"Because some Burodai long ago quarreled with a Mynah? Because of the sins of our ancestors?"

"Because I serve the chancellor," the boy muttered.

"Right now, you serve no one. You're a prisoner. My prisoner. That puts you under my command now. And I command you to shut your mouth and let my healers help you."

"Why?" the boy said, shuddering under the grip of the shamans.

"Because you're just a boy. Now bite down on this." Tori handed him the cloth. "I'll stay with you until it's over." She gripped his bloody hand, and to her surprise, he held on to her. The amputation was quick. The boy squeezed so hard, her fingers went pale and numb, but soon, he passed out. Which was for the best. The shamans worked swiftly to clean and dress the stump before he woke again.

It wasn't until she pried her fingers loose and moved on that she realized all the wounded Shadows had been watching her the entire time. Their eyes followed her as she walked over to Darien's makeshift bed. She had been avoiding it as long as she could. She feared the sight of him, feared he might be dead already, and feared even more what she would do if he lived.

Alyk finished dressing the wounds as she arrived. Darien's eyes were closed. His chest heaved with each breath, as though each one were strained. His skin had turned a yellowish color.

"He passed out while I was sewing him up," Alyk said. Like her, he had blood all over him.

"Will he live?" Tori asked tremulously.

"The saber missed his vital organs. But it will not heal easily. If it grows infected, he could fade into a burning nightmare. A terrible death. But for now, he looks all right."

"Thank you."

Alyk nodded wordlessly, his eyes passing from Tori to Darien. There was something unsaid in his gaze.

"You think I'm making a mistake letting him live," Tori ventured.

Alyk opened his mouth, about to speak, then shook his head. "It is not my place to say, my saint. I should tend to the other soldiers. Our soldiers. I'll see you later." He walked off without another word.

Tori stood by Darien's side for a short while but was soon interrupted from her thoughts.

"Can I speak with you, my saint?" Valeria Sardona asked.

Seemingly at the sound of her voice, Darien began to spasm. His eyes shot open. They were bloodshot, and they fixed on Valeria.

"You bitch!" he rasped, his voice shot. "You traitorous whore!" He tried to pull himself to a sitting position and toppled over, shrieking in pain. A pair of shamans came rushing over and eased him back onto the table. Darien closed his eyes, but continued to tremble violently.

"It might be best if you leave," one of the shamans said.

Fighting tears, Tori took Valeria by the arm and led her out onto the steps, where only hours ago, the bodies of Legions and Northmen had littered the snow. Now, the storm had ceased, and a fire had been lit, consuming the dead.

"I am sorry for that, my saint," Valeria said.

"You've saved my life twice now," she said. "Call me Tori."

"I am sorry for that, Tori."

"It's a fever dream."

"Perhaps. But I believe it shows the point I am about to make. It is a mistake to let him live."

"You love him," said Tori. "I saw it in the catacombs. And I saw it in your eyes during the battle."

Valeria nodded. "I didn't intend to. I was a fool."

"You believed in him."

Valeria crossed her arms over her chest. Even in uniform, she was beautiful. Her silver hair glinted in the moonlight. "I was sent by Queen Seren to infiltrate the Legions. I betrayed my queen for a man I was too smart to fall for. I wasted far too much time hoping he would turn. I nearly lost myself along the way. I should have left with you in those catacombs."

"If you had, this battle might have turned out very differently. You once told me that all Shadows are not as dark as they seem."

"I did," Valeria said. "And I meant it. I saw what you did for Yari, that boy in there. I believe some Shadows would serve you, in time."

"But not Darien?"

Valeria opened her mouth to answer, but then stopped. Tori could tell she wanted to believe it.

Tori gripped her wrist. "There's still good in him. Merri saw it. I've seen it. And I know you have too."

Valeria took hold of Tori's shoulder and met her gaze. "I wanted to see it. If there is good in him, it is a small portion buried deep. It nearly tore me apart to betray him, and even so, I didn't have the heart to kill him. Not until the end. But I knew, then, that I had to finish it. I couldn't let my hopes stand in the way. Darien is too great a threat to this revolution. If you let him live, Tori, he will betray you. He is the chancellor's through and through. If you let him live, he will bring this revolution to ruin."

Tori did not know what else to say. She thanked Valeria for her counsel, and for her bravery, then dismissed her.

Night had fallen. The infirmary had quieted down, and she'd seen Alyk head for the chambers he and the shamans had claimed in one of the towers. But Tori did not go to bed with the others. She stood by the pyre in the courtyard for hours, staring into the flames. The skulls of dead soldiers seemed to gape out at her, and in all their eyes, she saw deep brown ones staring back. The eyes of a boy from the mountains she had once known and loved.

A boy who had died long ago.

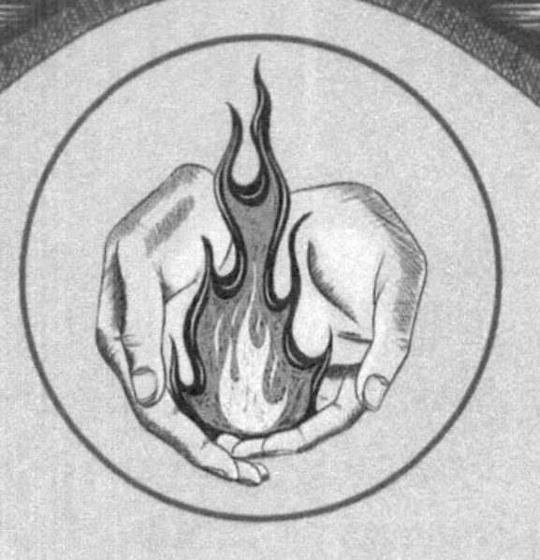

CHAPTER THIRTY-NINE

The channel approaching the island capital of Elya was narrow, and an eerie fog loomed over Seren's ship, making the water glow with a haunting green hue. It was the middle of the day, but it felt like twilight, and Mischa shivered despite the relative warmth of the Southern Isles. She felt as though she should be feeling a sense of coming home, returning to the islands of the southern world. Despite the terrible circumstances she'd fled, Mischa looked back with fondness on her homeland. The beaches and palm trees, the sweet smell of nightblooms and luscious fruits.

But this place was dark and muggy, and smelled like a fishing dock.

"We're close!" Queen Seren shouted from the helm.

Mischa was relieved. It had been two days of navigating these channels. They had not taken flight again after the Morph attack, which made for slower travel, and with tales of sea dragons as well as the Morphs, Mischa had been on edge the entire time. She was angry. Angry that the Morphs had tracked them. Angry that one of the Morphs had taken on Vashti's form to mess with her head. Angry that it had worked. Mischa hated that the Yan Avii princess still had a hold on her, even after her betrayal and Mischa's emerging feelings for Skya…

But Mischa had frozen up.

If not for Tes, they might all be dead.

They had not even begun this war, and Mischa already wished it was over. Now, the Alyut were marching to war, and Mischa felt helpless and hopeless. If the chancellor had tracked Seren to the Floating Mountains, what else did he know?

But Tes gave her courage and hope yet. Despite numerous attacks and watching both her parents die, despite killing someone for the first time, Tes somehow had not lost her childish wonder. She stood at the prow with Geryn dul Narsuk, watching the water for strange creatures and ghosts. If she was honest, Mischa wanted to run away, curl up in some safe place, and escape these horrors.

But Tes was different. She was ready to face what was to come. It was strange to think that a child could be so strong. And Mischa knew she had to be the same.

"Is it always this dark?" Mischa asked, joining the queen on the aft deck.

Seren nodded. "They say ghosts actually do live in these shallow channels," she said with a glance over at Tes.

"I thought that was just something Geryn told her to keep her occupied."

Seren smiled. "They say the waters teem with angry Islanders from Old World sea battles who long for revenge against the Oshans who overtook this place. That is why the water glows green. But my *scholai* told me a different tale. It is one that has haunted me ever since. From childhood, we Islanders are told romantic tales of the Old World when the islands were our own. Before the Oshans invaded, we were free and lived in peace in the lands the gods gave us. But in truth, we were not the first ones here.

"The Mandai roamed these seas before us. Maybe they were the first. Maybe they stole these islands from someone else. We were taught that we drove out the pagans who worshipped savage beasts and sacrificed their children on heathen altars."

"Those tales weren't true," Mischa said.

"They were twisted truths," Seren said. "An excuse. To reason away the slaughter of an entire race. My people killed the Mandai and took their islands. A people not so different than Melanesians in all likelihood. Wiped off the earth. If their ghosts truly linger in these waters, I shudder to face them."

Seren was quiet for some time before she continued. "I've never looked at my people the same way since. I don't mean that I see them as evil, but we were taught we were special. My *scholai* taught me that we are no different than the Oshans we so love to hate. We were oppressors too."

"Then why wage war against the Oshans? Isn't that just continuing the cycle?" Or perhaps she was looking for an excuse to run and hide.

Seren looked out into the deep, her breaths calm and steady. "Do you know how I've managed to unite the island kingdoms, Mischa?"

Mischa shook her head. "I thought it must have been your magic. Yet we are not arriving by air. So I guess they don't know everything you can do."

Seren nodded. "I prefer to keep some mysteries. I suppose some may have joined because of my magic. But I wanted them to follow me for more than power. We held an election among the lords and ladies. We maintained our separate kingdoms, ruled by a parliament, overseen by the kings and queens. I was honored to be selected as *the* Queen of the Southern Isles."

"Democracy," said Mischa.

"Of a sort."

"They attempted such things in the Old World."

"And they failed," said Seren knowingly. "My *scholai* taught me this. Many forms of government have risen up through the ages of the world. I suppose none of them truly work. But I believe in the unification of the Southern Isles. We won our freedom a hundred years ago, and the past century has been turbulent. We warred amongst ourselves. Kingdoms rose and fell. It could have destroyed us, but Osha was always too weak to seize the opportunity.

"But Osha is gaining power once more. If we do not fight, Cyrus Maro's tyranny will overtake the Isles and the rest of the southern world again. That is why we wage war. But this war is not ours alone. The Oshan Empire is a black stain on this world. This chancellor is not like the others. He is crafty and ambitious, and the Morph attack, I fear, is only the beginning. His eyes are on the Southern Isles now. Mischa, we must convince the island kingdoms to sail to war at once. Already, I fear it is too late."

Mischa touched the queen's arm and then pulled away, suddenly realizing how improper that was.

Seren smiled. "It's all right. Queens need friends, as well as warriors." She reached out and squeezed Mischa's hand.

"I am not a warrior. I am not a revolutionary. If I could, I would run away from all this, especially after the Morph attack."

"Why don't you?"

"I believe in Tori," said Mischa, reminding herself what she'd known all along. "I've seen the way people follow her. There is something mythic about what's happening. Like the Watchers of old. Like the tales of the gods."

"You believe she *is* a god?" Seren's eyebrows raised querulously.

"I don't know that I believe in gods at all. But I believe Osha is meant to fall. And I believe she is the one to lead us."

Seren nodded. "I believe in her too."

The queen went silent, and Mischa pulled away, crossing her arms to keep herself warm in the thick fog. After some time, Seren announced they were nearing their destination.

A great promontory jutted out into the channels ahead. Waves crashed against the towering cliffs. These shores were jagged and harsh. The trees dark and foreboding. Nothing like the pearl-white shores of Melanesia.

"I sent ravens ahead," said Seren. "The kingdoms will have gathered their fleets for the conclave. It may not compare to the Floating Mountains, but the sight of our war fleets all gathered in one place is wondrous to behold."

The sky had taken on a reddish hue. *It must already be sunset,* Mischa thought. It was strange to see it from within the haze.

The ship groaned as it reached the promontory, the waves growing choppier near the sharp cliffs. Mischa joined Tes and Elder Narsuk, excited to see the mighty fleet of war ships in the harbor, ready to sail for Osha.

Mischa's heart sank as they turned into the bay. The crimson clouds were not fashioned by the sun, but by flames. The Bay of Elya was on fire.

The water was littered with smoldering splinters of wood. Shards of war ships—masts, taffrails, and decking. The sails and rigging were long ago consumed. *This fire must have ignited hours ago. Maybe days.*

The water was dark as night, small flames lapping at the waves themselves. Pitch.

A foul sulfurous stench filled the air, and the smoke stung Mischa's eyes. The devastation stretched all the way to the grey city of Elya. No one aboard said a word for some time. The Kroqala navigated through the bay, weaving between flaming bits of wreckage.

Seren moaned bitterly. "It… can't be!"

"But the city is untouched," said Geryn with confusion. "What happened here?"

Seren didn't answer, and Mischa did not say a word. Nothing any of them could say mattered. The fleets of the Southern Isles were destroyed.

They would not be sailing to war.

———

IT TOOK NEARLY AN HOUR TO MAKE THEIR WAY TO ONE OF THE FEW trading docks that had not been consumed. Members of the parliament of the Southern Isles met them as they disembarked. The lords and ladies bowed before their queen, but Seren impatiently gestured for them to rise. Her lips were drawn tight. She had hardly spoken a word since they entered the flaming bay. Now, her voice teetered between rage and despair.

"What happened here, Lord Thiere?"

The queen spoke to a middle-aged man with a pale face and long silver hair drawn back in a tight ponytail. His face, too, was tense. The other lords and ladies shook their heads as he stepped forward to answer. He was clearly the leader of this group of nobles.

"They came in the night. From nowhere. We thought the rumors couldn't possibly be true."

"What are you saying?" Seren asked impatiently.

"S-sea dragons. They ruined our entire fleet."

"There was pitch in the water."

"A pair of trading vessels from the Trium were anchored offshore. There was an explosion. The fires ripped through our fleet like tinder."

"It was horrible, my queen," said a young lady of the city.

"Like watching the Abyss swallow our city," said another.

Seren cursed, then swiftly brushed past the entourage. Guards flanked her. The Kroqala remained with the ship. Mischa, Tes, and Elder Narsuk followed, but the lords and ladies stood back, confused.

Seren spun on her heel. "We're here for a war conclave. We do not have time to waste."

———

THE CITY WAS NOT MUCH MORE CHEERFUL THAN THE CHANNEL they'd arrived in. The grey stone was ancient and covered in moss, and the air was thick and suffocating. The parliamentary building looked to be an ancient temple that had been put to new use. Tall pillars marked the entrance to a large round chamber with circular rows of hand-carved seats. The room looked like it could hold hundreds of members but only about twenty men and women followed the queen into the chamber. Mischa, Tes, and Elder Narsuk stood beside the queen's throne at the edge of the circular floor.

Seren lè Tal commanded the room. All the lords' and ladies' eyes fell upon her expectantly. But Seren's scowl worsened.

"Where is Lord Lafet? Lady Mari?"

"My queen, the king and queen of the Thanes are tending to their people," said Lord Thiere, whom Mischa took to be another of the lesser kings of the Isles. "They were hit the hardest. Hundreds of sailors."

Seren gestured to those present. "You're all local representatives. Low nobles, except for Lord Thiere. Where are all the others?"

"My queen, they left with their liege lords," said Thiere. "Under the circumstances, we all trusted that we must first tend to our own people."

Tes tugged at Mischa's arm.

"Not now, Tes," Mischa hissed. And then apologized to the gathered nobles, realizing she had just interrupted a king.

"Must these strangers… er… be present for this conclave?" Lord Thiere murmured with annoyance. "These are… hmm… private affairs."

Seren glared. "They are emissaries from the North. Our allies. They will remain. How many ships survived?"

"My queen," said Lord Thiere, "surely you don't still think—"

"How many ships do we have?" Seren demanded.

Lord Thiere sighed. "Two dozen at best, my queen. But we are weak. Devastated. Our sailors and soldiers are in no state to be going to war. Gods, those beasts might still be lurking out there. We worried *you* would not return safely."

Seren sat forward. "We were attacked on our way here, by a company of Metamorphi. We barely survived. If not for this young Watcher, we might not have survived at all."

"A Watcher, my queen?" Thiere turned to Tes and nodded his apologies. "It is a pleasure to witness the return of Watchers to these halls, young lady."

Tes glared at the man without answer. Mischa pinched her arm, and Tes bowed respectfully. "Thank you, my lord. Mischa's a Watcher too."

"Oh my." His eyes went wide.

"We have no time for pleasantries, Lord Thiere. We survived the

Morph attack, and we have come back to this devastation. These are acts of war. And time is of the essence."

"M-my queen?"

"What part was unclear?" Seren said, clearly suppressing a shout.

The faces of the other nobles conveyed Thiere's same astonishment. "Our fleets were destroyed by sea dragons."

"Yes, and where did they come from?"

"No one knows, my queen. But surely you do not believe the ridiculous rumors that the chancellor somehow unleashed them."

"I know he did," Seren said evenly. "I've spoken to the one who was with him. The Gallows Girl."

"Yes, you said as much when you ordered this conclave." Lord Thiere's face was masking a grimace.

"My words are not sufficient for you? Then ask her comrade, who was there as well." Seren gestured to Mischa.

Suddenly, Mischa's throat felt dry as a desert. She coughed. "It is true," she said. "The chancellor is responsible for bringing back the beasts of the Old World. I saw him do it with stones of powerful sorcery. Ancient sorcery."

"You've heard the way his Darkling Witch subdued the Rulaqs in Maro'El," said Seren. "What do you suppose will happen if more beasts bend to the chancellor's will?"

Lord Thiere shook his head. "Even if all this is true—and I *do* believe you—we cannot go to war. My queen, your people need you. Here!"

"My people need to be protected from the Oshan savages who have ravaged us for centuries. And our opportunity is now. We do not have time to mourn. An army of Northmen sails south as we speak. They are attacking the Oshan fortress of Stormfall, and we must come to their aid. There is no other time. The Legions are weak. The citadel is in disrepair. This is our only chance to attack while Maro'El is still frail."

Lord Thiere crossed his arms. "I am innately cautious, my queen. You know this about me."

"A trait I admire in you, Lord Thiere. But if we wait, we doom our allies to die, and we merely bide our time for the day when the chancellor attacks with strength while we flounder. Our city stands, but it will not endure an Oshan attack. If the Morph attack was any indication, the chancellor has his eyes set on reclaiming the Isles."

Lord Thiere sighed, but nodded. The other lords and ladies in the room exchanged glances and nods.

"I wish there were another way, but I will side with you, my queen. Unfortunately, it is not up to me alone. Nor the lords and ladies gathered here."

"Send ravens to the other isles. We will reconvene in two days. The other lords and ladies cannot have made it far. Whoever is present will have a voice." Seren descended from the throne, no longer hiding her fear and anger. "The chancellor will pay for what he's done to our world." She gripped Lord Thiere's shoulder. "We have to make him pay."

Lord Thiere managed a grim smile. "I will send word to the other representatives. And I will do my best to convince them."

"Thank you."

The chamber emptied quietly, and Seren lè Tal slumped into her throne. It was not like the thrones Mischa had heard of in tales. It was plain. Made of cedar with a high back. It was finely carved, but otherwise, it hardly stood out from the other chairs in the room.

Mischa took Tes by the shoulder. "Let's leave the queen to her thoughts."

But Tes glared at her. "I need to speak with her."

Mischa tried to hold her back, but Tes slipped past.

"It's all right, Mischa," said Seren, managing a slight smile. "What is it you need to tell me, my young Watcher?"

Tes straightened up at the title. She leaned close and spoke softly. "They're lying."

"What do you mean?" said Seren.

"I heard them whispering as we were coming here. I couldn't make out all the words. But that Thiere was lying about where the other lords and ladies are."

———

THE FLAMES ACROSS THE BAY FADED AND THE CLOUDS TURNED GREY. Night descended slowly on the city of Elya. The clouds shifted from grey to the color of a vibrant flame, then to a dark shade of blue that glowed softly in the lantern light of the city. It was just enough for Mischa to keep her footing as she and Tes crept through the city, and just enough for her to worry that they would be seen.

Seren lè Tal occupied an ancient palace at the center of Elya, set upon a small knoll and visible from the port and most corners of the city. Long ago, it had been the magnificent high palace of the Elyan Empire. But the empire fell over a millennia ago, and the palace was destroyed near the fall of the Old World, and had only recently been rebuilt. It was functional, but the newly unified island nation was not wealthy, and the high palace was still in disrepair.

Upon her return from the North, the queen was attended by a Palace Guard of her own choosing, most hailing from the Isle of Tal. Many had attended her before she'd risen to power. Seren trusted them with her life. But even with the Kroqala, whose loyalties to the queen were unquestionable, Mischa had been wary about leaving her. But she couldn't very well leave Tes alone to this task.

There had been much discussion and speculation, but none of it mattered. There was something Lord Thiere was hiding. And they needed to know what. For now, Thiere thought Seren believed him, and they hoped this would work to their advantage.

Thiere lè Sard's palace was located near the southern edge of the city. If Mischa and Tes could get inside, perhaps they could unveil what the Sardic lords and ladies were up to.

Thankfully, the stone structures of the city seemed to gobble up the light. Mischa found a dark corridor where she could fly them over the palace walls, and they crept through the grounds. The place was dark save for a domed glass structure at the center that emanated golden light.

Tes pointed. "He's meeting with the others. I can just hear them."

Mischa held Tes around the waist and left the ground. They landed on crumbling stone, and Mischa nearly lost her footing. *Gods, this whole city is falling apart.*

Tes pointed to the dome, and they crept near, treading softly on the ramshackle roof. They hid in a dark corner where they could see below. A group of lords and ladies, the ones from earlier that day, were gathered around a long table. There was one woman Mischa didn't recognize at the end opposite Lord Thiere.

"Who is that?" Mischa whispered.

Tes shook her head. "Can't tell. Someone important."

The group was engaged in a heated conversation, but the strange woman sat back in her chair, arms crossed. She did not dress like most noblewomen. She wore pants and a tight-fitting tunic, and her dark hair was pulled back in a braid.

"What are they saying?" Mischa asked.

"They're arguing about what to do with Seren."

"What do you mean?"

"I don't think they want her to be their queen anymore. They keep saying her time is up."

Mischa's heart quickened. "Where are the other high lords? Like Thiere? Mari and Lafet?"

Tes shook her head. "I… I think they're on their way."

"To Elya?"

"I don't think so… I think they're going to overthrow Seren."

Mischa tensed all over. "That strange woman is not from the Isles, Tes. Why is she here?"

Tes did not need to answer. The woman stood. Her skin changed. Wings emerged from her back.

Tes and Mischa both jerked back into the shadows.

"We have to go!" Mischa whispered.

Within, the Morph looked up toward the sky, right at where they had been peeking through the glass.

"Gods, she knows we're here," Tes hissed.

She sensed our magic! She probably knew we were here the whole time.

Mischa's stomach churned as she took flight. She had never flown such a distance before, let alone with a young child. She gripped Tes tightly and soared over the city, toward the central palace. She hated the way the overcast sky glowed. She flew low, to not be easily spotted from afar. She kept expecting to hear the nauseating screech of the Morph coming after them, perhaps with more of her kind. Tes was trembling, and Mischa gripped her tight. Her arms were growing weak. The air had grown terribly cold. She reached deep, deep, deep for her magic.

Mischa landed on Seren's balcony and her legs gave out on impact. Her ankle twisted beneath her and she rolled into a jarring landing. Her body ached from the energy she had used. Two guards sprang out from the balcony doors, swords drawn. Seren appeared behind them and ordered them down.

"What happened?" the queen asked.

"Th-there's a Morph coming to kill you!" Tes cried. "We have to leave!"

One of the guards grabbed hold of Tes, his blade at the girl's throat.

"What in the Abyss are you doing?" cried Mischa.

"I've been betrayed," said Seren evenly. Mischa could sense the hurt in her tremulous voice. "Even by my own kin."

The guard did not loosen his grip on Tes. "I am sorry, my lady."

"I am not your lady, Kalren. I am your queen. Now, release the girl."

Kalren shook his head. "I cannot."

The other guard joined Kalren, sword drawn.

"You as well, Esre?"

Esre spoke through gritted teeth. "We are sworn to the Isles."

"And not to your queen?" Seren's fists clenched, and Mischa swore she saw energy emanating from her knuckles.

"You are not our queen any longer."

"Don't be a fool, Esre. You know what I am capable of."

Seren shed the dark cloak she'd been wearing. Mischa realized in that moment that she had never actually seen the queen's bare arms before. And she immediately realized why. Runes were etched deep into her skin, giving it a strange marbled appearance. The symbols covered every inch of her forearms and her biceps, all the way to the exposed shoulders of her regal gown, disappearing inside the bodice of her dress. The runes were glowing, the same way the symbols glowed on the skyship.

The source of her magic.

"Don't, my lady," Esre cautioned, extending her blade at Mischa.

Mischa tried to get up, but her strength was gone. Her ankle raged with pain. She reached for her Fieri magic, but managed only a waft of flame. She was utterly spent from the long flight.

Esre's blade pressed against Mischa's neck. "We don't want to kill them, but if you use sorcery against us, my lady, they will both be dead before we are."

A fierce energy teased from Seren's fingertips. Her arms glowed with a harsh light.

The doors to Seren's chambers sprang open and more guards poured in, followed by Thiere lè Sard.

"Stand down, my lady," he said softly.

"You traitorous bastard!" Seren cried. The energy in her hands surged.

Lord Thiere shook his head. "There has been no treachery. This is democracy. And you have been dethroned by unanimous vote."

"You hired a Morph to kill me!"

"We have no intentions of killing you if you cooperate, my lady. That Morph was here to ensure we completed our part of the alliance."

"Alliance?" said Seren angrily.

"In exchange for our remaining ships," said Thiere, "the chancellor has promised to rebuild our fleet. We had hoped after seeing the devastation, you would see reason."

"Spare me your excuses, Thiere. You voted before I arrived."

"You would lead us to destruction, my lady. We were forced to choose a better path. The world is changing. Enemies are becoming allies. Cyrus Maro is marrying a Yan Avii maiden. We must learn. We must set aside ancient feuds."

"Where are Mari and Lafet?" Seren demanded.

"Sailing for Osha with our last vessels, to go to war against the Gallows Girl."

Mischa cried out in desperation, squirming to get away from Esre's grasp. But Esre pressed her blade and drew more blood.

"NOOOOO!"

Tes's cry made the ground tremble. Esre lost her balance, and Mischa seized the moment.

Despite her ankle, she shirked Esre's grip and managed to disarm her. She was about to drive the blade into her chest when—

"Stop!" Seren shouted.

Mischa's sword froze in midair.

A bolt of light was wrapped around the blade.

Kalren had not let go of Tes. She was trembling in his grasp. Blood dripped from a wound in the Crooked girl's stomach.

Oh gods! No!

More guards surrounded Mischa and wrested Esre's blade from her grasp. She fell to her knees.

"No, no." Mischa murmured. "Seren, fight back. Help Tori!"

But Seren sighed defeatedly, shaking her head, then bent down and retrieved her cloak. *Why isn't she fighting?*

Seren's kinsman released Tes, then joined Thiere's side.

Seren leaned over the Crooked girl, who lay whimpering on the ground, a growing pool of blood forming beneath her. A small tendril of magic escaped Seren's fingers, like a tiny bolt of lightning, and the wound closed over. Then, the light of Seren's magic faded completely.

"I am sorry, my lady," Kalren murmured as he stepped away. "But our loyalties are to the Isles."

They turned to leave, but Thiere turned back. "Don't get any other foolish ideas about stopping this." He pointed out the window.

In the distance, a burst of flames glowed against the low-hanging clouds.

Seren's mouth gaped open, wordless.

Mischa was shaking from the pain in her ankle and the growing horror as she realized where the flames were coming from.

"My ship…" said Seren, her voice barely a whisper.

"I am sorry, my lady," said Lord Thiere. "Your secrets were not as well-kept as you thought. You won't be flying north to help the Gallows Girl. Your war is over."

With that, Thiere and the guards left.

Mischa held Tes as she cried for their friends marching straight into a trap. Her own heart shut down. They had failed everyone they cared for, and there was nothing they could do.

Seren lè Tal did not cry. Without expression, she watched the flames consuming her skyship flicker until they faded in the darkness.

PART ELEVEN
THE HUNTER &
THE PREY

What happened seemed obvious looking back. Nevertheless, it took us all by surprise. Nothing would be the same after Stormfall.

—from *Dawn of the Third World*

CHAPTER FORTY

It became a ritual, the Gallows Girl wandering through the makeshift infirmary in Lord Byrn's great hall. While her soldiers replenished themselves on Stormfall's winter stores, Tori helped feed the wounded. Including the Legions. Alaster Byrn had kept his halls relatively well stocked for the winter, and Tori insisted that all, including the prisoners and Lord Byrn himself, be fed hot meals each night. Though Fara dul Baruk had protested this act of mercy, it was proving to work as Tori hoped. The prisoners were calm, and there was even talk that some might pledge themselves to the Gallows Girl soon enough.

Tori knew it was a risk and a long shot, but she also knew that this revolution's hope was in the lowborns. The Legions were not the enemy. Even the nobles were not the enemy. She had invited Lord Byrn to dine with her last evening, and he had been honest in answering her questions concerning the other strongholds in northern Osha. He had offered up his weathered maps freely and thanked her for the civil treatment of his soldiers and family.

And if Lord Byrn had cooperated, then perhaps there truly was hope to turn the Legions in time.

Perhaps even…

Tori tried to push thoughts of Darien away, but they continued to creep back up, catching her off guard. This was the exact thing she had hoped to avoid. Her notions of killing Darien were long lost upon facing him in the flesh. This worried her, but she could not deny her lingering hope for him.

Sure, she was here, in the infirmary, to show the Legions there was another way than the chancellor's cruelty, but she was also here, serving their enemy, because she wanted to keep an eye on Darien.

He had been in a severe state for three days, easing in and out of dark fever dreams that left him screaming, whether from pain or rage, she did not know.

Tori drifted through the hall, handing out food, touching hands, and whispering words of hope for the wounded, but her eyes wandered frequently to Darien from across the room. He was unconscious now. Alyk was tending his wounds, and she was grateful he was not awake to feel the pain. Yesterday, the application of a shaman's salve had sent Darien into hysterics. Alyk suspected infection. Tori worried he might slip into sleep and never return, but his body seemed to be fighting death like a mother desperate to remain to look after her children.

What is Darien fighting to live for?

Valeria believed it would be best if he died. He would never change. But Tori couldn't believe that. She hated that she couldn't just let him die and be done with it. Instead, she had ordered extra guards to look after the infirmary. And she had kept her eye on Valeria, who was eating with the Alyut and Crooked folk presently.

The Southern Islander could not be trusted, for all she had done to aid this revolution. Not when it came to Darien. Valeria was too emotional. Bore too much regret for having trusted him.

But am I as much a fool as her?

Alyk stood from Darien's bedside, the wounds cleaned and dressed, Darien still unconscious. The shaman caught Tori looking. Alyk disapproved of her decision to spare Darien. She knew he did. He resented that he had been tasked with preserving him. But, of course, being Alyk dul Baruk, he would not say it to her face. He had hardly spoken to her since the battle ended. Alyk frowned, turned away, and moved on to another patient.

Am I pushing my true allies away for the sake of mercy? No, she knew this was the right decision. She had to lead in a different way. If not, what were they fighting for?

Tori was pulled from her thoughts by a sudden hand grasping her own. One of the Legion prisoners. But the touch did not alarm her, and the sight of the prisoner saddened her.

The woman's eyes were ruined and the surrounding skin was horribly scarred. For a moment, Tori thought it was the doing of the battle, but at closer inspection, the wounds were not fresh.

"I am sorry this happened to you," Tori whispered.

"Your shamans say I should heal. I consider it a victory." Her face was scarred and mended, though still red from healing. The soldier looked so fragile. Her entire stomach was bandaged. Tori squeezed her hand.

Tori smiled at the woman's optimism. She did not seem to harbor any hatred toward Tori, nor toward the Northmen who had inflicted her wounds. But judging by the woman's fragile grip and clammy skin, Tori feared her recovery might not be so sure. "I pray it is so," she murmured.

"And now I've finally come to meet the Gallows Girl. More reason to be grateful."

Tori squeezed her hand once more. "It's a pleasure to meet you…"

"Kirra," she said.

Why does that sound so familiar? Tori wondered.

"Interesting sentiment from a Shadow," she said.

"Not all Shadows bring darkness."

It echoed of something Valeria had once said to her in the catacombs beneath the Crooked Teeth, shortly before Tori escaped. Perhaps it was more true than even Valeria had realized.

"Why would the chancellor send a blind soldier into battle?" Tori asked. It was no wonder the woman found hope in the Gallows Girl.

Kirra smiled. "My weapons are not blades and muskets any more than yours."

"A Morph?" Tori asked.

The woman chuckled. "A Watcher."

Tori realized why her name was so familiar. Kirra was the woman Kale had gone to find in the Red City. The reason he had betrayed them to the chancellor. What was she doing here? Tori's guard went up.

"You know my name, I take it," Kirra said.

Should she hide it? No, the woman already knew. "You're Kale's Kirra."

She nodded without expression. "You could say that."

"You both turned against us."

"Depends on who you ask." Kirra lowered her voice. "I joined to bring you to Maro'El, but not for the reason the chancellor suspected."

A chill traveled up Tori's arms. "What do you mean?"

"You are wasting time here in the North, sitting around while the chancellor figures out his next move."

"He does not know yet. No one escaped this place."

"Perhaps you're right. But you are wasting your time, nonetheless. This army of yours is impressive, but in the face of the Legions, they will not stand a chance. If you linger long, you will be destroyed. Your true army waits in the South. That is where you should be heading."

Tori was not sure what to say.

"The Saints, Tori. Lowborns across the empire have found hope in you since the day of the Gallows. They are many. And they are stronger than the chancellor could ever dream. You need to go to Maro'El."

Tori's gut twisted. Something felt wrong about this. She backed away. "Sounds exactly like something the chancellor would want. You travel with Legions and Morphs, hunting me, and you expect me to believe you?"

"You expect *your enemies* to believe you when you show them mercy and spread rumors that you would take their allegiance. And I am not your enemy."

Tori did not know what to say. Her heart was racing.

"Believe what your heart tells you, Tori. The one that tells you to spare your enemies. That there is good in the ones who betrayed you. Even Commander Redvar."

"H-how could you—"

Kirra pointed to her ears. "I'm a Sonora. I've heard you. I know the Alyut elders want to march on the other northern fortresses, and you want to march south. I know you have an army of Southern Islanders, but you have not heard from them. And I know you check on the commander twice a day. I think your gut is right on all these things."

Tori backed further away, feeling strangely sick. She could not believe what this woman was saying. It was too good to be true. What she wanted to hear. And it was coming from the mouth of one who had joined the chancellor's Sky Guard. She hurried away, but the woman called after her.

"Darien's going to live."

Tori sprinted from the great hall.

———

ALYK CAME TO HER IN THE NIGHT, BUT TORI WAS NOT SLEEPING. She sat beside the warm hearth gazing out an open window at the empty night, unable to shake what Kirra had said. Was she right? Could Kirra be trusted? Were they truly wasting time here in the North?

Tori had held council with the elders, Lir'ghe, Alyk, and Skya that evening. There had been no word from Seren or Mischa. They had hoped to have the support of a fleet behind their movements. Fara dul Baruk proposed they move on the nearest stronghold, Falcon's Roost. Lir'ghe feared they would spread themselves too thin, and strongly suggested they wait for word from his queen. The others were divided on the matter. Tori thanked them for their counsel without resolution.

It was her decision, in the end, but she did not know what to do.

Without Seren, a plan to turn south was worthless. Tori did not like the idea of waiting, nor marching inland. She wished Mischa were here. Or better yet, Ren. So quickly she had gone from the apprentice to the leader who was supposed to have all the answers, but in truth, she knew no more than anyone else. Probably less. She kept thinking of the Saints, longing for what Kirra said to be true. But it was so great a risk.

Alyk knocked before entering Tori's chambers, an act that annoyed her.

"If I wanted you out, I would have locked it," she muttered as he sat beside her. It was the first time they'd been alone since the taking of Stormfall. She should have been glad for him to come.

"I… didn't want to disturb you," Alyk said softly. He sat close on the sofa, but they did not touch.

"You saw the light. You knew I was awake, or you wouldn't have come."

"I didn't want to assume anything."

Tori sighed. "You never do."

"What is that supposed to mean?"

"I like you, Alyk. I want you here. I want your counsel. Why are you so cautious all the damn time?"

Alyk met her gaze. His eyes betrayed sadness. "I will follow you into anything, Tori. I believe in this revolution, and in you. I know Stormfall is only one victory. And it could be our only one. But it doesn't matter. I will follow you into death. You have my loyalty."

"Then why don't you show it?" Tori asked. She grabbed his hand. "Why have you been avoiding me?"

He pulled away. "I'm not naïve enough to think that a shaman from the White North has a chance with the Gallows Girl."

"That's really what you think of me?"

"It's what I know. We are playing a deadly game of war and politics. Love has no place in that."

"Love?"

Alyk's smile was halfhearted. "You told me not to be cautious. But I know, even if you feel the same way, you can't return it."

"And why not?"

"Tori, don't play the fool. We haven't heard a word from Seren in a week. Something's gone wrong in the Isles. The chancellor will know we took Stormfall soon. The longer we sit here, the longer we wait for our demise. We can't march on Maro'El alone."

But what of the Saints? "So you've given up. Is that it?"

"Not on this revolution. No."

"On you and me?"

"You have to think strategy, Tori."

"Strategy."

"A strategic marriage to the Gallows Girl might be one of the greatest bargaining chips we have. We need more allies."

Tori said nothing. She knew it was true. A few scattered victories in the North would not be enough. Not without the Isles.

"A Faerish prince, perhaps," said Alyk. "Even an… Oshan commander."

Tori was growing hot despite the cold night. "So this is about Darien, then."

"I've seen the way you look at him when you visit the wounded."

"He's my enemy, Alyk."

"And you still care for him. And he cares for you. I saw the way you fought. Neither of you wanted to kill the other. And it's okay. It would be a powerful turn of events. The Gallows Boy betrays the chancellor."

Tori shook her head. "You're unbelievable. Do you know that? Darien has hardly been conscious in a week."

"And when he stirs, he looks for you. I've seen it. And in his dreams, I've heard him murmur your name. I'll admit, I questioned your decision to spare him, but perhaps you were right."

Tori stood up and glared at him. "I don't want Darien, or some Faerish lord. I want you."

Alyk faced her. "The world needs more than me. I've spent a lot of time thinking about it."

Tori pushed him in the chest. He almost lost his balance. She'd used a slight flare of her Conjuri magic. "To the Abyss with that."

"What?"

"Don't push me away because you're afraid you'll lose me. That's *shenzah*. The world's not pulling us apart. You are." She pushed him again. He stumbled and braced himself against the wall, eyes wide.

"Tori, don't…"

But she didn't let him finish. She moved in quick and kissed him, hard and long.

And he didn't push her away. Alyk pulled her closer. His skin was on fire. His hand held the back of her neck and her own hands gripped tight around his back. She felt her whole self coming to life in a way it never had before. But then he hesitated. He pulled back an inch or two. She could still taste his warm breath.

Tori kissed him again, softly, pulling him back toward her. "We don't have any assurances in this war, Alyk. All we have is right now."

She held his gaze. His dark eyes flickered in the low light.

He was about to speak, but Tori interrupted him. "Do you want this?"

He smiled. It was slight at first, and then it grew. "Too much."

"There are no alliances here. Just you and me."

She barely finished before Alyk pulled her close again. He smelled of healing herbs and salves, a strangely alluring scent. Tori's lips traveled to his neck, and he shuddered at the touch. His hands twisted into her wavy locks. Her body arched with pleasure.

Tori didn't realize what she was doing until Alyk made a startled cry. She had pulled him back toward the sofa, so he was lying on top of her. But they were not on the sofa any longer.

Intense energy wrapped around them, surging from inside her and binding her to him as she hovered in the air.

Alyk glanced up. "Th-this is incredible!"

Tori smiled and then kissed him again. "Quit talking. You're ruining the moment."

She closed her eyes, and it felt like they were in another world. A world of light and wonder and beauty. She had the vague thought that it was one of their own making. Not some dream world. Something real. A world where they could choose their destinies. Their loves. If only for a moment. And she wanted to create that world with him. Make it last forever.

———

They stayed together by the hearth late into the night, his head resting on her shoulder, both of them staring into the lapping flames. Tori stroked his long black hair and took in the scent of him. She felt momentarily at peace, so grateful that Alyk had found her in that Crooked village.

"I wish we could just stay here," she murmured.

Alyk nodded, a foolish grin on his lips.

She chuckled. "I mean in Stormfall. Well, here too."

He turned to her and smiled. "I know. We have a war to fight."

"I've been thinking. Your *madru* was right earlier. We can't just sit here and wait for allies. I think we should march on Falcon's Roost."

"What about it spreading us too thin? Lir'ghe made a good point."

"We need to show strength if we have any hopes of bringing others to our cause. But I think we could do it without sacrificing our soldiers' lives."

"How?" said Alyk, sitting up straight. "You think the lord of Falcon's Roost will yield?"

"I think the Shadows are beginning to see through the chancellor's brainwashing. I think it is time we make them an offer."

"They would follow if the commander of the Sky Guard pledged himself to you."

Tori had been thinking of Darien's actions during the battle. He had surrendered to save his soldiers when it was clear they would lose. She was sure she could convince him. "The next time he wakes, I want to speak with him."

"That was your plan all along, wasn't it?"

Tori hesitated. "Not all along. But there's still good in him. Valeria may not see it. You may not see it. But—"

A frantic knock thundered against the door. Then, it flew open.

It was Skya and Valeria.

"What's wrong?" Tori demanded.

"It's the prisoner. Commander Redvar. He's escaped."

CHAPTER FORTY-ONE

W hat?" Tori said. "He was barely alive a few hours ago."

Darien's escape could ruin any hope of turning the other Shadows. And if he reached the chancellor, their revolution would be over with one small victory to show for it.

Skya shook her head. "He must have been faking his weakness. He's disappeared from the infirmary. The guards are scouring the fortress, but I doubt they'll find anything."

"If he was faking it," Tori said, "he may have been strong enough to fly beyond the walls."

Valeria nodded. "But not far. Not with the wound I gave him." She sounded like someone trying too hard to convince herself. Tori should have let Valeria kill him. "Gather the rogues and the Riders. We'll hunt him down all night if we have to."

Skya and Valeria hurried out to ready the others. Alyk lingered for a moment.

"You were right," Tori said. "Valeria was right. I was a fool."

Alyk gritted his teeth. "We'll find him, Tori. Wear your thickest furs. It's cold as the Abyss out there."

With that, he left.

Tori dressed as quickly as she could, layering shirts and furs and leathern armor. Her skin was thrumming with magic desperate to be unleashed. She would not spare Darien this time. She strapped her saber to her back.

The door creaked open.

"Alyk, are the Riders ready?"

"I am not Alyk."

Tori spun, then froze.

Darien staggered in and closed the door behind him. He looked like *shenzah*. His greasy hair was matted to one side, his eyes were bloodshot, and he clutched his side with one hand. The other hand bore a small sack.

Tori reached for her magic. The force threw him against the door with a thud. She drew her saber. She had to act fast while she had the upper hand.

"Let's get this over with," she hissed, waiting for him to draw a hidden blade. But he had none. Only the bag.

"I'm not here to hurt you, Tori."

The door flew open, sending Darien to the ground. He moaned at the impact. Skya and Alyk rushed in, swords drawn.

"Wait!" Tori cried.

"What in the Abyss is he doing here?" Alyk shouted, his eyes fixed on Darien with hatred.

"I am not here to resist," Darien said with a groan. "Only to speak."

"Then speak and be done with it!" Alyk said angrily.

"It might be better alone," Darien said, rising to his feet. His bandages were turning crimson. He stepped forward, but Tori shoved him back against the door with her Conjuri power. He did not resist her.

"You'll speak to them, or not at all," Tori said. "What is in the bag?"

"I was worried it might have been lost in the battle. Or else that Valeria had disposed of it. I couldn't speak of it. Not until I was sure."

"Sure of what?"

Darien untied the leather strings and instantly a horrid stench filled the air.

"Gods!" said Alyk.

Skya drew nearer, her sword at the ready.

Darien reached in carefully and pulled out the object. It was a severed hand. Engorged and a disgusting purplish color, the wrist was caked with dried blood. On the middle finger was a symbol that filled Tori with dread. It was a golden ring with a round onyx stone. Carved into the stone's face was a white raven bearing a scroll. The emblem of House Andovier.

Ren's hand.

Bile filled Tori's mouth, and she nearly choked. Alyk touched her shoulder, but Tori pushed his hand away. "Leave us alone."

"Tori," Skya protested. "You can't be—"

"It's not a request!" Tori felt bad for snapping, but she knew she could not process this with them in the room.

"I am not leaving you alone with that bastard!" Alyk said.

"He can barely walk. I can handle him. Wait outside. And tell the Riders to go back to bed."

"Tori, this is foolishness." But still, Skya backed away.

Alyk shook his head, hurt evident in his eyes, but he said nothing.

Tori and Darien had not been alone since Scelero's estate. Not since the day of the draft. That felt so long ago. Those two people no longer existed.

"W-why?" she managed, fighting tears.

Darien's eyes narrowed at her, but she thought she sensed a softness in his voice. "Most of your old friends turned eventually, Tori. They saw the foolishness of resisting a ruler who lets them be who they truly are. It was what your Shadow Watch set out to do in the first place. They joined the Sky Guard. But not Captain Andovier. His pride is too great. You see it, don't you? The Shadow Watch was never about a revolution of magic. It was about Ren Andovier's grudge against the Maros."

Tori was silent for a moment. She knew Ren and Cyrus Maro had a fraught past. He had told her as much, though he had never revealed the details.

"They killed his family," said Darien.

"That wasn't the chancellor's doing."

"No, Ren helped the chancellor's experiments with magic, years ago. And then, he betrayed him."

"Because he saw what he was," Tori said.

"Are you so sure about that?"

Tori glanced at the hand. Tears welled at her eyelids. "Did you cut it off?"

Darien put the hand away. "No. But I would have, if the chancellor asked me to."

Ren had his flaws, but Tori still cared for him. He had taught her all she knew of magic. He had taught her to believe in herself. Without Ren, there would be no Gallows Saint. She could no longer hold back the tears.

"I know you think I'm a monster."

"Darien, I—"

"I don't blame you. But I've accepted what I am. You do what you got to survive. You told me that once."

"I remember," Tori murmured. "When we built the gallows. Is that all this is? Survival?"

"No. I thought you were a fool, then, actually."

She managed a half smile. "I was."

"Perhaps we both were. I was angry, you know. Angry you stole my resistance. Angry you sent me off to the Legions. Angry you were some sorceress in hiding. Angry you were dead and I was not. I felt like you were nothing but a lie. I suppose they used that to their advantage in the Shadow Camps. But I told myself I would survive long enough to do some good."

"Like killing those Watchers at the Watchtower? The Crooked folk?"

"I didn't kill them. Neither did the chancellor. You were the one who stirred up the Rulaqs, Tori. Remember?"

Tori bit her tongue. The memories flooded back of that horrible night.

She had tried so hard to convince herself it was not her fault, but the truth was the soldiers and Watchers would be alive if she had not resisted.

"You followed a fool," Darien said. His face was expressionless. "I don't blame you for that."

"You really think you're not a fool to trust the chancellor?"

Darien smirked. "There are worse people to follow. He's better than his father. Better than the damned nobles."

"He cuts the hands off his opponents."

"Most rulers in this world would have killed him long ago. Ren's a pompous fool."

"So this hand is supposed to convince me to surrender?" Tori asked. "To save the fool?"

"No." Darien held her gaze. His eyes were different than the ones she remembered from Scelero's estate. Narrower. Darker. The Morph bleeding through his human form. "The hand served another purpose back in Maro'El."

"Then why?"

"What are you fighting for, Tori? Because the way I see it, we have a bigger enemy. Monsters are ravaging the world, and we are fighting over who gets to bring magic back."

"I thought the chancellor was blaming *me* for those beasts."

Darien nodded. "That doesn't mean he believes it."

"Then who is it?"

"We believe it is someone else. Someone who has been trying to bring down Osha for some time. Someone who sent spies into the Legions. Someone who has been building her own sorcerous power in secret until very recently."

"Seren lè Tal." Tori had wondered at the source of Seren's power from the day they met. Could it be tied to the stones, somehow? Or was Darien making this up?

"The Witch Queen of the Southern Isles. The one you allied yourself with. There's another set of godstones in the world. The chancellor believes it is the source of her power."

"I never saw any stones."

"Did she reveal the source of her power to you?"

Tori shook her head.

"There is more to magic than Watchers, Tori. And that magic cannot fall to the wrong hands. No one has pure intentions. But you've, once again, chosen your allies poorly. I came north to offer you terms of peace. Before you declared war."

"Peace in exchange for my head?" Tori said, her fists clenching.

Darien looked upset. "The future queen wants your head because she believes you are responsible for the monsters that attacked the Red City."

"The chancellor still wants me dead."

"The chancellor wants an end to your rebellion, Tori. You were offered mercy on more than one occasion, as I recall."

"My rebellion is about more than magic. It's about justice. We were slaves, Darien. Or have you forgotten?"

Darien smirked. "Hardly. I told you I was angry. But I'm not angry anymore. I am alive, and I've come a long way from Scelero's estate."

"You're not free."

"There is no such thing as freedom, Tori. It's an illusion. There is better and worse. Do you think your rebellion has made things better for the slaves of Osha? It hasn't."

"So things should stay the way they've always been?"

Darien shook his head. "Things are already changing. Watchers fly beside Morphs and a Klavash boy leads them. And while we weaken ourselves fighting a needless war, the real enemy is waiting to ruin the world. So my question to you is if it's worth it. Is your doomed rebellion worth the lives lost? The bloodshed?"

Tori did not know what to say. They had won the Battle of Stormfall, and yet she felt as though they had lost. Could Darien be right about Seren? Was the Witch Queen merely using her?

"What is your plan exactly, Tori? You can't win. Even if the Witch Queen *were* coming to help you, you're leading them to—"

"W-what?" Tori cursed herself for letting slip that Darien was right about their plans. But it caught her off guard. "I... I don't know what you're talking about."

"That's why you haven't marched on Falcon's Roost. You're waiting on an army that is never coming. The rest of the Isles are not so eager to bring the world to ruin. And that will be your undoing. You're sitting here waiting like a fawn for a hunter. No one's coming to your rescue. You're fighting a war you can't possibly win. And for what? Some renegade Oshan noble who is too proud to admit the world doesn't need him to save them?"

Tori stood abruptly, her hands shaking. She shouted for Alyk and Skya. They entered immediately. "Please escort Commander Redvar to his new cell. We can't have him escaping again."

Darien did not protest the shackles. He went peacefully, but he turned at the door. "There is another way out of this, Tori. One where we all walk away with our heads."

———

ONCE SHE WAS ALONE, TORI RETRIEVED THE SACK DARIEN HAD brought her. The stench was growing in the warm bedroom, and it filled her senses as she opened it. She nearly retched, but she did not look away. She peered closely at the rotting flesh. She had held this hand, been taught with this hand. Darien could have taken any hand and put Ren's ring on it, and she doubted she would know it in this decaying state.

But she knew it was his. Deep down, she knew Darien was not lying. Not about that.

Tori walked over to the fire and cast the hand into the flames. She watched it burn. And she cried. *Ren, you gods-damned fool.*

And she had been a fool to follow him.

But she did not follow him anymore. This war was about Restoration. It was about outcasts and lowborns. Not magic. To surrender would be to turn her back on all these people who had looked to her for hope.

Osha was an oppressor. Just because the chancellor was no longer oppressing sorcerers did not cleanse him of his other evils. Darien was a fool for thinking so. She hated him for believing it. Hated him for casting doubt on everything she stood for. Hated herself for questioning her resolve.

Tori donned her cloak and left the suffocating warmth of her room. Outside, Lir'ghe flitted about between the towers but never came near enough to speak. Had he heard what Darien said about his queen?

She stood at the battlements, facing the east, letting the cold wind nip at her face. The sting felt good, made her feel alive.

A week previous, they had attacked from that direction. They had won the first battle of this war. Why didn't it feel sweeter? Why did Darien's words affect her this way?

Because you're afraid he's right.

Tori didn't notice Valeria arrive. The Southern Islander braced against the wall a short distance away, gazing out silently at the coming morning. She said nothing at first. All Tori could think was that Valeria served Seren, and a question had been gnawing at her. Tori had known the Witch Queen had ulterior motives, but was it possible she was the one bringing these beasts upon the world? Someone had to be. Someone had to have the other set of godstones.

"The way everything happened," Tori said, moving closer to the Morph spy. "In the catacombs. You set Mischa free at a moment when all the Legions were distracted. It was perfect."

Too perfect…

"I was waiting for the right moment," Valeria said. "When it came, I took it."

"It was the only possible moment. And before they could come after us, the Nosferati showed up like an invading army. As though it was planned."

Valeria was silent.

"Where did they come from?"

"I don't know, Tori. Perhaps it was the gods."

"The gods are an easy excuse for something that ought to have a better explanation," Tori said. "For a long time, I wondered if it was me. But that never felt right. I would have known if I was letting other creatures in from the Old World."

"Perhaps the Nosferati were always there."

"That never felt right either. They showed up for the first time in centuries right after the Rulaqs returned? Right before frost giants and

Xa'Rila and sea dragons came to ravage our world? No, the Nosferati came from the Old World too."

"How?"

"The same way the Rulaqs did," Tori said. "Someone *let* them in."

Valeria eyed her carefully. "What are you suggesting?"

Tori sighed. "I don't know."

"Whatever Darien told you, you can't believe it. He is full of lies. And the worst part is he believes them. I should have gone with you back in the catacombs. That is what my queen wanted, but I couldn't bring myself to leave. Because of Darien. I believed there was still good in him. I hate him for that. I betrayed my queen for him."

"Your queen," Tori said. "She's a powerful and mysterious sorceress."

"She's a good queen, and she will come through. She'll bring our fleet." And Tori sensed sincerity in that desire.

But will she bring more than a fleet?

Tori clapped Valeria on the shoulder. "I hope you're right. For all our sakes." She was about to leave and see if she could catch some sleep before breakfast, when she glimpsed a strange moving shadow in the distance.

Valeria's eyes perked up as well. The horizon was turning with morning. Was that what had caused it?

"Did you see that?" Tori asked.

Valeria nodded, her expression stern and concentrated.

Lir'ghe shot over to them. "I see movement in the distance."

Tori had a dark feeling about it. She hurried to the nearest tower. The guard manning it bowed as she approached.

"Where's your spyglass?" she demanded.

The Alyut man retrieved it from a cloth sack and handed it to her. "I doubt you'll see much at this hour, my saint."

Tori snatched the glass and held it to her eye. The glass enhanced the distant hills, though it made them slightly blurrier. She scanned the horizon, but saw nothing more.

"Do we have any scouts out?"

"Not at night, my saint."

"No one went out looking for the escaped prisoner?"

"They all came back, my saint."

Tori scanned the horizon again, wishing the sun would hurry and rise above the Teeth so she could see. It was probably nothing, but...

And then, she saw it.

Another shadow of movement to the southeast in the corner of her eye. And then another. And another. She adjusted the glass, and her heart sank.

Tori dropped the spyglass on the stone ground. It shattered.

Valeria touched her arm and asked if she was all right, but it was several moments before Tori realized what was happening. Her mind raced ahead of her body.

Valeria shook her.

"What did you see?"

Tori shrugged the girl's hand away. She stood and faced the guard with the strange feeling she was merely an automaton in a dark play, and this was the inevitable climax of some mummer's tale.

Had Darien known all along?

"My saint?" said the guard.

Tori spared one last glance. One last hope that it was some trick of the coming dawn.

A dark line began to appear at the horizon, stretching wide and growing thicker by the moment. "Sound the alarm. Stormfall is under attack."

"To battle, my saint?" the guard asked.

Tori bit her lip. Darien must have known. He was hoping she would see them and choose to surrender. "No, Sergeant. Prepare to flee. We must fly to the ships."

The guard saluted her and rang the warning bells. Tori was about to fly to her chambers and fetch her sword, but Valeria grabbed onto her.

"Flee?" Valeria said. "We can't give up Stormfall!"

Tori turned to her. The girl's eyes were wide. She gripped Tori's wrist, but Tori barely felt it. The world was turning without her. And it was turning against her.

"We have no other choice."

"We can hold this fortress, my saint! A horde from Falcon's Roost can't have more than a few hundred soldiers. Maybe a thousand. We outnumber them, and we hold a fortress."

Tori merely shook her head. "They are not from Falcon's Roost."

"What do you mean? Whose army is it? How many are there?"

Tori could now make out the shapes she'd seen through the spyglass. Even from this distance, the tall, serpentine necks were unmistakable. She felt nothing but inevitability.

"Rulaqs," said Tori. "The entire horde is marching on Stormfall. And the chancellor and his Darkling Witch are leading them."

CHAPTER FORTY-TWO

The ground quaked as Northern soldiers scrambled to grab weapons and any supplies they could manage. With their old master marching on Stormfall, the prisoners were barricaded in the great hall so they could not turn on the Northmen. Tori could not risk losing their one shot at escape.

The Alyut sailors had gone ahead to ready the ships. It was likely they would not fit, especially with the Bear Riders, but they had lost many in the battle, and Tori hoped it would not come to leaving anyone behind.

They would have to flee through the side gates of the stronghold, and quick, or else they would be going out to a slaughter.

Gone was the courage and strength of the people of the North who had taken this fortress a week previous. They were replaced with sheer terror. It was etched on their faces, young and old, man and woman. The horde would reach them within the hour. The elders attempted to maintain order, but it was quickly turning into a panicked retreat.

Tori took only her sword and her thickest cloak. When she left her chambers, Alyk nearly ran her over. His face was ashen. She touched his cheek. She had to be stronger than any of them, or they would descend into madness.

"We're getting out of this alive."

Alyk shook his head and pulled her toward the nearest tower. Smoke rose over the trees in thick plumes, from the fjords where they had anchored their ships. Tori felt like she'd been punched in the stomach by a frost giant.

"The chancellor knew," Alyk said stiffly. "A fleet of ships arrived just as our sailors reached the ships. Only one made it back to warn us before we marched to our deaths."

All Tori's strength left her. She collapsed to the ground. Alyk just stood there, gazing helplessly out at their ruined escape and the oncoming horde.

"How?" The Oshans didn't have a war fleet. They preferred to fight on land.

"They were from the Southern Isles, Tori. Seren failed."

The world pressed in on her. She could hardly breathe. Her chest heaved. She stooped forward and clutched her chest, pulling in short, desperate breaths. Her mind whirled, and she could barely see straight.

She pounded the ground over and over again. "GODS! No, no, no, no!" And then she went still.

Alyk joined her on the ground, taking her hand. She looked up into his dark, beautiful eyes. He gritted his teeth as he spoke. He was crying, not out of helplessness, but determination.

"We can still fight them, Tori. You've heard the songs. Some of the greatest heroes fell fighting battles they knew they would lose. The power of this rebellion does not have to come through victory. People will remember this battle. They will sing of our bravery. We may not win Restoration, but we can die in a way that my people will not give up hope. We defend a fortress surrounded by a chasm fifty feet wide. Accessible by only two bridges. We may lose. But we can bring many down with us."

There was a tale her mum once told her, of a band of Watchers in an ancient war from the Old World before the fall of the Elyan Empire. A few dozen sorcerers had held a fortress for days against an army of thousands. But they all died. What did it matter, if they didn't live? Tales were tales. Nothing more. Those Watchers had died useless deaths, and Tori could not let her followers share the same fate. Tori gripped Alyk's hand, but shook her head. "I can't ask that of you, let alone any of them."

"You've given up?"

Tori stood up, and Alyk's fingers slipped from her grasp. "Those old songs are the glorification of needless death. I will not let all of you die for me."

"We'll die for our people. For hope."

"The chancellor is here for me, Alyk. If I surrender, you all may have a chance. Don't give up your hope of Restoration for nothing. Darien offered me terms of peace, and I am going to accept them." Tori kissed him one last time and walked away.

"Terms of peace? Don't be a fool, Tori!"

Tori fought back tears as she turned back to him. "I've been a fool far too many times. But this is not one of them."

"He'll kill you!"

Tori could not meet his gaze. It was their only chance. She could not hope in the chancellor, but perhaps…

She descended the steps to the courtyard. Expectant eyes fell upon her as she approached her waiting troops. They had followed her through storm and bloodshed. They had watched her defeat death in the trial of fire and ice. And she knew they would follow her if she asked them.

"To war?" a young captain asked hopefully.

Tori did not answer him. She turned to Skya. "Bring me Commander Redvar," she ordered.

Skya's mouth hung open. "Tori, he's our bargaining chip!"

Tori shook her head. *I am our only bargaining chip.*

"That was an order, Captain Baruk."

Skya held her gaze for a long moment, then hurried off without another word. Murmurs struck up across the yard. Tori gave no answer, but Fara dul Baruk offered an explanation.

"She's turning herself in."

As the murmurs became a tumult of whispers, the High Elder approached.

"My mind is made," Tori said, grimacing. "You were right about this war."

"I wish I was not, Gallows Girl."

"I will do what I can to bring terms of peace for your people."

Fara dul Baruk crossed her arms. "For a minute, I thought we might have a chance. You gave even me a bit of hope, damn you."

Tori nodded. "Don't lose hope in your Restoration, Elder Baruk. Only in me."

Fara dul Baruk walked away. Skya escorted Darien out, chains linking the shackles on his wrists with those on his ankles.

"Unbind him," Tori ordered.

Skya did as she was told, but the others, understanding what was happening, began to voice their protests. Darien rubbed his wrists, but smiled grimly. "Thank you, my saint."

Was he mocking her? Suddenly, Tori doubted her hope, but it was all she had. "I have considered your terms and I have decided to accept them. Five hundred of your comrades are in the great hall of Stormfall. You can attest that we have treated them well. I would ask that my own soldiers receive equal treatment."

The murmurs grew to cries of outrage. But Tori raised her right fist, and they turned silent.

Darien nodded. "They will be allowed to return to their lands in peace, in exchange for your surrender."

"My saint, no! Let us fight!" cried a young Alyut man. Tori thought his name was Seldak.

Others echoed the sentiment.

Tori shook her head. "You all have fought bravely. And I have been proud to march beside you. But a good leader does not send her people to slaughter. I cannot ask you to die needlessly. This rebellion is over."

The people protested, but Tori had no more to say. She turned and gestured for Darien to walk out ahead of her.

The ground shook as the Rulaqs outside neared. The massive wooden gates of Stormfall groaned open. The sight beyond took Tori's breath away.

At least one hundred Rulaqs filled the fields of ice and scree. Behind them stood thousands of Legion soldiers. She had been a fool to think her ramshackle army stood any chance against such a force. A fool to trust the Witch Queen. A fool to believe in Ren. A fool to resist the chancellor.

Together, Tori and Darien marched out to face him. The cold northern air cut through Tori's cloak. Darien walked out in front of her across the snowy plain. The Rulaqs towered like battlements above them, still and tranquil, though their massive teeth were clenched threateningly. The chancellor and his Darkling Witch stood at the head of the force.

How did they subdue the beasts? Tori shivered at the sight.

The chancellor controlled these monsters, and if it was true that Seren lè Tal controlled the Nosferati, this would be one damned war for the ages. It might be best if the Northmen retreated back to the peace of the Ice City.

"You made the right choice, Tori."

She gritted her teeth at Darien's voice. "I'm not a fool, Darien. I know the chancellor will never let me live."

"No," Darien said emptily. "Likely not. But I promise you, I will do what I can."

"It doesn't matter. It's not about me. Save your breath to spare the Northmen."

Darien stopped. For a moment, his eyes looked like those of the old Darien. No hints of Morph. "You told me that I knew Merri hadn't turned. That I let her get close to you…"

His voice trailed off, and Tori steeled herself for his words. She had been wrong. She was wrong about everything. And this was her greatest mistake.

"You were right."

Tori didn't know what to say. Was that a tear in Darien's eye? She sighed.

"I loved Merri like a mother. I watched her die, and it killed me. I loved you too. No matter how far into the indoctrination of the Legions I fell, deep down, that never went away. Not completely."

Tori nearly choked. She bit her tongue, fighting back tears. "Why are you telling me this now?"

"I had to. Before it's too late." He walked on.

The chancellor was smiling when they reached him. He dismounted an ebony courser. The godstones glowed threateningly in Medea's right hand in case Tori tried to resist. But Tori was not trying to sense her magic. The chancellor wanted a lamb. She would give him what he wanted.

She could feel Medea pressing in on her mind from astride her snow-white mare. Tori did not fight her magic. "She has no ulterior motives," Medea whispered.

"The end has come at last," Cyrus Maro said.

Tori raised her hands in surrender. "Darien offered me your terms of peace."

The chancellor laughed. "Terms of peace? Darien was doing whatever was required to bring you here. No more. There are no terms."

"Then I will give them to you," Tori said obstinately. "I have five hundred of your Shadows within the fortress. We could easily have killed them or tortured them for information, Commander Redvar among them. Instead, we treated their wounds and fed them."

The chancellor raised his brows. "Why?"

"Because this is not their war. They followed a charismatic leader."

The chancellor laughed. "You turn my own words against me."

"You spared many Watchers for the same crime. I would ask that you extend the same treatment to the Northmen. Let them return to the White North, in peace."

"You are not exactly in a position to make demands, Gallows Girl."

Darien spoke up. "I can attest to her claims, milord. She treated us well."

"In exchange, I will come in peace," Tori said. "You may do as you will with me. I am through fighting."

"My queen wants your head," Cyrus Maro said.

Tori nodded grimly. "If that is her final request, then I will not fight it."

The chancellor thought for a while before answering. "If you come peacefully, then I will spare them. Medea, bring me the elements."

Medea handed him the bloodletting instruments Tori knew so well.

Her blood drained from her in a steady flow, until she was sufficiently weak. She held onto Darien's arm for support. It felt strange to touch him, but she did not feel the revulsion she had felt before. Darien grimaced when she met his gaze. He did not enjoy seeing her pain.

When it was finished, the chancellor prepared a vial of her blood, and drank. Then, a pair of Morphs fixed shackles on her wrists. The chancellor turned to Darien and Medea.

"Commander Redvar, you will remain until all of our soldiers have been released, and lead them back to Maro'El. We'll reward them all with a feast upon our return. Take Lord Byrn's men as well."

Darien's brow furrowed. "Milord, shouldn't Lord Byrn remain to rebuild his fortress?"

The chancellor shook his head. "Reconstruction of the fortress will take some time. It will be better this way. Medea will remain with the Rulaqs until our soldiers have been safely returned to us. Once Stormfall is clear, she will lead the attack."

Tori choked. "I spared your men! I came peacefully!"

"You never came peacefully," the chancellor spat. "You came with an army. You seized my fortress and showed me there is a force on Osha's borders we had all long forgotten. An enemy I will not allow to escape only to fight another day. I already made that mistake with you."

Tori looked to Darien. She had seen the good in him. Surely he would not stand for this senseless death.

He said nothing.

Tori let out a desperate shriek, hoping to warn the others, but it was stifled quickly as the Morphs fixed a gag over her mouth. She squirmed to get away, fought through the pain, but the chancellor's blow came from behind. The flare of Conjuri magic sent her to the ground, and her body ached from the jarring impact. Her eyes filled with tears. *No, no, no, oh gods, please, no!*

"Now," said the chancellor, "we have a wedding to prepare for."

The Morphs jerked Tori to her feet and dragged her off.

Tori caught Darien's gaze one last time, her eyes pleading. Only he could save them. In a way, she had known this from the moment she saw the Rulaqs. He was their only hope. The boy who had resisted at the gallows. The boy who had never stopped caring for her, who had allowed her to escape in the catacombs. The boy who would not stand for pointless death.

But the voice of hope did not come from Darien. It was not uttered aloud at all.

Your true army lies in the South, a voice said inside her mind, echoing the same words Kirra had spoken to her.

Tori's heart raced. It could only be one person.

CHAPTER FORTY-THREE

Medea met Darien's gaze and held it for a long time as the chancellor left with the Gallows Girl in tow. The Darkling Witch toyed with the chancellor's godstones in her hand, turning them over and over. Her wild dark hair shuddered in the northern wind, sweeping across the soft wrinkles under her eyes. Darien had always wondered how old she was. There was something unnerving about her that felt ancient and youthful at the same time.

Darien had spent so much time in her presence, but she was a mystery to him. He did not know where she came from. No one did. If he could believe those at court, she had joined the chancellor's company sometime after the day of the Gallows. Though most believed she had been secretly counseling him much longer. Perhaps when he first began to experiment with magic.

The unknown haunted her gaze. Darien glanced away.

The chancellor rode over the distant snowy hills, a small retinue of Morphs in his company, and disappeared over the horizon.

Tori had struggled at the news. One of the Morphs had beat her, after which she seemed to resign herself to the inevitable. Darien had nearly broken face, then. It had taken everything in him to hold himself back from pummeling the Morph that struck her.

He wondered what Medea was thinking and realized an instant too late that she was wondering the same thing about him. Except she could peer into his mind. He hastily attempted to guard himself.

Medea had given the order to convey the terms of peace to those within Stormfall. The lie that once the Legion prisoners were released, the Northern folk would be allowed to return to the White North.

The messengers had reached the front gates of Stormfall.

"You question the chancellor's decision," Medea whispered.

They stood at the front of the Rulaq horde, a host of Legions behind them. The beasts towered over them. Darien marveled at the way Medea had subdued them. She'd not only stopped their attack on Maro'El, but convinced them to fight for the chancellor. *Why would they choose to follow him?*

"Never," Darien said emphatically.

Medea smiled with thin pale lips. "It is not the first time I have sensed such conflict in you."

"I don't know what you're talking about."

"You were torn the day the chancellor chose you to become a Morph."

"I was not."

"Your friend was torn as well."

Darien's mind raced. He tried to ward off the thoughts, but there was no denying it. Medea knew. She had known him all along. He had not fooled her, not even when he had fooled himself. He resisted the urge to fly.

"Nevertheless, you served your chancellor well," Medea said.

The message delivered, the gates of Stormfall spread wide, and General Thuva and Lord Byrn led a large host across the bridge. Everything was going as the chancellor had planned.

Darien found his voice. "I have always been loyal to the chancellor. As I am now."

Medea smiled. "You underestimate my power, Commander Redvar. But you are not the only one."

"I am no traitor!"

Medea touched his arm and shivers shot through him. "No... but sometimes traitors are saints, my boy."

A sense of understanding passed between them. Darien could not quite believe it. Was it possible? "You don't mean to follow through on the chancellor's orders."

"I said no such thing, Commander."

But she had thought it. She had shared her mind with him for an instant. It had felt like the strangest thing. Like a thread weaving into his thoughts.

"Only you and I received the order," Darien realized aloud. "No one else knows this treaty is a trap."

"You have a choice to make, Commander Redvar. You have questioned the chancellor's actions since the day you became a Morph. You have obeyed your orders, but your heart, no matter how hard you've tried to suppress it, has not been fully invested in Cyrus Maro's cause. The Gallows Girl escaped in the midst of the Nosferati attack, under your watch. And now, you are faced with another opportunity. To do some good."

"You mean to let them go."

"I mean to do… what is just."

Darien looked into her dark eyes. Was she playing him for a fool? Or was she sincere? How could he know? If he said the wrong thing, she could turn his traitorous thoughts against him.

He thought of all the people in that fortress condemned to die. They were not evil. They had cared for him and his soldiers. Under no moral obligation. Tori had ordered that.

Meanwhile, the chancellor was growing erratic and cruel.

The de-handing of Ren Andovier was just the beginning. Now, he ordered the slaughter of people who had willfully surrendered. Who had returned their prisoners to them. He was going to execute Tori.

She had followed a fool, but Darien had seen good in her treatment of the Legions. He had seen her longing for justice for the Alyut. A people much like his own. Subdued by the Oshan Empire long ago. His people had not fought back. But now, he understood the source of his resentment toward his family, toward his people, toward himself.

His people were slaughtered, and he had been helpless to stop it. Untrained for warfare, they had been easy targets. They cowered. And ran. But when they came for his family, Darien had fought back with a shoddy hunting blade and an ax. He killed the man who'd raped his mother. He killed the woman who had clubbed a young girl to death and laughed at the way she whimpered after the first blow, the side of her face caved in. He killed the man who'd shot his father in the head.

Three soldiers he killed before he was brought down.

He could still see the Legion general's smile as he ordered the soldiers down before they killed the crazed Klavash boy.

Darien was the only one to kill a Shadow that day. And he was the only one spared.

It had never made sense to him.

Until now.

Darien had shown spirit, the general had said.

Darien had shown signs of bloodlust.

Signs he could be molded to do unspeakable things.

He had hated himself for surviving, and the Shadow Camp leaders used that hatred, twisted it. But he remembered now, something he had long forgotten. Darien had been motivated by justice that day. Not hatred.

Darien had ceased all care to guard his thoughts. He had let Medea into one of the deepest memories he held. Perhaps she had helped him remember. "What is just," he murmured, repeating Medea's words.

"You remember," Medea said. "The irony is that you might have been fully lost if you had not chosen to become the Morph that you are. Your mind was nearly gone when you let me in after the victory in Morgath."

General Thuva and Lord Byrn arrived. Darien greeted them warmly and informed them of the festivities to come in Maro'El, to which they had been invited. Lord Byrn protested at first, but Darien conveyed the chancellor's insistence that they join the city-wide festivities of the royal wedding.

Thuva and Byrn led the freed prisoners in the direction the chancellor had ridden shortly before. Near the end of the line, Darien spotted Kirra. The turned Watcher was hobbling along with the help of a young soldier. She had caught Medea's attention as well. Kirra smiled and turned her head their direction, ever so briefly.

Medea turned to him.

"Kirra never turned against her comrades, did she?" he said.

Medea shook her head. "She has played her part. So well, she nearly died."

"What do you have planned?"

"The Gallows Girl needed to come to Maro'El," Medea whispered. "We have great plans for her."

"We?"

Medea smiled. "Sometimes traitors are saints, my boy."

The Saints of the North. Darien could not believe it. But a great sense of relief washed over him. It was as though all the confusion and tension within him had evaporated. He was free to question, free to decide for himself.

For so long, he had felt so trapped.

"You've been helping Tori all this time."

"I've been seeking justice." Medea gestured to the Rulaqs. Their leader dipped one of its heads in a nod to her.

That was how she had won them over in Maro'El. They didn't serve the chancellor at all. She had convinced them to end their attack on the chancellor to join a greater cause.

"What do you want from me?" Darien said.

———

Medea told him what was to come, and Darien felt like he was coming alive, fully, for the first time in his life.

But he could not do it alone.

He morphed and flew to Stormfall. He spoke with Alyk dul Baruk and explained the chancellor's orders. And he explained the plan of the Saints. The Alyut shaman was wary at first, but he was desperate for hope. For his people. For Tori.

Just as Darien was.

The Northmen would march south tomorrow.

But there was one more piece to the plan. After her betrayal, Darien had thought she was the enemy. Valeria and her queen. But Medea showed him just how wrong he was.

Darien found her in the chambers where they had spent the night only a few short days ago. Her eyes were filled with anger at first. And then softened.

"I was a fool," he said, standing outside the door.

Her grim expression broke into the most beautiful smile he had ever seen. "I was the fool," she said. "For giving up on you."

They embraced. The wound in Darien's side hurt, but he didn't care. The anger that had consumed him before felt unfathomable. Like it had belonged to some other person. Valeria kissed him, fighting tears, and pulled him close, like she might never let him go. Yet, he thought in that moment, he had never felt such freedom. For the first time, there was nothing standing between them.

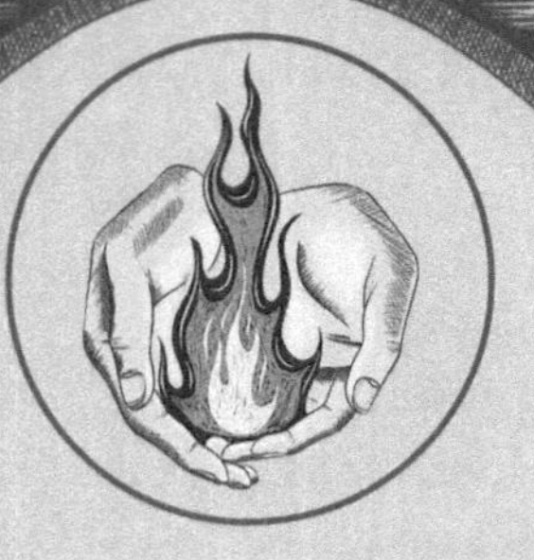

CHAPTER FORTY-FOUR

They sailed for the Isle of Tal on a ship manned by Seren's kinsmen. Kin who had betrayed her. The queen of the Southern Isles remained belowdecks for most of the journey through the narrow channels between islands, and a dark mood had begun to consume her.

There had been no sign of the Kroqala since the night Seren was betrayed, and Mischa feared they had died in the flames that consumed the skyship. The queen had hardly spoken since that dark night, but her rage and sorrow were growing. Each night of their voyage, Mischa could see a fierce glow skirting under the door and flickering off the shifting corridors of the ship.

The glow of magic.

At all other times, Seren kept her magic tamed, as she'd vowed to Lord Thiere in exchange for safe passage to her homeland. The strange rune markings in her skin were covered by dark sleeves again.

Mischa and Tes kept close to one another during the slow voyage, and Mischa often found herself comforting the Crooked girl over the failure of their rebellion. In truth, Tes proved as much of a comfort for Mischa. She could not descend into the depths of despair, no matter how tempting it was, not with Tes around.

Mischa claimed the last vestiges of hope for Tes, but kept none for herself. She was grateful Tes was alive, but she hated how easily Seren had been subdued.

She had never felt so hopeless.

At night, Mischa would lie with Tes in their cabin until the girl fell asleep, then Mischa would venture to the deck and watch the stars and the moons trekking across the sky, oblivious to the fragility of the dark world below. The world they had abandoned.

———

WHEN THEY CAME TO PORT IN THE TRADING CITY OF HESSA, THE largest city on the Isle of Tal, Mischa's spirits were further crushed. News had come swiftly of the capture of the Gallows Girl. Her execution would take place in a matter of days, if Mischa believed the teller.

There was a small Alyut trading vessel tethered at the port, and after hearing the news, Geryn dul Narsuk left them to join his kinsmen.

That was it, then.

The revolution was over.

The news pressed on Mischa's chest like a great stone. It was all she could do to place one foot before the other as they left the docks.

The rebel army in the North had been crushed. Were they all dead? Even Skya and the Alyut?

Her vision clouded as she fought back tears. But she held Tes's hand and pressed on through the streets of Hessa toward the palace. The girl was trembling, but Mischa insisted things would be all right.

"We have to go!" Tes said. "We have to help!"

But there was nowhere to go, no way to help. They were two young Watchers opposing a world turned against them.

Seren remained queen of the Isle of Tal, but she received a lackluster welcome. The crowds were small and disinterested. Palace guards escorted them through the grid-like streets, but they were hardly needed. Favor drifted like currents of the wind, and Seren lè Tal had lost favor across the Southern Isles. Even in her own home.

Nonetheless, the three were escorted to Seren's palace, set upon a hill in the midst of the city. Mischa and Tes were provided temporary quarters until Mischa could decide what to do. Mischa instructed Tes to rest up for their journey from the Isles the following day. She was not sure where they would go. Perhaps the Trium.

Seren was about to leave as well, but Mischa stopped her. "My queen, may we speak?"

Seren offered a grim, defeated smile, but nodded her assent. "There's no need to call me that any longer, Mischa. My reign is at its end."

"That's all there is to it? You've given up entirely?"

"It's the will of my people, and I must honor it. You do not hail from the Isles. You could not understand."

"But you united them," Mischa said, still bewildered at how swiftly the change had occurred. She could not imagine the chancellor bending to the will of others so easily. She supposed that was what separated rulers like Seren lè Tal from Cyrus Maro. But she wondered if it was the best way to rule. She felt so helpless. She wanted to fight. To resist.

The Isles had made a deadly mistake. They should be made to pay for their betrayal.

Yet she knew, deep down, that there was nothing they could have done. Three sorcerers against a kingdom were no match.

"The Isles have united against me," Seren said. "Even my own people. When the time comes, parliament will select a new ruler, and I will not even be Lady Seren any longer. I will be Seren Taldona, as I was as a child. A brief anomaly in the histories of the world. The witch who ruled the Isles for a moment and then faded into oblivion. The magic of our time will belong to the Oshans, gods damn them."

"But Tori—"

"At the rate news reaches us here in the South, she's probably been dead several days."

"That depends on the messenger, my queen."

The sudden voice made them both turn sharply. Mischa's hand went straight to her blade.

The face she saw took her by surprise. "Valeria?" The silver-haired Morph nodded and bowed to one knee before her queen.

Seren crossed her arms. "How did you get here?"

"The guards let me in. One of them remembered me from the days before you sent me to infiltrate the Legions. They did not seem to be on high alert."

"No, indeed," said Seren. "I thought you'd died. It's been long since we heard report from you in the Legions."

"I am sorry, my queen. But I promise you, my loyalties have never wavered. That is why I'm here."

"Why is that?"

"I was the one who brought the news from the North. Tori is to be executed in two days. And I've come to bring you to Maro'El. To stop it."

Although Mischa had no idea how Valeria could possibly think they could stop the execution, her heart stirred with hope. But she knew they could not fly there in two days, not even if they had Seren's skyship.

"Impossible," said Seren. "Our war is over."

"We have more allies than we thought," Valeria said.

A swirl of mist formed behind her, and Mischa could not believe her eyes. She ought to have reached for her blade, but she felt peace in her mind. The mist faded. Medea did not attack. She smiled.

Lir'ghe the Kroqala darted from the last wisps of mist and hovered at his queen's shoulder.

"Our war is far from being over," Lir'ghe said in his guttural buzz of a voice. It sounded almost cheerful.

Valeria and the demon faerie told them of what happened at Storm-fall. Tori's sacrifice. The chancellor's orders to slaughter the Northmen. How Darien had refused and joined Medea. The plot of the Saints in Osha to overthrow the chancellor. Mischa was overwhelmed by the stir-rings of hope.

"We must be swift." Medea closed her fingers around the gemstones, and they glowed with a fierce emerald light. A space opened in the invis-ible fabric of the air, and on the other side was a narrow street in a city dusted with snow.

Seren hesitated. "What can we do? I have no army. Nothing to offer."

"You're a witch, my queen," Medea said. "What we need is your magic. And when the world is set right, when Osha falls, the Isles will realize their mistake. You will be queen of the Southern Isles again."

Seren was silent for a moment, but Mischa noted the way Seren's demeanor sparked at the potential to remain queen.

Mischa didn't notice Tes arrive. She was still dressed. She gripped the queen's hand, her eyes wide with hope. "I heard you from the other room."

The queen smiled. "Of course you did."

"We have to go! We have to help them… my queen."

Seren looked down at the young Crooked girl. "You're right, young Watcher." The Witch Queen squeezed Tes's hand tight. They were the first to cross through the portal, Lir'ghe shooting through the mists after them.

Before Mischa went through, she hugged Valeria and kissed her cheek. The fierce soldier was taken aback. "What's that for?"

"You've saved me again, Valeria."

The Morph gripped her shoulder. "I haven't saved anyone yet."

Mischa stepped through the portal and Valeria followed.

They stood in a dingy street, somewhere in the Merching district of Maro'El, Mischa suspected. The bright towers of the Oshan capital shot up around them like great teeth, but the largest of them was visible even from this distant corner of the city. And Mischa had the dark sense they had just entered the jaws of the beast.

PART TWELVE
THE WHITE CITADEL

The citadel was one of the last remaining structures from the Age of the Watchers. Forged by magic, it withstood millennia of war and turmoil. Kingdoms and empires rose and fell, but still, the tower stood.

—from *New Histories of the Old World*

CHAPTER FORTY-FIVE

The chancellor was the first to arrive in Maro'El. He paraded the Gallows Girl through the streets to thunderous applause. High lords and the people of their estates, merchants, bankers, and other middleborn tradesmen—all of them roared at the sight of the Gallows Girl in chains. The city was nearly rebuilt. The Rulaqs now marched for the chancellor. The world was being restored after the devastation wreaked by the Gallows Girl and her monsters from the Old World. Even the monsters themselves might not be the curse they had first thought.

The Sky Guard escorted the chancellor's entourage down the main thoroughfare, and Kale was among them. Amidst the pomp and revelry, his mind was consumed by Kirra.

Or rather her absence.

The chancellor assured him she would be alive. Commander Redvar was supposed to arrive with the others soon, but Kale could not stop himself from worrying she had been killed. There was never meant to be a battle. Redvar was supposed to negotiate in the North, quick and simple.

Instead, the chancellor and his Darkling Witch had marched an army to the North.

After Medea had revealed herself in his mind the day she had channeled his power to locate the Gallows Girl, Kale ought to have been relieved to know that the powerful sorceress had turned against the chancellor. But there was so much at stake. So much could fail.

Nevertheless, the Battle of Stormfall had proved fortunate in its own way. Patrols had been scarce in Maro'El with such a great force sent to Stormfall. It had allowed the Hangman and his Saints to prepare the city for the wedding.

And now, the Gallows Girl had arrived in Maro'El.

The Hellfire Plot was going as planned, at least as far as Lazarus Delahi had let him know.

The procession reached Maro Square and the people crowded in to listen as the chancellor declared the death sentence on the Gallows Girl to cacophonous cheers.

The wedding was to be held in two days. It would be the greatest spectacle in the empire in centuries. Delegations from the Southern Isles and the Yan Avii would be in attendance, in addition to every lord house in Osha. Despite the descent of winter, delegations were pouring into Maro'El by the hour. The chancellor would be throwing a feast across the city to celebrate his union.

As soon as he could escape, Kale left the triumphal festivities and retreated to his quarters in the upper levels of the White Citadel. He was on guard duty in the palace later that evening, so he would need to rest.

The sun set in the middle of the afternoon. Soon, there would only be a few hours of daylight per day. But it did not matter. The lights of Maro'El warred with the stars in the heavens in their brilliance, and despite his fatigue, Kale could not sleep.

Perhaps it was the fine bed. After so many years spent on the move, Kale had never slept well in feather beds and blankets. He tried lying on the floor, but that proved useless as well.

When the door opened, Kale shot up from the ground, reaching for his blade.

It was only Ashi. She slipped in without a word and gave him a querulous look. "Why are you on the floor?"

"How did you get in my room?" Kale demanded.

She smiled with thin lips. "I attend the queen-to-be. And you are a palace guard. Your quarters are not off-limits."

"What do you want? Is it about—"

Ashi shushed him before he could mention the Saints of the North. Now that Tori was safely in Maro'El, he was expecting to hear from one of Lazarus's messengers soon.

Ashi lowered her voice. "Do not mention them here. The palace is not safe. The queen has need of you."

Kale crossed his arms and waited for her to elaborate. She did not.

"For what? I have never guarded Vashti before."

The door opened again, and in walked Vashti Burodai, arrayed in ruby-red Yan Avii silks. Kale nearly forgot his formalities, but he caught himself before protesting her intrusion. He bowed dutifully.

Vashti waved him off. "There is no need to bow, Kale. We are old friends. And there is no one else around."

Old friends? Despite having aided her escape from her father's execution two years previous, Kale and Vashti had hardly been close during their years at the Watchtower. She wanted something.

A chill coursed through him. Neither he nor Ashi knew just how dedicated Salla and Vashti were to their alliance with the chancellor. Would they get in the way of the plans of the Saints? Would they join? Ashi had wanted to speak with Salla after their visit to the Fringes, but Kale rejected that idea. When it came time, Salla might choose. But it would be foolish to reveal the plot to anyone else.

Kale had been hesitant to trust even Ashi, so great was her loyalty to her prince. But as best he could tell, the Ilya woman had kept their secret. He had felt her mind when she saw the Saints the first time, and he had felt her outrage at the treatment of Oshan slaves in the Fringes. He had to trust her.

But Vashti? He did not imagine her visit would be pleasant for him.

"How can I serve you, my queen?" he said at last.

Vashti betrayed a smile at this, her lips pursed in noble fashion. She fit in well with the high nobility of the citadel. And she blamed Tori for the attack on the Red City. He could sense pleasure, even now, that the Gallows Girl had been brought to the citadel in chains. Salla's loyalties might be swayed, but he sensed the queen would not let go of her hatred. She saw what she wanted to see.

"You are a guard of the palace," Vashti said at last. "I need you to guard me."

Kale considered telling her that he was not on duty for several hours, but thought better of it. "Of course, my queen. Where may I escort you?"

Why me specifically? he wanted to ask.

"The dungeons."

"The dungeons?" Kale said. Ashi caught his gaze, and he detected sympathy. "The Gallows Girl?"

"No," Vashti said. "We're going to see Ren."

At the sound of his brother's name, Kale tensed all over. An overwhelming sense of guilt enveloped him. He could not face his brother again.

But he was only a pawn, and so he had no choice.

———

Vashti, Kale, and Ashi descended into the dark belly of the White Citadel. There were many levels to the tower below the city. Above, the world consisted of shimmering crystals, extravagant jewels, and fine tapestries. Below, the world was molded of ancient stones that had withstood centuries. The steps were worn smooth. The engravings on the walls had faded.

"They say these walls were formed by magic," said Vashti.

Kale nodded, the act casting frantic shadows in the flickering lamplight. "It's the reason it has stood so long, they say."

"How long?"

"No one knows."

Vashti chuckled. "You're from Maro'El. Surely you know their histories."

"History that ancient fades into myth, in my experience."

"What do the myths say?"

"The myths have evolved since the fall of the Old World, my queen. But my family preserved some ancient stories. According to my mother…"

A lump formed in his throat. Kale had not thought of his mother in some time. She had been dead for so long, her memory had begun to grow faint and fleeting. Once, the sight of violet gowns or the scent of Trium lilac might have brought him to tears. But he had learned to block her out, once he was able to control his Cerebro gifts. He could not let himself dwell on the past.

The corridors wended deeper and deeper.

"Your mother?" said Vashti.

"Sorry," Kale said, clearing his throat. "She has been dead for many years."

"I am sorry to hear it."

"She taught me that the first Oshans arrived over a thousand years ago. Magic was becoming a powerful and devastating force in the Elyan world. There were great travesties in that age. Renegade sorcerers used their power for greed and vile intent. Great lords sought to use sorcerers as weapons. They were hunted and often enslaved.

"Many with the gift fled north, along with other groups. Religious outcasts, low-class folk looking for a better life. The newcomers fought off the original inhabitants and built a new civilization. It led to the formation of the Watcher Orders. And eventually to the Great Empire of the Old World…"

Vashti was silent for a while. "My people tell a different tale about the pale-skinned savages from the South. The Sky Bloods were a curse from Votan, an ancient sky god, who turned his back on us long ago. My people were but scattered tribes back then. We were forced to unite to defend against the flying devils and their hordes. Everything changed when your people arrived."

"I don't defend their actions, my queen."

"No, but your mother's stories do. History is written by the conquerors, but my people find hope in the ashes. The arrival of the Oshans led to warfare that still has not ended, but it also brought us together. War still unites the Yan Avii. But I pray my brother can unite them in days of peace."

"I… I hope it is so, my queen."

"I hold no delusions about the chancellor, Kale. But this wedding is a great step toward that peace."

Why is she telling me all this? Does she suspect something?

"I pray it is so," Kale said.

"You never believed in the Shadow Watch," Vashti said. "I could always tell."

"My brother was full of ideas. Some of them good. But the Shadow Watch was doomed to fail."

Vashti went quiet. The walls deep below the citadel bore a strange film and smelled of ancient dampness.

"Why are we going to see Ren?" Kale asked as they neared the dungeons.

Vashti touched his shoulder from behind, and he stopped and turned to her. Her skin emanated warmth, and her jewelry glinted in the lamplight.

"I never thanked you for what you did for my people, Kale. When you betrayed your brother."

Kale did not know what to say. He had not thought of the Yan Avii in that moment at all.

"I know you did it for other reasons," Vashti went on. "But your decision made this wedding possible. And I am grateful."

"You're welcome, my queen."

"You asked why we're going to see your brother. I've just received word that the chancellor plans to execute him alongside the Gallows Girl…" Her voice drifted off.

Kale walked on. He didn't know what to think. He felt hollowed out. He had for so long. The rise of the Saints was meant to be his redemption. It had taken everything in him to remain collected when Ren lost his hand. Now, Kirra was still missing, and Ren was to be sacrificed?

Vashti grimaced. "If he had not been such a fool, things would not have gone the way they did at the Watchtower. I never wished for this when I betrayed him. There are things I cannot change, but that does not mean I don't have regrets. I needed to tell him that before the end."

They reached the depths of the dungeons, where the Watcher prisoners were kept. The Morph guards protested only momentarily before standing down before their queen-to-be. A scowling female Morph escorted them to Ren's cell. They passed several doors, and Kale wondered whether Tori was chained within one of them.

The Morph unlocked a cell at the end of a hall. The latch clanked as it opened, and Ren looked up, feebly. His skin was nearly translucent. His eyes vacant. He sat hunched in the corner, clutching his stump arm to his chest. He tried to speak and then fell into a fit of coughs. His eyes settled on Kale for a moment, but Ren seemed to look through him.

Vashti went forward and knelt beside him. She touched his forehead. "Arayeva, you're on fire." The Morph was about to leave, but Vashti ordered that he bring bandages and alcohol. The Morph scowled but knew better than to argue with her queen.

The bandaged stump was caked in dried blood. The dressings had not been changed in days. When Vashti reached to unwrap them, Ren pulled away.

"It's infected, Ren. Let me help you."

"I'm going to die. What does it matter?"

Kale remained back in the doorway. He could sense Vashti's brokenness at the sight of the man she had once loved.

Ren held out his stump weakly. "Why are you here?" Ren murmured.

Vashti turned to Kale and Ashi. "Give us a moment, will you?"

Kale was frozen in place. He nearly threw up as Vashti unwrapped the oozing wound. Ashi took his forearm and pulled him away, and Kale was grateful that Ren hadn't seemed to realize who he was.

Kale and Ashi lingered in the corridor while Vashti spoke with Ren in indistinguishable murmurs. Kale did not try to detect their meaning. The Morph returned to her post at the base of the staircase and left them alone.

"There is still good in her, Kale," Ashi whispered.

"Vashti cares for your people. Nothing more."

"My people's interest *is* the interest of the Saints. My queen cannot even be herself in this marriage. Posing as Fer Zora's daughter? This wedding is a temporary solution. Vashti knows this. Salla knows this. This entire alliance is but biding time. Osha must fall. Why not now? When the time is right, they will join us."

Kale shook his head and gripped Ashi's wrist tightly. "You must not jeopardize this."

Ashi shook off his grip. "You are not my lord, Kale."

"I'm sorry. But please, let Lazarus enact his plan. Vashti and Salla may choose then, when the time comes."

The door creaked open and Vashti exited. Kale caught a glimpse of Ren's face and was sure that he had recognized him. He made a decision on impulse. "My queen... may I have a word with my brother?"

Vashti nodded. "A quick word."

Kale entered the reeking cell. Some color had returned to Ren's face. He looked up. Kale could sense the hatred pouring from his brother's mind uninhibited. There was so much to say, and yet nothing.

Ren spoke first. "I told Vashti I didn't think you'd have the guts to face me."

Then he *had* seen him from the start. Kale remained near the door.

"Vashti betrayed the Shadow Watch for her people," Ren said. "A noble purpose in its own way. Your reasons were pathetic."

Kale nodded wordlessly.

"Is that all you're here for? To stand and nod?"

Kale wanted to tell him of the Saints. Of the ways he was trying to redeem his wrongs.

"You spineless *skazha*! Your fear is what killed our mother. And now it is going to kill me. You make me sick. I'm about to die, and your face is not what I want to see before the end. Leave me be."

Kale fought back tears. He backed away.

"Nothing to say for yourself?" Ren seethed. "No excuses?"

Kale choked, but he found words. "Nothing can excuse what I've done, brother. All I can do is make it right."

"By joining the Sky Guard? By helping them find the Gallows Girl?"

Kale shook his head. He had to tell him something. He drew closer and whispered, "Tori's greatest army is here in this city. You're not dying at this wedding. And neither is she. Not if I can help it."

Kale spun and left the cell, heart racing, hoping no one had heard him from the other side. The door clanked shut behind him. But the corridor was empty. Where was Vashti?

He hurried down the hall and found the Morphs at their post, looking bored.

"Where's the queen?" Kale asked.

"Gone to see the Gallows Girl."

CHAPTER FORTY-SIX

Tori trembled with shivers as she waited to die. Waited to see if her hopes proved true.

She had to believe.

In Darien. In the symbol of the Gallows Girl.

The last time she had been in this cell, she had felt no hope. She felt little now, for herself. But the Gallows Girl was something beyond her, even her life. Her death might not be the end. There were Saints across the empire. Saints throughout this city.

Even Saints within the chancellor's inner circle.

Even now, Tori could barely believe it. But she had felt Medea in her mind as she left with the chancellor and his entourage.

Your true army lies in the South…

The same words Kirra had spoken to her. If Medea and Kirra were working with the Saints, then there was hope for the Alyut and the Crooked folk. For Skya. Alyk. Seren. Even Darien.

Of course, there was the possibility that all of it was a lie. Darien. Medea. The army in Osha. But she could not believe that. She had to cling to hope.

When the door opened, the sudden light blinded her for a moment. Tori heard soft footsteps. The door closed, but the light remained. Her eyes slowly grew accustomed. The visitor said nothing until their eyes locked.

The Yan Avii princess's eyes were filled with hate. But to her surprise, Tori did not return the animosity she had once felt so strongly toward her.

She pitied Vashti. The daughter of a father who had become a monster, who had sacrificed his daughter to save face before his people, in the same way his father had tried to save face when his affair with Tori's mum was discovered.

Finally, the princess spoke. "I've waited long for this day, Gallows Girl."

Tori nodded weakly. "I know you have… For what it's worth, I was sorry to hear what happened to the Red City."

"Save your groveling. You will die for what you've done to this world."

"I regret many things, but resisting the chancellor… I can't apologize for that. But I wish it had turned out differently for our people."

"Our people…" Vashti seethed. "Don't you dare claim loyalty to my people, you half-blood bitch! You unleashed hell on this world! You stirred up the Rulaqs and you let the other beasts through. The beasts that destroyed *my* city."

Tori said nothing. She thought of what Darien had said. Was this entire rebellion aimed at the wrong foe? Had she allied herself with the enemy of the world? Did Seren possess the other stones? Was it someone else?

Or was Vashti right? Tori had never ruled it out. It might have been her.

"You don't deny it," Vashti said with satisfaction.

"I don't know what happened. I've thought it through over and over again. I don't know what power lay in the gateway the chancellor used. I never tried to let anything else through. But I don't know."

"You don't know…"

"I did the best I could in the moment when I resisted the chancellor. I was trying to save the Watchers. You did the same for your people."

Vashti rolled her eyes. "Spare me your flattery. It will not save you now."

"I've accepted my fate," Tori said, holding Vashti's gaze. "I just haven't accepted yours."

Vashti's eyes bore into her. "What are you talking about?"

"It was my choice to come to Maro'El. Too much blood has already been spilled on my account. I accept what's to come. The road ends here for me. But it doesn't have to end for you. Or for our people. Watchers or Yan Avii."

"What are you saying?"

"Your loyalties are not yet set in stone. Are you happy with the choices you've made?"

Vashti crossed her arms and huffed, and Tori expected the conversation was over. But then Vashti spoke. "I don't regret my intentions… but I blame myself for what happened to the Watchers. I never wanted them to die. Zaya, Joran, Gany, and Lena. Their faces haunt me every day."

"Me too," Tori said.

"I hate you all the more for that."

"I don't blame you."

Silence hung over them.

"You despised me at the Watchtower," Vashti said at last. "You have more reason than ever now. But you don't anymore. Not after I betrayed the Shadow Watch. Not after I asked for your head. Why?"

"You despised me at the Watchtower. I despised you back."

"I still despise you, Tori."

Tori breathed deeply. "I never knew my father. My mum raised me on the Steppe. But he was a Burodai."

"I already know that. It doesn't change anything."

"What you don't know—what I didn't know—is that we are more than just related by tribe. My father was Aron Burodai."

Vashti's face turned to stone. "Impossible. That is *shenzah*!"

Tori shook her head. The chains binding her wrists to the floor rattled with the movement. "I didn't want to believe it either. But my mum showed me."

"How? She's dead!"

"There is a temple in the North where the veil between the Aether and our own world is thin. My mum came to me. In a sort of vision. I saw *him* too, through her eyes."

Vashti was biting her lip, fighting tears. She would not look at Tori. "Really? Then, what did he look like?"

Tori had memorized every moment of her mum's vision. It was the most beautiful thing she'd ever seen. Her parents in love.

"It was the year I was born. He was tall and muscular. He rode a magnificent white horse with a grey mane. His face was narrow and smooth except for a thin mustache. Long dark hair he pulled back in a long braid. Skin that radiated in the sun. He had a scar on the side of his neck, just below his ear."

Vashti's expression had fallen.

"We're sisters, Vashti. I know it's hard to believe. And I know that your father was—"

"Don't speak of him!" Vashti screamed

Two more people rushed into the room. Kale and a woman Tori didn't recognize, who appeared to be a servant. Tori's heart quickened at the sight of Kale Andovier. She thought again of what Kirra had said. If it was true, then Kale was part of this as well.

"My queen," said the servant woman, noting her mistress's distress. She touched Vashti's arm, but the Yan Avii princess pulled away and fled the room.

The servant hurried after her, but Kale Andovier remained. It seemed like so many months ago that Tori had said goodbye to him at the Watchtower. Before he'd betrayed them to the chancellor.

He looked from her to the door, as though contemplating something. There was no one else there. A distant clamor echoed down the halls. Guards.

"Kale…" Tori began.

Kale touched a finger to his lips. He reached within his cloak and retrieved a piece of parchment. He placed it in her hand and backed away.

On the parchment was inscribed the symbol of a gallows cleft in two. Her heart thundered in her chest. When she looked up, Kale was leaving.

"Wait!" Tori called. "Please!"

He turned.

The guards neared

"The wedding must go on as planned," Kale said. "And then Saints will rise."

He closed the door and was gone. Tori cried with relief. She closed her fingers around the parchment, clutching it like a babe to her mother's breast. It was but a slip of paper, and yet it contained the hope of the world.

CHAPTER FORTY-SEVEN

Before the wedding, Cyrus Maro spent a blissful last night with his favorite nightling. A night of passion and little sleep. He lay awake beside her deep into the night, pushing aside all the pressing thoughts that plagued rulers of great empires. He stroked Rhaena's dark hair as she laid her head on his chest.

She was so beautiful. Her charcoal eyes. Her copper skin. Her slender waist and curved hips. The way she softly whimpered with each breath in her sleep. The rhythm of it usually helped Cyrus sleep himself after the throes of passion had faded. But not tonight.

His mind was like a skiff tossed by violent waves upon the shores of sleep.

So much was about to change.

He had never wanted to marry. Not after Elara.

That had been so long ago, yet Cyrus Maro could see her face when he closed his eyes. Rhaena reminded him of her. Not in looks, as Elara had been Oshan of the purest blood. House Barra.

It was the fire in her eyes. Her playful, almost mischievous nature. Elara's fire had not gone out. Not even as she died. Cyrus Maro allowed himself no regrets but one. After all that happened those years ago, he wished she had lived. Despite what she'd done to him.

When he was with Rhaena, she returned. Not the Elara he had

known, but the Elara he wished he would have known. An Elara who loved him back. Even if it was but an illusion.

He reached for Rhaena and realized her side of the bed was empty. He shot up in bed.

The Faerish girl, draped in nearly transparent scarlet silks, stood silently at the window beside the hearth, gazing out at the city. He hadn't felt her stir. The fire was dancing fervently. She must have stoked it after he had drifted off to sleep. It was nearly morning. Cyrus donned his kendrak robes and approached her from behind, wrapping his arms about her.

"Why aren't you sleeping?" he asked. It was not like her. Usually Rhaena slept as sound as a child in his feather bed.

The nightling did not look to him. Something was wrong. "What becomes of me now?" she murmured.

The chancellor straightened up. "What do you mean?"

"I don't want to return to the nighthouses. All nightlings envy girls like me. Chambers in the palace. Warm meals and fine clothes. The pleasures of only one fine patron. They will hate me if I go back."

"How could anyone hate you?"

Rhaena pulled away from him. It was not like her. Perhaps out of play, but this was different. "The other girls might envy me, but they don't look fondly on the playthings of nobles. Let alone the chancellor."

"Then… well, then you won't return to the nighthouses. The kings of Jurka keep palace harems. Why shouldn't you stay in the citadel?"

Rhaena turned to look him in the eyes. "I may be a whore, but I am not a fool, milord. You can't have nightlings running around the citadel with a new bride to please. Alliances to maintain. I know enough about politics to know I'm used up."

"I'll find a way, my dear." He touched her cheek tenderly, but he could have sworn she flinched at his touch.

Truth be told, the chancellor had not given Rhaena a second thought amidst all his other pressures. She was supposed to be an escape from those pressures, gods damn her.

He felt a twinge of guilt for this. But of course, Rhaena was right. She would have to leave. And if she were to return to the nighthouses, he would not want her back, no matter how beautiful she was. She would be used by others. The thought sickened him.

But he had greater things to worry about. For now, he would ease her mind. To shut her up. He needed sleep, and she was supposed to help with that. "It will be fine. I promise you."

Rhaena glared at him. "Fine… that's the problem with you Oshans."

Cyrus Maro was growing irritated. He liked her spark, but this was bordering on defiance. "Excuse me?"

"You use things up and cast them away. Human things. Like we are pigs or dogs. You call yourselves civilized, but you're no better than any other kingdom in this wretched world."

"Hold your tongue, whore. I've indulged your fire, but I will not be spoken to like some mercher on the street. I've treated you far better than any woman of your station deserves."

"Oh yes, thank you, milord. I ought to grovel at your feet." She turned so quickly and unexpectedly, Cyrus Maro lost his balance and fell to the floor. His head thudded against the fine marble.

He clutched the back of his head, dazed.

She pushed me?

He swelled with anger, about to cry out, when he realized he couldn't speak. It was as though invisible hands were covering his mouth. He must have hit his head even harder than he thought.

Rhaena stood by the fire. Her back was to him for a moment. He tried to scramble away, but his limbs wouldn't work. He was paralyzed. *Oh gods! What is happening?*

Rhaena turned to him. She held a wrought iron poker above her head. Why in the Abyss had his attendants left something like that in his chambers?

"Here's my thanks, milord!" Rhaena cried and brought the iron poker down upon his head.

———

The chancellor shot up in bed, his head pounding like a hammer upon an anvil.

The bedroom doors flew open and a servant rushed to him. He pushed the boy away madly, fearing for his life. "Don't touch me!"

The sheets were soaked with sweat. "Where's Rhaena?" he demanded.

"Who?" the boy asked dumbly.

"The whore, you imbecile." The boy didn't even know her name.

"S-sorry, milord. She left at dawn." The boy threw open the curtains, nearly blinding Cyrus Maro. His head throbbed worse.

It was dawn already?

"Shut them!" the chancellor demanded. "What are you doing in my chambers?"

The boy stammered fearfully. Tears welled in the corners of his eyes. "I-I-I'm sorry, milord. The Lady Medea ordered me to wake you."

The chancellor breathed with some relief. "She's returned?"

"Aye, milord. Just now she returned from the North."

"Then send her in and leave us be." The boy made to run away, but Cyrus called him back. "And don't you ever enter my chambers again without admittance, or I will have your head."

The boy nodded tearfully and ran away.

The chancellor donned furs and sat in the chair by the hearth, double-checking that there was no fire poker left behind.

There wasn't.

His chest rose and fell turbulently, and he tried to catch his breath. He drank some water, and then some wine, but nothing remedied the terror he felt. The dream had been so real.

It was the damned Gallows Girl. So long as she was alive, he could trust no one. Not the nameless servant boy. Not Rhaena.

Especially not Rhaena. He would have her sent back to the night-houses. Or better yet, have her executed. He could not let someone live who had spent so much time close to him.

Medea entered and he felt some relief.

"All went according to plan?" the chancellor said.

The sorceress nodded. "The Northmen will be no further trouble, my lord."

"Good. Very good."

"Pardon me for saying this, but you don't look well. Is there anything I can do for you?" The sorceress touched his arm kindly.

"I need this day to be over with," Cyrus Maro said. "I need the Gallows Girl to be dealt with once and for all."

"The execution will commence after the wedding, according to the queen's request. Her head will be served during the wedding feast."

The chancellor shook his head, running his hands through his hair. "No, I would have her killed before."

"My lord?" Medea's dark eyes spread wide. "Before the wedding?"

"Wait until the crowds have gathered for the ceremony in the square. The Gallows Girl will be executed on the balcony before the entire city. I will not parade my bride in the square while the Saints still have their Gallows Girl. She dies before the wedding."

"Of course, my lord. I will have Commander Redvar wear his sword."

"Don't bother," Cyrus said.

"I thought you wanted him to do the deed."

"I will do it. With my own sword."

"My lord, on your wedding day?"

"This alliance is built on the Gallows Girl's blood. What do I care if that blood is on my robes when we are wed?"

CHAPTER FORTY-EIGHT

When Kale saw Kirra, his heart filled with rage. She was broken. Even worse than she'd been when she left him. She came in the early hours of the morning, knocking at his door. He pulled her into an embrace and she nearly screamed in pain.

She had been badly injured at Stormfall. Ashi led her into his chambers.

"What happened?" he demanded, helping Kirra into the room. Her skin was pale with exhaustion and fighting infection. She felt clammy all over.

Kirra huffed with dark laughter. "That Morph from the Red City. Turns out she was on our side."

The Morph who had pretended to be Kirra, who had tried to convince him to kill Salla, to prevent the alliance this wedding would bring. Valeria. "But why would she—"

"She tried to save the Gallows Girl, but she didn't know that Tori's hope for victory was not at Stormfall, but in coming to Maro'El. She nearly killed me. An unfortunate misunderstanding to say the least." Kirra's voice was weak, but she smirked at her own dark jest.

"We have no more time to waste," Ashi said.

"What do you mean?" said Kale.

Kirra coughed violently. She gripped his arm for balance.

"Come," he said, gesturing to the bed. She looked nearly as fragile as she had after her encounter with the chancellor in the Red City. "We need to get you to a healer!"

"No time. The streets are filling."

"For the celebrations, sure. But the wedding is not for hours. Your work is done."

Ashi shook her head as Kirra fell into another fit of coughs. "The chancellor means to execute Tori this morning. Before the wedding."

Kale cursed. "Before?"

"Where are the Saints?" Kirra asked.

"The plan is moving forward. The Saints have infiltrated the city."

"What is Lazarus planning?"

"To take the city," Kale said. "No one knows the whole of it. Those of us in the citadel are meant to ensure the takeover goes as planned, before the chancellor can execute Tori."

"Forget that," Kirra said. "You must warn Lazarus and the others. The execution is three hours ahead of schedule."

"But what about Tori?"

Ashi shook her head. "If the Saints aren't ready, none of it matters."

Kale gripped Kirra's hand, a dark fear creeping through him. This plan was crumbling, as he had feared it would. For weeks he had been anticipating Kirra's return and now he had to leave her right before the few Saints in the citadel rose up.

And she was so weak.

"This is our moment," Kirra said, squeezing his hand back. "Our redemption. Our revenge for what was done to the others on Jallaa. So much evil has been done by the chancellors. Today it ends."

"It will work. We'll make it work." Gods, he hated to leave her.

She touched his face and warmth shot through him. "Don't worry for me, Kale. I was always the stronger one, anyway."

He chuckled in spite of his fear. "I love you," he said.

Kirra's fingers traced his face and found his lips, and she kissed him. "Me too. I always have. Now, go!"

He turned to Ashi. "Stay with her."

Keep her alive!

"I will," Ashi said.

Kale leapt from his bedroom window and disappeared into the thick morning fog that hung over Maro'El. He flew across the city toward the Merching district, grateful for the cover of mist.

He found the nightling, Nyla, and a host of others preparing themselves for the festivities at Lazarus's estate. Vendor carts that appeared to sell food and ribbons and banners were being loaded with weaponry that would soon fill the streets.

Nyla's eyes went wide at the sight of him. "What are you doing here? Your post is in the citadel! The processions have begun for the wedding!"

"The chancellor is executing the Gallows Girl. Before the wedding."

"What?" Nyla said, too loudly.

The Saints gathered around drew nearer.

"Get back to work!" she shouted. "And be quick about it! I need those carts in the streets yesterday!"

The Saints set back to work.

"Where is Lazarus?" Kale demanded,

Nyla shook her head, cursing. "I can't tell you. Lazarus's orders."

"He has to know what's going on!"

The girl bit her lip and pulled him away from the others. "No one is supposed to know."

"He will understand. Our success depends on it."

"Someone had to do it," she said. "Of course it had to be him. But he didn't want anyone to know until it was done."

"Until what was done?" Kale demanded. He searched her mind and felt nothing but darkness.

"Lazarus is in the sewage tunnels below the city. He's going to set it off."

"Set what off?"

"The Morgathian shipments. Remember? The ones we hijacked. They contained the secret to the Morgathian firebombs. That's what Lazarus has been planning all this time."

"*Shenzah*," Kale said. "Lazarus is going to blow up the citadel!"

Tears welled in Nyla's eyes as she nodded. "We have to warn him or it will go off hours late." The nightling barked orders at the remaining Saints, then grabbed Kale's wrist. Together, they sprinted through the crowded streets and made for the vents at the heart of the city. Maro'El was brimming with people making for Maro Square. They thought they were coming for a wedding. They had no idea what was to come.

Kale feared there was no time.

He saw movement at the top of the White Citadel.

They were readying for the execution.

CHAPTER FORTY-NINE

Darien's heart thundered in his chest as he escorted Astoria to the palace at the pinnacle of the White Citadel. A great fear plagued him, but his path had already been set when he spared the Northmen.

Northmen who were now marching toward Maro'El.

Darien had betrayed the chancellor. There was no undoing that. But he feared he had made a mistake.

Medea had sent Valeria after the Witch Queen, and the thought of the sorceress from the Southern Isles still unnerved him. The chancellor needed to be deposed. The order to slaughter the Northmen had been the final breaking point, when the chancellor's cruelty was made plain to him. But Darien still did not see the chancellor as the great enemy of the world that Tori and Medea and the Saints saw him as. Darien still feared there was another enemy.

Chaos was about to take this city.

And though he had chosen betrayal, his heart remained ill at ease. But he could not turn back. He had set himself down a path through a dark and twisted wood, and all he could do was hope there were no monsters at the end of it.

He escorted Tori, by the arm, up the winding stairs from the dungeons, up through the many levels of the citadel. Behind them, the Morphs followed.

There was commotion in an adjacent hall. Soldiers hurried past, toward the main staircase used by the lords and ladies. Many of them were being ferried up to the central palace upon magnificent litters, so as not to overexert themselves.

"The Alyut?" Tori whispered to him as Morphs turned aside to the let the soldiers pass. It was the first time it had been safe enough for her to risk the words. Even so, he barely heard them.

Darien did not meet her gaze. He merely nodded and squeezed her arm, indistinctly. Tori held her blank expression, but there was a spark in her eyes, a renewed fire. Her fist closed over something, hidden in her palm, which she had held onto from her cell.

He wished he could speak with her. There was so much to say, and no time. The chancellor had changed the order of the day, and the entire city was scrambling, and Darien feared Tori might not make it out alive.

What would happen if the Saints were not ready?

He could only pray they were.

He could only pray all of this was not one great mistake.

He prayed as he had never prayed before in his life. To Rivka, the god of his ancestors.

He had not believed in gods since the day the Legions killed his family. But he felt a sense that he had been spared death, despite the many opportunities for it to take him, for this moment. His actions could dictate the trajectory of the world.

If there were benevolent gods, somewhere, surely they must help him now. He needed strength and wisdom because the task before him was insurmountable. *What if this is the wrong choice?*

His chest echoed with the turbulent drumming of his heart. With each step upward, the tempo grew fiercer.

Darien felt courage walking beside Tori. After all this time, he had never stopped caring for her. Seeing her leadership, her sacrifice for her followers, he could not help but admire her. It had taken their fight at Stormfall for him to come to terms with this.

And he had made his choice, but still, he feared. Or perhaps that fear was merely the lingering effects of the Shadow Camp indoctrinations. He could not be sure. In truth, he thought the Shadow Camps were an excuse for a change in himself he had stopped fighting, not from lack of will, but of belief.

He had truly believed in his service to the chancellor. And what was stranger still was he did not regret the things he had done in the chancellor's name. He had ended a rebellion. He had saved Maro'El from the attack of monsters.

But he had made his choice now. Calm focus settled over him, the way it did before every battle.

The palace doors spread wide, ushering them into the chancellor's magnificent inner halls. The morning sun bent the light into a thousand brilliant shimmers. The chancellor sat upon his crystal throne, a seat that would soon be taken by another.

Darien was about to commit treason.

He was about to turn the world on its head.

The chancellor smiled as they entered. His bride-to-be was dressed in the traditional scarlet silks of Yan Avii matrimony. The lords and ladies of the High Council were gathered, along with many other highborn nobles adorned in fine jewels and raiments of intricate tailorship.

Darien gripped Tori's arm one last time. The chancellor descended from his throne.

There was no turning back.

His task was before him. His part of the grand scheme of the Saints.

Darien Redvar was to be the one to kill the chancellor.

PART THIRTEEN
WEDDING OF FIRE

The Wedding of Fire will forever be remembered as the day the New World ended.

—from *Dawn of the Third World*

CHAPTER FIFTY

The chancellor descended his throne, pale blue eyes alight. He had waited for this moment for months, and he did not hide his pleasure at the sight of the Gallows Girl in chains, her blood drained, her head hanging in defeat.

Astoria clenched her fists tighter as she approached.

She kept the gift in her right hand. It had come with her last meal. She did not know who had brought it.

But it was the last sign of her hope in the Saints.

Darien released her and stepped back. Tori breathed slowly, in and out, in and out, forming wisps of vapor in the frigid winter air. The great doors of the chancellor's throne room were thrown open to the balcony. The lords and ladies were dressed in thick furs, and Tori shivered in her threadbare cloak.

Cyrus Maro wore all white, the way he had the day Darien was drafted into the Legions. But there was one stark difference. At his side, he wore a saber. Vashti stood stoically before a second throne that had been set beside the chancellor's. When Tori looked to her, Vashti held her gaze. But her dark eyes were unreadable.

Had *she* brought Tori the gift?

Tori felt warmth course through her body.

Salla stood nearby, accompanied by a large retinue of Yan Avii chieftains and their families and attendants. On the opposite side of the room stood lords and ladies from the Southern Isles, who had betrayed Seren and destroyed the Alyut fleet. Oshan lords and ladies composed the majority of the crowd. Medea remained at the foot of the steps leading to the thrones. There was a small company of Morphs and a few members of the Sky Guard, including Kirra. The Watcher looked frail. She clung to a Yan Avii woman. The same one who had been in her cell with Vashti and Kale. *Did Kale bring the gift?*

Kale was nowhere to be seen. There were few allies here as far as she could tell.

How did the Saints expect to stop this execution?

The chancellor reached her and touched her chin with cold hands, forcing her to look into his eyes. She betrayed no emotion, but the chancellor did not seem to care.

"Astoria Burodai," the chancellor began. "You have sought to destroy us. You unleashed monsters upon the New World. You allied yourself with traitors."

A pair of guards brought Ren forward. One of them was Dajha. He would not look at Tori.

Ren looked so frail, it made Tori sick. His rotting, blood-drenched clothes hung loosely over his scrawny frame. His cheeks were sunken and his eyes glazed over. But he held his head high and nodded to her as he came to her side. They had been in this situation once before, but this time, the chancellor would have no mercy.

"Today, you are sentenced to death for rebellion against the empire. I can think of no better way to celebrate the unity between Osha and the Yan Avii than to destroy those who would tear us apart."

Those gathered in the throne room applauded.

Guards seized Tori by both arms, and she and Ren were dragged out of the room to the great balcony of the White Citadel. Tori trembled despite herself, wondering if the Saints were there, wondering who had delivered what she held clenched in her fist.

The warmth in her body increased, despite the cold air outside on the balcony overlooking Maro Square.

She could feel.

More than the chancellor could know.

She would not die a martyr. Not without a fight. Tori looked out at the city. Maro Square was filled with people, and at the sight of her, they all went silent. Thousands of them. Gathered there to watch her die.

The chancellor's voice boomed across the city.

"Behold, the Gallows Girl, the great enemy of Osha!"

The gathered masses erupted with jeers, and Tori's stomach knotted. There were no Saints down there. She looked away and glanced around the crowded balcony.

There were faces she knew. Dajha. The boy, Jann. Vonn, who had taught her the ways of the Conjuri. Sahra, the Watcher healer. It seemed all of the Watchers, except Ren, had joined the Sky Guard.

Had it been one of them? Was there hope for the Watchers who had betrayed her?

Tori could feel the blood in her veins, every pulse of her heart.

"Osha must remain unified," the chancellor went on. "Osha must remain strong in the face of those who would destroy us."

At this, the lords and ladies nodded their assent. Were they as loyal as they appeared?

"The New World must remain strong! Together!"

Vashti and Salla nodded. Vashti's brother. *My brother.* What would they do when everything exploded?

The lords from the Southern Isles offered their agreement at the chancellor's words. They had betrayed Seren, but were they loyal to the chancellor?

"We must unite against those who would destroy us. In truth, the Gallows Girl is not the true enemy. She is merely a symbol, an idea, that has turned us against ourselves. Monsters have returned to this world. They have destroyed the Red City and fleets across the Boundless Sea. They tried to lay low our own city, but we have prevailed."

Cheers rose up across the city.

"The chancellor and his Darkling Witch! The chancellor and his Darkling Witch!"

Tori's heart fell. The Oshans were more united than she had realized. But they were united by a lie.

Medea stood by the chancellor's side. The Darkling Witch who had betrayed him. Or had she? Where was her army in the South?

Tori would find out in a few moments.

"While our true enemies seek to return our world to an age of darkness," the chancellor went on, "the Gallows Girl has sought to destroy us from within, to seize a fragile moment in the history of the world and use it to her advantage. But she has failed. And now, she will die."

The guards shoved Tori and Ren to their knees at the edge of the long arm of the balcony, so all the square could see. Jarring spasms shot through her at the impact, but even so, Tori could feel her mind awakening. She clenched her fist tighter. For a moment, she met Ren's gaze. His eyes did not look hazy anymore. He nodded to her, gritting his teeth at the movement. Then, he dropped his head, ready to die.

Tori looked out at the city one last time. She looked beyond the walls of Maro'El. For a moment, she thought she saw something beyond the haze that hung over the city.

But then it was gone. Just a shimmer in the clouds.

The cold chill of the chancellor's saber on her skin brought her back from the realm of hope. Perhaps it had all been an illusion, one final trick of the chancellor. But Tori's senses did not lie. She could feel the energy behind the world again.

A flash of golden light emerged from the clouds. A tiny face appeared in front of her.

Lir'ghe's face was lit with a twisted smile. *The Saints are here!*

The chancellor raised his saber high. "Farewell, Gallows Girl."

Tori clenched her fist so tight that the vial in her hand shattered.

It was empty.

She had already drunk the blood.

Tori spun around, and with a surge of Conjuri magic, she sent the shards of glass flying into the chancellor's chest.

He stumbled back.

And the world plunged into chaos.

CHAPTER FIFTY-ONE

Muskets exploded in the streets below. Tori glanced down for a fraction of a moment. Maro Square had become a raging battlefield. Blades clashed. Shots ignited. Smoke rose. And bodies fell. Legions charged from all sides, but it was hard to tell Saint from citizen in the madness. The crowd was a great swirling realm of violence as the Saints of the North rose up to take the city.

The balcony had turned into a battleground of its own.

Tori's hands quickly healed from the shattered vial. With a surge of Conjuri magic, her chains fell from her wrists. She spun, searching for the chancellor, but he had disappeared. The shards of glass were left behind, scattered on the balcony floor.

The godstones! Tori cursed.

The world blurred around Tori as lords and ladies scrambled away from the mayhem. A pair of Morphs attacked Tori from either side. Darien cut the first down. Tori reached out with her magic, and the dead Morph's blade shot through the air. She seized it and exchanged blows with the second Morph. The soldier was a skilled fighter. And quick. She took to the air, leaping over Tori, but Tori did not need to follow. She reached out with her sense. The shards of glass shot through the air, shredding the Morph's wings. The creature plunged back toward her, and Tori's saber speared her through the chest. The body landed on top of her, knocking her to the ground.

A hand reached for her and pulled the body aside.

It was not Darien.

"Dajha!"

"Good to see yeh again, Gallows Girl!"

Tori clasped his dark fingers. "You too!"

A blade swung at her head and she ducked. Dajha leapt forward and made quick work of the soldier.

"You turned back," Tori said.

Dajha gripped his saber tightly. "I made a grave mistake. Realized it bad when the chancellor took Ren's 'and! Been 'elping the Saints ever since."

"Glad to have you back."

"Me too." Dajha nodded to her and leapt out to take on another guard. The man aimed a long musket, but with a flare of magic, Tori made his aim waver, and Dajha ran him through.

Lords and ladies shrieked and ran for cover as blood began to pour on the crystal floor. The balcony was clearing quickly, but there was nowhere for the highborns to go. A figure stood at the doors. Bolts of something like lightning swirled around her.

Tori couldn't believe it.

It was Seren lè Tal. The Witch Queen wore a dark strapless gown, and Tori realized that she had never before seen the queen without her cloak on. Her body glowed with a haunting green light emanating from strange markings etched into her skin.

Hers was a powerful magic. Something entirely different than Tori's own. The sight of it stopped the nobles in their tracks. Light went shooting from her fingers and struck down a pair of Morphs. The energy was so powerful it lifted her from the ground.

Morphs and Legion soldiers fell all around. Dajha was not the only Watcher who had turned against the chancellor. Vonn joined the fray. Sahra helped Ren get free of his chains. In the madness, Tori spotted Mischa.

Her friend clashed with a Morph in the air, and they spun like hawks fighting over a bite of flesh. Swords sparked, and for a moment, it seemed the Morph was winning. But with a flash of Fieri power, Mischa threw off the Morph's concentration, and the creature plummeted to the city below.

Tori dispatched another Morph. The soldier's blade clipped her shoulder, but she healed quickly. Meanwhile, Darien faced off with the chancellor. Tori was unsure when Cyrus Maro had returned to the fray. He used the stones to appear and disappear between blows, but Darien's reflex for battle was remarkable. He reacted to the chancellor's reappearances so quickly, it was as though he knew where he was going to come from. The chancellor had healed himself from the glass, but his white clothes were drenched with dark stains where he'd been pierced. His magic was fueled by Watcher blood, but how long would it last?

Blades clashed in a blur, Darien and the chancellor spinning and dancing through the air. The chancellor might have used the stones to escape, but it seemed he could not quite comprehend just how great this betrayal was. Until it was too late. The battle was dwindling around him, and the Morphs on the balcony were falling fast.

This realization was distraction enough for Darien to disarm him. The chancellor was about to use the stones to flee when Medea came to his aid. She blocked Darien's attack, knocking him to the ground. She helped the chancellor back to his feet.

The chancellor turned to Darien, eyes alight. "You little shit! After all I've done for you."

Too late, Cyrus Maro realized Medea, too, had betrayed him.

In her fingers, she held the godstones. Energy shot from her palms, sending Cyrus Maro to the ground, writhing in pain. The chancellor curled into a ball. Suddenly, he seemed little more than a child.

Medea eased up, and the chancellor lay still, groaning.

The battle on the balcony lasted mere minutes at best.

But the mayhem in the square was growing more intense. More regiments of Legions had joined the fight. The Saints looked to be falling back as the square filled with Legion uniforms.

A great horn bellowed across the city.

Tori knew that horn and it filled her heart with hope.

At the outskirts of Maro'El, the first of the Bear Riders were descending the hills from the north to join the fray. *The Legions won't stand a chance.*

Tori could hardly contain her amazement. The chancellor was defeated and the Legions would soon follow. Kirra and Medea had not lied. Tori's army was here in the South, after all. A greater army than she ever could have realized.

Valeria Sardona landed on the balcony in her Morph form beside Seren lè Tal. Valeria had helped lead the attack in the streets. "The city is ready to fall, my queen."

Seren clasped her shoulder in a matronly manner. "Well done."

Lir'ghe hovered over his queen's shoulder. Valeria rushed to help Darien to his feet. She pulled him into an embrace and kissed him. Tori was glad to see them restored.

Mischa pulled Tori into a hug. Tori did not try to hide her tears—she was so glad that her friend was there and alive. After the fleet from the Southern Isles had attacked at Stormfall, she had feared the worst for her and the queen. It was difficult to fathom how much had changed in moments. Tori was alive, and the Saints had all but won.

"How did you get here?" Tori said.

Mischa smiled. "Valeria came for us. But it was really Medea. She was behind this all along."

"You traitorous whore!" the chancellor shouted as he struggled to his feet, extending his sword pathetically out in front of him. He was shaking from the agony of Medea's energy.

Cyrus Maro stood alone.

The Oshan lords and ladies backed away. Vashti had disappeared in the chaos, and Tori guessed the Yan Avii princess had flown off when it was clear the chancellor was about to lose this fight. Salla stood back with his kinsmen. He had not joined the fight on either side.

The Southern Islanders kept their distance from Seren, who brandished bolts of light threateningly between her palms.

"You are a ruler of traitors, Cyrus Maro," Seren shouted. "You turn kin against kin. Blood against blood. Did you really think it would never happen to you?"

Medea, Seren, and Tori closed in and surrounded the chancellor. Lir'ghe hovered over his queen. Darien came to Tori's side, and she was glad to stand beside him on the same side of this war. Merri had been right about him all along.

Cheers rose up in the streets as the Bear Riders of the North came thundering into the city. The Legions fought bravely, but the tide seemed to be turning as Valeria had predicted.

"Do you hear that?" Tori said with dark delight. "That is the sound of your empire crumbling."

The chancellor seethed. "You won't prevail. I have thousands of Legions, dozens of Morphs."

But no Morphs had come to his aid, after the first had fallen on the balcony. Either they were more loyal to Darien than the chancellor, or they, like Vashti, understood a lost cause when they saw it.

"You do not command them anymore," said a voice Tori did not recognize. It was one of the noble ladies, a fierce-looking woman in a sapphire gown that hugged her slender form.

"Lady Dragonis!" the chancellor cried, realization dawning. He turned to Medea. "You took her to the Old World!"

Medea smiled. "You thought I was striking fear into her heart, but in truth, I was revealing the power that you were growing too afraid to wield after your flight from the Nosferati. I convinced her to bide her time. Even your own people have turned against you."

Dragonis smiled a darkly satisfied smile. It made Tori uneasy for some reason. "I never feared you. Nor any of you Maros. The council has spoken. The Maro reign ends with you."

"And I suppose you think *you'll* rule now?" the chancellor said with a sardonic laugh.

"We've chosen another." Tori was surprised to find it was Ren who had spoken. He stepped forward weakly, leaning on Sahra for support. Lady Dragonis grasped his hand with both of her own. A greeting of comrades. Tori had nearly forgotten that Ren had friends in the White Citadel.

"Andovier!"

"You cut off my hand and left me to rot," Ren said. "How do you think I survived for so long? I've had friends on your council for years."

Dragonis smiled and nodded. "I've been waiting for this day for quite some time."

The chancellor laughed. "You think you could rule, Andovier? This city would crumble within days."

Ren was unfazed. He stood tall, despite his frailty. "I never said it was me. Medea is the one who saved this city. She subdued the Rulaqs. And *she* will usher in our Third World. A world where sorcerers will not be hunted. Nor will they be pawns in the games of nobles. Our world will be greater than any age of this world."

Tori felt a rush of relief, as though she had completed her task. The future of the world was a weight she had dreaded to bear, and she was glad to see it falling into other, more capable hands.

"You are the face of the old regime," Medea said to the chancellor. "Your ancestors tried to rid the world of our kind. You never deserved these stones. And now, they will be your undoing."

The godstones glowed with bright light in Medea's palm. She grimaced, and a portal opened up on the balcony of the White Citadel. With a flare of magic, Tori wrenched the chancellor's sword from his hand. Darien leapt forward and seized the chancellor by the arm. Valeria took hold of the other. Medea led the way through the portal between the worlds. Darien and Valeria shoved the chancellor through, and Tori, Ren, Lady Dragonis, and Seren lè Tal, with Lir'ghe darting after, followed them into the Old World.

Tori could feel the dark pull on her heart the moment she returned to that dreaded hell world.

They stood upon a hill in the very same valley the chancellor had brought her to at the Watchtower. The ruined necropolis spanned in every direction, jagged white stone splayed out like so many ancient bones, but there was something different.

There was no longer a single gateway. There were dozens of stone arches, spanned by the strange film-like substance that held back the Old World from the New.

The valley was filled with hundreds, no, thousands of beasts.

Rulaqs and Nosferati and frost giants. The once calm sea to the west roiled with the tails of mighty sea dragons. But there were other creatures too. Ones Tori had never heard of. Enormous ape-like creatures with long tusks, bearing spears made of shattered bone. Swift reptilian beasts with bony spines and claws the size of daggers. There was a host of dark shadowy figures that seemed to dart in and out of existence like wisps of black smoke.

Tori shuddered at the sight of them. The creatures turned slowly toward them as they became aware of the presence of the intruders from the world beyond the gates. They did not attack. They looked up the hill as though they'd been waiting for them to arrive.

The chancellor's face betrayed a fear Tori doubted he had ever felt before.

"Behold, the army of the Third World!" Medea cried.

CHAPTER FIFTY-TWO

Medea led the way down the hillside into the midst of the hellish inhabitants of the Old World. Tori and the others were speechless as they walked beside monsters that could devour them in moments, especially here, where their magic was useless. However, the beasts seemed to notice none of them but Medea. Their eyes followed her with rapt interest.

Tori watched the others. Ren and Dragonis and Seren. All of them took in the sight with wide eyes. They had put their hope in Medea, the Darkling Witch who had subdued the Rulaqs. None of them seemed to have realized just how great her power was. She walked among the beasts, and they dipped their heads. She brushed their arms and their snouts, and they murmured with satisfaction and expectancy. These beasts were hers, and she was their mistress. It was the most terrifying army Tori had ever seen. Darien and Valeria stood guard over the chancellor, but Darien's expression was not as joyous as Valeria's. He took in the sight and muttered what Tori was thinking. "It's a gods-damned army of monsters."

Tori was reminded of what Darien had said back at Stormfall. He had been wrong. The beasts were not Seren's doing. They were Medea's.

"Still think your Legions will last?" Medea asked the chancellor.

The chancellor shook his head. He seemed to have moved past anger to some overwhelmed acceptance of defeat. "I... I was a fool," he murmured.

Tori enjoyed hearing him say the words.

Medea smiled. "The illusion of power makes fools of most men."

"I thought it was such fortune when you came to me. I needed a guide to my experiments. And you appeared."

"Fortune is for the entitled, Cyrus Maro."

"I was good to you. I brought you into my inner circle. You were but a woman of the road."

"Aye, you brought me in. But you saw me as an opportunity. Something to be used."

"Did you plan it all along?" the chancellor said.

Medea brushed the long neck of a nearby Rulaq. "I did not plan it from the start," she said. "For some time, I thought you might be the one to restore the world. And I wanted to aid you in that effort."

"Restore it?"

Medea gestured around. "The world was split apart. A portion was stolen from it. At a time when sorcerers were hunted down and killed, you spared me. You took me in."

Tori had always wondered where the witch had come from. She realized that Medea had become for the chancellor exactly what he had offered Tori after the day of the Gallows. While Tori had rotted in his dungeons, Medea had been the sorceress at his side.

"I saw what your ancestors did to the Old World," she went on. "I was there, many lifetimes ago."

"Lifetimes?"

Medea smiled. "You used to say there is more to this world than our small corner. You never knew how true that was."

"What are you?" the chancellor asked.

"I've been called many things. An ancient. A witch. A goddess. Words are but a lilting breeze. Shifting, shapeless things. But I've watched the world. I've seen ages rise and fall. You call this the Third World, but you do not know just how many ages have come before."

"You brought the Nosferati upon us in the catacombs," the chancellor said. Darien's grip had gone tight on the chancellor's shoulder.

"I'm afraid not," said Medea. "You had the godstones, remember? The Nosferati were a mystery to me as well for some time. But after enough traveling between worlds I realized the truth."

They had reached one of the gateways at the edge of the city. What looked like a shimmer of the strange film-like substance from afar proved to be a flickering. Briefly, the lethal film between the worlds vanished, and the gate opened completely. Medea stuck her hand into the empty space. A few moments later, the gate flickered again, and the portal sealed once more.

"Your ancestors never meant for the gateway to be opened. They intended to lock away the beasts of the Old World forever. Your own experiments brought the Nosferati upon you. These gates are wearing down."

Across the city, one of the arches flickered and several of the ape-like beasts passed through into a jungle world before the gate sealed up again. When the film returned, three of the creatures were killed by the barrier that kept them out of the New World.

"All the destruction that has plagued the New World these past months was your doing, Cyrus Maro. But I intend to rectify that wrong. For all creatures, just as I did with the Rulaqs. It is time for the Old World to end."

The chancellor shook his head. "You will bring our world to ruin."

Medea gestured around. "Worse than this?"

The grey world was taking its toll on Tori, the nothingness beginning to seep in. She hoped Medea would hurry on with the end of the Old World. Darien grimaced, still holding tightly to the chancellor's arm. *He must be feeling it too.*

Darien met her gaze and shook his head. There was something in his eyes, but Tori couldn't place it.

"You'll need more than a set of godstones to end this world," the chancellor said.

Medea grinned. "Aye. Two sets of stones it took to create this world, so many years ago. And two sets of stones we have."

The realization came slowly for all of them. Perhaps it was an effect of the Old World. Medea gestured to Seren. The runes in the Witch Queen's skin glowed, even here in the nothing world. A primal greenish hue.

Seren caught Tori's gaze and smiled apologetically. "I'm sorry I kept it a secret, Tori."

"How?" said Cyrus Maro.

"In the South, magic is practiced differently than the ways of the Watchers," said the Witch Queen. "Its power lies in knowledge. It must be taught and shared."

"The godstones are a part of you," said the chancellor. "How is that possible?"

"That, too, was something shared. I was given this power by another.

The *scholai* of my youth. He taught me the ways of sorcery until I was ready. Every rune upon my body was a spell, hard-earned. And when I was ready, he passed his power on to me." A tear formed in the queen's eye. "I did not know it would kill him. But the great magic of the South can only be wielded by one. He sacrificed himself so that I might change the world."

"And now," said Medea, "for the first time since the Old World, the two great powers are reunited. And we shall change the world forever. We shall undo the evils your forefathers brought upon us. The Third World will be ruled by those who have been left behind, persecuted, enslaved, and forgotten. You will watch the New World be replaced with one much greater than you ever could have imagined. And then, Cyrus Maro, you will die."

Seren took hold of Medea's outstretched hand, and together, they strode toward the gateway. The strange film dissolved in their hands. Tori glanced around the hell world. All of the gates had begun to dissolve.

Medea let out a cry, whether from pain or triumph, Tori did not know.

The army of the Third World poured through the many gateways in long lines. They emerged into realms of mountain and desert, jungle and sea.

It was different than the way the Rulaqs had entered the New World.

This was not a stampede. It was ordered, the march of otherworldly regiments. As the last of the army poured through, the ground trembled. One by one, the gateways began to crack. One near the sea toppled over, great stones splaying across the Old World.

Medea and Seren grimaced with the pain. The stones glowed brightly in Medea's palm and Seren's skin rushed with something like green fire.

The sky began to morph, almost as though it were bleeding. And then, Tori realized what it was. Color returning to the sky. It seemed to drip down from the clouds and coat the grass with splatters of green.

The Old World was coming to an end.

The cracks and rumbles were so loud, they nearly drowned out another sound. Tori had been so enamored by the transformation of the Old World, she had not realized the transformation that had come over Seren. The green fire was growing stronger. It was consuming her.

The Witch Queen shrieked with agony.

Valeria let go of the chancellor and rushed to help her. She pulled Seren away from the gate. There was an explosion of light. The queen collapsed onto the grass. She did not move. Lir'ghe buzzed around her frantically, crying out in an ancient tongue.

Tori hurried over to help, her heart racing.

Medea had managed to pull herself away from the gate. She staggered forward, weak but unscathed. The godstones glowed with a blinding fury.

Seren's eyes were wide and empty. A greenish smoke emanated from her skin, but the runes did not glow any longer.

Tori checked her pulse, but she knew what she would find. Lir'ghe's cries turned into a high-pitched wail, one of the most haunting sounds Tori had ever heard.

"She's dead," Valeria cried, turning toward Medea with tears streaming down her face.

The sorceress was shaking visibly. More gateways crumbled and the Old World filled with light and color.

"Th-the stones demand a blood tithe," Medea muttered with raw realization. "I didn't..."

The last gateway, the one Medea and Seren had opened, began to crack. The film that had covered it was gone. The world shook. Tori grabbed Valeria by the arm and pulled her away from Seren's body.

A stone fell, and with a flash of magic, Medea defended herself.

As the Old World came to an end, her magic worked. Medea leapt aside, narrowly missing another shard of pale stone. Beyond the gateway, for a moment, Tori saw a vast desert. More stones fell.

Tori and Valeria scrambled away from the crumbling arch, and in the chaos, Tori glimpsed two dark figures flying upon dark wings. One of them turned back, and caught Tori's gaze. Only for a fraction of a moment.

Then, the two Morphs disappeared through the last traces of the remnant portal to the New World.

Medea cried out, reaching with her magic, but it was too late.

The gate crumbled.

Tori glanced around the newly-colored world, mortified, as she realized what had happened.

The chancellor had escaped. And Darien had gone with him.

CHAPTER FIFTY-THREE

Kale and the nightling revolutionary hurried through the dark sewage tunnels beneath the city. Dimly, Kale wondered if this was the same tunnel Tori had once escaped through when he had helped bring her to the Watchtower.

They entered from the streets and wended their way deep into the narrow underground passage. He and Nyla were both Cerebros, and knew what the other was thinking as they crept through the dark.

Shenzah…

The stench was overwhelming. It squelched with each footfall and coated the walls. The fumes seemed to press in on them. Ahead shone a faint light. There was the dim rumble of thunder in the distance.

"The Saints have risen," murmured Nyla. "We must hurry!"

Kale hoped it was so. He hoped Kirra and Ashi and the others would make it out alive. He knew it was wishful thinking. The sound made him sick. Made him regret his decision. These thoughts had been plaguing his mind as they raced through the dark. He felt so helpless. But he could not let it sway his resolve.

Nyla hoped to ensure that Lazarus was ready to blow the citadel.

The capstone of months of planning the Hellfire Plot, the act would ensure the victory of the Saints.

And Kale meant to stop him.

He knew it was what Kirra would want. And more importantly, he realized now, it was what he wanted. The Saints needed to rise. The chancellor needed to fall. But not like this.

He displaced these thoughts with thoughts of excrement, letting Nyla see something in his mind, but not the thoughts he wanted to hide. He was a far more practiced Cerebro than she.

When they found Lazarus Delahi, the ancient man was frantically arranging a system of fuses, attaching them to large barrels and sacks. The floor was dry here in the depths of the tunnels, and it was covered with Morgathian firebombs. A strange dark powder coated the floor. The place was eerily quiet so far beneath the city.

Nyla rushed to his side. "The chancellor has rushed the executions. The Saints are rising as we speak."

Lazarus cursed. "It's nearly ready, but I'll need your help."

Kale and Nyla rushed to arrange the last of the long strands of fuse. There was a bundle of thick cords in a heap near the entrance to the room, connecting the network of firebombs. Lazarus picked them up, but as he turned his back, Kale drew his dagger, seizing Nyla from behind.

She cried out.

Lazarus's face turned to ice. "What in the Abyss are you doing, Andovier?" He drew his own blade.

"I can't let you do this." Kale steeled his resolve.

"You *skazha*!" cried Nyla, squirming against his grip.

Kale pressed the blade against Nyla's neck until it drew blood, and she stopped moving. "Don't make me kill her, Laz."

"I told you he was a mistake," Nyla said. "His woman is in the gods-damned tower!"

"Shut up!" Kale hissed.

"You would betray the Saints?" Lazarus said carefully.

"This is not a resistance," said Kale. "This is madness. You will bring in a regime just as violent as the one before it if you do this. There are innocent people in that palace, Laz. Servants. Your own Saints." *Kirra and Ashi, Tori and Ren.*

"They knew the risk."

"Do the Saints know about this?" Kale shouted.

Lazarus shook his head. "They believe the bombs will aid their fight in the streets. The true plan is known only to a select few. But we all joined this cause willing to die to end Osha's rule of tyranny."

"You will kill every person in that palace. And thousands more in the streets."

"Medea and all your Watcher friends will fly to safety. The Gallows Girl will live. And so will Kirra."

That might be true, but Kale could not help but think of Ashi. All the Yan Avii. He thought of those he had lost on the Isle of Jallaa. The ghosts that had haunted him all these years. Lazarus had been the lone survivor of that attack. Just as he would survive this one. If he died in the explosion, he would be hailed a martyr and return in some other fool's body.

"That's not good enough," Kale growled.

"There are twenty thousand Legion soldiers defending this city!" Lazarus gritted his teeth. "We may gain an advantage by surprise, but we do not have nearly enough Saints to win this battle. This citadel has stood since the Old World. It is the symbol of Oshan oppression. If it falls, the city is ours."

Kale shook his head. "I can't let you do this, Laz."

"Then kill her and be done with it. I trained you, Kale. And I have a younger body again. Do you really think you can stop me?"

But Kale called his bluff. "You would sacrifice your own daughter?"

"My…" Lazarus's eyes betrayed the truth.

Kale had long wondered at the strange connection between a young nightling and this merchant turned revolutionary. He had known the look of those who had been used for noble pleasure. Nyla was too naïve, too optimistic. She was no nightling. She had been playing a part in Pendra and Maro'El for the sake of the Saints, serving her father to bring Kale into the fold. And it had worked. But not well enough.

"I will kill her if you do not back down."

"D-don't do it, Laz!" Nyla said.

Kale covered her mouth and pressed the blade harder. A slow stream dripped down her neck.

"You won't do it," Lazarus murmured. "You don't have the guts, and you know it. Now, release her and help us run this fuse out of here." Lazarus turned his back and began winding the length of dark cord toward the next chamber.

"Stop!" Kale shouted.

"Enough games, Kale! This revolution depends on—"

Before he could finish, Kale drew his blade hard against Nyla's throat. The spluttering sound made him sick. Her body spasmed violently. Lazarus dropped the fuse in horror.

"No! Oh Other! No!"

Kale let the girl slump to the ground. He held out his sword toward his old master. "I can't let you do this. Don't make me kill you too!"

The old man cradled his daughter in his arms, blood bubbling from the wound as she tried desperately to breathe. Lazarus tried to stop the blood with his tunic, but there was nothing he could do. Nyla's eyes glazed over. He settled her head gently against the ground, then rose to his feet, drawing his sword.

"You traitorous bastard!"

He flew through the air. Kale met him, and their swords sparked in the dim lantern light. Lazarus moved with fury, but his attacks were predictable. Angry attacks always were. His blows were strong, but they were easily parried. The ancient man began to tire quickly, and that was when Kale strengthened his own blows. Their swords darted between flickering shadows. Finally, Kale landed a blow.

Lazarus's fine tunic quickly drenched with crimson. He dropped his saber and fell back against a giant barrel of explosives.

Kale stood over him, sword extended. "I don't want to kill you, Laz."

All Kale sensed was rage and sadness in his old master's mind, but those thoughts masked something else. And he realized it a moment too late.

Lazarus Delahi reached out with all his strength, summoning a magic Kale had never seen him wield. The energy sent Kale flying out of the room and into the tunnel of sewage. He collapsed and struggled to his feet, trembling from the shock.

Within the room, Lazarus slumped against the explosives, clutching his side. "You forget, Kale. I do not cling to this life. It is but one of many. Pray we never meet in the next."

With that, the room lit up with a blinding light, and the entrance crumbled before his eyes, sealing off the room.

Kale braced for the explosion that would follow. But it did not come. Perhaps Lazarus was dead. Perhaps he'd expended too much energy sealing off the room of firebombs.

All Kale knew was that there might still be time to save the others. He took flight and darted through the narrow tunnels. The passages wended nonsensically, but he was guided by a desperate hope.

CHAPTER FIFTY-FOUR

Tori staggered back into the New World with tears in her eyes. Seren was dead. The chancellor was still alive and only the gods knew where. And Darien…

Gods, why did he let the chancellor go?

Valeria trembled. Tori helped her through the opening formed between the worlds with the godstones. Lir'ghe darted through and vanished from sight, wailing at having left his queen behind. Ren and Lady Dragonis followed. And lastly, Medea. The opening closed in a swirl of mists.

They emerged in the throne room of the central palace to gaping mouths and wide eyes. The crowd from the balcony. The Yan Avii and Southern Islanders stood in the corner, guarded by several Watchers.

The godstones still glowed violently, but Medea stowed them in her robes. The sorceress did not speak, but her expression said everything. Three people who had passed through the portal had not returned, and everyone knew that something was dreadfully wrong.

Mischa hugged Tori tightly. They said nothing. The silence was answer enough. But not for the nobles of Osha.

"What happened in there?"

"What do you think happened?" Medea snapped.

"The chancellor…"

"Is alive, Lord Barra. He escaped with the aid of his gods-damned minion. And the Witch Queen is dead."

The expressions of the Southern Islanders were not as mournful as they ought to have been at the news.

"What now?" said a noble lady. "Without the chancellor, the Legions will never surrender. The battle has turned down below. The Legions are gaining strength. More reinforcements are marching across the Meridian. Without the chancellor—"

"It matters little, Lady Tindeir," said Medea, seething.

"It matters a *great* deal," said Lady Tindeir bitterly. "Look outside!" She gestured out toward the city beyond the great doors to the balcony. "Where is your army of the Third World?"

Medea glowered. "We cannot set them upon our own city after centuries of being locked away. They would kill everything in sight."

"Of course not!" cried Lord Barra. "That would be much too convenient. We have no army. No chancellor. No Witch Queen. We made this uprising happen. And you have sent our plans to—"

"We will win this war!" Medea shouted.

The room went silent. Lady Dragonis paced back and forth. The other nobles muttered to themselves but offered no further protests.

"We should… convene," said Dragonis. "The High Council should decide what to do next."

"Aye!" said Lord Barra. The other nobles nodded their assent.

Medea clenched her fists, but she nodded. "Very well." She turned to Valeria. "Captain Sardona, have the Southern Islanders and the Yan Avii taken to chambers in the middle levels. Lock them in until this is over. Lady Dragonis, take the lords and ladies to the council chambers. I will join you once I have spoken with the Sky Guard."

"Yes, of course, Lady Medea," said Dragonis.

Lord Barra began to protest about the need to convene immediately, but Dragonis barked at him, and he and the others followed her obediently into a chamber adjacent to the throne room.

Valeria and Mischa led a company of Watchers to escort the Southern Islanders and the Yan Avii away. Tori pitied Valeria. Her queen was dead, and the man she loved had betrayed them. *But gods, why did he do it? What changed at the end?*

Soon, the throne room was occupied only by Medea, Tori, and Ren. Lady Dragonis returned shortly.

"The nobles are secure?" Medea asked.

Dragonis nodded. Then, she turned to Ren. "How do you feel?" She touched his shoulder tenderly. The fierce woman was not just a noble ally. She cared for Ren.

Everything had been so chaotic, Tori had nearly forgotten how terrible Ren looked when he was brought up from the dungeons. Color had returned to his skin now. Sahra's Medici magic had helped him. He was still missing a hand, but he looked recognizable as the captain of the Watchers she had once known at the Watchtower.

Those days felt like a dimly remembered dream. He looked older now. It felt strange to think Tori had once felt something for him.

Ren smiled a thin smile. "I'd feel a lot better if Cyrus Maro was dead."

"For the time being, we must be content with what we have accomplished," Medea said. "The Old World is ended. The city *will* soon be ours. And the ruling class will be dealt with. Are you well enough to fly, Captain Andovier?"

"Fly where?" asked Tori carefully. "What do you mean about the ruling class? How do you know the city will be ours?"

Medea smiled at her like a mother to a naïve child. The look made Tori's stomach twist. There was something Medea and Ren and Dragonis had been keeping from them. She sensed it now. Suddenly she wondered if Darien had sensed it earlier. *Was that the meaning behind his gaze in the Old World?*

"My dear," said Medea, "you are strong and you have led a revolution, but you know nothing of war."

"Thankfully, neither do the nobles of Osha," said Dragonis. "They are so worried about their own petty squabbles for power, it never occurred to them that we don't need them any longer."

"What are you talking about?" said Tori.

"The nobles are the vestiges of another time," said Medea. "A time that has come to an end. Do you know where the White Citadel came from, Astoria?"

"The Old World."

"Aye," said Medea. "It was once a beacon of hope. Before Osha defiled it. Before it became a symbol of their power. Before it donned their banners. This tower may have been forged with sorcery by the Watchers of old, but that means nothing to the people of this world. This tower housed the First Chancellor, who ushered in the New World. And this tower has been the Oshan symbol ever since. It is true, the chancellor still lives, but this tower is the symbol of his power. Without it, the Legions will yield and Maro'El will be ours."

"What do you intend to do?" Tori asked.

"It was the Morgathians who developed the technology. We stole it, unraveled its secrets. And we planted their firebombs beneath the foundations of this great tower."

"You're not going to tell the nobles," Tori muttered.

"We have no intention of sharing power with those self-absorbed autocrats," said Lady Dragonis. "They created this world as much as the chancellors. The only reason they turned was because they saw this revolution was inevitable."

"You'll leave them to die," said Tori.

Dragonis glowered. "They deserve to die, Gallows Girl."

Tori shook her head, feeling sick. She bore no love for the nobles of Osha, but they were not all bad. Her mum had come from a noble family. So had Commander Scelero. Ren's family too. And Lady Dragonis's. "They helped us."

"They betrayed their ruler when it suited them," said Ren. "They'll do the same to us, should the opportunity arise."

"Ren, this is wrong."

But Ren shook his head. He held up his stump. The bandages were still black with dried blood. "The nobles did this. The chancellor ordered it, and they stood by. Just as they stood by when the Maros ruined my family."

Tori realized this was what Ren had desired all along. He had convinced them it was about magic, but it was about power and revenge. Just as Darien had told her at Stormfall.

"And what of the Southern Islanders? The Yan Avii chieftains?" Tori demanded. Vashti might have fled, but her brother was down there, along with the other *soltaynes* of her people.

"The Southern Islanders betrayed their own queen," said Ren. "They sided with the chancellor, just like the *soltaynes*. Salla betrayed the Watchtower, Tori. There is no room for them in the Third World. And besides, there is no way to save them. We are nearly out of time."

Tori couldn't believe what Ren was saying. He grimaced, but shook his head. He took hold of her hand. "They are our enemies, Tori. How did you think things would go when we took the world from them? You can't leave your enemies alive. If we spared them, they would undermine us at every turn."

Tori said nothing. She hoped the others would side with her, but when Valeria and the others returned from the lower levels, no one uttered a word of protest.

"Are *you* all right with this?" Tori muttered to Mischa.

Mischa gripped her hand. Her fingers were trembling, but she nodded. "We have to win this war, Tori. Our people are in the streets. Skya and Alyk. The Alyut and the Crooked folk. All the Saints. Their lives are on the line. Too many have already died. The death of a few enemy leaders is a small price to pay."

Tori felt sick, but she said no more. She knew Mischa was right. This was war. Death and betrayal were part of it. She didn't have to like it, but she would have to accept it. For the sake of their friends. For the sake of the world.

Medea led the Watchers from the throne room to the balcony. Below, the Saints retreated from the square. Legions cheered, but their victory below was an illusion. The square at the base of the White Citadel was filled with grey uniforms. All in one place.

"We fly for the tower of the Sky Guard!" Medea shouted.

The Watchers took flight, Vonn and Dajha carrying Lady Dragonis, as she could not fly. Mischa gripped Tori's hand reassuringly, then took off.

But Medea held Tori back. "We are the faces of this rising world. We should be the last to leave."

Medea reached into her cloak. It was lined with vials of blood. She held one up. "The chancellor was such a fool. He had no idea what I was capable of." She laughed and tossed the vial aside. It shattered on the crystal floor, coating it in a dark stain. Medea shed the cloak and pitched it over the edge of the balcony.

The Watchers soared over the city, brilliant dark streaks against the hazy sky.

"I don't blame you for disliking my methods, Tori. You are still young. But I have seen ages and ages of the world. And the world is not changed by the meek, I'm afraid."

She stepped back into the throne room. Her hand glowed and a surge of magic shot from her fingers. The doors to the council chambers clinked as the locks turned. A great pounding erupted from the other side. The pounding grew louder and louder, as the nobles tried to get out. Tori tried to tell herself that this was right. That they deserved this.

Medea led the way toward the balcony.

Then, the ground began to shake.

The floor was like a rug that had been ripped from beneath her. The world swayed. The streets filled with shrieks. And Tori crumpled to the floor.

"That is our cue," said Medea.

Tori lifted herself from the ground. But the world shook all the harder, and she felt as though the floor was sucking her down. The crystal walls began to crack. Pieces of the crystal ceiling rained down. A large shard speared Tori's thigh, and she shrieked. Medea hurried to her side. Energy passed from her fingers and filled Tori up with a strange warmth. And then it was gone.

The shard of crystal still impaled her leg. She felt cold and hollow with the pain.

Medea stood.

Tori reached for her Conjuri power, but her connection to her magic was cut off. She couldn't feel it at all. The pain in her leg was blinding.

"W-what's happening to me?"

Medea shook her head. "I am sorry, Gallows Girl. But there is room for only one savior in the Third World." More crystal fell and Tori's body was pierced with more shards. Her blood poured onto the floor, and the wounds did not heal. Tori's head felt light, but she knew the crystals had fallen with the aid of Medea's magic. Conjuri magic. The magic that Tori could not manage to wield.

Medea took flight from the balcony and left Tori alone in the crumbling tower.

Tori reached one last time for her magic, but it was gone.

CHAPTER FIFTY-FIVE

The White Citadel had stood centuries, through two ages of the world, the greatest architectural feat in the New World, but as Kale landed on Kirra's balcony halfway up the tower, it felt as though he were landing on a roiling sea. Great plumes of smoke and dust rose up from the streets. Smaller buildings were crumbling and streets were caving in. Maro Square had been filled with soldiers, but they were gone now. It was as though the streets had vaporized.

The tower shifted violently beneath his feet. Kale hovered above the ground and focused his senses. The minds of thousands of dying people overwhelmed him, the weight of their agony crushing his mind. And he feared there was little hope of finding Kirra by his sense.

He had seen many Watchers take flight moments before the explosion, but he had still sensed Kirra somewhere in the tower before the dying minds had crashed over him like a monsoon.

Kirra's chambers were empty. There was a great clamor beyond the doors. The tower shifted, and Kale nearly lost his footing. He gripped the handle of the door to stabilize and then turned it hard.

Smoke and dust poured into the bedroom from the hallways. Lanterns were shattered upon the floor. Some had ignited large tapestries, and flames darted across the fabric. Servants were in a mad dash for the central staircase of the citadel, choking on smoke, trampling over one another to get out before the tower collapsed.

A young servant girl was caught in the stampede and shrieked for only an instant before her cries were silenced. Blood and specks of flesh and brain matter splattered across the stairs.

Kale felt sick. His eyes watered.

Lazarus had done this to these innocent lowborns, and Kale knew it was unlikely any of them would make it out alive.

He was about to return to the window and fly to another level when he saw someone flying in the narrow space between the mob and the ceiling.

Vashti Burodai.

Kale took flight and followed her. In finer parts of the citadel, the staircases were wide open, but not here. Kale worried he would strike his head against the stone with the next shift of the tower, but he reached the next level safely. Vashti landed beyond the staircase in a great empty hall similar to the one Kale had just left. The smoke was even thicker here.

"Vashti, what are you doing here?" he shouted between violent coughs as he landed beside her.

The fierce princess's bronze face was ashen. "My people are here. Your Darkling Witch sent the Yan Avii below before the explosion. My brother is with them."

"The Yan Avii?" Kale knew then where he would find Kirra. With Ashi and her people. He took hold of Vashti's hand. She was trembling, her eyes red and misty. She had been in the smoke much longer than he had. "We'll find them."

They took turns checking doors on that level, but there was no one there. They flew from level to level, great chunks of marble cascading from the ceiling. The building swayed, and Kale nearly collided with a toppling pillar as he flew. The tower teetered sharply, and the world seemed to have turned on end. But then it righted itself and held still for a while.

Kale was amazed the citadel was still standing at all. Was it possible the explosion hadn't been great enough to bring down the ancient sorcerous craftsmanship? Maybe they *could* save the Yan Avii.

The staircase was thinning out, as most of the servants had either been trampled to death or made it to lower corridors.

Finally, they reached a level with two great doors that had been barricaded shut by fallen debris. The doors were splintered from impact on the other side. Vashti and Kale quickly freed the doors as more fragments cascaded around them. The doors flew open and the Yan Avii came pouring out with hardly a glance at who had freed them. Smoke and dust rushed out with them.

Kale watched for Kirra and Ashi in the crowd, but they were not with the others. When the chambers had emptied, he and Vashti darted inside. There were several bodies left behind. A whole section of the roof had collapsed within these halls. He found Ashi and Salla kneeling beside a figure half covered in rubble. Ashi was weeping, and Salla stared off in a daze. He barely noticed when his sister pulled him into an embrace.

The tears came instantly. Kale's throat felt raw.

He ran to Kirra's side.

"Sky Blood," Ashi whimpered. "I... I told her to go with the other Watchers! But she wouldn't leave us. The Watchers brought us down here, and she knew something was wrong. She refused to..." Ashi's voice broke off into sobs.

Salla was kneeling beside her still. "She saved me."

"What?" Kale said.

"Right before the roof caved in. She pushed me out of the way."

Kale took Kirra's hand. At his touch, she stirred to life. Her frail fingers wrapped around his own, and he had never been more grateful for her touch. *Oh, thank the gods she's alive!*

Kirra smiled weakly. "Get out of here, Kale. Get Ashi and Salla out. Y-you have to leave me."

"No! Oh gods! No, I'm getting you out of here." Kale knew it was futile, but he pressed all his weight against the great slab of marble that covered her body from the waist down. He screamed with the effort, but it accomplished nothing. If only he were a Conjuri.

He sobbed uncontrollably, but Kirra's face was tranquil as a mountain lake.

Vashti helped her brother to his feet, and then Ashi. She led them toward the window. "We have to go."

But Kale couldn't bring himself to follow. He looked at Kirra's beautiful scarred face. The chancellor might have done that to her, but her death, this was the work of the Saints.

He gripped Kirra's hand. If only he had found her sooner. If only he hadn't tried to stop Lazarus, he might have saved her. Kirra muttered something unintelligible.

"What?"

"The Gallows Girl."

"She did this," he said angrily. "Her and the Saints."

Kirra shook her head. Her voice slurred. He leaned right up to her face.

"No, Kale. She's… still here. She didn't want… Medea betrayed…"

Kale shook his head. "I saw them fly away."

Kirra gestured to her head. "I heard it. Right before the explosion. She's still up there." She pointed. "You have to leave me. You have to save her."

The tower shook violently. More debris fell around them.

Vashti hollered at him. "Kale! We have to go! I'm sorry!"

Kirra nodded to him, her head lolling like a drunk's. "I… I love… you…"

Kale choked back tears, forcing himself to take in the moment in all its horror. Imprinting the memory forever in his mind. "I love you too. Always."

She took a deep, agonizing breath, then went still.

Kale staggered away. A large chunk of marble narrowly missed his head. Without a word, he took hold of Ashi by the waist. Vashti took hold of her brother, and the four of them took flight. They landed on a rooftop at the edge of the decimated square.

Vashti led the way to a staircase leading to the streets. "We have horses at the edge of the city," Vashti said. "The Merching gates."

But Kale didn't follow. He looked up at the great tower. It swayed in the smoke, like the giant trees of Parjha when they were felled for timber. It groaned and splintered as the ancient stone began to give way.

"Tori is still up there," Kale said.

"You don't know that," Vashti said. "Kirra was dying. She didn't know what she was saying. You can't go back!"

"I have to try! She wanted me to try!"

"That tower is about to collapse any moment. We have to get clear of this square or we will die in the fall."

Kale shook his head. "I'll meet you at the Merching gates." He took flight. Tears and smoke stung his eyes as he rose high above the city. Streams of people fled in the streets.

The balcony, where only an hour ago the chancellor had been conducting an execution, was empty. The giant doors to the throne room were thrown wide. Kale could hardly believe what he saw inside. Astoria Burodai was crawling across the floor, leaving a horrific streak of blood in her wake. There was a strange golden light surrounding her.

"Tori!" he cried, rushing to her.

Her face had gone pale and she was trembling violently. The wound in her leg looked even worse up close. There were more wounds in her chest. It was a wonder she was not dead. But then, Kale realized what the golden light was. A hideous flying creature was hovering over her. The light was pouring into her body from his fingers.

"Medea," Tori muttered.

"The witch betray us!" the creature said in a buzzing voice.

Lying a short distance away was a shard of crystal the size of a large dagger, covered in blood. Tori must have pulled it from her own leg, which explained the blood loss.

"Can you fly?"

Tori was crying from the pain. "I can't do anything. M-my magic. It's gone."

"What?" That wasn't possible. But he could sense the truth in her mind, the horror and fear at what was happening to her, mixed with the delirium of blood loss. Perhaps that was the cause of it, but there was no time to wonder.

"Medea. I... I don't know how. It's just gone."

Massive shards of crystal came cascading from the ceiling. Kale pulled Tori out of the way. The tower teetered sharply, but this time it didn't right itself. The floor sloped down toward the city, pulling them like a great weight.

Kale seized Tori around the waist, and they ran for the edge of the balcony. But then the floor disappeared. The world rushed with smoke and dust, blinding Kale's vision. The sound of the tower collapsing was more violent than any storm. So loud it pierced his ears like a blade.

He focused all his senses and took flight, his fingers clutching at Tori's sides. She was so weak, she could barely hold on. It was like carrying a dead body, and the weight jerked him violently, but he managed to hold his flight.

They shot through the opening as the ceiling collapsed behind them. They flew through thick smoke and dust and debris, and Kale worried the tower was going to collapse upon their heads.

The world became like the darkest cave. An infinite expanse of darkness stretched before them. Growing and growing.

Kale couldn't breathe.

He could feel his strength waning. Tori's body pulled him toward the ground, which was the only way he could tell where the ground was. He could not carry them both on his own much longer.

Then, in an instant, the darkness evaporated, and they emerged into open air. The world was a raging wave of debris exploding across the city. It took all the strength he had left to reach the Merching gates.

He set Tori down, and they collapsed in the grass beside a narrow trader's road.

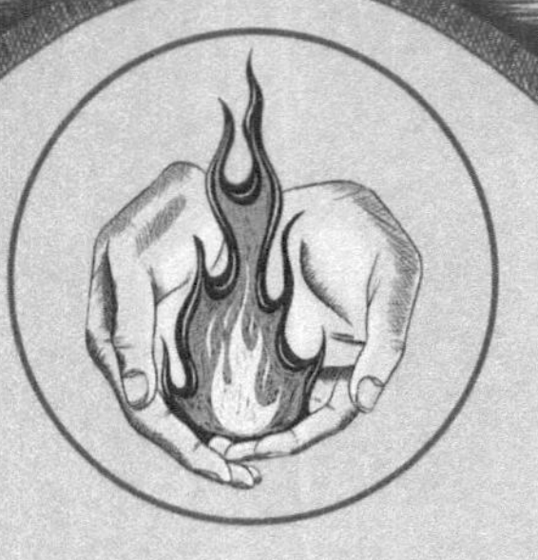

CHAPTER FIFTY-SIX

Mischa could not sleep for a moment that night. Neither could Tesleh. The Crooked girl came to Mischa's room in the dead of night and crawled into bed with her. Mischa pulled her close, and eventually Tes dozed off into fitful sleep. But not Mischa.

She replayed the events of the day over and over and over again.

Seeing the horrors of the explosion, Mischa had instantly doubted her resolve that it was the right thing to do. But Medea had been right. The Legions had been decimated, and the ones who survived had surrendered immediately. With one disastrous stroke, the battle was over.

The Wedding of Fire.

That was what the Saints were calling it.

Of course, there had not even been a wedding, but it was a trivial point to the triumphant lowborns.

The Darkling Witch narrowly escaped the explosion.

And Mischa had found out too late that Tori had not made it out at all. At the last moment, Tori had decided to go back into the building, to try to help the nobles. Medea had gone back to reason with her, and that was when the explosion came. The roof fell. Tori was crushed. Medea tried to help her, but there was nothing she could do. She barely made it out alive herself. The Darkling Witch was visibly shaken by the tragedy.

Medea hailed the Gallows Girl a great hero. A martyr.

Tomorrow, there would be a ceremony held in honor of her as well as all the other Saints who had died in the name of freedom. And then, Medea was to be crowned high queen of a new nation, one in which sorcery was celebrated and lowborns were lifted to their rightful place. The northern realms of the Empire of Osha were to be returned to the Alyut, where Fara dul Baruk would continue to rule her people, but now, they would finally live once again in their homeland.

It was the dream of the Saints, the Shadow Watch, the Alyut.

It had all come true.

But the cost had been so high.

Mischa cried into her pillow until she felt raw all over. Tori was gone. Seren was gone.

The chancellor had been defeated. She should have been happy, but nothing felt sweet about this victory. If only Mischa had realized Tori was not with them when she was flying away. She might have gone back. She might have helped. Somehow.

But her mind had been preoccupied with Tes. The girl had been left at the tower of the Sky Guard, safe from the battle, but Mischa had not stopped worrying about her through the entire battle. What if the Legions came? Or a Morph?

Mischa had thought the battle was over.

She thought Tori was with the other Watchers.

She was wrong.

Mischa wandered from her chambers at the first hints of light, letting Tes keep sleeping. The tower of the Sky Guard had become the temporary center of the new nation until the city was restored and a new palace was built.

Skya dul Baruk was already sitting in the dining hall of the Sky Guard quarters, sipping on a mug of steaming coffee.

Skya glanced up and held out the mug. "This Southern dreg is disgusting, but it works well enough, I guess."

Mischa took it and let the steam waft across her face. She had not had coffee in months. The smell took her back to the islands.

Skya brushed her shoulder, and Mischa leaned into the touch. She was deeply grateful that Skya and Alyk had survived the battle. There was much to be thankful for. She knew that.

Skya smiled grimly at her. "Couldn't sleep?"

Mischa nodded. "Thought eating something might help. I don't think I've had anything since yesterday morning."

Skya squeezed her hand. "Let me make you something." It was funny to watch the warrior scurry around the kitchen with her blade strapped to her side, dressed in her thick leathers. Her tattooed shoulders were bare, and Mischa liked to watch her. Skya had a dressed wound on her left forearm, which she insisted was nothing, but as she moved, Mischa noticed specks of blood begin to seep through the bandage.

Skya finished a shoddy porridge that smelled peculiar, but Mischa didn't mind. She barely tasted it anyway. Skya took up her own bowl and ate a spoonful. "Gods… that needs something. Don't feel obligated to eat it."

Mischa managed a slight smile. "It's not… bad."

"You don't need to flatter me."

She took another bite. "How's Alyk?"

Skya tried another bite or two, then switched to bread. "As can be expected, I think. He's in the courtyard now. Praying to the gods, I think. Or cursing them…"

Skya's voice drifted off, but she sat close, and Mischa was glad for her company.

"She was an amazing woman. You should have seen her lead in the Battle of Stormfall… I'm sorry. We don't have to talk about it."

"Maybe not yet… sometime."

"I've been thinking," Skya said. "My *madru* and the tribes. Most of them will be heading north soon. She'll stay to establish the new council, but the Alyut want to start building our new lives soon. We'll probably stay in the Oshan fortresses for the winter, but we aren't a people of castles. My *madru* wants to tear them down. Build up something Alyut."

"Like the Ice City?"

Skya smiled. "That was always temporary. A way to survive. It wasn't the Alyut way. Not the old way. Although that's been centuries. No one remembers the true Alyut way. Maybe it will be something new."

"That would be fitting," Mischa said.

Tes wandered in, looking shaken. Mischa pulled her into an embrace. "Bad dreams?"

"My brother," Tes said. "I dreamed Jordie was freezing to death up north."

"Don't worry, Tes," Skya said, mussing her hair, "Alyk is going to bring him south soon."

"He is?" Mischa asked.

"Alyk is taking a company back to Iqala in a couple days. So long as the weather holds, he will try to take them through the Teeth."

Tes looked satisfied at this and began to eat some bread, opting against the porridge due to the smell.

"What about you?" Mischa asked, nervous about the answer.

"My *madru* wants the Riders to go north. We don't expect the Oshans there to oppose us, but I'll need to be there to be sure there's no trouble. But after that…"

Mischa felt herself growing hopeful.

"We need Alyut representatives on the new council. My *madru* is thinking of appointing one of the elders. But the new army will need commanders. There are other Riders who could do it, but… I think I'd like to stay."

She squeezed Mischa's hand and warmth passed through her. "I hope you do," Mischa said.

Dajha came running into the room. "Ah'right, ah'right, get your own room."

More Watchers came pouring in. Valeria came in last and sat in the back of the room. Mischa pitied her. She had lost more than anyone. The soldier left the moment she finished eating.

The room filled with soft chatter. The mood was somber, but hopeful. Mischa was glad to see her old friends. Glad they were alive. Glad their betrayal had not been final.

But it was not the same. This was not the Watchtower anymore.

It was something different.

Perhaps that wasn't all bad.

———

THE SUN SHONE BRIGHT FOR THE CEREMONY, THOUGH A HAZE STILL hung over the city. Thousands gathered in the training green and the streets surrounding the compound that had once been the central grounds for the Morphs and the Night Legions.

Few people seemed to share the bittersweet feeling that overwhelmed Mischa. There were cheers and banners. Gallows symbols were raised all over the place. And there were chants for the "Darkling Queen."

Rumor had it, the minstrels had already begun composing ballads about the Wedding of Fire and the Darkling Queen and the sacrifice of the Gallows Girl in order to secure their freedom.

The ceremony was a celebration.

The Saints had prevailed.

Medea gave a fine speech after she was crowned queen. She praised the fallen, including Seren and the Hangman. She spoke of their daring sacrifices for the sake of this victory. She spoke of a new age. She said nothing of the details she had shared with the Watchers surrounding Tori's death. History would not remember a saint who questioned herself at the end. Who tried to free their enemies. Tori was hailed an unadulterated martyr.

Mischa was grateful for that.

In the end, Medea declared it was time for the image of the gallows to be taken down. "The revolution is over. Our Third World has dawned. And here in the North, we shall be a beacon. An Empire of Light that will consume the world."

The new banner was revealed.

A red flag emblazoned with a flaming golden sun.

The symbol of the Empire of Light.

Tes held Mischa's hand throughout the ceremony. She was enamored as the new banners shot up around them. Skya kept close too. She held Mischa's other hand, and Mischa tried to force herself to think less of the sad events and more about the hope of the future.

They had won. And the sacrifice was surely worth it. Though Tori had been torn in the end, Mischa knew she had always longed for this moment.

Alyk kept close as well, but he did not smile or cheer. Mischa lingered beside him as the crowds began to dissipate.

Together, they looked down at a gallows banner that had been cast aside and left in the mud and snow. It was a warm day. The kind of early winter tease that felt more like spring, but soon, the darkness and cold would descend again. And last for many months.

"I never really thought she could die," Alyk said at last, meeting Mischa's gaze.

She held back tears. "Me either."

"A martyr," he murmured. "She served her purpose. And now she's gone. Do you think she'll be forgotten now?"

Mischa grasped his shoulder, then pulled him into an embrace. "We won't let her be forgotten, Alyk. I'll always remember her bravery. Her heart. Her friendship."

"Her love," Alyk said.

Hints of a smile traced across his face as she pulled away. It lasted only a moment.

"This world needs us," Mischa said. "We must mourn. And we must remember. But we must be strong, and we must keep on."

Alyk didn't respond to this. He merely nodded.

They walked together back into the tower of the Sky Guard as the city broke out into wild celebration behind them.

CHAPTER FIFTY-SEVEN

Tori woke in a strange tent, lying on a blanket upon the cold ground. Her leg felt as though it were on fire. It was so stiff, she could not move it. Her whole body ached in a way it never had before. Her body was not healing. Not as it always had. Not by her Regenero gift.

A *thrasii* named Azrahi came in and tended her wounds. "You lost much blood," he said in Yan Avii as he replaced the dressing. He had stitched her injuries while she was unconscious. "It is a miracle you are alive."

It was the opposite, though. The miracle had been the fact she had healed so many times. This was the absence of miracle. If not for Lir'ghe and Kale, she would be dead.

But Tori was grateful for his help. He prattled on about her wounds in her father's language. He did not seem to realize who she was. Tori had forgotten much of the language since her childhood, but she knew he was talking about her wounds and the battle and miracles. Azrahi finished with her bandages and left.

Outside, the camp was silent. The Yan Avii mourned those who had been in the tower when it collapsed. Only Ashi, Salla, and a handful of others had made it out of the city alive. Thankfully, much of the camp had not been granted invitation to the palace. But it was the greatest among them who had been there. Their chieftains and the great families.

The others had been in the streets. Many had died, caught in the crossfire, when the battle broke out.

Vashti and Salla came to see Tori early that evening. Vashti did not seem pleased, but then again, the princess could have had her killed. Her people had been slaughtered in the name of Tori's Saints.

Salla knelt beside her bedroll, a grim expression on his face. "Your people did this," he said.

Tori nodded. "I did not know the extent of their plan."

"That is not an excuse."

"No… it's not."

"The greatest members of the tribes were lost," Salla said. "All the chieftains except myself. I hated some of them, but I did not wish them dead. Not like this. My people have lost everything that held them together."

Tori didn't know what to say. She realized she was not as Yan Avii as she had always liked to think. She had not even understood, until now, just how great this tragedy was.

Eleven chieftains dead in one day. This would change her people forever.

"I do not wish to excuse what the Saints did," Tori said.

"What do you want?"

Tori bit her tongue. "I don't deserve your kindness. You've helped me live. I cannot ask for more."

"Will you go back to them?" Salla's eyes narrowed, as though peering through her.

"Medea tried to kill me. She made it look like a tragedy. I don't know what to do. But I can't go back there."

"They call you a martyr," said Vashti, nearly spitting the words. "They praise your name in the streets, hold your banner. They celebrate what happened in your name."

"If Medea finds out I'm still alive, she will have me killed."

"I ought to kill you," Salla said. "If my people knew who you were, they would demand it."

"I would not blame you," Tori said. "But I am not the Gallows Girl anymore. She died in that tower."

"Kale says you lost your magic," Vashti said. "How?"

"The godstones… there is nothing left. I don't feel that connection to the world at all. I feel like a part of my soul has been… sucked out of me." Tori's body was consumed by a dull ache. And it was more than her wounds.

Vashti's cold expression did not break. Tori wondered if she was glad for what happened. If the Yan Avii princess was thinking about how easy it would be to kill her now.

But Salla sat back, crossing his legs beneath him on the ground. "The dilemma over what to do with you is more complicated than all that. My sister informed me of what you told her in the dungeons. About your father... our father."

His eyes bore into her. Tori broke his gaze.

"She believes you," Salla said.

Tori sighed and glanced at the princess. Vashti merely nodded.

"And I believe my sister," Salla said. "And so, I cannot kill you."

"Thank you," was all Tori could think to say. Then she remembered the only reason she was there at all. "Where is Kale? How is he?"

"In mourning," said Vashti. "Ashi is with him. But he will see no one else. He is devastated over the loss of Kirra."

"Kirra is dead?"

Salla nodded. "She died saving me."

Tori was overwhelmed with how wrong this revolution had gone. She did not know what to think or what to do. So many innocent people had died.

"Medea has been declared queen," Salla said. "And so, my people must leave. Tomorrow, we've been told. We are leaving tonight, before they have the chance to change their minds and kill the rest of us in our sleep. We will take nothing with us. We ride for Pendra tonight to gather the rest of our tribesmen."

"And from there?"

"Our city is ruined. Our alliances are crushed. But we are a people of the plains. We will make for the southern Steppe along the banks of the Spillway. The winter will be hard with so little food stores, but we have lived through worse. We survived the New World. We will survive this one as well."

Vashti came closer. She did not smile, but she met Tori's gaze. "Kale is coming with us. It is the least we can do after what happened to the woman he loved. You may come too. If you want."

Tori teared up. It happened all at once like a breached dam. After all they had been through, this gesture of peace was more than Tori could hope for. More than she deserved.

"Th-thank you, Vashti."

"You must take on a new name now that you're no longer the Gallows Girl. Something Yan Avii. Astoria was always such an awkward name, anyway," Vashti said. "In my opinion," she added.

"I'll think on it," Tori said.

"I am partial to Eszti."

"It's lovely."

"It's a family name. It means *lost one*. Seems fitting."

"Eszti." It sounded strange in her ears, but Tori didn't hate it.

THE YAN AVII LEFT THEIR TENTS IN THE DARK AND RODE SOUTH IN the dead of night. They avoided the roads when possible, and they rode hard. The wounds in Tori's leg and chest throbbed like she was being stabbed again with each stride of her steed. She gritted her teeth and fought through the pain. This was her life now. No more healing. No more flying. Nothing.

Despite her gratitude to Vashti and Salla, Tori felt hollow. She glanced back at Maro'El, now but a faint shadow on the horizon. No tower prominent against the sky.

It was where her friends were. Mischa and Skya and Alyk. Ren and the Watchers. But it was also where her enemies were. Had Medea been alone in her treachery? Or were there others? Had she always been meant to be a martyr? Would she ever feel the thrum of magic in her body again?

Tori cried as she rode, whether from sadness or pain, she was not sure. The cold tears stung her cheeks and reminded her that she was alive. It was something, at least.

She looked away from Maro'El, wondering if she would ever see Mischa or Alyk again.

For so long, she had thought overthrowing the chancellor would end her troubles. She would live in peace after that.

Now, the chancellor was gone.

And a new evil had taken his place.

But Tori was alive, and she was not alone. She rode behind Vashti and Salla out into the night. Lir'ghe darted along, always hovering nearby. And Kale and Ashi rode beside her.

This is not over, she thought. *It can't be.*

Kale spoke to her for the first time since he'd rescued her from the citadel. "Someday, we will come back. Someday Medea will pay for what she's done."

No one responded, but they seemed to ride all the harder through the night, a desperate determination in their pace. The Sisters hid their faces from the world all through the night. Tori felt she had never known such darkness. Even their daughters were shrouded by clouds, turning away from the dark deeds of the world.

END OF BOOK TWO

APPENDIX ONE
MAGIC OF THE WATCHERS

In the Old World, magic was partitioned according to the dominant gift of each Watcher. This helped bring order for the purposes of sorting and training young Watchers in their budding abilities. Each were separated into two schools of knowledge:

> **Corporeal** - magic that manipulated the bodily elements
> **Material** - magic that manipulated the physical elements

On occasion, a Watcher would defy the neatly segregated orders of magic. These multifaceted Watchers, known as Mages, were gifted with multiple abilities. They were seen as especially blessed by the gods in the eyes of the people they served.

However, the Watchers did not look upon these Mages so fondly. To their fellows in training, they were seen as threats, Watchers who sought to rise above them. To the masters of the Order, they were seen as overly ambitious, even dangerous.

Contrary to common belief, the magic of the Watchers did not belong only to them. Though the Watchers were the most famous and practiced wielders of magic in the Old World, they were not the only ones with access to such knowledge and power. Magic could not be confined to the realms of the Watchers, nor to their orderly systems. Before the fall of the Old World, one Watcher sought to defy this system. It did not end well.

Nevertheless, here are the orders of magic, as they were known in both the Old World and among the remnant at the Watchtower:

CORPOREAL ORDERS

Medici: the healers
Regenero: the regenerators
Cerebro: the mentalists
Metamorphi: the shapeshifters
Enduro: the ultra-swift

<u>**MATERIAL ORDERS**</u>

Conjuri: *the manipulators of matter*
Fieri: *the manipulators of fire*
Lumeni: *the manipulators of light*
Sonora: *the manipulators of sound*

APPENDIX TWO
REGIONS, CITIES, AND NATIONS OF THE NEW WORLD

<u>Osha and the North</u>

Crooked Folk: the wild peoples of the North populate the few remote settlements in the mountains of the Crooked Teeth; they come from a variety of nations, but hold no real political loyalties; known for being a hardy people, fitting of their environment

Crooked Teeth: remote mountains of Osha; the highest range in the New World, and serves as the eastern border of Osha

Forest of Ghen: the large haunted forest on the eastern border of

Osha; it is said the severity of the ghosts' torment is dependent on the state of the soul who dares enter the forest

The Fringes: a sprawling slum city at the northernmost edge of Greater Osha

Glacier Sound: a narrow channel, fed by the glaciers of the Crooked Teeth and the fjords that line the western coast of Osha

Greater Osha: the nation of Osha is partitioned by Glacier Sound; Osha proper resides to the north of the body of water and contains the capital city of Osha, Maro'El

The Green Sea: an expanse of grass and farmlands, composing much of Greater Osha

Hatia: a small Oshan village at the easternmost edge of Greater Osha, near the edge of the Yan Avii Steppe

Maro'El: capital of the Oshan Empire; named after Darius Maro, of House Maro, the First Chancellor of Osha, whose family has served as chancellors of the empire since the dawn of the New World

The Meridian: a large bridge that spans Glacier Sound near the Fringes

Osha: a fragmented nation in the New World, ruled by the chancellor and a High Council composed of highborn nobles; though the Oshan Empire once spanned the entire continent, the nation now struggles to maintain power as conquered nations have slowly withdrawn or rebelled

Pendra: an important Oshan trading city along the eastern border of Greater Osha

Stormfall: a small fortress in the remote northern regions of Osha

Ytala: a little known mountain village in the Crooked Teeth

<u>The Yan Avii Steppe</u>

The Great Spillway: a long river that runs south from the Grey Waste, all the way across the continent of the New World; the Spillway runs through the Steppe, and the Wandering Dunes lie across its eastern banks

The Grey Waste: an expanse of barren tundra to the north of the Steppe

The Steppe: the great expanse of rolling hills where the nomadic tribes of the Yan Avii make their homes

Vlyanii: the capital city of the Yan Avii, commonly called the Red City, due to the sandstone bricks used in its structure; it is the home of the Red Palace of the Great Soltayne, as well as the Golden Temple of Arayeva; it lies on the border between the Steppe and the Wandering Dunes

Wandering Dunes: a large desert to the east of the Steppe; according to Yan Avii folklore, after the fall of the Old World, the Yan Avii were once exiled to wander the desert of the Wandering Dunes, but were rallied and unified by their First Soltayne, who was purportedly visited by Arayeva herself

Yan Avii: the twelve unified tribes who inhabit the Steppe; each tribe is led by a *soltayne*, and all pay tribute to the elected Great Soltayne; since returning from their exile, the Yan Avii have warred with Osha over portions of the high plains for centuries

<u>Alyut Icelands</u>

Alyut: a tribe of native Northmen, who first inhabited the region now known as Osha; when the first Elyan invaders came, the Alyut people fled north; little is known about their whereabouts, except for the rumors spread by the few Alyut traders that venture to the southern realms of the world

Ever Winter Forest: a remote forest north of the Steppe; west of the Grey Waste

Frozen Sea: northernmost sea in the New World; passage is impossible in winter, and remains treacherous in other seasons due to the presence of icebergs

The Great White North: the harsh northern regions of the New World, largely consisting of vast plains of ice; few living things can survive in the cruel conditions

Iqala: the lone Alyut city in the Great White North; formed out of the ice itself; much of the city lies underground where a mysterious crystal known as icefire provides light, and firestone serves as a source of warmth

Mouth of the Gods: a glacial expanse between the mountain ranges of the Crooked Teeth and the Spine of the North

Uluq: small village of the Tu'va clan

<u>The Southern Isles</u>

Bay of Souls: passage near the Elyan capital; supposedly haunted by the peoples that the ancient Elyans conquered in the Old World

Channel Sea: narrow passages that weave amongst the Southern Isles and the mainland continent

Elya: capital of the Isles; established by the ancient Elyan conquerors when they first arrived in the Old World from the Lost Continent

Sard: island kingdom ruled by Lord Thiere

Tal: island kingdom and home to Seren the Witch Queen

APPENDIX THREE
PRONUNCIATION GUIDE

<u>Yan Avii</u>

Arayeva [air-uh-YAY-vuh]: the sun goddess of the Yan Avii

Ilya [IL-yuh]: an insurgent group of assassins, bent on rescuing the Yan Avii from the corruption of the soltaynes; they were formed and led by Salla Burodai

lynti [LIN-tee]: a female slave garment of the Yan Avii, fashioned of leather; tailoring varies, but typically worn to cover the chest, while leaving shoulders and midriff bare

sera [seh-RAH]: a formal address given to a Yan Avii woman of noble birth, akin to "My Lady" in the Common Tongue

shenzah [SHEN-zuh]: a vulgar Yan Avii exclamation conveying disgust or anger; something that is seen as an obvious lie; also a reference to literal excrement

Sol [SOLE]: a common term used to refer to Arayeva; also a reference to the literal sun

soltaya [sole-TAH-yuh]: a broad term referring to all noble-born members of the Yan Avii, from any of the twelve tribes, who would reside in the Red Palace during gatherings in Vlyanii

soltayne [sole-TANE]: a chieftain of one of the twelve Yan Avii tribes; each tribe is led by their own soltayne; however, the twelve tribes are ultimately led by the Great Soltayne, the Chosen of Arayeva

thrasii [THRAH-see]: a Yan Avii healer

xadjar [ZAH-jhar]: a billowy, woven pant, commonly worn by slaves of the Red Palace

Xa'Rila [ZAH ree-LAH]: ancient beast that has long been told to haunt the Wandering Dunes

ylkii [IL-kee]: a buttered flatbread, a staple of Yan Avii cuisine

<u>Alyut</u>

Anora [ah-NO-ruh]: goddess of the night, whose Lights guide the way for the people of the Great White North

baru [BAH-roo]: a formal address for a male sibling

Iqu'vara [EE-koo-VAH-ruh]: the hunters upon the ice; primarily live above ground, providing meat for the clans

Karu'va [KAH-roo-vuh]: the people of the caverns below the ice; live below ground, except for tribal gatherings; they harvest gemstars and other northern plant life that grows in the warm Alyut Under Realm

madram [MAH-druhm]: a formal address for a grandmother

madru [MAH-droo]: a formal address for a mother

muqbluq [MUHK-bluhk]: a frame of wood or bone, attached to the bottoms of boots for foot travel in deep snow

Nuq'vana [nook-VAH-nuh]: the Bear Riders; serve as warriors and protectors, both from predators and the peoples of the Rogue clans

saru [SAH-roo]: a formal address for a female sibling

Shalam [shuh-LAHM]: god of the day, who provides food, strength, and peace for the people of the Great White North

Tu'va [TOO-vuh]: the people of the trees; primarily live in the sparse forests in the southernmost regions of the Great White North; provide timber for the clans

APPENDIX FOUR
DRAMATIS PERSONAE

<u>The Great White North</u>

Alyk dul Baruk [AL-ik dul BAH-rook]: shaman of the Alyut people; close companion of the Gallows Girl; son of Fara dul Baruk

Astoria Burodai [uh-STORE-ee-uh BOOR-uh-die]: a Watcher of the Regenero and Conjuri orders; Oshan slave of Yan Avii and Oshan heritage; also known as the Gallows Girl, the famed sorceress rebel of Osha

Fara dul Baruk [FAH-ruh dul BAH-rook]: High Elder of the Alyut clans; mother to Alyk and Skya

Geryn dul Narsuk [GEH-rihn dul NAHR-sook]: elder of the Iqu'-vara; companion of Mischa, Tesleh, and Seren

Lir'ghe [LEER-ghay]: a Kroqala demon faerie; a close companion to both Seren and Tori

Mischa Sufai [MEE-shuh soo-FIE]: a Watcher of the Fieri order; daughter of a Melanesian merchant

Seren lè Tal [Seh-REHN lay TAHL]: the queen of the Southern Isles; also known as the Witch Queen

Skya dul Baruk [SKY-uh dul BAH-rook]: leader of the Bear Riders; daughter of Fara dul Baruk

Tesleh Falzen [TES-leh FAHL-zehn]: a young orphaned girl of the Crooked folk; Watcher of the Sonora order; goes by Tes

Maro'El

Cyrus Maro [SIE-russ MAH-roe]: the sixteenth Chancellor of Osha; second-born of Aleksander and Lysette Maro, ascended to the throne of Osha after his entire family tragically died

Dajha Bhati [DAH-jhuh BAH-tee]: a Watcher of the Enduro order; son of a notorious Parjhan privateer in the Silver Sea; member of the Sky Guard

Darien Redvar [DARE-ee-uhn RED-var]: commander of the Sky Guard; raised among the tribes in the Klavash mountains; also known as the Gallows Boy

Ilyana Dragonis [il-YAH-nuh druh-GO-nihs]: leading member of the High Council of Osha

Jann [Jan]: a young Watcher recruit of the Fieri order; member of the Sky Guard, taken under the tutelage of Darien

Lazarus Delahi [LAH-zuh-ruhs deh-LIE]: leader of the Gallows Saints; also known as the Hangman

Medea Lorzarre [meh-DEE-yuh lor-ZAHR]: powerful sorceress; close companion and advisor to Cyrus Maro; also known as the Darkling Witch

Nyla [NY-luh]: a nightling of Osha; member of the Gallows Saints

Ren Andovier [Rehn An-DOE-veer]: a Watcher of the Conjuri order; leader of the Shadow Watch; imprisoned in the Citadel

Rhaena [RAY-nuh]: a nightling of the White Citadel favored by Cyrus Maro

Sahra Elra [SAH-ruh EL-rah]: a Watcher of the Medici order; of Alyut descent; imprisoned in the Citadel

Commander Scelero: [Seh-LAIR-oh]: former commander of the Metamorphi; secret conspirator against the chancellor; Tori's former master

Valeria Sardona [vuh-LEER-ee-uh Sahr-DOE-nuh]: a leader of the Sky Guard; of Southern Islander descent; chosen alongside Darien Redvar to join the ranks of the Metamorphi

Vashti Burodai [VAHSH-tee BOOR-uh-die]: a Watcher of the Regenero order; daughter of the late Great Soltayne, sister of Salla; betrothed to Cyrus Maro

Vonn Elra [Vahn EL-rah]: a Watcher of the Conjuri order; from the Kingdom of Malai; imprisoned in the Citadel

Commander Zamel: [ZAY-mehl]: one of the highest-ranking officers in the Night Legions; commander of the attacks on Goran'El and the Watchtower

<u>The Steppe</u>

Ashi Burodai [AH-shee BOOR-uh-die]: a slave of the Red Palace, and the only female member of the Ilya; deeply devoted to Prince Salla Burodai

Kale Andovier [Kayl An-DOE-veer]: a Watcher of the Cerebro order; former Oshan noble of House Andovier, one of the great houses of Osha; also known as the Exiled Lord, after he fled the empire in the wake of unwittingly betraying his mother's magic to Chancellor Aleksander Maro

Kirra Fehn [KEER-uh FAIN]: a Watcher of the Lumeni and Sonora orders; close companion and former lover of Kale Andovier

Salla Burodai: [SAHL-uh BOOR-uh-die]: Great Soltayne of the Yan Avii tribes; brother of Vashti; leader of the Ilya

APPENDIX FIVE
BEASTS OF THE NEW WORLD

Metamorphi

Morph soldiers take on two typical forms. Though Morphs can also take on other transformations with blood magic.

The winged Morphs were a favorite of Cyrus Maro, retaining most human capabilities with the addition of flight.

The warg-like beasts were terrors in battle, known for losing their minds to predatorial instincts.

Rulaq

The unleashing of the
terrors of the North
from their Old World
prison would change
the world forever.

And hide is thick as
leathern armor.

Teeth the size of
large daggers.

Rulaqs are large enough
to trample trees.

Frost Giant

Fists large enough to hold a grown man.

Known to haunt the Icelands of the Great White North.

Gargantuan in size and a demeanor of pure malice. Few survive an encounter.

Body formed of rock and ice.

Xa'Rila

Head can become fully
enclosed for protection, while
traveling underground.

It is believed that the many Rilas
travel in packs and communicate with
a shared consciousness, functioning
in many ways as one horrific monster.

Thick armored carapace
built for burrowing through
sand and stone.

Known for ravaging the Yan
Avii people during their exile,
Xa'Rila was generally regarded
as a myth by outsiders.

Until the dawn of the
Third World.

Krogala

The true origins of the demon faeries are unknown, even to them. Krogala speak mysteriously of a great loss of memory.

Their magic is intricately bound to a mysterious form of rune magic. Perhaps there are answers here about their tragic past.

Four tiny wings bear them at remarkable speeds.

Diminutive in stature, many Krogala are no larger than a man's hand.

WOLVES OF THE CITADEL

(A SHADOW WATCH PREQUEL)

ONE
DARK GAMES

The Year 317 N.W.
Five years before the Day of the Gallows

The young lordling's skin shifted on the table. Pale hues morphed, turning to grey, and then pitch black. Slender arms bulged with newly-taut muscles. His handsome, youthful face became a hideous leathery thing with a monstrous red maw filled with elongated teeth.

In less than a second, the man looked nothing like the simpering lordling Ren Andovier had known from childhood. That Cyrus Maro was timid, always lingering in the background, fuming quietly to himself. That Cyrus Maro had drowned in the shadow of his elder brother.

Now, a dark grin twisted across Cyrus Maro's gruesome face. He sat up from the table and soft gasps filled the chamber.

Cyrus Maro's back shuddered. From the space between his shoulder blades and his spine, bone protruded from the skin and dark wings clawed their way out.

For months, their little band of lordlings—the Wolves of the Citadel—had been gathering discreetly, parsing through ancient secrets that might lead to such a break-through. And now, their newest member had done more in his first week than all of them combined. Giving their leader his first taste of true magic.

Cyrus Maro groaned softly as he stretched his freshly-sprouted wings.

"Hurts for a spell," said Captain Scelero, the man who had performed the ritual usually reserved only for the chancellor's magic hunting order.

Ren scoffed at the blood-infused draught in the captain's hands. The draught Scelero had given to the chancellor's youngest son.

This magic was nothing like Ren's own.

Blood magic…

It was not the sort of secret he'd expected to unearth.

According to Scelero, this was the magic that had always created the Metamorphi, ever since the fall of the Old World, when the First Chancellor had eradicated magic and formed the Morph orders that hunted them. Preserving the Oshan Empire from the sorcerous Watchers that had destroyed the Old World.

It was all a facade, of course. The chancellors used magic to create their magic hunters. Many Oshan lords and ladies possessed the shades of magical ability. The same Watcher blood that coursed through Ren's veins ran in many others. Had Ren been lowborn, the Morphs would have killed him long ago, but so long as they were not a threat, Oshan highborns' affinity for magic was permissible.

So long as they were not a threat.

House Andovier had learned this lesson the hard way. Now, Lady Andovier slept in the family crypt; Ren's brother lived in exile, gods knew where; and the future of the house lay in Ren's hands.

When Cyrus Maro first came to see him, Ren had thought it a trick. For months after his mother's untimely death, Ren had not dared dabble with his Conjuri ability. So, when the chancellor's own son came asking about his family's magic heritage, bandying about the idea of a secret society within the halls of the noble academy—surely, it was a setup.

But no.

Cyrus Maro was not like the other lordlings. He was nothing like his father, who feared everyone, and yet continued to slowly lose his hold on the empire, both in the farthest borders and within the Great Houses themselves. To Aleksander Maro, and all his forebears, Watchers posed the greatest threat of all. And when anyone appeared to be using magic for ill, even a lady from a noble house, it was a threat that must be eradicated.

But to Cyrus Maro, magic was neither a threat nor something to be trifled with, as the other lords treated it.

It was a future that had been buried, and simply needed the right hands to tend it. To coax it back from a centuries-long hibernation.

That was their mission. To explore.

To practice. To learn.

The Wolves of the Citadel. And now, this new recruit from a little-known house had offered Cyrus Maro the secret of the Metamorphi.

Cyrus Maro admired his new wings with fascination. Leathery skin expanded six feet on either side of him. Stretched over bony appendages like that of a bat, or the depictions of mythic dragons.

His body was some strange amalgamation of man and beast. His face hideous, yet still retaining traces of the man within.

"You're one of us now," Cyrus said, clasping Captain Scelero's hand with a toothy grin.

"As are you," said Scelero. The man looked around at the small group of young nobles, a glint in his eyes.

All nine members met his gaze with a mix of envy and admiration. And Ren along with them.

Ren had brought Cyrus Maro one thing of value, months ago. A series of ancient runes. Words of power that could be performed without the natural-born gifts of Watchers. Secret words to bind a secret place. That knowledge had created the possibility of the chamber where they had conducted their meetings this term. The magic formed a shield around the room from outside ears. Even the sense of magic hunters.

But Cyrus Maro needed more. And this newest member had brought exactly what he was searching for. What the other Wolves had, thus far, been unable to do.

Unlike his elder brother, Loras—unlike every other member of this group—Cyrus Maro possessed no natural affinity for magic.

Until now.

Ren Andovier did not despise Ruben Scelero.

The man had simply made the first move in one of many dark games nobles played. The same sort of game that had brought about the downfall of his house.

But by the gods, Ren would not lose this one.

TWO
INVITATION

What's your problem, Andovier?"

Two months with no breakthroughs, and they had just left the last true gathering of the Wolves until next term.

Once again, the Morph captain had brought something new. A means of morphing into other human likenesses. The greatest of Morph abilities.

For two months, Ren had smiled and congratulated, but today, he'd left the end of the meeting with no word. And damn him, Scelero had noticed and followed.

"I thought we were all in this together," said Scelero.

Ren glowered at the man, glancing around the empty halls. "Keep your voice down."

They stood in a vast hall near the academy library. The long winter had turned to a swift spring, and now, the beginning of the short summer. The halls of the academy had emptied as nobles fled the city to enjoy the warm weather in the countryside or on the coasts of Greater Osha.

Ren intended to spend his summer poring over the ancient tomes his family had kept stowed away since the Fall of the Old World. Tales of Watchers. Wellsprings of magic. Portals. Myths. But could they contain something more? Something that could make up the ground he'd lost to Scelero?

"What?" demanded Scelero. "Lordlings tinker with magic all the time.

The Metamorphi barely even monitor the academy. Those runes are a nice effect, but barely even needed."

Great, Ren thought bitterly. *My one contribution…*

"Blood magic on the other hand," Ren retorted, "very needed."

"You got a problem with blood magic?"

Ren rolled his eyes. "Depends whose blood."

"Right," said Scelero. "You know what your problem is, Andovier?"

"Enlighten me."

"The same with everyone else in this damn little club. Same thing that's kept Osha receding for decades."

Ren huffed. "Yeah?"

Scelero sighed, crossed his arms over his chest. He spoke softly. "All you high lords connive in isolation. Leaves you vulnerable."

"What do you know?"

"I know what happened to your mother—what they said publicly—was bullshit."

Ren glared at him for bringing his mother into it. "Everyone knows that."

"Sure, but do they know exactly what happened?"

No, only a precious few, though Ren supposed it made sense that a Morph might be privy to the truth. But all knew House Andovier had fallen out of favor with the Great Houses.

"What do you think happened?"

Scelero barely whispered his response. "Same thing that happened to my sister."

"I… I think I remember hearing something about that."

"It was years ago. You would have been a child."

Scelero had about ten years on Ren, older than most at the academy. Though that wasn't uncommon for a soldier from a low house.

"Fell out of favor," Ren muttered.

Scelero nodded solemnly.

"What happened to her?" Ren asked. "Actually?"

"She posed a threat, and she fled Maro'El. Few years later, the Morphs hunted her down somewhere on the Steppe. She's dead now."

"Is that… why you became one of them? A Morph?"

Few Morphs came from the lord houses of Osha, it was said. In fact, Ren did not know much about where they came from at all. They were spies stationed across the empire. Across the world. There was no honor or glory in being a Morph.

Scelero shrugged. "All of it was quiet. And we were barely a middling house. So, it was not hard to keep it so. But it put my house on even shakier ground. I was given little other recourse. A lowly little magic hunter, clawing back his redemption."

Ren shivered. Was all this a trap?

"Now, I'm here, learning military tactics at the academy with a bunch of bloody youths, and Cyrus Maro comes calling."

Ren nodded warily.

"I think I've said enough for now. I've my reasons for being here, and you have yours. But you and I both know the fate of a Morph who blows their cover. I am here at my own risk, just as you. But… I'm not here to bare my sordid past. If you should decide you're ready to quit trying to unravel all the lost secrets of magic on your own, here's where you can find me."

Scelero handed him a bit of parchment with an address.

The Morph captain walked off, footsteps echoing in the high-pillared hall.

———

A WEEK LATER, REN KNOCKED AT SCELERO'S DOOR.

The man smiled and welcomed him into the modest townhome near the Legion training grounds. They passed through a sparsely furnished sitting room, and descended stairs into the basement. The entire level was a sort of laboratory filled with tubes and vials.

"I've been thinking about the nature of Morph magic," said Ren.

Scelero raised a brow. "Not what I was expecting, but go on."

"You Morphs… create new members of your order."

"Indeed," said Scelero. "The process requires a complete transmutation of the recipient's blood."

Ren scowled.

"Our prince insisted we only reveal the final stage of the process to the Wolves. To safeguard the secrets of the order."

"Right," said Ren.

"It requires a particular alchemical process. Magic blood from another Morph."

"Not from a creature?"

"It is freely given from other members of the order. That is how it has always been done."

"So you mix the old Morph blood with the new…and put it back?"

Light flashed in Scelero's eyes. He winked. "Simple as that."

Ren glowered. "I thought you said you were tired of working alone."

"Wrong, I suggested that *you* might be tired of going at it alone, and implied that I might possibly be convinced to collaborate."

"Same difference."

"There are some secrets that cannot be freely shared, Andovier."

"Well, fortunately for both of us, you are not the sole harbinger of lost legends of magic."

"Go on."

"Like I said," Ren continued, "I've been thinking about the creation of your Morphs. I knew what was shown at the meeting was performative. But what had gone on behind the scenes, that nagged at my mind. To accomplish such an act of transformation, a shapeshifting beast out of magic-less blood, that must require a mighty act of creation. Power brushing up against that of the gods."

Scelero offered no expression.

"Godstones," said Ren.

"You… think they're real."

Ren rolled his eyes, dug into the satchel on his shoulder, and produced a short tube of leather. Once he removed the fastenings and unlocked a brass runemarked mechanism, the leather unraveled, revealing an extraordinarily well-preserved parchment written in the Common Tongue.

Scelero drew in a sharp breath, recognizing the symbol at the top. A castle tower surrounded by sharp mountains on both sides, like jaws of a beast.

"The Watchtower," he whispered. "Sigil of the Watcher orders of old."

Ren nodded.

"Few now would recognize it," said Scelero. "But after the Fall of the Old World, possessing one of the old Watcher texts would have resulted in death. Where did you come by this?"

There was no holding back now. Ren had chosen his path, whatever may come. He needed a way to get closer to Cyrus Maro, and Scelero could be the key.

"My mother," said Ren. "It's a copy, of course. My family has transcribed them several times over the centuries."

"There's more than one."

Ren shrugged. "Some secrets can't be freely shared, Scelero."

The Morph captain smiled.

"This scroll is a history of sorts," Ren went on. "Of the end of the Old World. Written by one of the last masters of the order."

He handed the copy to Scelero. The man read the inscriptions quietly regarding the fate of the mythic godstones for sometime, then shook his head and sighed. "Those are remarkable claims."

"All sorcerers. All the monsters that inhabited this world, gone like that—" Ren snapped his fingers. "How else would you explain it?"

"The First Chancellor created... another world?"

"A shade of a world," said Ren. "According to Master Alasar."

"That sounds like a myth, if I ever heard one. And suggests that the First Chancellor was much more powerful than any histories claim."

"Any surviving histories," Ren clarified.

Scelero drummed his fingers against his chin. "Well... I certainly know nothing of other worlds or wells of magic. But that Watcher master got one thing correct at any rate. The chancellors did possess a pair of powerful stones. They've been used to create each Metamorphi. Including Cyrus Maro. And myself. But godstones... could it be..."

Ren smiled. He did not possess the perceptive abilities of his brother or his late mother. But he sensed Scelero was telling the truth.

"Why did you show me this?" asked Scelero.

"You're not the only one who holds secrets to the past," said Ren. "I've been delving deep, but thus far, have been unable to come up with the break-through Cyrus Maro desires."

"You don't think Morph magic is enough?"

Ren smiled sardonically. "I think we both know the answer to that. I have keys to the past. I need help to decipher what is myth and what will lead us into the future."

"What do you have in mind?"

THREE
BLOOD HARVEST

A month later, Ren and Scelero met with Cyrus Maro in private at Scelero's laboratory.

The chancellor's youngest son eyed the pair of vials with trepidation. One contained a clear alchemical concoction Ren and Scelero had worked tirelessly on the past several weeks. The other contained Ren's blood. Carefully, Cyrus Maro poured them both into a chalice.

"The ancient Watchers believed that magic resides in the spirit," said Ren. "And from the spirit, it flows to the rest of the body. The Metamorphi orders, on the other hand, have shown that this magic is also contained in the blood. My best guess is that the initial morphing alters not just the body, but your very essence itself."

"So... this will do it in another way?"

"Not exactly," said Ren. "Did you know the Metamorphi were one of the Watcher orders long ago?"

Cyrus Maro leaned forward. "I did not."

"It was a broader power. But most Morphs specialized in one or two transformations. The First Chancellor must have honed on the ones he found most desirable for his purposes."

"Wargs and winged beasts, yes," said Cyrus.

"What's most important for our purposes is that you now possess Watcher blood," Scelero said.

"And this?" Cyrus asked, holding up the chalice.

"The ancient Watchers held the potential for greater power. Not just multiple transformations. There were some with multiple gifts. And the Magi held the possibility for all, which is why the orders feared them so."

Cyrus Maro pondered this. "This vial…"

"It contains Conjuri blood," said Ren. "My blood."

"Just as my blood was key to your becoming a Metamorphi," Scelero went on. "Or perhaps, more comparable, just as the host's blood is vital to complete a Metamorphi transformation into another human's likeness."

"This is temporary," said Cyrus.

They both nodded.

"The effect lasts a few hours," said Scelero.

"And what is the effect on my Morph abilities?" asked Cyrus.

"It remains," said Scelero.

Cyrus grinned as he held the chalice up to his lips. He drank. A sip at first, and then, one long swig that emptied the glass.

His lips darkened, and Cyrus licked them clean.

Ren watched the young man carefully. Cyrus closed his eyes, concentrating.

"I.. feel no different," he said, opening them.

"Exactly," said Scelero, eyes flashing with excitement.

"Your spirit already contains the potential for magic. This merely helps awaken you to the potential that is already there."

Ren reached out with his Conjuri sense. With great concentration, he could feel forces in the world beyond what his eyes could see. There was energy in all things, even solid matter. The material world itself was an illusion. Particles bound by magic, composing all things. With his Conjuri ability, he recognized this in some ethereal sense, and could manipulate the energy between himself and the world.

The dagger in his belt shifted in its sheath with a soft ring. A subtle resonance rippled between his own mind and the dagger. He pressed against that energy, gently at first.

And then, shoved—

The dagger shot across the room and buried itself in the laboratory door with a thud and a clatter.

Cyrus Maro smiled greedily. "I'm impressed Master Andovier."

"Master?"

"That is what the Watchers of old called leaders of their orders, yes?"

He glanced at Scelero, whose gaze shifted slightly. Then, he smiled.

"I like the sound of it," Scelero said. "Now, it's your turn, my prince."

On the first vial, Cyrus Maro was barely able to make the dagger move on the table.

But over the next several days, they met again.

A week later, a blade shot across the room at his own behest.

Ren and Scelero grinned at one another.

A true break-through.

"By the gods, you may both prove to be masters," Cyrus said.

————

"I've a theory," said Scelero, weeks later.

It was just Ren and him once more.

"You have… not truly honed your skills," Scelero finished.

Ren grimaced. "Not until recently, no."

Same as most lordlings, but perhaps even less after what happened to his mother. Until Cyrus Maro came knocking, Ren had been avoiding his magic abilities.

"Far as I can tell, Cyrus lingers right around your own limited ability at this point."

"Limited?"

"I don't mean it as an offense, surely. But… well, that's part of the reason a seasoned Metamorphi's blood is used on new recruits… higher potential, I suppose."

"What are you suggesting?"

"I'm theorizing that perhaps a more powerful Watcher's blood might have a greater impact."

Ren scowled. "And where might we get more powerful blood?"

Scelero shrugged. "There's a Conjuri that one of the scouts brought in from across the Green Sea. A powerful one. Morgathian bastard. We drain prisoners' blood to weaken their abilities. At least, until questioning is complete. I could fill a few vials easy enough, I think, during my next security duty."

Ren felt queasy. It was one thing for him to offer his blood freely, but to use that of one of the hunted?

"You want to… harvest blood."

"Gods damn it, of course, I don't *want* to. I despise the practice, just as I've despised the order I'm part of ever since…"

Silence fell over the lab. Ren's fists were clenched tight, nails burrowing into his palms.

Scelero sighed. "It's drained either way, Ren. Why let it go to waste? We could use it for some good at the very least."

Ren felt like he might be sick. He turned and left the room. He strode swiftly up the stairs. Footsteps echoed behind him.

"Andovier! Wait!"

Ren turned, anger flaring. "All that shit you said. About your sister. About us being of the same ilk. I should've known you were just like the rest of them. A damn hunter claiming the greater good in the name of your own ambition."

Scelero pounded the door at the top of the stairs, slamming it shut behind him. They stood, glaring across the sitting room at one another. "You've no idea! I've despised the order I'm part of since the day my sister died!"

"Harvesting Watcher blood?" Ren demanded. "That Watcher could be me had I been born a lesser lord."

"Yes," Scelero said. "My sister knows that all too well!"

"Then why in the bloody Abyss did you join them?"

"I joined the Morphs to try to protect her. I failed. When she was deemed a threat, she fled to the Steppe. Bore a child. Everyone believed I disowned her. Joined the Morphs out of rage and disgust and penance. But no, I joined to protect my sister and her daughter. And I failed. I thought when they brought her in, I could help her escape. But instead…"

"What happened?"

"She resisted them. And paid the price."

"And… the child?"

Scelero shook his head. "I don't know what happened to her."

"Was she…"

"A Watcher? Yes, very powerful. So my sister said. I never met her. Only heard in the one letter she ever sent."

Scelero strode to the mantle across the room and pulled a parchment from a leather-bound book.

Ren remained quiet.

Scelero looked it over, then replaced it where he found it.

"You asked why I became a Morph. But the question you should be asking is why I am here. Why a magic hunter is a member of the Wolves. Helping Cyrus Maro learn magic. Helping you."

"Why, then?" Ren asked.

"Because deep down, I know that there was no world in which I could not have failed my sister. Not yet. The order found her across the world. But with Cyrus Maro... perhaps my niece may yet grow up in a world where sorcerers are not hunted, but celebrated as they were in the Old World. A world where your mother was not executed and those Watcher texts are held sacred, once more."

Ren swallowed, unsure what to say.

"So, yes, if that world comes because I dared make good use of Watcher blood already stolen. So be it. The question is will you dare the same?"

FOUR

DREAMING

Cyrus Maro grunted as he pulled the dagger from his own shoulder.

He had turned the blade mid-air, with a flash of Conjuri magic. Blood poured from his shoulder, and Ren grabbed his other arm to steady him.

"Gods damn it!" Cyrus groaned.

"Give it a moment," Scelero said softly.

"Ah!" The prince's body convulsed, and the wound began to close over. He panted heavily as his body healed itself, fueled by Regenero blood.

A minute later, he removed his shirt and stood before a mirror, admiring his shoulder. "Not even a damn scar," he said, shaking his head. Cyrus rotated his arm. "Like nothing happened at all. Brilliant!"

Ren and Scelero both dipped their heads in a bow.

"You've outdone yourselves this time."

"Thank you, my lord," Ren said.

Summer was nearing its end. Soon, the halls of the academy would fill, and the rest of the Wolves would return.

"I'll see you both rewarded one day, I promise you. Scelero, you'll make a fine Commander of the Metamorphi, I daresay."

"I could only dream of such an honor, my lord."

Of course, only the chancellor himself appointed Morph commanders. And Cyrus was second in line. It was an uncharacteristically empty promise from him.

"Never stop dreaming," Cyrus said. "And you, Andovier, what is it you desire?"

Ren thought a moment. "My dream... is the chance to demonstrate the possibilities of magic to your father, my lord."

Cyrus remained expressionless. "For what purpose?"

"Look what we've accomplished in a matter of months? Imagine what we could do as a true order!"

Cyrus grimaced, and sighed. "I'm afraid you don't know my father as I do, Ren. He has little ambition, and even less courage. To bring back a true Watcher order, it would be feared, resisted by every bloody house in this gods-forsaken city."

"And when you said not to stop dreaming?"

Cyrus smiled. "I meant it. But put no faith in my father."

"And the other Wolves?" asked Ren. "They could be the key to shifting opinions among the Great Houses."

"We'll show them our progress soon."

"Our first meeting is tomorrow night, why not—"

Cyrus brushed him off. "Afraid I shall miss the gathering tonight. A family matter, unfortunately. We're going to the coast for a few days before term begins."

"A vacation?" Scelero asked.

Cyrus nodded. "At my father's insistence. As I said. No ambition. No courage. We'll be lucky if there's an empire left by the end of my father's reign..."

Neither Ren nor Scelero knew what to say.

"Anyway," Cyrus said. "We'll save our reveal for the next gathering of the Wolves."

Cyrus Maro gripped each of their hands in turn. "But I meant what I said. The future is bright."

———

"Dreaming," Ren mused in Scelero's lab the next day. "That's for sure."

"What?" asked Scelero.

"What in the Abyss are we doing?" Ren asked. "Three hundred years. That's how long the chancellors and the Great Houses and everyone else has kept magic in the shadows. Three hundred years of hunting threats, while nobles joke around in their bloody estates."

"You think these things happen overnight?" Scelero demanded.

"I think the chancellor already knows Cyrus is dabbling. I think little noble experiments like this have happened before, and they'll happen again. And the chancellor will keep it in the shadows. Like always."

"Ren, enough!"

"Don't you see this is all a game to him? And if the Wolves ever do become a threat, who do you think will pay the price? Not Cyrus Maro. And—gods damn it—he knows straight away that nothing will ever come of all this. Noble gods-damned dabbling, that's all this ever was."

Ren's chest ached. He braced himself against the edge of Scelero's table. Fuming.

"Well?" Ren demanded.

"What would you have me say? It seems your mind is made up. This is a futile endeavor. Nothing will come of it. Maybe you're right. Maybe you should run off, just like your brother. Go to the Southern Isles or Parjha. And guess what? If you practiced magic there, even at the edge of the New World, the Morphs would hunt you."

"Pah! If I were going to run off, I wouldn't go to the ends of the world. I'd go to the Crooked Teeth, look for the Watchtower."

Scelero sighed. "And what would you do if you found the Watcher haven of myth?"

"I'd change this damn world."

Scelero was quiet for some time. "I think you should go, Ren."

"To the Teeth? I was only—"

"No... I'd like to be alone."

"Scelero, look, I—"

"No, if you think all this is futile. Too great a risk, perhaps it's best we part ways. You're right. Most of the Wolves are just like the other nobles. Fiddling around. But not you. Not me. And certainly not Cyrus Maro. He is different. And if you can't see that..."

"You heard him. His father will never consider a Watcher order. And he's bloody second in—"

"I think you should go, Ren."

"Fine by me!"

Ren stormed out of Scelero's townhome and wandered the city, before venturing to the edges of the noble district. Soon, he found himself in his family's modest estate for the first time in months. A cloud drifted across the sun, casting long shadows, and he stepped inside.

Since his mother's death, the place had grown slowly mustier. Dust everywhere. Windows clouding over. Every day, House Andovier was fading. Every day growing shorter, just like the northern summer.

Ren found his father slumped over the sweeping socha desk in his study, hand still cradling a half-empty glass of wine. It would spill over any minute. Ren took the glass. His father didn't move. A few blocks away, his uncle was likely in similar straits.

They had never been a truly powerful house, and there had always been risks of harboring Watcher secrets. But Ren feared if he didn't do something soon, his house would fall into oblivion.

Maybe you should go. Run off like your brother.

No, Kale was a gods-damned coward!

All their family had spent centuries cowering, running, hiding.

It was time to do something.

Time to act.

Perhaps Scelero was right. Cyrus Maro could be the key. And besides, there was no time for the Andoviers to hope in some distant future.

Ren left his father in his stupor and crossed the city for the second time that afternoon.

It was nearly dark, and clouds loomed on the horizon. Bolts of lightning flashed, somewhere high in the mountains of the Crooked Teeth.

Ren crossed through the academy grounds. It was the quickest way to reach Scelero's home near the Morph headquarters.

Wind picked up, rushing across the cobbled streets, kicking up dust. The grounds were nearly vacant, though a handful of students were already milling about in dark robes. All of them hurrying toward doors.

City bells began to ring. An utter clamor, unlike anything Ren had ever heard at the academy. Soldiers replaced the robed figures in the academy lanes.

One caught his gaze and shouted.

"Inside! Everyone off the streets!"

Ren froze, confused.

Another soldier of the Night Legions shoved him from behind.

"You heard him, lordling! Get inside!"

"What's happening?"

"The royal family is dead. Only Cyrus survived."

FIVE
OVER THE EDGE

The entire city remained under curfew for days of mourning. And the true reason—investigation.

Slowly, rumors turned from blind speculation into something Ren found believable. The Maro family had been vacationing in the southern regions of the empire. There was a fire. Cyrus Maro was found outside with minor burns.

A miracle, the rumors said, to be able to survive such a horror.

Most of the estate burned to the ground, but Cyrus Maro had managed to crawl his way out before the roof collapsed.

The gods spared him, the rumors said.

Ren remained holed up with his drunken father for three treacherous days wondering what in the Abyss was to come.

If the rumors could be believed, he knew how Cyrus Maro had survived. And what did that mean about the rest? About what Cyrus had said before he left?

And why was Ren left in the dark?

On the third day, there was a great funeral procession. All the city walked the streets in black, gathering in Maro Square beneath the shadow of the White Citadel. By then, Ren had heard from several other members of the Wolves.

None had heard from Cyrus Maro. Or Captain Scelero.

On the fourth day, when the curfew was lifted, Ren returned to

Scelero's home. His servant insisted he was not there. All Morphs were on high alert.

When the servant left, Ren peeked through the windows. It was hard to tell through the slit in the curtains, especially with how sparsely Scelero had furnished the place, but Ren saw nothing.

Empty.

Ren returned to campus. Next term was delayed another week until after the coronation.

Cyrus Maro—the new chancellor.

Ren wanted some gods-damned answers. He weaved through the milling crowds of highborn students, conversations buzzing with speculation.

The High Council was in an uproar.

Ren closed himself up in his dormitory, waiting for news. A few of the Wolves came by, pestering him with questions. Had he heard anything new?

No one seemed to have known that Ren had been meeting with Scelero and Cyrus Maro over the summer. And they accepted that Ren knew nothing more than they.

The day before the coronation, there was a firmer knock on his door.

Ren answered slowly.

A legion guard shoved the door open. He pushed past Ren, and began to scour the room, lifting up papers off the desk, pulling out drawers.

"What the Abyss is going on?" Ren demanded.

"Shut your mouth and wait," said another man.

Ren turned.

"Commander, m-my apologies."

A legion high officer. Here?

Another guard pulled Ren out into the hall and began to check him for weapons, running his hands up and down Ren's body.

Satisfied, he stood back. A moment later, his comrade returned from Ren's room.

"All clear, milord!"

"Good," said the commander. "I will take it from here, comrades."

The legion soldiers marched away, leaving Ren and the imperial officer alone. He motioned to Ren's dormitory, and they stepped in.

"What is this about?" Ren asked.

The man closed the door, and immediately his face shuddered, morphing from the visage of a seasoned warrior to that of a much younger man.

Ren glowered at Ruben Scelero.

"I'm sorry for the charade, my friend," Scelero said. "Officers are interrogating members of the Wolves across the campus as we speak. I expect this won't be your last interrogation."

"Where the Abyss have you been? I stopped by your home. It looked—"

"There is nothing to find there," said Scelero. He glanced around the room. "And here?"

"I don't keep anything here in my own—"

"Good!" Scelero removed a satchel from his shoulder and produced two leather-bound scrolls for him to see.

Ren trembled with rage and confusion.

"My mother's scrolls, how could you possibly—"

He reached for them, but Scelero drew back and shook his head.

"I'm afraid I can't give these to you."

"Like the Abyss, you can't!"

Scelero's hand rested on the handle of a short musket at his hip. Ren had no weapon. "Don't do anything rash until you've heard me out, Andovier. I wanted you to know your family's secrets are safe."

"You knew," Ren muttered bitterly. "What Cyrus's plans were all along."

Scelero nodded. "He always knew you held the key to unlocking his potential, and he was right. You just needed a little prodding to give up your secrets."

"So that he could k—"

"Don't," Scelero cut him off.

"That's why they're investigating, right?"

"The high lords have suspicions, but there is no evidence. No other Wolves knew the extent of our experimentation. No one but you and me. And it must remain that way."

Ren eyed the scrolls. "How did you know where they were?"

"I'm a hunter, remember? You were elusive, but eventually, I tracked down the hiding spot. Far more public than anyone would have guessed. But as I said, your secrets are quite safe with me."

Ren stared at the man who had outplayed him. "You used me. Both of you did."

"Oh, don't be high and mighty, Andovier. You said it yourself, the chancellor would never have approved of our true aims. What's done had to be done."

"And I'm complicit."

Scelero nodded and put the scrolls away in his satchel again. "No one can ever know what we've done, Ren. I need assurances, I'm afraid. If anything were to go wrong… well, I would hate for any further harm to come to your house."

"Are you threatening my family?"

"Never, my friend. I just want to be sure you're thinking through *all* the ramifications, if the High Council were to discover what we were doing. I think you knew those risks already when you first joined the Wolves. But I am sorry for how it played out. I know you hated to be left out."

Ren glared at him. That was the truth of it, whether he wanted to admit it or not. Ren had wanted action, and Cyrus Maro had taken it. Without him. "What do you want from me, then?"

"We stand at the cusp of fulfilling all our dreams, Ren. Yours included. Cyrus and I both hope you'll continue to aid us with what's to come."

Ren nodded evenly. "And what is to come?"

"The interrogations will go on for a while, I expect. You'll need to lay low. Stay quiet. Have a good story for what you've been up to this summer. You won't hear from either of us for some time. But believe me, Ren, Cyrus has great plans."

Ren felt queasy, the same way he had when Scelero had suggested using that captured Watcher's blood. He pictured himself standing at the edge of a great precipice, and Scelero was drawing him downward. Over the ledge.

There would be no going back after this. But then, he'd already committed the day Cyrus Maro came calling. How else could one learn to fly, but to leap?

House Andovier had no future. Ren had no future. Not without burning the ships of the past and committing fully to this path. He expected Scelero and Cyrus Maro had both known this all along.

Ren met the man's gaze and nodded. "You don't have to worry about me."

Not yet, he thought.

"Good." Scelero's face shifted again, changing visages once more. One Ren had never seen.

"I've never seen your true face, have I?" Ren asked.

Scelero shrugged. "You've seen more of my true self than any but my sister, Ren. That is the truth."

Yes, Ren thought. *That is what I feared. But these dark games are only beginning.*

Scelero saluted him.

Ren merely nodded in return.

Scelero opened the door, and looked back. "Goodbye, Andovier. I'll see you again. In a glorious future."

ACKNOWLEDGMENTS

First thanks goes to the incredible artists I've had the privilege of collaborating with on this project: Joe Requeza, Andrew Maleski, Rachel St. Clair of Claymore Covers, Denis Kornev, Sebastian Breit, Sabzdunz, and Sutthiwat Dechakamphu. It is truly special when characters and scenes that have lived in your head for years come to life in a whole new way. It's been a pleasure!

Thanks to the online indie fantasy community for all their support and enthusiasm for these editions. Petrik Leo and Johan from Library of a Viking were kind enough to help me out with the Campaign and Art Reveals. And thanks to Andrew, and the whole team at Merrick Books.

To my wife, Kaitlin, whose artistic eye was invaluable throughout the process of developing this illustrated edition.

And most importantly, a huge and heartfelt thank you to all the wonderful backers on Kickstarter who made this edition possible. In alphabetical order, they are:

A-E

Hank A. | Chris Ackman | Aldchad | Matt Allen | Walter E. Alvarez Jr. | Jace Andreassen | Ria Angell | Adam Arvidsson | Padraig Ayre | Jan B. | Lex B. | Helena Balogova | Peter "Tonour" Basak | Jayden Bell | Jack Bilton | Brett Blakley | Peter Blomberg | David Bobbitt | Justise Briones | Shanon M. Brown | Jason Bruening | Adam Bryant | Gregory Butt | Ashley Byrd | Cal | Dan Calderman | Marena Callahan | Evett Cardwell | Meredith Carstens | Matthew Chau | Tyler Cheek | Cliff Chen | Scott Chisholm | Gianna Christopher | Convinton | Bernhard Conz | Zach Cooper | Heather Cooper | Kathryn Craig | Tim Cross | Beth Culp | Andy Culver | Starr D. | Zoe D. | Graham Dauncey | Chase de Groot | Andrew Deans | David DeHaan | Julian Delgado | Monica Dempsey |

Aaron DeWaard | Zack Dewell | Ben DiDonato | Martin Dovina | Angelo Drakontaidis | Alex Dummer | Lucas Edwards | Elbert Family | Troy Erickson | Hugo Essink

F-I

Janito F. | Kristyna F. | Amber Ferguson | Irinel Finco | Conall Fisher | Emma Flaws | Kimberly Florendo | Leniel Isaac Flores-Neris | Jacob Fox | Athena Franks | Caleb Friesen | Joe G. | Mike Galligan | Zeke Gates | Luke Ghensi | GhostCat | Katrina Gilles | Sam Gollings | Eric Gossett | Alex Grade | Melissa Graham | Alisha Green | Vance Green | Mark Griffith | Connor Grove | Michael Grovenburg | David H. | Matthew H. | Jonathan Hamm | Ñólálissë Han | Matias Hansen | Sophia Harlow | Sian Harris | Alex & Kathryn Hastings | Jeffery Heileson | Cady Henry | Kyle Hermans | Billye Herndon | Joseph Hill | Alicia Hintzen | T. Hise | Christopher Hofer | B. Holloway | David Holzborn | Devon Hood | Liana Houdershell | Terry Mitchell Hulett | Justin Huntress | Ashton Hurley | Corbin I. | Marin I. | John Idlor

J-M

Fred W. Johnson | Michael Johnson | Eddie Joo | Jacob Joseph | Kala Judd | Ryzahna Juliano | Mick Kasemeier | James Kaylor | Boe Kelley | John Kern | Tanvir Khan | Callie Klopfenstein | Kodiak | A.L. Knorr | L. Haymond | Brandon L. | Megan Lagarde | Dakota Land | Matt Landberg | Samantha Landström | Mathieu Lefebvre | Hampus Lind | Zhanna Lisser | Nicolas Lobotsky | Makayden Lofthouse | Rhys Lowcock | Lulu | Adriane M. | Michael M. | Zach M. | Ben Madeley | Erick Madrid | Rachel Maifret | Katherine Malloy | Gianluca Marcheselli | Jacob Marquez | In loving memory of Basil Martin | Craig Mayne | Rory McCabe | Austin McClain | Larry McConville | Gerald McDaniel | Chase McGlinchey | RC McKinney | Cathy McLoughlin | Elivin Mendez | Agnès Metanomski | Angela Mitchell | Ricardo Monascal | Cristiana Monteiro | Nathan Morgan | Damon Morton | MykeTea

N-R

Korbyn N. | L. Nabeta | E. Nabeta | Brandon Neal | Kaedyn Nedopak | Benjamin Newton | David Nolan | Adam Nooney | Jason Nugent | Mike

Olson | Toby Otto | Salvatore P. | Brendan Papz | Jonah Pavlicek | Nicholas Paynter | Paul Perez | Neil Phillips | Gernot Pressinger | Qavee | Marea Quijano | Christopher R. | Dami R. | Michael R. | Vicki R. | Marcos Ramirez | Morgen Raney | Jason Rhine | Annie Richer aka Lawrichai | Nancy Richey | James Richmond | Douglas Rist | Joe Rixman | Gina Rochester | Roseking | J.D.L. Rosell | Natasha Rueschhoff | Tomas Rydland

S-Z

Bryce S. | James S. | Nicholas S. | Seamus Sands | SafePondDemon | David Sanders | Armin Schopfer | Blake Severson | Patricia Sleiman | Smiddy | Clayton Smith | Heather Smith | Kent M. Smith | Paul Smith | Richard Sorden | Anders Sørensen | Kitty Sparrow | Jeffrey Speight | Melissa St-Pierre | Kelsey Stenberg | Dallin Stgelais | Kelly Stirling | Gordon Sturgeon | Matt Swinnerton | Adam T. | Melissa T. | Mike T. | Andrea Tolu | Zach Tomlinson | Elizabeth Grace Tresslar | Atakean Trishria | Cheyenne Trujillo | Arild Tvedt | Christoph van Dommelen | Kristy VanWyhe | Eric Vilbert | Phil W. | Madge Watson | Jacob Watt | Russell Weeden | Kenyon Wensing | Kyle Westjohn | Duncan Wilcox | Annarose Willhite | Trevor Wilson | David Wolfson | Lin L. Wong | Adam Wood | Spencer Wright | Jasmine Young | Troy Young | Kian Young | Trey Zyvoloski

www.ingramcontent.com/pod-product-compliance
Lightning Source LLC
Chambersburg PA
CBHW061103310726
48974CB00002B/377